I stomp across the shadowy room to unlock the door of the diner. "What the heck are you doing here this time of night?"

"I'm not really sure, to tell you the truth." Reese pushes past me. "I was due to fly out this afternoon. But that new truck—it steered itself over here." He sets his phone on the nearest booth and taps the screen. "You're too busy to go dancing, so I brought the dancing to you."

Norah Jones's sultry voice fills the room with melancholy.

"Oh." My hand flies to my mouth. "I love that song."

With a soft smile, he holds out a hand. "Dance with me?"

My brain whispers that I look like roadkill and smell like the deep fryer. My feet ignore all that, and I step into his arms.

"Come away with me," he sings softly in my ear, and a shiver starts at the back of my neck and shoots down my body.

His hand is at my shoulder blade, supportive but not intrusive. He leads me across the floor, and we glide, perfectly in sync. Knowing we're sharing the exact same joy shifts something in me. In spite of our differences, we have more in common than I knew. Happiness is like champagne, bubbling up from my chest.

When the singer's voice trails off, he dips me, deep and low. The light of the streetlamp blinds me, and I tip my head back until my ponytail brushes the floor. He holds the dip three beats too long. When I raise my head to see why, he's right there. His face blocks out the light and is less than an inch away.

His lips hover so close that I feel his breath on mine. He holds, one second, two, three…

Praise for Laura Drake and Her Novels

"Laura Drake writes real cowboys with heart and soul."
—Carolyn Brown, *New York Times* **bestselling author**

"Brilliant writing, just brilliant!"
—Lori Wilde, *New York Times* **bestselling author**

"Drake writes excellent contemporary westerns that show the real American West."
—RT Book Reviews

HOME AT CHESTNUT CREEK

"This fast-paced romance has just enough suspense to give it spice."
—Publishers Weekly

THE LAST TRUE COWBOY

"Drake takes readers on a beautifully imperfect journey."
—Publishers Weekly

"For readers who love romances that pack an emotional punch, *The Last True Cowboy* delivers on all fronts. This is a romance with grit, heart and just the right amount of sizzle."
—Book Page

A Cowboy for Keeps

A CHESTNUT CREEK NOVEL

LAURA DRAKE

FOREVER

NEW YORK BOSTON

Copyright © 2020 by Laura Drake
Excerpt from *Last True Cowboy* copyright © 2018 by Laura Drake

Cover design by Elizabeth Turner Stokes. Cover images by Rob Lang.
Cover copyright © 2020 by Hachette Book Group, Inc.

Forever
Hachette Book Group
1290 Avenue of the Americas, New York, NY 10104
read-forever.com
twitter.com/readforeverpub

First Edition: July 2020

Forever is an imprint of Grand Central Publishing. The Forever name and logo are trademarks of Hachette Book Group, Inc.

The publisher is not responsible for websites (or their content) that are not owned by the publisher.

The Hachette Speakers Bureau provides a wide range of authors for speaking events. To find out more, go to www.hachettespeakersbureau.com or call (866) 376-6591.

ISBN: 978-1-5387-4647-9 (mass market); 978-1-5387-4648-6 (ebook)

Printed in the United States of America

OPM 10   9   8   7   6   5   4   3   2   1

To Mr. Rasmussen, my high school English teacher (may he rest in peace), who taught me to love Shakespeare, Chaucer, and John Donne. If you can do that with a fifteen-year-old, you're one hell of a teacher.

CHAPTER 1

Lorelei

It's been the normal crazy-hectic twelve-hour Saturday at the Chestnut Creek Café, and I'm beat.

Nevada, our cook, ducks her head into my office. "See you on Monday, Lorelei."

"Enjoy your day off. Say 'hey' to Fish for me."

"Will do." She waves and the door falls closed. I'm glad Nevada's happy. Of course I am. She and Joseph "Fishing Eagle" King may be total opposites, but they fit together like layers of a Kit Kat bar.

My sister, Patsy, has her pick of cowboys on the rodeo circuit. Carly has Austin and her baby (soon to be babies). Nevada has Fish, and I...I'm just blue tonight, I guess. I shut down the computer and pull my saddlebag-size purse from the drawer. I'm proud that our railroad-station-turned-café is the social hub of Unforgiven. I'm proud to be the manager, feeding hungry people. It's a good, clean, honest job. Maybe not the job I dreamed of when I was young, but I like it. I just wish sometimes that I weren't so... invisible.

I'm a human golden retriever: loving, loyal, dependable. But in my experience, humans with those traits tend to go unnoticed. The dogs, on the other hand, people find adorable.

I walk through the pristine kitchen and push through the swinging door into the diner. The streetlight outside makes little inroads in the room's deep shadows. In the quiet, the earworm that's floated through my head all night cranks up, an old melancholy song of yearning and broken hearts. I raise my arms and waltz with a shadow partner across the floor. I try to imagine his face, but of course, a shadow man has none. It's better that way. Shadow men can't let you down.

My feet slow, and I drop my arms. My dream of competitive ballroom dancing died years ago, along with my hope of romance, after my great love affair ended with Prince Charming turning into a married, smooth-talking loser. See, happily-ever-afters only happen to stray golden retrievers, not their human counterparts.

That's okay. Let everyone else have the messy love lives: the heartache, the loss, the pain. I'll stay above that fray, thank you very much. I have friends. But the last time I had a date, we had a different president. I have so little time for whatever single people do for fun that I sometimes feel like I'm watching life from behind a pane of glass.

But I'm the one who installed the glass. When you put your young heart into the hands of a casual liar the first time, you scrutinize men's hands after that. I sure didn't plan to be single at thirty-seven, with no hope of a partner or babies. But the years slipped away, and here I am.

Talking to myself.

"Stop it, Lorelei. You sound whiny. You're not a whiner." I take the few steps to the door, unlock it. "Besides, Momma's waiting." I step out and lock the door behind me.

Unforgiven doesn't literally roll up the sidewalks after dark, but if they did, no one would notice. Everyone is home with their families. I drive from the light of one streetlamp to the next, past dark stores, far too many with windows dressed in butcher paper. The square and its dingy gazebo look tired and a bit spooky this time of night. Unforgiven is miles off the interstate, and we've struggled since the railroad shut down years ago. Sure, some tourists come through, but fewer every year. Route 66 means nothing to Gen Z.

I turn off the town square and head for home. No streetlights out here to break the vast blackness of a New Mexico summer night. The only beacons are safety lights on poles and outbuildings. Three miles out, I stop at the mailbox with WEST on the side, with the little yellow tube below for the *Unforgiven Patriot*. Just the usual flyers and bills. I'm silly to think my sister would write when she doesn't answer calls or texts, but still there's that little letdown every time I open the box.

Patsy's living an exciting rodeo-road life. That life isn't for me, but it would be nice to get a glimpse of it now and again—from a safe distance, of course. Living vicariously would suit me just fine.

The headlights of my old Smart car sweep the house, highlighting that it needs a coat of paint—or three. But I have no time, and there's no money to pay someone to do it. Besides, if I had the money, it'd go for a new roof. The warm light from the kitchen spills onto the porch, raising my smile. That light has welcomed me home every one of my thirty-seven years. Well, since I was old enough to leave it, anyway.

The screen door shushes over the lintel, and home wraps around me with the smell of meat loaf and the sound of laughter.

"That piece doesn't go there, Mary."

"Yes it does, see?"

"No, you can't force it. You know better than that."

I cross the worn linoleum to the living room. Mom and Mrs. Wheelwright are at the card table, putting together their latest jigsaw puzzle.

"What's up, ladies?"

Mom's small, dried-apple face comes up, wreathed in smiles. "Oh, Patsy's home!" She stands and, ignoring her walker, shuffles over and throws her arms around me. I hug her back, inhaling her dusting-powder scent, choking back the sticky wad of disappointment in my throat. "It's Lorelei, Momma."

She backs up enough to look into my face, a wrinkle of worry between her brows. "When is Patsy coming home?"

"Don't know, Momma."

"Mary, I need help. Can you find where this piece goes?"

Momma totters off, Patsy forgotten. For now.

Mrs. Wheelwright gives me a small, sad smile. She is a godsend, staying days with Momma for next to nothing. She's only a few years younger than my mother, but she's a former nurse and says she's happy to help out. I think she wants to escape her too-quiet house since her husband passed last year. I blow her a kiss and wander back to the kitchen to get dinner finished and on the table.

Momma mistaking me for Patsy usually doesn't bother me, but tonight it does. I have been the constant in Momma's life even before her stroke two years ago. I've stayed in Unforgiven, kept up the house, worked to pay the bills, and taken care of her.

Still, she longs for Patsy.

Not that I blame her. My younger sister got all the charm, looks, and glitter—everyone's favorite. I don't begrudge her that—I'm right there in her pack of admirers. You can't not like Patsy. She's so full of herself, and confidence, and...life. She lights up the room when she walks in, and when her focus is on you, you feel special, smart, important.

I pull on the worn oven mitts and take the meat loaf pan from the oven, setting it on the back of the stove to cool. I cross to the pantry by the back door, reach behind the gingham curtain, and pull out the Potato Buds without looking. They've been on the same shelf, always. It would be great if Patsy could make it home sometime. The last time we saw her was after Momma's stroke. But she was antsy and made more work than she helped. My sister is many great things, but a caregiver isn't one of them. Within the week, she was gone, back on the road with her latest cowboy boyfriend. And except for a sporadic text or two, checking on Momma, nothing since. But I know she cares. We love each other in this family—it's our superpower.

I pour the tea, finish whipping the potatoes, and move everything to the table. "Dinner's ready!" Mrs. Wheelwright starts dinner, I finish it—that's the deal. When they're seated, we hold hands, I say a quick prayer over the food, then pass the plates.

After dinner, when Mrs. Wheelwright has left and I've gotten Momma into her nightgown and in bed, I sit in her rocker and pick up the book we've been waiting to start. Reading is beyond Momma now, but she loves to be read to. I enjoy it, too; it calms me, helping me put the day down, relaxing my mind for sleep.

Momma loves all romance, but ever since I happened on a sci-fi romance last year, she's been hooked on intergalactic love battles. I picked up this one by Fae Rowen at the library. "You ready, Momma?"

She fists her hands on the sheet and nods, her eyes bright. Her stroke mostly affected her mind, making her childlike and apt to forgetting. Her face is as full of delight as a ten-year-old's—in bad need of ironing. I lean over and kiss her forehead. "Do you know how much I love you?"

"I love you too, dear." She pats my face. "Where would I be without you?"

"Well, you'll never have to find out, so you settle in." I turn to the first page. "'O'Neill never expected a glorious red and purple sunset to be her enemy...'"

* * *

I love late spring for a lot of reasons, but especially because I can drive to work on a Monday with the sun coming up over the Sandia Mountains.

The opening notes of "Amarillo by Morning" ping from my phone. If this is our busboy calling in sick, I swear... "Hello?"

"Is this Lorelei West?"

"Yes. Who is this?"

"Officer Beaumont, New Mexico State Police. Do you know a Patsy Lynn West?"

"What?" My hand jerks, and the car takes a sharp swerve. My heart beats timpani in my ears; my blood swirls in a dizzying storm surge. I pull off the road, skid to a stop in the gravel, and throw the car into park. "She's my sister. What—"

"Ma'am. I'm sorry to do this over the phone, but I need to inform you there was a vehicular accident last night—"

"Where?"

"Out on Highway 10—"

"No, where are you calling from? What *city*?"

"Oh, Las Cruces. Ma'am, I'm so sorry to inform you, but your sister died on the way to the hospital last night."

I'm dreaming. I'm in my bed, and this is just a nightmare, probably from the chilis in the meat loaf—

"Ma'am? Are you there?"

"Yes." The word comes out on an emphysemic wheeze.

"I'm very sorry for your loss, ma'am, but I need to know—"

"You're sorry?" The word spirals up as pounding blood spreads over my vision in a red-tinged haze. "Where do you get off, calling at"—I check the clock on the dash, like the time of day could make the least bit of difference—"five a.m. to tell me you're sorry?" My shout echoing off the windshield slaps me, making me realize I could be a tad hysterical.

"Ma'am."

I heave in a lungful of air and come back to myself. "No, *I'm* sorry. Give me a second here." My arm loses function, and the phone drops to my lap. I rest my forehead on the steering wheel. I'm not dreaming. Patsy is...gone. A picture flashes, of the last time I saw her. She gave me a hug and a dazzling smile, told me she loved me to pieces. Then she hopped in her truck, threw me a kiss in the rearview, and dust billowing, rode into the sunset.

If I'd had any inkling of the future, I'd still be holding on to her, even though she'd be kicking and screaming; she loved the excitement of the next rodeo down the road. How could she be gone for good? Forever? I feel like I've fallen into an alternate universe. Because *this* world has my baby sister in it.

"Ma'am? Ms. West?"

When I become aware of a faraway chirping, I realize I've been hearing it for a while. The phone weighs a ton when I lift it to my ear. "I'm here."

"I am truly sorry, ma'am. I just need to know what you plan to do about the baby, since neither the mother nor the father survived the accident."

I pull the phone from my ear and stare at it. Either I *am* sleeping, or he's crazy. Or maybe both. "What are you talking about?"

"Your sister's baby."

"You're telling me Patsy had a baby." Yeah, sleeping. This has the same tilted, off-the-rails feel to it. I dig my nails into my palm hard enough to draw blood. Funny, I never felt pain in a dream bef—

"Yes, ma'am. A"—papers shuffle—"Sybil Renfrow was apparently babysitting and called us when Ms. West didn't return." For the first time, his voice shifts from administrative to human. "I know this is a shock, but if you don't want custody of the baby, I need to let Social Services know. Are you aware of any other—"

"Stop! Stop right there!" My brain does a slow, sluggish turn from the past to the present. "I'll be there, okay? I'm on my way." I check the clock again. "I'll be there by lunchtime. I'll take the baby. Text your address to my phone. You called me, so you have the number."

"I do."

"And, sir?" I take a breath. "How old is the baby? Do you know its name?"

More rustling. "Six months old, ma'am. Her name is Sawyer. Sawyer West."

Somehow knowing her name makes this real. A *baby*.
Oh, Patsy.

CHAPTER 2

Lorelei

I hang up and sit, trying to absorb what is unabsorbable. My baby sister, dead. All that beauty, that love of life, all that potential. Why on *earth* didn't she tell us she had a baby?

It's wrong to hate the dead, but I'm powerless to halt the searing, self-righteous fury that takes over my body, rattling my bones and putting the taste of bile in my mouth. Six months. For six months I didn't know there was a baby on the planet that shared my blood. My DNA.

"Sawyer." I try it out on my tongue.

A big truck blows by, and Einstein rocks on his shocks. I'm wasting time. I jerk myself from my anger and force my mind to work. Oh God, *Momma*. I'm going to have to tell Momma. Somehow.

First things first. I focus on the red-brown mountains in the distance. How can the view be the same as before the phone call that changed everything? I lift my phone and hit speed dial.

"Lorelei, hi. I was just getting Faith up."

"Carly. I need your help." My voice sounds shocky, like *I* was the one in a car wreck.

"What's wrong? Oh no, not your momma?"

"Not Momma. Patsy. Carly, Patsy's dead." The words are cracked, like broken chunks of granite falling into my lap. Saying it out loud just made this high-def real.

"What?" Her voice is shrill. Patsy and Carly were in the same class at Unforgiven High, though they traveled in different circles. "Oh my God, I'm so sorry. What happened?"

"I just got the call from Las Cruces. There was a car wreck last night. I'm sorry to do this to you when you're due to deliver soon, but I've got to go—"

"Of course you do. Look, you're in no condition to drive. Come by here, and—"

"Carly, someone has to cover for me at the diner. You going to leave Nevada in charge?"

"Oh, good point. Put her and my nana together and we'd have no customers left. I'll go in."

"I'm so sorry to ask. Your feet will swell, and—"

"Are you kidding? The regulars will take over, just like they did after I fainted in the middle of the dinner rush the night Faith was born. They won't let me lift a finger. You go. What else can I do? Wait. Your mom…"

"Mrs. Wheelwright is with her. I'll call them later."

"Are you okay, hon?"

Her cottony tone and softer sympathy pull a sob-filled cough from my chest. There's a wad of something down there. Soft, sticky, and a little nasty—like chewed-up black licorice. I push it deeper. I'll fall apart when I can afford to. "There's more, but I can't talk about it right now. I've got to git, Carly."

"I know, but you call me the minute you hit the Las Cruces city limits, y'hear? I'm going to worry until then. It won't help, but it's all I can do."

I check traffic and take the car out of park. "Don't you worry, or you'll end up popping out that baby, and then where'll we be? I'll call you later." I hit End, knowing she'll understand the hang-up. Thinking about any baby makes my voice wobble, and I can't afford that right now.

Tossing the phone in the passenger seat, I check the mirror and ease onto the road. Two hundred miles is four hours, but if Einstein holds up, I can make it in three and a half. And God help the cop that stops me. When the message pings, I punch the address into my phone's program and let the GPS lady tell me what to do. I drive, my vision narrowing to only the pavement unrolling ahead, my thoughts zipping past like the white dashed lines down the middle—here, then gone.

Patsy at four, hair tousled from sleep, opens her faded blue eyes and reaches for me. Will the baby have her eyes? The fight we had when she borrowed my favorite sweater for a date, then hot-water washed it to Barbie-size. How do I tell Momma her daughter is gone? I hope Carly's okay on her feet today. I still need to call Mrs. Wheelwright. Who was the baby's father? How can there be a future without my sister in it? I'm so sorry, Patsy.

I'm washed out on a surge of helplessness, into a sea of sadness, and the road shimmers. *Stop. Stop. Stop it.* Look only at the next thing to be done. Then the next. That's how you'll do this. I look at the dashboard. The next thing is gas, or I'm going to have to walk to Las Cruces.

* * *

Reese

Late afternoon, I push back from the desk in my bedroom/
office to stretch. My muscles are the good kind of tired from
a day of riding and checking the herd. I've got to solve the
breeding problem. God knows, we've got land, but keeping
the test herd separate is a challenge.

I glance at the shelf over my desk, to the carved wooden
pony, an Appaloosa, painted in pastels, prancing. My mother
got it for me when I was just little. It's one of my favorite re-
membrances of her—a sepia-tinged memory of her warmth
and smile, filled with the scent of her perfume.

Hi, Mom.

My phone buzzes on the desk. A number I don't recognize. "Reese St. James."

"Mr. St. James, this is Officer Morales, of the New Mexico
State Police. Do you have a brother, Carson St. James?"

What has he gotten into now? "I do. Why?"

"Sir, I'm sorry to inform you..."

The rest is a buzz in my ear as shock, like liquid lead,
races through my body. The call is short, just the facts. I hang
up, thoughts hitting like shrapnel. How can my twin be dead
and I'm still here? Bo would be so pissed; his favorite son is
gone, and his least is left—the sole surviving St. James.

I toss clothes in a bag and jog for my Cessna. On the
way, I stop to inform my ranch manager, and in minutes
I'm in the air, the plane on autopilot, and try to absorb the
enormity of what's happened. I always thought that if my
crazy brother died in an accident, it would be a collision with
a bull's head, not a deer. The statie said there was a woman
driving—another fatality. Carson always had a taste for the
wild ones, and this one did more damage than any bull.

I'm not unfeeling; I'm sure his death will sink in and I'll mourn. But despite being identical twins, we've never been close. I was born considered and deliberate (weak, according to Carson and my father), and my brother lives like his ass is on fire.

Lived.

This news would have killed our father, if he weren't already dead. Bo "Balls-Out" St. James was bigger than life and believed himself bigger than death, until a massive heart attack a year ago proved him wrong. And if he could talk now, I doubt he'd admit his mistake.

Then it hits me; I'm now the sole owner of Katy Cattle Co. Bo began it before we were born, named it after my mother, and through his bullheadedness, brawn, and (some say) bribery made it into one of the largest cattle ranches in the state. And this is Texas—four hundred thousand acres. A business that big has contingencies to put in motion. I've got calls to make, starting with our attorney.

* * *

Lorelei

Three hours, forty-three minutes later, I pull into the state police annex parking lot and sit listening to the wind moan around the window's worn weather stripping, feeling the push-pull of my wants. Wanting to see Patsy's baby is a throbbing, bone-deep ache that's gotten stronger the closer I got to Las Cruces. But pulling open that glass door will mean crossing a barrier, a point of no return, leaving my bigger-than-life sister behind. If I stay here, could it remain not real? Oh, if that were true, I swear I'd sit here until the car rotted out from under me.

Except, there's a baby. She's the most innocent victim, and she has to be all that matters right now. I open my door and step out, snatch my purse from the floorboards, and clutch it to my chest like a shield. I force my feet across the tarmac, schooling myself with each step: *You can do this. You have to do this. It isn't about you. Or Momma, or even Patsy. It's about a baby.*

I pull open the door and hike across the dull linoleum to the reception desk. It's manned by a handsome young man in blue.

"I'm Lorelei West. I'm here about"—*focus on what you can handle*—"the West baby."

A line appears between his brows, but when he figures it out, his face falls to official planes. "Could I see some ID, miss?"

He's just being polite. Thirty-seven is a bit past the "miss" stage. I root in my bag and finally come up with my wallet and flip it open to my license.

He studies it, then me. "I'm sorry for your loss, Ms. West."

Not going there. Not now. "Can you tell me where the baby is?"

He shuffles papers. "The bod—um—your sister is at the hospital. You'll need to go there and fill out paperwork about who to expect to pick up..."

I just stare at him, trying not to think ahead. "The baby?"

"Since you said you'd be here this afternoon, they are keeping her at CYFD." He pulls off a Post-it and writes. "Here is their address, and the hospital's. And in case you didn't know, the passenger in the car also died in the crash."

"Patsy was driving?"

He looks down at his papers. "Yes. It seems they hit a

deer, and she lost control of the vehicle." He looks up, and his blue eyes find mine. "It doesn't appear that alcohol was involved, but toxicology reports aren't back yet."

I haven't spared a thought for the passenger. And I can't right now. "Thank you." I take the directions and step away from the desk.

"Ma'am?"

I stop.

"They're running your background check now, and depending, they might release the baby."

It hadn't occurred to me I could be going home without the baby. "Depending on what?"

"They'll have questions for you there." He points to the note in my hand.

My anger flares, then dies. Of course they have to be sure they're giving Sawyer to a relative and a good person, not some degenerate. It's now critical that I hold it together. "Okay, got it."

My need to see Patsy's baby propels me to a low-slung building in a not-so-great section of town. I get out and jog to the door, but before I pull it open, I check my shadow in the window and stop to smooth my windblown hair. I don't want to look unhinged to the decision makers. Thank God they can't glimpse what's going on inside. I take a deep breath.

Lord, if you're not too busy, I could use a hand here.

I pull open the door.

The office is as utilitarian as the DMV, with cubicles marching away into the distance. I tell the receptionist why I'm here, and she buzzes someone, then asks me to have a seat; they'll be with me in a few.

I sit but can't keep still. My foot taps and I squirm like a toddler who has to go.

A *baby*. A shot of adrenaline hits my bloodstream, speeding my heart and weakening my knees.

I gave up hope of a family of my own years ago. I remember my parents when I was young. Loving. Not in big ways, but the small ones that spoke louder: a brush of his hand at her waist when he walked by. Her fixing his collar every morning before he left for work. The way her eyes lit when he walked in the door at the end of the day and said, "There you are." I'm not sure I ever even saw them kiss, but the love was as plain as the no-smoking sign on the wall in front of me. Daddy knew how to love my momma. I've always held out for *that*.

But I was real about my chances. I'm one of those girls who is so average, I blend in. The beige undertone compared to the bold colors of girls in the high school halls. I'm not saying I don't have anything to offer. I'm reasonably intelligent, even-keeled and loyal, steadfast and…boring. I have none of Patsy's fireworks. Oh, I got asked out. Still do, now and again, but I believe there's a time for everything in life, and that time has passed me by. The men left in the dating pool are the ones who never married (and it's obvious why), or the divorced men wanting a do-over, trailing kids in their wake and desperate to recapture what they had before they married—youth.

No thanks.

I stand and pace the seven steps between the walls of the reception area. But a baby. God, I love babies. I love kids. I may not ever forgive my poor sister for robbing Momma and me of experiencing her pregnancy and birth.

I sit. Patsy…the details and decisions yet to be made swoop and dive like wasps in my head. Were she and the cowboy married? Surely we'd have heard about that, wouldn't we? Maybe not. A baby trumps a wedding, and she didn't tell us about that.

"Ms. West?" A woman about my age in a blue polyester pantsuit stands at the desk.

I hop up like the chair shocked me. "That's me. I'm here." I sound like a first-day kindergarten teacher, full of fake cheeriness.

She pushes open the little spring-loaded gate to the side of the counter. "I'm Ms. Brown. Come with me, won't you?" She leads me to a small conference room and sits next to a file folder with pages of forms on top. "Make yourself comfortable."

Like that's going to happen. I perch on the edge of an office chair.

"First, could you show me some ID?"

I pull it out and lay it on the table.

She looks from the license to me, as if it's fake. "We've tried to contact the father's family but haven't reached them yet, as far as I've heard. As of now, you are the closest next of kin."

I want to ask her if they were married, but how would that look? Oh yes, we were close. No, she didn't tell us about the baby, or much of anything, apparently. "If I satisfy all your questions, I can take the baby home today?"

"First things first, shall we?" She opens the file folder. On top is a blown-up photocopy of Patsy's driver's license.

Such an ordinary, everyday thing. But seeing my gorgeous sister smiling for the camera ratchets taut the muscles in my chest. Patsy is the only person I've ever known who can make a DMV photo look like a model shoot. I still can't—

"She listed her address as yours."

"Of course she did. That's where she lives. At least, that's her permanent address."

"Is that a house or an apartment?"

"A home."

"Who lives there?" She looks up, and her eyes seem to penetrate my skin to root around inside, searching for lies.

Well, I have nothing to hide. "My mother, me, and Patsy, when she's home."

"No other children in the home?"

"No."

"Are you employed?"

"Yes. I'm the manager of the Chestnut Creek Café in Unforgiven. Have been for seven years."

She's checking a paper as I speak. I read upside down—it's my background report. "Isn't all this in there?"

"I need to have a feel for any potential guardian."

The strain of today tugs on my last nerve. "By asking me questions you already have the answers to?" I'm trying, but really.

Her head snaps up.

"Look, you don't know me, but trust me when I tell you, I do not lie. I detest liars. Ask me anything you want. You want to know about the bubble gum I stole from O'Grady's when I was six? I did it. Momma about snatched me bald. Want to know when I last had sex? It was—"

"Ms. West." She puts up a hand. "I know this is stressful. You've had what I'm sure is a very bad day. I appreciate that. But I am responsible for this baby, and—"

"She's not 'this baby.' Her name is Sawyer." The woman cocks one eyebrow, and I know I need to stop. But it's like someone threw a bath bomb of emotion in my chest, and there's no pushing it down this time. "She's not just any baby. She's my baby sister Patsy's baby. I'll fill out paperwork until I'm gray if you want me to"—my voice goes all wobbly—"and I know you have a very hard job to do. But please, if you have the least bit of empathy in you, can I see the baby?" I clench my hands in my lap and lock my jaw to make the words stop. She's either going to agree, or say no, and there isn't screw-all I can do about it. I make myself still and send up a prayer.

She looks me over hard for what seems like forever. Then she stands and walks out.

I sit on my hands and try to hold it together. Has she just ended the interview?

Two minutes later, she walks back in, carrying my niece.

"Oh." I'm on my feet, my hand over my mouth. I've been trying so hard to get to this point, I realize I haven't thought one nanosecond beyond it.

Her eyes are big and round as a Disney bunny's. Patsy's pale-blue eyes stare back at me, like the sky some days: a watercolor wash of white on blue. She has straight brown hair, from her father, I assume, since the Wests are blond. She's wearing a red-and-white-striped onesie that makes her look like a little pixie.

Her cheeks aren't pink; they're red. "Does she have a fever?"

"No. She's just starting to teethe."

Without warning, the long, horrific day catches up to me. My knees give way and I plop into the chair. A strangled wail works its way past the licorice glob in my throat. I stick my fist in my mouth and bite down, but it gets around that, too. "Oh, Patsy." I put my face in my hands, bend double as the shocked grief I've stuffed all day spews.

This woman has got to think I'm unhinged. Stop, stop, stop it. She won't give you Sawyer.

It makes no difference. I have no control.

Something brushes my hand, and I turn my head to see a tissue dangling. I snatch it like it's a life jacket and cry some more.

In time, the worst is over. Oh, I don't kid myself. I'm raw and seeping, and it's going to build again, but for now...I look up.

The lady bounces Sawyer on her hip and hands me the tissue box.

"I'm so sorry. I can't imagine what you're thinking." I pull tissues, blow my nose, and mop my face.

"I think that this baby is *wanted*." Her eyes are a bit shiny, and her smile is lopsided. "We'll have someone visit, of course, to be sure the home is appropriate and safe, but for today, I'm comfortable turning her over to you."

She hands the baby down, into my lap.

Sawyer is warm and soft and looks up at me with wise eyes. Then she reaches up and touches my wet cheek.

"It's okay, hon." Another tear tracks down my face. "You had a long, hard fall, but I've got you. I'm going to make everything okay from now on. I *swear* it."

* * *

Reese

It's dusk when I land in Las Cruces. It takes forever to get a rental car and longer to get to the hospital: a modern, three-story structure overlooking barren landscape.

The lobby is almost deserted.

I explain to the security guard at the desk that I want to see my brother.

He tells me he's sorry for my loss, picks up a phone, and relays the message. When he hangs up, he directs me to the basement.

I'm ushered into a "viewing room," where they leave me

alone with Carson. I take off my Stetson. Doing this would never be easy, but pulling a sheet down to see your own face? Except for the scar across my forehead, the reminder of just how different we are—were. I gulp deep lungfuls of air until the dizziness passes and do it. His face escaped injury, a detail I know he'd be happy about. For whatever good that does.

Anger forms under my breastbone, pushing out. Hard to believe they hadn't been drinking, but the statie said it didn't look that way. Yeah, they hit a deer, but a bull rider's reaction time is better than a normal human's. "Dammit, Carson, why weren't you driving?"

I search for something profound to say but find I have even less to say to him than I did when he was alive. We take after our mother in looks and build, but Carson got Bo's personality. He was Bo's legacy—the favorite child.

According to the will, we were to work together to run the ranch, but Carson wasn't done rodeoing. I'd always hoped we'd find more in common when we were both back on the ranch. I mean, we're twins, for cripes' sake. But now the chance to get close to my brother—to understand him—is gone, and I'm only just beginning to realize how much I'd wanted that. Could we have forged a relationship without Bo between us? I'll never know. Shit. The unfairness ignites my anger like sulfur in a burning flash of heat.

And when it consumes itself, I'm left empty and cold. I don't know what I expected to gain by coming here. To make it real, maybe? Well, it is that. "I'll take good care of the ranch. You know you don't have to worry about that." Not that he worried about it much when he was alive. God, I sound cold. But screw it. I'm not enough of a hypocrite to try to conjure soft memories from my childhood when there weren't any.

But there's a greasy feel of guilt slicking my guts. Guilt for being alive, when Carson isn't. Guilt for not staying in touch much the past couple of years.

Guilt for lost chances.

I've been spending every minute working, for what? Carson and I were the end of the line. Since my first and only bull ride ended my chances of having children, when I die, the ranch will probably go to the state. My whole life, and what have I done that will last? What will I leave? Nothing that matters to anyone. Least of all me.

"God, Carson, I'm so sorry." I raise the sheet over his face, turn on my heel, and walk out.

I drive out to the rodeo grounds. This is Carson's world. They'll know him here. Maybe I can get more information than the scanty cold facts the police dispensed. The packed-dirt parking lot is deserted, but the floodlights form a halo around the empty stands.

Crap. It's Monday. The cowboys that were here last weekend are scattered to the winds of rodeo. But I notice a trailer under the stands with lights on, so I head that way.

I open the door and step inside.

It's a small room, filled with two paper-buried desks. An older man and woman sit behind them, shuffling through the mess. They look up. The man's jaw drops, and the woman lets out a little "eek."

When I haven't been around my brother in a while, it's easy to forget that we have the same face. I take off my hat. "I'm Reese St. James, Carson's brother."

The woman crosses herself.

The man stands and sticks out a hand. "I'm Ben Davis. I put on the rodeo here. I didn't know your brother well, only saw him a couple of days every year, but he was a good kid—he'll be missed."

The woman's eyes are shiny. "Oh, I'm so very sorry for your loss."

"Thank you, ma'am. I appreciate it."

"They left your brother's things with us, figuring someone would come looking for them. They're in the back of my truck. I'll just—"

"No need. I'll get them on the way out. What I'm really looking for is information."

"Don't know much, only what I heard from the cowboys." Ben leans his thin butt on the edge of the desk. "They were heading out to the bar, and a deer ran out and—"

"The police told me. Do you know the woman who was with him?" Carson had as many commitment issues as me, so I'm pretty sure this'll be a buckle-chaser dead end, but still...

The woman squints. "I heard her name. Let me think. Pam? No. Peggy?" She shakes her head. "That's not right. It's some singer's name, from way back, remember, Ben?"

He crosses his arms and stares at the notice-covered wall. "I don't—"

"Patsy!" Her face lights up. "Like Patsy Cline. I knew I was gonna remember."

"Do you know her last name? I feel like I should get in touch with the family." And finding out more about her will tell me more about my brother.

"Oh, that's sweet. No, I'm sorry. I never heard her last name."

"Do you happen to know where she was from?"

They both shake their heads.

I should just let it go. Sentimentality was drummed out of me at an early age. But I can't. I'd like to know more about my brother in his last months. Surely her family would know more about that than me.

CHAPTER 3

Lorelei

ONE WEEK LATER

I'm sitting on a folding chair at the graveside, listening to our minister recite the well-worn platitudes meant to ease grief. Since I'm immune to them, I'll pray that they'll help Momma. She looks older since Patsy's accident—folded in on herself physically, mentally, emotionally. She shifts between grieving for her youngest daughter and not remembering her at all, which I think is more a coping mechanism than the effects of the stroke. I get it; you're wired to protect yourself from things you can't face. I wish I could seek refuge there myself, but someone has to handle things.

The only pinpoint of light at the end of the dark tunnel of the past week lies sleeping in my arms. Sawyer is a delightful baby, easygoing and content, unless there's reason not to be. She seems happiest in my arms, and I'm glad of it; I need the comfort as much as she. She shifts and whimpers in her sleep, and I bounce my knee to calm her. She won't remember her mother, but I'll be sure she knows her, through my memories. What kind of a mother was Patsy? Leaving a six-month-old to go drinking isn't a great indicator, but I know my sister. She may not have been perfect, but she loved this baby with everything she was capable of.

And I'll do the same.

My mind drifts to the father, and I push the thought away, worried that even thinking about him will conjure his family. Social Services has been out to the house and okayed Sawyer's living environment. It helped that Mrs. Wheelwright is a retired nurse and loves babies. I now have legal custody, which should ease my unease. But there's still a cactus prick of conscience. Sawyer is their blood, too. They have a right to know she exists.

But how do I know they don't know? Just because Patsy didn't tell us doesn't mean the father didn't tell his family. And even if they didn't know, it wouldn't take much digging to find us, right?

Either way, Sawyer is mine now. It's like God heard what I hadn't thought to ask for and gave it to me. The past few years, I've been restless, and I finally figured out why. It was my eggs, lying around like lazy kids, living in the basement, going nowhere. And with no likely prospects for a father, I thought they'd just die off, unrequited. Having this baby makes me sated in ways I couldn't have imagined a week ago.

When the reverend begins with the "ashes to ashes" part, I know we're almost done here.

The white casket with gold trim shines so pretty in the sun, just like Patsy did. It was worth every bit of the money

I couldn't afford. We'll pay it off over time, because it's all I could do for my sister, and I have so much to be grateful to her for. The lightness she brought to my childhood. All the memories she left behind. Last and especially, Sawyer.

Thank you, dear sister. I know you didn't mean to give me this gift. But you can rest easy—you know I'll love and protect her with my life.

Goodbye, sweet Patsy. We so loved you.

The sermon over, people shuffle toward Momma and me. I wipe tears and brace myself, dreading their questions. Was Patsy married? Why had she never brought the father home to meet us? How could she have not told us she'd had a baby? All I have is facts, but they don't give me answers.

* * *

It turns out, I didn't give the townspeople enough credit. In the church basement, the reception has turned into an impromptu baby shower. Momma pulls an adorable stuffed cow from a gift bag. "Oh, how sweet! Thank you..."

"It's Nevada, Mary. It's okay, you don't have to remember. The gift is from me and Joseph." She leans over and pulls up the orange-and-brown granny-square throw that's falling off Momma's lap.

Who'd have thought that tough Nevada would be sweet with my mother? But Fish has brought out a softer side in her that we never guessed was there. Skirt and all, she drops to the floor beside Momma and helps her open the presents that are more than welcome. I had to buy a car seat before we left Las Cruces, and I found a used crib on the local garage sale Internet site, but between that and formula and diapers, my bank balance is nearing the red. Pray God that Einstein's tires hold out and the rain holds off so the roof of the house doesn't leak for a few months.

"She's so precious." Carly reaches over my shoulder to stroke Sawyer's cheek and is rewarded with a smile. "Are you holding up okay, sweetie? If you need more time off, I can—"

"Don't you dare say it." I turn to her massive bulk of belly. "You are on maternity leave. I'll be back in the morning. I can't believe you closed the diner today."

She shrugs. "Don't be silly. There wouldn't have been any customers, since just about the whole town is here."

She's right. I look around the room, grateful for our tight-knit community. Kids in their Sunday-best clothes chase one another, mothers snatching at them on the way by. Austin, Carly's husband, is talking to a group of old farmers in the corner. He'd fit right in, if he weren't holding Faith, their child. The garden and historical society ladies sip tea in another corner. The townsfolk may squabble among themselves, but let something bad happen and they're there, offering everything they have. "I'm so thankful. For everything." I blink back tears I thought I was done with.

"Aw, com'ere." Carly gives me a hug, made awkward since both our babies are between us.

My baby. How can I be elated and grieving all at the same time?

Fish steps out of the kitchen to give me a hug.

I sniff. "Nevada stole your cooking job, yet still you're in the kitchen."

He offers his finger to Sawyer, who tries to put it in her mouth. "Everyone brought the food. I'm just serving it."

"Still. Thank you."

"I'll be out to take a look at your roof this week. It wasn't in great shape before, and you had to have lost shingles in that last storm." He retrieves his finger and runs the back of it down Sawyer's cheek. "I'm so sorry for your troubles, Lorelei."

I shake my head. "A funeral is meant to put an end to the sadness and the 'sorrys.' Starting tomorrow, we're looking ahead and thanking God for the amazing blessing we've been given." I drop my head and look at him from under my brows. "And you are not messing with my roof. You have enough to do with your farm. Don't worry about us. We'll be fine."

He can look fierce when he wants to. "That is my gift to Sawyer, so you have no say. It's between her and me. Right, baby?"

Sawyer smiles at him and kicks her feet.

"I love you, Fish. Thank you."

* * *

Reese

Bo somehow got around local laws to bury my mother on the ranch, on a pretty mesa overlooking the river about a quarter mile from the house. We buried Bo there a year ago, leaving me the only one left to bury Carson.

I invited the crowd back to the ranch house after. Friends, neighbors, and employees drink whiskey from cut-crystal glasses in the great room. Afternoon sun pours in the two-story window wall that juts like the prow of a ship. My father didn't do anything by halves.

I'm weary of the pomp and politeness. I wish everyone would just leave, but Bo drilled into us from a young age never to judge a man's pocketbook by his dress and always use your Sunday manners if you don't know who you're talking to. I know almost everyone here, but not well enough to feel comfortable with herding them to the door.

I look around. Friends of Bo, friends of Carson. I have acquaintances and business associates, but no one I'd expect to fly in for this.

"Mr. St. James?"

A kid in pressed Wranglers, dusty boots, and a starched white dress shirt walks up. He's carrying a can of beer in one hand, his hat in the other. Not sure how he got the bartender to give him the can instead of a glass, but… "Yes."

"I'm Shane Grayson. I rodeoed with Carson. He showed me the ropes and helped me out a bunch over the past year, so I wanted to be here. To tell you how sorry I am."

"Thank you, Shane." I hold my face in somber lines in spite of my heart banging my ribs. Finally, someone with information. "Can I talk to you for a minute?"

"Yessir."

I lead him down the hall. Bo's study is like the rest of the house—made to impress. Mounted trophy animals line the dark-paneled walls, and the fieldstone fireplace is big enough to roast a pig in. Teddy Roosevelt would have felt at home here. I lead Shane to one of the burgundy leather chairs and he perches on the edge.

I'd rather stand, but I don't want to intimidate him any more than he is already. He looks like a fresh-faced kid, though I know he can't be much younger than me. "I know the basic facts, but Carson wasn't so great about staying in touch. Can you tell me a little about his life on the road?"

His face lights in a smile. "Carson, he was cowboy from the ground up. I saw him get stomped by a bull in the first round of the finals in Pecos. Broke two ribs, and he still rode his last bull. Made the whistle, too."

"Yeah, that sounds like Carson." I only rode that one bull, after Carson double-dog dared me. I ended up with a scar on the outside, a bigger one on the inside, and a lifelong lesson Carson never learned.

"But he was a nice guy, too. Him and Patsy, they kinda took me under their wing."

I cough to cover my gasp. "Patsy. Tell me about Patsy."

"Aw, she was the best. All the guys were half in love with her. She had that spark, you know, how some women have? Makes you want to be close to them. She liked to have a good time, but she didn't have eyes for nobody but Carson. And he was the same, even if they weren't married. I think they'd a probably gotten around to it eventually." He sets the untouched beer on the antler table beside him. "And that baby..." He shakes his head. "They loved that baby like nobody's business."

"Wait. What?"

He cocks his head. "The baby. Sawyer. You didn't know about her?"

There's never been an earthquake near here, but I swear the ground just shifted. "A *baby*," I breathe.

"Sure. Precious little thing she was, too."

My gut drops. "Was? She wasn't in the car—"

"Oh, no, sir. I didn't mean to scare you. Sybil—she's a can chaser and a looker her own self—she was babysitting that night."

"Where is the baby now?"

His face scrunches. "I don't know. Never thought about it until just now."

Possibilities I thought long dead bloom like squid's ink in my brain.

A *baby*.

A piece of Carson still exists. I'll see that his baby is safe and cared for with the best money can buy. It's the least I can do for my brother.

But I've got to find her first.

* * *

Lorelei

"Nevada." My cook stands at the grill, flipping burgers and twisting her hips. Her earbud headbanger music stutters and stumbles across the floor to me. I shoulder my heavy purse and walk over to tap her on the shoulder.

"Holy crap!" She whirls, crouching, holding the spatula like a weapon. "Oh." She straightens and pulls out one bud. The volume surges.

"Turn that danged thing down already. The place could be on fire and you wouldn't know it."

"If it were on fire, it'd most likely start right here." She waves the spatula at the grill.

"We didn't buy you those danged things to blow out your eardrums." The patrons chipped in to buy them two months ago, so *they* wouldn't have to listen to that god-awful stuff. Except for Manny Stipple; he likes it. But I think Carly's grandpa's moonshine has destroyed his taste in music, right along with his liver.

The irritation fades from Nevada's face. She reaches for her phone at the back of her waistband and the sound fades. "You're right. Sorry."

In the old days (pre-Fish) she'd have gone to the mat with me on this. I heartily approve of Nevada 2.0. "Thank you. I'm making a run to O'Grady's. I forgot to order artificial sweetener, and we're almost out. Need anything?"

"Can you get me six tomatoes? The delivery will be here in the morning, but that should hold me for tonight."

"Sure. That it?"

The swinging door to the diner opens, and Sassy Medina, our waitress, steps through. "Lorelei, there's a guy here to see you."

"Who is it?"

"I never saw him before. But if you don't want him, I'm giving him my number."

I shake my head. Probably a new produce vendor, trying to poach customers. I push through the door.

The guy standing next to the front door is no vendor. He's not tall: about my height, with broad shoulders and a small waist, in Wranglers, tooled boots, a plaid work shirt, and a cream straw cowboy hat that he sweeps off as I walk up. Short brown hair. He looks like a young James Garner, except for the scar that bisects his left eyebrow and disappears into his hairline. It saves him from looking like a pretty boy.

"I'm Lorelei West. What can I do for you?"

He looks around, steps to an open booth, and slides in, assuming I'll follow. This one is used to getting his way.

He waves across the booth. "Please, have a seat. Would you like some coffee?"

His gaze is warm and appreciative. This guy is selling *something*, but I'm not buying. I sit and cross my arms on the table. "This is my restaurant. If I want coffee, I know where it is."

"Oh, you own this place?"

My cheeks flush. "I'm the manager. And I have a job to do, so…"

He puts out a hand. "I'd like to talk to you for just a minute, if I could. I'm Reese St. James."

His hand is strong and smooth. That name sends tingles down the synapses in my brain.

Who does he think he—the name drops into a slot in my memory, and all the other slots drop cargo. Patsy. Her boyfriend was a St. James.

Oh no. *Sawyer.*

My stomach clenches as if anticipating a blow. I eye him like the sidewinder that got into the house once. "What can I do for you?"

He laces his fingers on the table, leans in, and what's in his dark eyes makes my nerves jangle. It's longing. No, *yearning.* "The baby. My brother was the father of the baby."

My brain is whirling, but nothing helpful is coming out. All my worry is sitting right in front of me, and my flight reflex is just as strong as my fight. But I'm going to have to use words, because my legs wouldn't hold me anyway. "How do I know you're who you say you are? You could be a...child-napper."

That pulls his lips to a half grin. He reaches for his wallet, flips it open. Texas driver's license, and the name matches the photo. I pull it across the table to read better. "Where is Carrizo Springs?"

"South Texas. Between Laredo and Eagle Pass, on the Rio Grande."

"What do you do there?"

His scarred eyebrow rises.

I stare him down. "I have to be careful."

"Guess I can't blame you." He puts out a hand. "Can I have my wallet back? Or do you want to take a copy of my license?"

I don't know if he's kidding or not, but I consider doing just that for a second or two, then hand it back to him.

"Let me set your mind at ease. I have no criminal record, I don't have a drug problem, and I'm gainfully employed."

"Doing what?"

His eyes cut to the sidewalk outside the window. "I work on a ranch down there."

My liar radar is pinging. "You're a cowboy." I manage to keep the scoff out of my voice. He's tanned, but not the deep-down wind-beaten skin of a man who works in the sun for a living. I should know. I feed men like that every day. His hands aren't calloused, and ranch hands don't usually worry about whitening their teeth.

"Yep."

The bitter taste of ashes from an old fire crawls from my stomach and tightens my throat. What am I, some kind of liar-magnet? "What do you want?"

"To see the baby, of course." He sits back, stretches his arm along the top of the booth, and gives me a charming, confident smile.

A guy like this is used to barking orders, not taking them. "I don't know why you'd think I'm stupid or what game you're playing." I look at him through narrowed eyes. "But you're not a simple cowboy, and I'm not letting a liar anywhere near Sawyer."

CHAPTER 4

Reese

She slides out of the booth and, with one last glare over her shoulder, flounces out the front door.

Okay, so skirting the truth wasn't the best idea I've ever had. But I thought long and hard about how to play this on the thirteen-hour drive out. When I hit the town limits, I knew I was right to dress down. This is a raggedy small town, and I didn't want to intimidate her or seem uppity.

So instead I came off like a weasel. Fantastic.

"Don't look so sad. She'll be back." The curvy waitress holds aloft a pot of coffee. "Want some while you wait?"

I flip over the cup on the table. "You bet. Thanks."

She pours, then continues her rounds.

Lorelei West is a honey badger wrapped in blue jeans. Not a woman who'd stop traffic maybe, but her features are pleasing. A too-long face, shoulder-length blond hair. Her full, kiss-me lips are nice, but it's her eyes that get me. Faded denim blue, intelligent, expressive. I hope she's not a card player, because they show everything going on behind them. Lorelei West is a handsome woman.

Who hates me.

Which is fine. I'm not here looking for a date. It doesn't matter if the obstacle is good-looking or a brick wall, I'm getting past it. I've never tried to charm a honey badger, but charm runs in my family, so I'll give it another shot, because I'm not leaving without seeing my niece. I had hope that Lorelei took the baby only out of obligation. Hoped that she'd let me take Sawyer home to the ranch, where she belongs. That hope is now shattered, pieces scattering the floor. *Cleanup on booth five!*

But then again, Ms. Lorelei West never came up against a St. James when he wants something. After all, I have Bo in my DNA, and God knows, his genes are strong.

I pull my phone and hit speed dial.

"Travis and Partners, attorneys at law."

Travis had been my father's attorney for forty years, and though his crassness and lechery set my teeth on edge, he knows where all Katy Cattle Company's bodies are buried, and I don't. Yet. "It's Reese. Is Mr. Travis in?"

"I'm sure he will be for you, Mr. St. James. Hold just a moment."

"What can I do you for, Reese?" Travis's bigger-than-life voice booms, and I can picture him leaning back, custom boots up on his mahogany desk.

"What do you know about child custody law in New Mexico?"

"You going to get that kid? Good. That baby is a St. James. Bo would want it raised on his land."

The "it" rankles, and I don't think the "his land" is a slip of the tongue. I don't need this puffed-up rooster telling me what my father would want. "The mother's sister has the baby. She lives outside of Albuquerque. I want you to report back to me about my chances of getting custody."

"Is the woman unfit to care for the child?"

"Not that I can see, but I don't know her. I'm going to try to find out."

"Okay, I'm on it. Your father would be proud of you."

I click End. His proprietary tone started after my father died, like he's now the purveyor of what Bo would think. The man is odious, but good his job. A necessary evil. I sip coffee and wait.

Strange, how a little human I've never met has become so important to me. The feeling is gut deep. It wasn't until I hit the wall that is Lorelei West that I discovered a wall in me, too. Getting this baby is something I *need* to do.

I want a do-over.

There may be no shame in being different. I know that now. But growing up in Bo's house, different meant I was the butt of jokes, derision, and pressure to conform. I tried. I worked harder than the lowest hand on the ranch. But those three seconds on a bull proved what I'd known all along. I didn't fit the St. James mold. So I decided if I couldn't join them, I'd beat them. Book learning came easy to me, so I read every book in Bo's huge library on breeding and ranching. Carson barely made it out of high school. I went to college, then on to an MBA.

They say every kid needs one champion, one person who loves them and believes in them. Maybe if my mother had lived…I've come to realize the stuff you missed as a kid, you can't make up for later.

But maybe Sawyer and I could be our own family. I could be the champion that she'll need. I'm sure Lorelei means well, but I have almost unlimited resources. I can give Sawyer so much more.

I drink coffee and imagine my new future until Lorelei walks in forty minutes later, arms full of grocery bags. She glances my way, flinches, frowns, then pushes through the swinging door to the kitchen. A minute later, she pushes back through.

I stand as she stomps up, plants a fist on her hip, and looks down her nose at me. "You're still here?"

"I'm sorry. You're right. I lied. But I had a good reason. Could I impose on you for just ten minutes of your time? I'd like to explain."

"Why do liars always say that? I manage to make it through every day without lying, good reason or not." She may be frowning, but her eyes are assessing.

I push down on the frustration and try to mimic Carson's deadly puppy-dog look. "Please?"

She blows out exasperation with her sigh, then sits.

"I just want you to know that I didn't lie about everything. I am from Carrizo Springs, and I am a cowboy. At least some of the time. Ever heard of the Katy Cattle Ranch?"

From her widened eyes, she has. The big ranches are legendary.

"Well, since the car wreck, I'm the sole owner."

She whistles. "Wow, when you lied about being a cowboy, you went for the gold, didn't you?"

I rush on. "I just didn't want to barge in here and intimidate—"

Her face goes stiff, except for the nostril flare.

It's a gift I have, saying the exact wrong thing. "I mean—"

"*I* should be intimidated?" She looks me over, long and slow, and her lip curls just a bit. "By *you*?"

If Bo were around to see me ball up a negotiation this bad, he'd cuff the back of my head. And this is beginning to feel like the most important negotiation of my life. "I didn't mean it that way." My face heats at the thought of how I must look to her: arrogant, presumptuous. Maybe I do have Bo in me after all.

Her eyes are slits. "Then just how did you mean it?"

I force the frustration down. I can't afford it. "Look, can I start over? I'm not usually an ass, though I know I seem well practiced." I sit on my hands so I can't spill my coffee on her, which is about the only stupid thing I haven't done yet. "My parents are dead. My twin brother is dead. All I'm asking is to see the last person on the planet I'm related to."

She winces. "You and Patsy's... boyfriend were twins?"

"People had a hard time telling us apart until I got this." I point to the scar on my forehead.

Her eyes ease the tightness at the edges. "Losing your twin, that's horrific. I'm sorry for your loss." Softness turns her eyes a darker shade of blue.

"And I'm sorry for yours. Truly."

"Why didn't you come before now?"

"I didn't know about the baby."

Her mouth drops to a small O of surprise. "He didn't tell you, either?"

"You mean *you* didn't know about the baby before the accident?"

She shakes her head slowly. I can see the wheels turning. She's deciding. I sit motionless under her scrutiny and try to look harmless.

"I'm off in two hours. I can take you to the house to see Sawyer then." She slides out and stands.

"Thank you."

"Just don't make me sorry for being soft." She walks away.

* * *

Lorelei

Two hours later Sassy stands at the door of my office, untying her apron. "That cute guy is back."

I glance at the clock on my computer. "He may be a liar, but he's a punctual one." Okay, the lie wasn't that extreme, and given my past, my BS radar is set higher than most, but the thought of some rich dude not wanting to *intimidate* me…What a jerk.

She leans against the doorjamb. "I've got a dentist appointment tomorrow, so I'm going to be about an hour late."

I haven't been to a dentist in a decade (not that I could afford one, even if I had the time). I've noticed how other people have no problem putting themselves before their jobs. I'm going to have to take a lesson from them—I have Sawyer now, and she comes first. "Just get here as soon as you can, okay?"

"Sure." She unties and folds her apron and, with a wave to Nevada, walks out the back door.

I power down my computer, throw my purse strap over my shoulder, and walk into the kitchen. "You almost done, Nevada?"

"On my way out now."

The kitchen is neat, the grill clean. At least there's someone I can depend on. I push through to the shadowy dining area. Reese St. James is sitting, one hip on a stool at the bar.

I've cashed out the till, coffee setups are ready for morning, but Sassy forgot to lower the blinds. I drop my purse on the counter with a thud, walk to the first booth, kneel on the cushions, and slide the canvas shade down. I move on to the next and notice that Reese is doing the same on the other side. We meet in the middle. "Thank you."

"No problem. Can we go now?"

"Just one more thing. It'll only take a second." I grab the bag of burgers Nevada left on the counter, check the dead bolt on the back door, then push through the swinging door to the dining area. With the shades down, the only light is the streetlamp through the glass door. I step to it, and our shoulders brush.

He holds the door open, and I walk out to the warm night. The streetlight gleams off a new GMC Denali pickup. His, obviously.

I lock the door behind us. Reese jumps as a dark shape rushes out of the shadows.

"It's okay." The small black dog flattens his belly to the sidewalk, his tail whipping happiness.

"Is that yours?"

"No, just a stray." I pull one of the burger patties from the bag, and the dog eases forward to take it from my fingers, backs up, and with a nervous eye on us, wolfs it down. "I should call the pound, but I keep hoping someone will take him home with them." I toss the other patty to him, then crumple the bag. "My car is behind the café. I'll meet you out here."

"I'll walk you back."

"Don't be silly. I do this every night."

He glances around the empty sidewalks and across the street to the dark square. "And tonight, you won't do it alone."

I want to argue with his proprietary tone, but it's been a long day and I want to get home. "Suit yourself." I take off at a brisk walk, and he trots to catch up.

"You're not used to people helping you."

"And you're used to giving orders." I step over the old railroad tracks only partially embedded in asphalt. "Mind the rails."

"This place really did used to be a rail station, huh?"

"Yes, before the spur shut down in the fifties."

"The town doesn't appear to be…thriving."

"We do all right." We've reached my car, in the alley behind the diner.

"Wow, you don't see many tiny cars in Texas."

"Here, either. But me and Einstein, we—"

"Einstein?"

"He's a Smart car, right?" I ignore his chuckle, put the key in the door (the clicker died two years ago), and unlock it. I feel like I should drive him to his car, but after seeing his wheels, there's no way I'm inviting him to scrunch into mine. "I'll meet you out front."

"Okay, I'll follow you to your house." He puts his hands in his pockets and walks into the dark of the alley.

I pull around front, then drive out to the house with the headlights of his massive truck in the rearview mirror, blinding me.

I feel like I'm walking barefoot in a field of stickers. He's grieving, too. He should be able to see his brother's baby, but my instinct is to go all dog-in-the-manger with Sawyer. It's all twisted up in my head, but Sawyer is the innocent in all this. It's my job to keep her from any more heartbreak. What's the right thing to do?

Is he going to fight for custody? He's a man. Even in our enlightened decade where sexes are supposed to be equal, I believe I'd still have the edge with a judge. I flip up the rearview mirror. I don't need it out here, and the headlights on that tank are giving me a headache.

But he's rich. More than Unforgiven rich; he's Texas-high-roller, stinking rich. Sweat slicks between my palms and the steering wheel, and I shove the thought under the floor mat. I'll deal with that if I have to. *Pray God I don't have to.*

I'm tired. It's been a long, emotional day. I'll give him an hour, then I'll shoo him out.

I pull into our dirt drive, imagining the house through his eyes. Compared to his life, we must seem worn-down, weathered, weary.

Well, he can judge all he wants. We are rich in what's important—love. And whatever he has, nothing trumps that. I park, hop out, and am beside his door when he steps out. "I'm going to try to explain who you are to my momma, but she's had a stroke, and she may or may not understand. I just want you to know, so you're not surprised." I shoot him a pointed look, hoping I don't have to say the rest. *If you so much as look at my momma wrong, I'll take you apart.*

"I know I haven't presented myself well so far, but I do have manners, and I promise to use them."

"Okay, then." I turn on my heel and head for the screen door. I'm nervous. That's why I notice the hole in the screen, the worn-through linoleum and the chipped plaster where Patsy rammed the table in the wall while turning cartwheels in the kitchen when we were little. Our house may look battered to someone who doesn't know every nick and imperfection is a memory.

My irritation eases, thinking about the memories we'll make together in this house, Sawyer, Momma, and me. The doorjamb in the pantry will be her growth chart—a line and her age, right beside Patsy's and mine. I wonder what the tooth fairy pays these days. Then there's back-to-school shopping, school plays... I sigh.

Patsy's death left a huge hole, but it made me a mother. Momma has accepted the baby with open arms and heart. If Reese tried to wrench Sawyer away, with Momma's delicate mental state... My heart taps a Morse code SOS on my breastbone. Well, he just better not, or he's going to come up against one rabid New Mexican momma bear.

I pull the screen door open. "Momma?"

* * *

Reese

I'll bet this farmhouse was something in its day. But that day is long past. There's a wide front porch with wooden rockers set back from the railing. Weed-choked rosebushes climb through the railing, trailing leaves. A partially collapsed barn looms behind the house, spooky in the shadows. Hard years and neglect have taken their toll. They either don't care that the house is falling down around them or they don't have any money to put into it. To be fair, it'd cost a fortune to rehab it. Probably better to leave it to the barn's fate.

My world, solid just a week ago, feels like this house looks: shaky, with the underpinnings falling out. And I know my life will change again after meeting Carson's baby. I like kids fine, but I haven't been around them much. What if I don't feel a thing for her? What if she hates me? What is the proper protocol in this situation? I like to be prepared, but there's no way to study for something like this.

Suck it up, boy. A St. James does what needs be done. The voice in my head is Bo's. It gets my feet moving.

Lorelei is holding the sagging screen door open. When it slaps behind me, I'm in a kitchen dating from the '60s. An old porcelain stove and oven, a Formica table and chairs covered in cracked vinyl. But there are fresh gingham curtains at the window, and on the sill, a flowering violet in a planter shaped like a burro. Everything is worn, but spotless.

"Momma?"

"We're in here," comes a voice from the other side of the old-fashioned arched doorway.

I follow her into a "parlor," where two older women sit on a couch complete with doilies, playing with a baby.

Carson's baby.

"Momma, this is Reese St. James. His brother was—" She halts when the other lady on the couch shakes her head. "He's Sawyer's uncle. Reese, this is my mother, Mary West, and Mrs. Wheelwright, the angel who helps us around here."

"Pleased to meet you both." The words are for the women, but I can't take my gaze off my niece. Her eyes are Lorelei's, but the rest is 100 percent St. James. I have photos of Carson and me as babies, and... "Do you mind if I sit down?" I drop into an overstuffed armchair without waiting for permission. There's something wrong with my legs.

"Are you all right, young man?" Mrs. Whatever asks, alarm in her eyes.

"I'm okay."

She stands and hands Sawyer to Lorelei. "I'll get you a glass of water. Don't you move."

My heart beats a tattoo on my ribs. I've been going through the motions the past week, wondering why I wasn't feeling any of the emotion I'd expected. Now I know why. It's been building like a summer storm that just hit, catching me out in the open. My eyes are watery, and my fingers tighten on the chair arms so as not to reach for her. This baby, my brother's child, is a St. James. A tiny, beautiful miracle.

"How sweet of you to come visit," Lorelei's mother says with a smile, then looks to her daughter. "Do we know this man?"

The lady comes back with a glass of water, and I gulp some and put it down.

"It's okay, Momma." Lorelei clutches the baby like she's afraid someone will tear her from her arms. She frowns down at me. "Do you want to hold her?"

I'm on my feet. "Yes."

Lorelei leans over the baby, whispers something, kisses her forehead. Then, after a long pause, hands her over.

I don't know how to hold a baby. But apparently, my arms do. She lies trusting, looking up at me with somber eyes. She's perfect. Fine brown hair, delicate-as-moth-wing brows over extraordinary eyes the color of the sky on a scorching August day, when the sun is so fierce it washes out the blue. A tiny nose upturned just a bit and full lips. She looks like a cherub in a Renaissance painting.

She's studying me just as closely.

"I wonder if she thinks you're her daddy," Lorelei says. "You being twins and all."

The lady who brought me the water says, "Twins. Oh, that's even more sad, if such a thing is possible."

"What's sad?" Lorelei's mother asks.

"Nothing, Momma. Everything is fine."

"If he's related to that baby, that makes him family, right?"

"I…I guess so." She doesn't look happy about it.

The old lady breaks into a wrinkly smile. "That fixes it, then. You'll stay for supper."

"Momma—"

"Oh no, ma'am. I—"

Mary sticks out her chin. "Don't you be silly. Turn family out without feeding them? Not in my house."

"But, Momma, I don't think—"

"You sit and talk." The other old lady stands. "Come on, Mary, you and I will get dinner on the table." She pulls a walker from beside the couch and helps Lorelei's mother up.

Lorelei looks like she was just offered creamed bugs on toast for an entrée.

The baby wraps her hand around my finger, but it's my heart she's squeezing. "Hey, Sawyer. I'm your uncle." Liquid gushes to my eyes, and I blink it back. *I know, Bo. Men don't cry, either.*

I needn't have worried about bonding. I'm already dreading having to hand her back. She sticks out her tongue and gums it. When she squirms, I rock from foot to foot.

"She's teething."

"Ouch. I'll bet that hurts." She tries to pull my finger to her mouth, but Lorelei is there with a little blue plastic ring.

Lorelei smells of hamburger grease and underneath it, some old-fashioned flower. Roses? Lilacs? I don't know from flowers, but the scent suits this house, suits her.

"Go ahead and sit. She gets heavy."

She isn't, but I settle into the chair anyway, cross my legs, and lean the baby in the crook. It frees up my hands to touch her. Her silky hair, the warm softness of her cheek, her tiny feet. She's in some kind of unitard made of nubbly fabric. "God, she's beautiful."

"She is." Lorelei looks as helpless as Sawyer.

I find I want to know more about this woman, so different from the ones I've known. "Were you close to your sister?"

"I thought I was." She dips her head and closes her eyes. "I don't understand why they didn't tell us. I mean, it doesn't make logical sense."

"Had you met my brother?" Carson, in a committed relationship—I still can't get my head around it.

"No. We hadn't seen Patsy in…a while."

She doesn't meet my eyes. They were together at least the nine months Patsy was pregnant, and six months after. I guess it's not only my family who had issues. I want to make Lorelei feel better but have little experience with women's soft feelings.

"I'd give a lot to know why, but I guess we'll never know."

I came to town to take Sawyer home with me. I may suck at decoding the mystery of women, but even I can see that's a hard sell. Lorelei's a proud, independent woman who loves this baby with everything she's got.

"Dinner's ready."

I'm not exactly sad to be interrupted. But it won't get easier, putting it off. "Lorelei, would you—"

She stands. "Let's go. Momma gets fussy if her routine is disrupted." She takes the two steps to me and reaches for the baby.

I stand. "I can take her in."

"I'm going to put her down while we're eating."

"Oh, okay." But still, it's hard to relax my arms enough to let the baby go. The back of my hand brushes Lorelei's soft breast on the handoff, and my face heats.

I watch the sway of her hips as she carries the baby to a dark room off the parlor, then wander to the kitchen. I shouldn't stay. I know Lorelei doesn't want me here. But I can't seem to leave.

Lorelei's mother is seated, and the other lady is putting a casserole dish on the table.

"It smells wonderful."

"*Psshhhht.* It's hash." Lorelei's mother flops a hand. "You sit right here." She pats the chair to her right.

"Thank you, ma'am." I pull out the chair and sit.

"My name is Mary."

Lorelei walks in just as the other woman seats herself. "I'm so sorry to put finishing dinner on you, Mrs. Wheelwright."

"No trouble at all."

Lorelei sits.

Mary extends a hand to me and Mrs. Wheelwright. "Will you say grace...what is your name?"

"It's Reese, Mary, and I'd be proud to." My mind shuffles data it hasn't used in a decade.

Lorelei flushes and offers her hand to me and to Mrs. Wheelwright.

Her skin is soft, but her fingers are calloused. "Lord, thank you for unexpected gifts, sent to fill our hearts. We will do our best to honor that precious responsibility. Please look after those who have gone before us. Oh. And thank you for this food." The words stumble out. Words I hope are adequate, and probably aren't. "Amen."

"Amen." Lorelei frowns and snatches her hand back.

Dishes are passed. Hash turns out to be hamburger, Tater Tots, onion, and green pepper. There's a green salad to go alongside.

"Where are you from, son?" Mary watches as the other lady pours iced tea.

"I'm from a little Texan town near the Mexico border called Carrizo Springs."

"Who's your family?"

"I just found out that you are." I glance to Lorelei.

She ducks and her hair curtains her face.

I take a forkful of hash. Interesting, in a greasy-spoon kind of way. "Ma'am—Mary, tell me about this house. Has your family always owned it?"

Her face lights up. "My grandfather built it. My momma was born here, I was born here, and my daughters, too. We used to own all the lands around it, but over the years they were sold off." She frowns, like she just remembered something. "So now there's just the house and the acre it sits on."

She looks around the room. "I wouldn't trade it for all the world's riches."

I understand now what she sees. "It's a lovely place."

Lorelei slaps her napkin on the table, her face a mask of disgust. "I'll put the kettle on for tea."

Mary chatters through the rest of the meal, unaware of her daughter's temper. Her memory of the past is remarkable; it's when you get to current events that things get muddled.

She's a happy, charming woman, and I'll bet she was something in her day.

Finally dinner is over, Mrs. Wheelwright has gone home, and I'm standing at the back door, getting ready to leave. Except I'm not ready. I turn, and Lorelei barely misses bumping into me.

She leaps back.

"If it's okay with you, I'd like to stay a few days, to spend some time with Sawyer. Can you recommend a hotel in town?"

Her jaw is tight enough to crack walnuts. "We don't have a hotel."

"The closest one, then."

"I don't think—"

"Look." I wait until her eyes finally settle on me, then whisper, "I know you don't like me, and I'm sorry for that. But I'd really like to spend some time with my niece, to get to know her. For just a couple of days." I put all my hope into my gaze. "Please?"

She lets out an exasperated sigh. "Oh, suit yourself. There's a budget motel on I-40, five miles out of town, but it won't be up to your standards. I'll let Mrs. Wheelwright know to expect you tomorrow."

She wants to push me out the door, I know. But I don't

want to leave. There's a vulnerability in those eyes that tugs at something in my chest. It makes me want to unravel this woman's secrets, in hope of understanding my own. I let out the breath I was holding. "Thank you, Lorelei. Really."

The line of her jaw is tight, and she doesn't meet my gaze. "I didn't do it for you. I did it for Sawyer."

CHAPTER 5

Reese

The hotel Lorelei directed me to was one of those old motor motels from the '60s, long, low-slung, and lousy. The neon sign out front is flaking and flickering like something out of a horror movie. But there's a light on in the office, and this beats sleeping in my car. I hope.

A buzzer goes off when I walk in, and a sleepy-looking college-age kid steps from the back.

"I need a room."

"You're lucky. We just happen to have an open one."

I'm assuming that's sarcasm, since I saw all of two trucks parked outside. "Great."

He pushes a form across the counter. "That'll be forty-five dollars."

"I'm planning on staying a couple of days." I scribble information.

His eyebrows disappear into his floppy bangs. "It's two hundred dollars a week."

I pass my credit card across the counter along with his form. "I'll take it." I look around the shabby little room, wondering if there's a by-the-hour rate, but decide I really don't want to know.

"You're in number two, our executive suite."

"Thanks." I take the plastic key fob with the old brass key attached.

When I walk in, I'm smacked by the smell of cheap disinfectant so strong, it makes my eyes water, but it's still not enough to cover the stale smell of ancient cigarettes. Bare light bulb overhead, heavy vinyl blackout curtains, nasty avocado shag carpet, and a creaky bed. If this is the executive suite, I'd hate to see a regular room. But given the outside, it's about what I expected.

The red numbers on the alarm clock read 8:00. Not too late to get some business done. I sit on the bed and fire up my laptop.

Three hours later, I'm lying on top of the covers, trying to sleep. I should be home. The ranch is all my responsibility now. But even this fleabag motel won't drive me away. Not until I get what I came for.

If only I knew what that was.

I mean, I'm staying for my niece, of course. But like it or not, I have to admit I'm staying for me, too. Since the accident, I've discovered a hole in me. A blind spot so dark, I only know it's there by crawling and feeling around the edges. It's big. And deep. And it feels like lonesome. Which is crazy, because I've always been separate. I was relegated to that growing up, have chosen it since.

Two pair of washed-blue eyes drift through my mind. What if the connection I felt tonight is a clue to what's missing in me?

I've been to therapy (something else Bo and Carson would

have laughed at, if they'd known). Guess it's not surprising I have "commitment issues"—the tendencies fit me better than my astrological sign. Self-sabotaging relationships, attracted to unavailable people, poor communicators.

Check, check, and check.

My track record with women nowadays is shorter than a fifty-yard dash. I hope that won't be true with little ones of the gender.

* * *

The next morning, I pull the door to the room closed, realizing that Lorelei and I didn't settle on a time for me to go out to the house. I also neglected to get her cell number. This is so not like me. It seems I've been wrong-footed since I rolled into this town. Or maybe it's just the aftershock of Carson's death and discovering he had a daughter. I'll stop by the café and ask. I've got to eat, regardless.

The town square looks less spooky but not much better in daylight. Butcher paper curtains many of the store windows, the old-fashioned movie house is showing a month-old release, and a dingy gazebo sits amid weeds in the center square. Unforgiven looks like it died a while back but the townsfolk missed the obituary.

The Chestnut Creek Café seems to be the one exception to the decline. I can't find a space in front, so I park down the block and walk back. When I open the door, a brass bell jangles against the glass. The booths are full of high school kids, old men in overalls, a few blue-collar workers and businessmen. I walk across the black-and-white mosaic floor to take the last stool at the bar, next to two grizzled old-timers.

"I got 'em both footballs."

"Manny, you been drinking Sterno again?" the one with crumbs in his gray-shot beard asks his disheveled neighbor. "You can't get a baby a football for a present. And one's a girl, you fool."

"Way I figure it, this way she'll have what the boys want when she gets outta diapers."

"Dude, that is so non-PC." He raises a grizzled brow, and his friend wheezes a laugh.

A petite waitress stops to fill their mugs, then raises the coffeepot my way. I flip the mug in front of me and she pours.

"Are y'all talking about Lorelei West's niece?"

Their heads swivel my way. "You're not from around here, are ya?"

I'm beginning to realize Mr. Football is more than a little drunk. "Nope. Texas."

"Like the drawl wasn't a dead giveaway. Why're you here?"

"That's not polite, you mule-eared idiot." Mr. Beard Crumbs sticks out a hand. "I'm Moss Jones, and this here is Manny Stipple."

I shake his hand. "Reese St. James."

The drunk leans across his friend to offer a hand. "You're that rich rancher guy. Pleased ta meet'cha. I got nothing against money."

Moss takes off his dirty cap and puts it over his heart. "Real sorry to hear about your brother." He slaps it back on his head. "You're here about the baby, I guess."

I'm not surprised. Gossip flies fast in small towns. "Sawyer." I like the sound of her name coming out of my mouth.

"She's a cutie, that one."

The waitress is back, order pad in hand. "What can I get you to eat?"

I glance up at the specials on the chalkboard above the serving window. "I'll have the breakfast burrito."

"Oh, Nevada does that up really good," Manny slurs. "Order a side order of her fry bread. She learned how to make it from her live-in, Fish. It's the best."

I don't want to know what a "live-in fish" is, but when in Rome...I nod at the waitress, she jots it down, tears the slip off, turns, and slides it onto the order wheel just inside the window. I glimpse a compact ponytailed blonde cooking at the grill. The back of her T-shirt declares *Silence is golden— duct tape is silver.*

"I think I like her already."

"Yeah, our Nevada, she's special."

I want to ask about Lorelei and her family, but I know if I come at it head-on, it will remind them I'm a stranger. "What did this town do to get a name like Unforgiven?"

They light up like football fans walking into a ten-TV sports bar in November. Moss says, "Well, that's a matter of some debate hereabouts."

"It's cuz they strung up Greg Paredes for branding cattle that weren't his, back in the 1800s," Manny says, then slurps his coffee.

"Nah, it's from when—"

There's a hollow *boom*. The door to the kitchen swings open and Lorelei walks through. Her gaze circles the room, then lands on me. "What are *you* doing here?"

The waitress sets my breakfast in front of me.

"A man's gotta eat."

"Oh."

She's even prettier when she blushes.

"Besides, I realized we hadn't worked out when I could go by the house, and I didn't have your number to call you."

"Right. Sorry." She jots her number on the back of an order slip and hands it to me. "Anytime after ten should be fine. It'll give Mrs. Wheelwright time to get Momma's and Sawyer's breakfast."

"And here's my number." I hand her one of my Katy Cattle Company business cards with my cell phone number. "Is there anything I can do for you out at the house?"

Her eyes darken when she's angry. I should know, since it's about the only way I've seen them. "I mean, if there's anything you need a man to do—"

"I'm perfectly capable of taking care of things, thank you so very much." She lifts a massive iced tea jug. "And if I wanted a man, I'd have one by now."

Why is it I can't see the stupidity of my remark until after it's out of my mouth? But her blush hints at something she's not saying.

"You're in it now, boy," Moss mumbles out of the corner of his mouth.

"I'm sorry. I didn't mean to insinuate—" But I'm talking to her back, because she's walked over to the first booth.

"Our Lorelei's about the nicest woman we got in Unforgiven. What'd you do to piss her off?" Moss looks me up and down, reassessing.

"Breathed, I think." The fry bread is crispy and delicious, and the burrito is huge. I decide it's safest if I eat. Can't stick my foot in my mouth if there's food in it.

When I'm done, I say goodbye to my new buds and walk to the car. On the way, I pass an old-fashioned five-and-dime, just opening. I decide to stop in to get a present for the baby.

As I pull open the door, I happen to look down to the corner of the window display. I stop, then squat to look closer.

A carved wooden black-and-white Pinto with a painted rope bridle, standing proud. It's not a match for mine, but it's damned close. One of my most prized possessions is a small hand-carved wooden horse my mother brought back for me from a trip. Its war paint is pastels with geometric lines and symbols. I inherited the one she brought back for Carson as well. I've searched hours online over the years and have never been able to find ones to match them. I straighten and pull open the door.

"Well, good morning." A little lady with big brown hair at odds with her lined grandma face greets me. "What can I help you find?"

"Could I see that horse in the window?"

"Certainly." She bends over the display and hands me the horse.

It's smooth and warm from the sun. Remembering my mother's elegant, long-fingered hands holding my horse, moisture pricks at the back of my eyes. "Do you know who made this?"

"It's hand carved by a local artist."

"Do you know how I can get in touch with him?"

She gives me a side-eye that reminds me I'm a stranger in a small town, then takes a half step back and pats her hair. "I'm afraid I can't. But if you care to leave me your number, I'll let you know when we get another in."

I pull a business card from my back pocket and hand it over. "I'd appreciate that, very much. I'll take this one." I tuck the horse under my arm. "I'm also looking for a present for a baby."

"Ah, Carly's newest. You'll for sure find something in the baby corner." She points to the back of the store.

That must be the baby the guys in the diner were talking about. I follow her back, the old wood floors creaking. We pass tables of overalls, underwear, kitchen goods, and hardware. I haven't been in a catch-all store like this in ages. I pull in the smell of the old building and realize I'm smiling. I know I'm in the right section when I reach an explosion of pink and blue. I look around, realizing I don't know what half this stuff is used for. What size would Sawyer be? What do I know from babies?

My eyes are drawn to a rack of stuffed animals. Hard to go wrong there. Bears and monkeys, lambs and...Oh, now, that's cute. I pick up a lavender stuffed goat with rainbow horns and a little bell around its neck that tinkles a happy sound. I take it with me and keep walking.

On the floor against the back wall is a tiny wooden rocking horse that looks to be handmade. Chocolate brown with a rope mane and tail, a red heart brand on its hip, and a big smile. Oh yeah, what little girl wouldn't want that? Besides, best get her started early; Sawyer comes from ranching stock.

"My husband makes those."

"It's beautiful." I tuck it under my arm. "I want to buy some clothes, but I don't know the size."

"You'll want the newborn."

"I'm actually shopping for my niece. Sawyer West?"

"Such a sad story. I'm sorry for you and your family." She sighs and shakes her head. "She's six months, but I'd get nine months. She'll stay in them longer. Follow me."

Fifteen minutes later, I pay for my purchases, and it takes me two trips to get them all in the car. Baby stuff is so darned cute, it's impossible to resist buying a bunch. Besides, I'm buying for me and Carson both.

I drive three miles out of town to the address Lorelei

gave me. A broken and dragging barbed-wire fence runs alongside the road near the house. It looks like nothing's been done with the land for years. I pass a Realtor's sign: THREE HUNDRED ACRES OF PRIME RANCHLAND. So much for truth in advertising. A cow per ten acres is my guess.

The house stands all alone, a half mile from any neighbor. The gold morning light highlights the battered exterior. It reminds me of a grand but shabby Southern lady after the war, trying to keep up appearances in spite of the wolves at the door. A shame, really.

I pull in the rutted dirt drive, and Mrs. Wheelwright pushes open the screen door to wave me in. "Lorelei called. Do you want some breakfast?"

"Very kind of you, ma'am"—I wipe my feet on the mat before stepping in—"but I ate in town."

"I'm not 'ma'am.' I'm Sarah."

"Who's there?" Mary's thready voice comes from the parlor.

I walk through the arched doorway. "It's me, Mary. Reese. Remember?"

"Of course I do." She looks like her daughter when she frowns. "It was only yesterday. I'm old, not addled, young man."

I can see it's not easy to win with either of the Wests. "I've come to visit with you and Sawyer today."

"Oh, that's nice. But the baby is napping, so you just come sit by me." She pats the couch cushion next to her.

"I think I heard her fussing." Sarah takes a step to the nursery.

"Would you mind if I check on her?" I have only a vague idea of what to do, but the cooing coming from that room tugs me that way.

"Not at all. You go on."

"Mary, do you mind?"

She shoos me with her hands. "Babies trump old ladies any day."

I step into the room where Lorelei took the baby last night. On one wall is an inexpert but endearing mural of an undersea world complete with mermaids, starfish, and...is that a shark or a whale? I dictate a note in my phone to order a mermaid twirly thingy for over the crib.

Irritated sounds pull my head around. In a battered crib against the wall, Sawyer is squirming. I step to it and reach a hand in. "What's the matter, little one?"

Her face scrunches, and she lets out another blat.

I put my hands under her armpits, lift her, and lay her against my chest. "I've got you. It's oka—" But it's not. She's soaked, and she smells like..."Mrs. Wheelwright, could you come in here, please?"

I hear tittering from the living room, but her face is carefully blank when she comes around the corner. "Yes? And it's Sarah, remember."

"Sawyer's a bit..." I hold her away from me. "Indisposed." I look down. My dress shirt has a dark spot, and my eyes are watering from ripeness so strong I can almost taste it. I swallow, queasy.

Sarah can't hold a straight face any longer. She chuckles. "Babies do that, you know."

"Will you show me what to do?"

She tips her head and studies me from the corner of her eye. "You want to change her diaper?"

"Of course I do. She's my niece."

"I was right about you." She winks. "Follow me." She walks out.

I don't know what that's about, and it doesn't matter,

because I'm starting to gag. I follow, holding a wriggling Sawyer out in front of me.

She takes me to a small bathroom in the hall. "She needs a bath, too. Might as well do both at the same time."

A pedestal sink stands across from a doily-draped, white-washed cabinet, and an old toilet, and a clawfoot tub with a shower curtain tucked into it. There's hardly room for me and the baby, much less two adults.

Sarah lays a towel over the doilies. "Put her here."

"Now, pull the tapes."

"Huh?"

"On the diaper." She points.

"Oh, okay." I pull, one on each side. The diaper flops open, fanning a miasma of stench into my face. "Huah." I gag, then swallow the fry bread that surges into my throat on a wave of grease. "Sweet mother of . . . huah."

Sarah snorts a shot of laughter.

"How can something this small—huah—smell this . . . ? Huah. Is she sick?" At least I have only to turn to the toilet if I lose the fight and hurl.

"No. Pretty much every morning she serves up a present like this."

She takes out a flat box of wet disposable cloths. "Here, I'll do it." She tries to elbow me out of the way.

"No. I can . . . do this."

She looks skeptical but backs up a half step, grabs a small plastic bag, and holds it out.

I'm surprised it doesn't have a nuclear-waste warning label. I start mopping and scraping and—Oh. My. God.

Sawyer, now happy (and who could blame her), kicks her feet and chortles at me. I try to focus on *that*.

Sarah pulls aside the shower curtain, and I glimpse a pink plastic tub—either a baby tub or a footbath . . . or maybe both. She runs the water, testing with her fingers until she's happy with it.

I put the last wipe in the bag and tie a knot in the top, hoping to contain the funk.

"Hey, stinky, you ready for a bath?" She smiles and waves her limbs at me. Her body is long, but she has cute little chubbers around her thighs and arms. Her skin is so soft and delicate, I'm afraid my rough hands will hurt her.

"Okay, ready here."

I gather Sawyer and carry her to the tub. Sarah backs up, and when I kneel on the tile, she perches on the toilet lid to coach me. Compared to the diaper, this is easy. Sawyer seems to love the water, splashing and pursing her lips to make a *hoo-hoo* sound. By the time she's clean, I'm soaked and laughing.

Sarah lays a new towel on the cabinet, and I carry Sawyer over, dry her, and Sarah shows me how to wrap her up like a burrito.

"I'll go get her clothes." She walks out, leaving Sawyer and me alone.

Our features are similar enough to be remarkable, really: the straight hairline against her tall forehead, the so-shallow dimples when she smiles. I lift her and lay her on my chest and whisper, "You and me, kid, we're going to have fun. I'll get you the smallest, gentlest pony ever, and we'll go riding together. We're a long way from the school, but maybe I'll bring in tutors. What do you think?" I run my lips over her wispy hair, inhaling the smell of baby and sweetness. "Then, when you're older, we'll—" I look up.

Sarah is leaning against the doorframe, looking smug. "Oh, this is going to be fun to watch."

"What is?"

"Never mind. I'll get her dressed. You go visit with Mary."

"Thanks for letting me help." I hand the baby over.

She gives me a warm smile that makes me feel like I've passed some kind of test. I rub the towel over my wet shirt and pants and head to the parlor. I don't kid myself that Lorelei will be anywhere near this easy.

I lower myself to the butt-sprung green couch beside Mary, and the scent of old-fashioned dusting powder fills my nose.

She looks up at me from a sea of wrinkles. "So. Tell me about your people."

If I bring up Carson or Patsy, will she get upset? Will she even remember her daughter? It seems I've been walking in a minefield since I hit this town, and if I make Lorelei's mother cry, she will flat tear me up.

I take a breath and try to tiptoe. "My parents were Bo and Katy St. James. Bo inherited a bit of land in West Texas from his dad, so he tried to raise cattle. But there was a drought, and he had to sell them off. Then he tried cotton, but he didn't take to farming much and he didn't have enough land to make a living at it anyway."

"I've known hard times myself. No shame in that." She pats the back of my hand.

"There were some lean years, for sure. But then his luck changed. Turns out the land was good for one thing. The oil beneath it."

"Oil money been the ruination of many families." An impish smile makes her eyes sparkle. "But I wouldn't squawk about a big old ugly oil well in my backyard."

I smile. I like this lady. "But he really hit the jackpot when he met my mom. She was working at a soda fountain at her dad's drugstore in town. He did some research on her favorite things and wooed her with yellow roses and love notes until she agreed to marry him. He promised her a big house with rosebushes all around and room for lots of kids."

She clasps her hands to her chest. "Oh, I like this story."

"He saved all his money and bought a ranch, had that house built, and planted those rosebushes."

"And did they fill that house with children?"

I look down at my hands. "Only two, ma'am. My mother passed away when I was eight."

"Oh, that's so sad. I'm sorry."

"It was hard on my father. He changed. He was always driven, but after that he was obsessed with the ranch. He turned hard and remote."

Mary nods. "He was grieving. Men grieve different than women."

Maybe, but he gets no absolution from me. "Yes'm."

"Here's the star of the show." Sarah walks in, holding Sawyer, turning me from thoughts of the past to the hope of the future. She puts the baby in my lap, and my heart beats softer, my hands are gentler. Everything in me reaches for this sweet, tiny thread of family.

* * *

Lorelei

I'm driving home, nodding to one of my ballroom-music mix tapes, imagining myself gliding across a floor. Turn, step, step, dip, and turn...Momma said I went from crawling to dancing. I'm sure she's exaggerating, but I've loved dancing as far back as my memory goes. Momma squirreled away her change so I could take lessons from a lady in town who taught kids on Saturday afternoons. I sigh.

I reach to massage my lower back. It has been a brutally busy day and I'm looking forward to a hot bath, snuggle time with Sawyer, and reading to Momma. When I pull into the drive, Einstein's headlights spotlight that Texan's massive showy pickup.

My mood plummets like a dead cat down a well. Crap. I should have known. You give a Texan an inch and he'll take a hundred-acre chunk, then start drilling for oil.

I park and drag my aching feet to the door and into the house.

"Oh my goodness, will you look at that?"

I haven't heard that much excitement in Momma's voice since the last time Patsy came home.

"Well, I'm not surprised. Sawyer's smart. She can't help it—she's got good genes." His deep voice holds a smile.

I doubt he's referring to *our* half of the gene pool. I walk around the corner. Mrs. Wheelwright is sitting on the couch. Momma is beside her, hands over her mouth, watching Sawyer and Reese lying on their stomachs on the floor.

"Okay, you ready?" he whispers to Sawyer, and rolls onto his back.

Sawyer does the same.

"She's rolling over!" They look up at my screech. I step over and lift Sawyer to put a loud smack on her cheek. "Oh, you are the most brilliant baby ever." I slap on a smile. Of course I'm happy; she and I have been working on this for a week. But there's a little bruise on my heart that she did it when I was gone. And for *him*.

Reese pushes to his knees and stands. "I was just demonstrating, and she did it. I couldn't believe it."

I hug Sawyer to me and sniff the sweet-smelling spot on the very top of her head. "I'm so proud of you," I whisper.

This is just one of the millions of firsts she'll have. I won't even remember this one in a year.

But that's a lie. I will. I hold my face in happy lines and try not to glare at the interloper. "Why are you still here?" The bitterness dripping from the words betrays me.

A quick wince flashes across his face before a mask of indifference falls. Good.

He brushes off nonexistent lint from his tailored dress pants (no homey Wranglers today; we're seeing the true St. James). "You're right. I didn't mean to stay so late. I got caught up, and...I'm sorry."

Even before Momma's death-ray stare, I know I should apologize. But that would be letting down my guard, and I can't do that. What if he wants to take Sawyer from me? We really don't know this man. Who is he to walk in and make us share her? Indignation surges, and I open my mouth to spew it.

What if she likes him better?

I close my mouth and bury the nasty thought I didn't want to know about myself deeper in my mind.

"Don't go. You must stay for dinner." Momma smiles.

"Oh yes," Mrs. Wheelwright croons, "say you'll stay."

Momma's voice holds a shake. So do her hands. Her face is relaxed, edging to slack. Today was too much for her.

"Not tonight, Momma. You're tired, and so am I. It's been a long day for both of us." I carry Sawyer to her room, to put her to bed.

Reese's steps shush over the carpet behind me. "Look, I'm sorry..."

I step through the doorway. A little rocking horse is in one corner, a giant stuffed bear in the other. Unopened packages of clothes are stacked on the dresser. In the crib, a lavender stuffed goat. All the shiny new things make my secondhand furniture and the mural that I worked so hard on look shabby and...poor.

Something tears inside me, and a putrid mixture of envy, shame, and bitterness oozes out. I lay Sawyer in the crib and turn on him. "Where do you get off? Do you think you can waltz in here and buy us? Buy Sawyer?"

That hurt is back on his handsome face, but I whip up another spurt of anger. "I see that you've charmed Momma and Mrs. Wheelwright into your corner today. You won't find me so easy."

"News flash," he mumbles under his breath.

"This is all just a game to you, isn't it?" I hiss. "Why don't you leave the unsophisticated yokels alone and go pick on someone your own size? Corporate bigwigs or something?"

"Pick on? I'm not—"

Sawyer takes a deep breath and lets out a wail of despair.

"Now see what you did? I'll never get her down." I lift her out of the crib and put her on my shoulder, rubbing soothing circles on her back.

"Hey, that's not fair."

"*You* want to talk fair?" I hiss and bounce on the balls of my feet, not sure if I'm trying to soothe the baby or the monster loose inside me. "Look around this room. It's a perfect example of the unfairness of life. So you know what? You can just deal." I turn and stalk to the parlor and give Sawyer to a wide-eyed Mrs. Wheelwright.

"What's wrong? Who is that man?" Momma's voice is high and whiny. She gets worse in the evenings, but she's even more confused when she's upset.

I whirl, and almost bump into Reese. He takes a startled step back. "Thanks. Now Momma's upset." I know I'm being mean and unfair. And I don't care. I march to the kitchen, push the screen door, and hold it open. "Please, can you just go?"

He steps past me, onto the porch, then turns, brows drawn over fire in his dark eyes. "I didn't come here to cause problems for you. I came here to see my niece. I'm staying a week, and I hope to be back tomorrow...if it's okay."

"You've seen her all day today." *Which is more than I get.* I cross my arms over my vulnerable chest. Underneath the anger, his face is so sad, reminding me that he's lost a lot, too. My soft heart is starting to regret my snit-fit.

"I have. And she's amazing. Perfect, really." Some of the fight goes out of his eyes. "Look, you're seeing me as a stereotype, and I don't deserve that. I'm not judging you, or your family."

I lift my chin. "We may not have money, but we have something all your money can't buy. Love."

He glances away, and this vulnerable little-boy look comes over his face. "You're one of the lucky ones, then."

He turns, shoves his hands in his pockets, steps off the porch, and walks to his truck.

God, how could someone as coldhearted as me ever hope to be a good mother? I wish I could take it all back; I know I've hurt him. "Hey," I call after him.

He is at his car and glares back at me over his shoulder. Then he climbs up into the massive interior.

"I'm sorry."

But he's already slammed the door and fired the engine.

CHAPTER 6

Lorelei

The next morning, I find any excuse to be in the dining room: coffee patrol, refilling sugar on the tables, chatting up the customers. When Sassy asks if I want to trade jobs with her, I head back to my office. It's ten, and Reese is obviously not coming in. I wanted to apologize the proper way, the hard way, face-to-face.

I close my door and pull his card from my purse. It's like him: crisp, clean, and consequential. *Reese St. James, Manager.* Probably hasn't had a chance to replace *Manager* with *Owner.*

That's mean-spirited and rude. So not me, but this guy seems to irritate me just by breathing. I don't know him well enough for my code-red animosity. Yes, he's rich and a bit high-horsed, but he's human, and I hurt him last night. And I'm worried about him wanting Sawyer, but I have court papers; *I have custody.* He'd have to prove legal grounds to take her from us, and there aren't any.

And on the porch last night, I saw through him, to the sadness. He lost his mother, his father, and now his brother. He looked so all alone. It's pulled at me, ever since.

Besides, Sawyer deserves better. If a friend told me this story, I'd tell her to be happy that Sawyer has more than just me and Momma. So why am I so mad?

After my fit last night, I have to admit—I'm jealous. Not of his money. Well, not mostly. It's the time his money affords him. He can walk away from his life and spend a week playing with his niece, not worrying a minute about the expense, or if he'll have a job when he gets back. He's so entitled that he has no idea that he is. I know he has a right to be in Sawyer's life. I just don't know how to fit him into our lives. He's like a spring in an old couch, pushing and uncomfortable. And as long as I'm admitting…he's charming and good-looking, and when he looks at me with those melted-chocolate eyes, he reminds me of dreams I tucked away years ago. Silly, young-woman dreams of romance and love and babies.

Maybe that's part of why this guy irritates me. Better to let sleeping dreams lie.

I eye the computer. Maybe I can research somewhere to buy the organic cornmeal that Nevada wants for her fry bread. "No. Your Momma taught you to do the hard stuff first. Quit frittering and get it done."

I plop into my chair and dial. Maybe he'll be on the phone. Maybe it'll just go to voice—

"Hello?" His voice is warm as liquid sunshine, and it isn't a recording.

"Yes. Um. Reese? This is Lorelei."

"Yes."

Chilly and abrupt, but he hasn't hung up yet. Better than I expected. Better than I'd have done in his place. "I looked for you this morning, but you didn't come in for breakfast."

"I thought you'd be more comfortable if I didn't. I went to the Lunch Box Diner, down the street."

"Oh no. You didn't eat the chili, did you? It'll give you the runs."

"At eight in the morning?" He chuckles, and I'm glad he can't see me blush. "No, I had eggs."

"Oh, good. I don't know how Dusty could ruin eggs. Listen. I just called to tell you I'm sorry. About last night. I was rude, and you did nothing to deserve it. That's not like me, though you probably think it is, from the impression I've given you, and—"

"You sound like me, the first time we met."

I smile, remembering his stuttered apology. "I kinda do, don't I?"

He sighs. "Let's agree that neither of us is at our best right now. We've lost family, and Sawyer was a surprise to us both. I feel like my life stopped and I've been thrown into a new, strange one."

It's as if he looked inside my head and described what he saw. "Yes, it feels just like that."

"Okay then…" I hear him take a breath to say goodbye.

"I'm not done. It's not a good apology until I give a reason for my actions. I came home last night and saw Sawyer rolling over for you and…I was jealous. I'm sorry I'm that petty, but apparently, I am. You're more than welcome to visit." A flush climbs my neck, and I have to admit that I'm looking forward to learning more about him. If he's still there when I get home, that is.

"You don't need to fall on your sword, but thank you. I accept your apology." There's a smile in his voice. "I'm heading out there now. Oh, and I'm cooking dinner."

Click.

I sit staring at the phone. He's presumptuous and bossy,

but for once I'm not complaining. I go through my days doing what needs to be done. He has no idea what a treat it is for me not to do this one chore, for one night.

And I'm sure not telling him.

But it's sweet of him just the same.

* * *

Reese

The attorney emailed me the background check on Lorelei West early this morning while I was working in my hotel room. She's just what she appears to be: honest, hardworking, broke. Her bank account balance explains part of why she's so snippy about money. She's one appliance breakdown from bankruptcy.

I pull up the drive, shut the truck down, and watch the wind dance with the long grass of the yard. I can't claim that Sawyer isn't being taken care of. I sure can't claim she's not loved.

If only I'd found out about Sawyer first. Once I had her, a court would be crazy to take her away from me.

I glance to the back door of the house. Would I have been as open and free with visitation as Lorelei has been? I open the car door and slide the long step to the ground. Moot point—Lorelei couldn't afford the trip to Texas. Maybe I'll try to give her some money to help with Sawyer's expenses. Just until I can work out joint custody.

"Come on in," Sarah calls when I knock on the screen door.

"Who's there?" Mary's tremulous voice comes from the parlor.

I drop the grocery sacks on the table and step to the doorway. "It's me, Mary."

"What is that man doing in the house?" Mary's voice spirals just short of panic.

"It's all right, hon. I invited him." Sarah pats Mary's hands, and mouths *Bad day*. Poor Mary. Poor Lorelei.

"Why don't I get Sawyer up?" I say.

"I'll do the diaper. You can do the bath." Sarah scoots to the edge of the couch.

"No. You keep Mary company. I'll handle it." Like Bo always told us, fake it 'til you make it. "I'd like to help."

She raises one eyebrow. "You sure?"

"Oh yeah. It'll be easier today."

Turns out, I'm an optimist. The smell hits me at the doorway—the stench rolls over me. Still, Sawyer smiles to see me and waves her arms. I didn't know it was possible to gag and smile at the same time.

I lift her and, holding her at arm's length in front of me, trot for the bathroom, lay her on the dresser, and flip the light switch. Nothing happens. I tap it but don't hear the jingle of a blown bulb. No time to deal with it now—I've *got* to get her out of that diaper. Good thing there's enough light from the frosted window over the tub to see by. I break my personal best getting her cleaned up. Once the nuclear waste is tied in a plastic bag, the air clears and my stomach settles.

I tickle her belly, and she chortles at me.

"Oh yeah, you think it's funny now. Wait until I tell this story to your first boyfriend. Who will be laughing then, huh?" Keeping a hand on Sawyer to be sure she doesn't roll off the dresser, I unbutton my shirt. I learned yesterday that there's no way to do bath time without getting wet myself, and this is my last clean shirt. I check behind the door for somewhere to hang it. There's a hook with a small pink bra hanging from it that I doubt is Mary's. I imagine it on Lorelei's long torso. I finger the lacy edge. When I realize I must look like a pervert, I rip off my shirt and hang it on the hook. "Okay, button, let's do this."

We both enjoy the bath, though I end up almost as wet as her. Every once in a while, she lets out "mmmmmmm" or "iiiiiii," which must be the beginning of words. While I'm getting her dressed, I make a mental note to look up when babies start talking and how to help them learn.

Whoever created snaps on baby clothes didn't consider man-size hands. Have they not heard of Velcro?

Eventually we're both presentable, and I carry her to where Mary and Sarah are working on a puzzle. Well, Sarah is. Mary is playing with a piece, turning it this way and that as if trying to understand what it's for.

"Ah, here's our girl, Mary." Sarah reaches up to take Sawyer from me.

"Why is that man here, again?"

"I'll go to put away the groceries. I'm cooking dinner tonight, Mary."

"Oh, you're from the Meals on Wheels."

I walk to the kitchen and leave it to Sarah to explain... or not.

Once I put away the steaks and other perishables, I glance around, thinking about the conversation with Lorelei this morning. Not surprising she feels overwhelmed; she has so much on her shoulders. Maybe there's some way I can make myself useful. It might go a ways to making up for my bumbling yesterday. I need to forge some kind of relationship here. "Sarah?"

"Yes?"

"Do you know where the electrical breaker is and where tools are kept?"

"Check in the pantry for the breaker box, and I think the tools are under the kitchen sink."

"Thanks." I find the circuit box in the back corner of the sparsely populated pantry. I flip the breaker for that part of the house, then wander back to the sink and pull open the cabinet door beneath it. There's a worn cardboard box full of screws, washers, nails, wood glue, zip ties, a hammer, and a screwdriver with multiple size attachments. I pull it out and head for the bathroom.

I was right—the bulb is fine. I check the switch, and it's fine, too. I unscrew the switch plate, trace the wires a few inches, to find the break. Simple fix. I put it back together and flip the switch. The light comes on. I dust my hands, feeling pretty smug.

I have all day, and Sawyer naps through a lot of it. Might as well be useful. "I'll be outside for a bit," I call to the ladies, then head out the door and stroll to the rickety barn. Dust-mote-filtered sunlight streams through the gaps between the boards. I peer through the doorway to the shadowed interior. The hayloft collapsed at some point, and ancient hay bales are scattered like a giant's Legos across the dirt floor. The support beams have given way at the very back, and who knows where else. If tools are in there, they're staying here.

From here I can see into the backyard. The grass is a sickly straw color, shin-high. Only the weeds seem to be thriving. There's a metal shed near the barbed-wire boundary at the back of the property. Here's something I can do; I'll see if there's a mower in there. Not that it would help the weeds, but at least the yard would look more presentable.

The door squeals when I pull it open to reveal an ancient push lawn mower. I pull it out, knowing my shoulders are going to ache tonight. How in the heck does Lorelei wrangle this dinosaur?

Looking from the outside, her burdens are too many and too heavy for her delicate shoulders. The mower's tank is empty, so I rig a siphon to pull gas out of my truck's. I take off my shirt and hang it on the outside mirror. Lorelei seems to be as genuine, honest, and loving as she appears. The women I've known aren't anything like that. In fact, they're the opposite: high-maintenance, cliquish, and shallow. I'm jaded and a bit…crispy when it comes to women.

But I have to admit, I admire this one.

The mower fires on the tenth pull, and I start pushing, imagining Lorelei in that pink bra.

* * *

Lorelei

I pull up and park in the driveway, but something's niggling. Something's different. I step out of Einstein and look around. The crickets' night song is the same. The driveway is the same. The yard…the yard. It's neatly mowed, and the smoke drifting from the back of the house makes my stomach growl. Meat—steak, if I don't miss my guess. I walk around to where the light over the back door spotlights the small cement porch. The Weber grill is smoking, but no one is around. The backyard's shaggy grass is shorn short as well. Where did Sarah find house elves in Unforgiven?

I turn at the sound of water hissing from the hose. On the far side of the house, a shirtless Reese is bending over, dousing his head. His biceps flex, and the drips down his broad back glisten in the yellow porch light.

"I-yiy-yiy!" He drops the hose and tosses his head back like a wild horse. Water flies in a fan. "Man, that's cold."

Water rolls down to the two small dimples in his lower

back. I know I should announce myself, but it's been too long since I've been this close to a young, good-looking male body.

Besides, I don't trust my voice.

He runs his hands down his torso, squeegeeing water, then turns. "Oh. Hi." He reaches for his shirt on the plastic chair as if it's the most natural thing to be half-naked in front of a woman he hardly knows.

He's got one of those epic chests: almost hairless except the line of dark hair running down the front of his water-spotted Wranglers. *Shut up, Lorelei and say something.* "Um. Hi." I'm hoping he can't see my flaming cheeks. "I'll see you inside." And I flee. Well, I don't actually run, but it's a near thing.

I'm in the kitchen when he steps in, this time wearing a shirt—and Momma's apron, a plate in one hand, a set of tongs in the other. "Welcome home." He smiles that all-American-boy smile my way. "Dinner is in ten minutes."

You just have to respect a man who is secure enough in himself to wear a ruffled pink-flowered apron.

I run up the stairs to my room, grab my holey jean shorts and a ratty T-shirt, but stop at the closet on my way out. We don't often have company. Or meat that isn't ground, for that matter. Wouldn't hurt me to dress *one* step up from grubby. I pull out a sleeveless yellow-and-white gingham blouse, yellow shorts, and sandals. Clean and summery, but not special. I can live with it. I head downstairs to wash up.

I close the bathroom door and, out of old habit, flip the light switch. The lamp over the sink comes on, and I stare at it for a minute. It's been out so long, I'd almost forgotten what the room looked like lit. I notice the towel from Sawyer's bath is tossed over the towel rod instead of hanging in its usual place, on the peg behind the...Oh hell.

My pink bra is dangling from the hook like a whorehouse invitation.

Hot blood throbs in my cheeks. Him imagining me with no clothes on is mortifying. And kinda...hot.

Wow, Lorelei, that's flat pathetic. The next time a guy asks you out, you need to accept.

I turn on the water in the sink and wash the smell of fryer oil off my skin. It could have been worse; it could easily have been the ratty bra I have on. I'm going to hope Reese has forgotten about this. In five minutes, I've changed and go in search of Sawyer.

She's lying on her back in her crib, sleeping in a onesie I've never seen before, with a cartoon lion on the breast. Her eyelashes are feathery shadows against her pink cheeks, her thumb an inch from her mouth.

My heart swells, pushing almost painfully against my breastbone. How can love be this fierce, when three weeks ago I didn't know this baby existed? I don't know, but I don't care. The love is just there, beating in my chest along with my heart—just as strong, just as essential.

She's a part of me now.

Funny how I didn't feel I was missing anything before. But now it's like my life has gone from black-and-white to color. It's so much richer, so much fuller. Details I hadn't noticed stand out in bold relief.

The responsibility for this tiny life weighs heavy some days. Did Patsy feel that way? Sawyer is so little and delicate. And the world is hard.

I run my finger over the silk of her superfine hair, then make myself step away. It isn't easy. It's probably good that I have to work. I think I'd just end up staring at her all day.

In the kitchen, Momma is buttering corn on the cob

at the table. Mrs. Wheelwright is at the sink, draining green beans.

"How you doing, Momma?"

"That boy from Meals on Wheels is so nice. I didn't know they cook and everything."

I manage to hold back a snort of laughter. "Yeah, county services are stepping up, huh?"

Mrs. Wheelwright's smug smile sends a little jangle of awareness down my spine. She's on Team Reese, I can tell. She'd just better not start matchmaking. "What can I do to help?"

She waves at the stove. "You can stir the gravy and take the mashed potatoes out. We're almost ready."

I grab the stained pot holders from the counter and pull out a baking dish of mashed potatoes. The consistency of the little peaks makes it obvious that these aren't from a box. I carry it to the table, then stir the zero-lumps gravy.

No way a spoiled rich boy did this. "Was all this delivered?"

"Nope." Mrs. Wheelwright carries over the dish of green beans and sets it on the table. There's that smile again.

"Cooking, mowing, electrical work...quite a Mr. Fix It, isn't he?" He may be handsome enough to play Prince Charming, but I can't afford to forget: I'm no Cinderella. I didn't lose a shoe and I don't need saving.

She studies my face. "Before you mount that tall horse and ride, you may want to rein in and watch for a few minutes."

The screen door opens and Reese walks in, a platter of sizzling meat held high. "Steaks are done."

"So is everything else." Mrs. Wheelwright pulls out the chair at the head of the table. Daddy's chair. "You sit right here."

He sets the steaks on the table, unties the apron, pulls it over his head, puts it in Mrs. Wheelwright's outstretched hand, and sits.

"What a treat." Momma clasps her hands under her chin like a starry-eyed ingenue. "Do you know how long it's been since we've had steak?"

"It hasn't been *that* long, Momma," I mumble, looking down at my plate and tucking hair behind my ear that has escaped my ponytail.

"Will you say grace, Lorelei?" Mrs. Wheelwright reaches for Momma's hand and mine, leaving me with . . . his.

It's warm and dry, and distracting enough that I'm grateful the words come by rote. "Thank you, Lord, for this food, our home, Momma, and our angel, Mrs. Wheelwright—"

"And the Meals on Wheels man," Momma says. "Amen."

"Amen." I jump when he squeezes my hand before he lets it go. I fire a glance at him, but he's looking at Momma.

He lifts the serving spoon. "Mary, would you like corn or green beans?"

The meal is a treat; I have to admit that. He teases and charms Momma and Mrs. Wheelwright, making them giggle like schoolgirls. He more or less ignores me. Which is good. Of course it's good. No reason for it to put my teeth on edge.

When I'm done, I lift my plate and several others, balancing them with the years of practice I got as a waitress before Carly promoted me to manager.

"I'll do the dishes," Mrs. Wheelwright says. "Why don't y'all get Sawyer up from her nap and go out on the front porch? It's a beautiful evening."

Her too-sweet smile confirms my suspicions. There's a matchmaker among us.

"I've got to—"

"You entertain your guest, Patsy." Momma wags a finger at me. "I taught you better manners."

Reese is looking at me, pity painted on his face.

Suddenly, it's all too much. I'm tired, and heartsore, and just wishing I could pause the world for a bit—to put everything down. I turn to the sink and stack the dishes, my sinuses prickling with emotion.

A chair squeals across the linoleum behind me. "I'll get Button and meet you out there."

My daddy's words ring in my head: *Buck up, Lorelei. You start from where you are and make the best with what you have.* I dampen a dish towel to wipe down the rockers and pick up a lap blanket on my way by the couch.

As always, the front door sticks. We use it so seldom.

"Here, I'll do that." Reese hands Sawyer into my arms, grasps the doorknob, and tugs. Nothing. Tugs again. Nothing. "Step back."

I do, turning Sawyer away, just in case.

He braces his foot against the wall. His shirt pulls tight, outlining the V of his torso, muscles straining. He pulls, and the door pops open. He bows and waves me through.

Fixed a switch, mowed the yard, got the front door open. A trifecta of little things I can cross off my list, which is still long enough to wrap around the porch. "Thank you."

He pulls the blanket from my shoulder and spreads it over the boards, then takes Sawyer from me. She clings to his neck, kicking her legs and making a "buh, buh, buh" sound.

She likes him. Momma likes him, and Mrs. Wheelwright is leading the St. James fan club. Heck, after today, even I kinda like him.

And he's pretty much ignoring me. A mesquite thorn of melancholy pierces my heart. I should be used to it by now—being a fixture, like a toaster or a dishwasher, noticed only when it stops working. I wipe down two rockers that are covered in dust.

He lays Sawyer on the blanket and hands her a teething ring. "You okay?"

My throat closes on a nasty wad of self-pity. "I'm fine." I drop the dish towel and sit. I'm just so tired.

He settles in the other rocker. "Why do I get the feeling you say that a lot, even when it's not true?"

How does he know that? "How old are you, Reese?"

"Thirty-two. You?"

I didn't realize the gap was that much. "Thirty-seven. Have you ever been married?"

A snort comes from the shadows. "Nope. You?"

"Nope." I'm certainly not going down that rabbit hole, telling him what a fool I was dreaming myself almost engaged to a guy who turned out to be married. I lay my head against the chair back and set the chair to gently rocking. The crickets start up again, and the smell of cut grass hangs in the still air. The dark envelops me like the hug of an old friend. "I'd forgotten how nice it is out here."

"Did you used to hang out on the porch?"

"Oh yes. Momma and Daddy used to sit here in the summer and watch Patsy and me play hide-and-seek in the dark."

We rock in silence, punctuated now and again by Sawyer's syllables.

Somehow, it's easier to talk in the dark. "What were summers like when you grew up?"

"Work, mostly." His voice rumbles like the water in Chestnut Creek, calm and deep.

"Oh, come on. You never played hide-and-seek, or kick the can, or rover?"

"Nope."

Sounds like such a lonely childhood. "What did you do in the evenings?"

"Read in my room, mostly."

"Ah, you're a reader." There's something we have in common.

"Mostly trade journals and the like, nowadays. But when I get time, I like a good political thriller. You like to read?"

I nod. "Momma, too. I read romance to her every night."

"Ah, a romantic." There's a smile in his voice.

"In fiction, yes."

"Not in real life?" The tone is too serious to be a tease.

Just how did we get into this conversation? "Nope." I pick up my carving knife and the chunk of wood that is only beginning to look like a horse.

"What's that?"

"Ah, just a hobby."

"Are you whittling?"

"Carving, actually. It was my dad's thing. I learned from him."

"Let me see."

I hand over the chunk of wood. "Just a new project."

I can hear the slide of his hands over it. Something about his big hands fondling my wood makes me want to squirm on my seat.

"A horse?" His voice is an awed whisper.

"Always. Why?"

"Do you sell these at the five-and-dime?"

"I mostly make them for friends, but yeah, sometimes."

"I found you," he breathes.

How can a whisper touch my skin? Goose bumps engulf me in a wave. I swallow. "Found me?"

He tells me a story of what had to be my father's ponies

and a dying mother's gifts. But it's the tone in his voice that whispers the grief of a lonely child. "I'm so sorry. I can only hope that my dad's pony reminds you of your mother."

"It does." He rocks. "What a coincidence that we meet, all these years later."

"It's amazing, really."

We sit, the creak of the chairs answering the cricket's calls. Silence between people who don't know each other is almost always awkward. But this isn't. It vaguely occurs to me that that in itself should make me nervous. But I'm not. My muscles relax into the gentle rocking, and the night sounds blur...

"Lorelei." He's shaking my shoulder.

"Huh? What?" Panic takes my breath. "Sawyer?"

"I put her down for the night." Reese is squatting before my chair, hand on the arm. "You fell asleep. Sarah got your mother to bed and left about ten minutes ago."

"Oh." I run the back of my hand over my mouth to be sure I haven't drooled on myself. "I'm sorry." I push to my feet. "I never do that."

"Don't apologize for being tired." He stands. "I'm going back to the hotel. Walk me to my car?"

"Sure." When I go to stand, his hand is there, and I take it without thinking. It's strong. Warm. Solid. I duck my head, my heart brushing hummingbird wings against the walls of my chest. We take the broad front steps, his hand warm and solid under my elbow. "Thank you for dinner. And for mowing. And the bathroom light." I remember my bra, and I'm glad it's too dark for him to see my blush.

"It was my pleasure."

"It's very kind of you. I appreciate it, but you have to stop." When we round the corner, the kitchen porch light spills onto the drive.

"Why?"

I feel the warmth of his gaze on the side of my face. "Because it's not yours to do. I'm not comfortable with owing favors."

"You don't owe me anything. Family helps each other."

"Oh, come on. We're not family. Not really." I stop, and his hand falls away. He looks at me so long, I have to turn to face him.

"You don't think anyone notices, but I do." He frowns, studying my face. "You do what needs to be done, without complaint, every day. I've seen you with your employees, the townsfolk, even stray dogs. You have a huge heart, and if there's something I can do to help, I'm going to." He turns, shoves his hands in his pockets, and strolls to his truck.

Like he hasn't just laid bare my deepest secrets. My deepest want.

Like he's *seen* me.

CHAPTER 7

Reese

The next days fly by at Mach one, and before I'm ready, it's time to leave. There's no question of delaying departure: my breeding manager has problems, a prize bull tangled with a barbed-wire fence, and a small grass fire has started in the canyon south of my land. I zip my suitcase and look around for anything I might have forgotten. This room is nasty, but I'm grateful for my time here. I pull the suitcase off the bed and roll it to the door.

At Lorelei's request, I didn't call about the roof. I didn't buy Sawyer more things. I backed off "helping," but nothing could stop me from spending time with my niece. I've learned a lot this week about diapers, baths, and babies, but I need to know more. I've ordered a bunch of books on baby husbandry, and they should be waiting for me at home.

I let the door fall closed behind me and head for the truck. One more thing to do before I go. My empty stomach jitters as I pick up and discard arguments, trying to find just the right tone.

I'm usually a great negotiator. But the first rule of negotiations is that you have to be ready to walk away from a deal, and there's no way I'm doing that. Maybe, if I find just the right words, just the right expression... Who am I kidding? If I were any good at doing this, I'd have negotiated a place for myself in the house I grew up in.

I drive to the Chestnut Creek Café in a cloud of potential disaster that mirrors the iron sky hanging just overhead. I park on the square, and as I get out, a low rumble of thunder rattles through me.

I step into the café's after-breakfast/before-lunch lull. I timed it right. I flag down the waitress and ask if I can speak to Lorelei.

Moss pats the stool beside him. "Hey, Reese, sit down here and help me pound some sense into this mule."

Manny protests, and I tune out the rest of their daily grousing.

Lorelei pushes through the swinging door, her brow scrunched with concern. "What's wrong? I thought you were already gone."

"I need to talk to you." I look around. The few diners are studying their plates... and eavesdropping. "Is there somewhere?"

She leads me to the front door, out to the sidewalk, across the street, to the scruffy patch of grass that constitutes the town square.

Thunder rolls, and a huge drop of rain hits me square on the top of my head.

She squints up at the sky, then heads for the gazebo in the center.

I trot behind, and we just make the steps when the sky lets

loose with a crash of thunder and torrents of rain. It drums on the roof like it's trying to beat its way in.

She turns, crosses her arms, and her face falls into those wary lines that she wears most when I'm around. "What did you want?"

Even concerned, she's pretty. And I so wish I didn't cause her concern; she has so many already. The negotiations class I took recommended leading with the positive. "I know you don't care for me much, and you've been generous and kind to me this week, letting me visit and get to know Sawyer. Thank you."

"It's not that I don't like you." Her mouth twists. She studies me for a few seconds before turning to look out at the rain. "I don't like who I become when I'm around you."

Her honesty tugs the same from me. "I like who you are."

Cheeks pink, she looks at her feet. "It's just that, since Sawyer came, I'm so afraid all the time." She wraps her fingers around her biceps and hunches her shoulders.

"Here." I shrug out of my jacket and spread it over her shoulders. "Why are you afraid?"

"Thanks." Thunder cracks overhead, and she flinches. "I don't know. Before it was just me and Momma. Adults. Now I'm responsible for a helpless human. What if she gets sick? What if she falls? What if . . . ?" She looks at her feet. "What if I'm not a good enough person to be her mother?"

The naked vulnerability in her words raises something strong and protective in me, making me want to go find a white horse and sword. *Oh yeah, that's me. Bet Carson and Bo are laughing their asses off right now.* I look down at her big eyes, dusty blue, so much like Sawyer's. "I think you're an amazing woman. You handle more in a day than I could in a week."

I take a deep breath. "That's what I wanted to talk to you

about. You have so much on your shoulders. I'd like to share some of the responsibility for Sawyer."

She's shaking her head before I get the words out.

I came here for this. I have to say it, even though I know from her look it won't help. "What if we shared custody? I could take Sawyer for a couple of weeks. I'll be responsible for getting her to and from—"

"What?" Her eyes widen with panic as red rises up her neck to splash her cheeks in a flush of crimson. "No, no, no, no, *no*."

"But I could help—"

"Oh, right. I see. Let me *help* you, Lorelei. Really, I'm just trying to lighten your *burden*." Her lip curls. "I open up to you, and you use it to get your way."

"That's not fair." Anger fires down my nerves, and I don't feel the loss of my jacket for the heat. I've groveled and apologized all I'm going to. "I have more resources. I can give her—"

"I can't believe I fell for your charm. You told me that first day that you wanted Sawyer, but you've been so nice, I let myself forget."

"I *am* nice." I spread my hands. "Look. You are an intelligent woman. Why would you let your pride and stubbornness deny Sawyer—"

"Well, don't worry. It won't happen again because—"

"A chance at things you can't give her? This doesn't have to be either/or, you know—"

Lightning cracks close enough to make me duck. Her mouth is moving, but the thunder drowns out the words.

"...arrogant, pushy man I've ever met. I have zero intention of sharing custody. Do you hear me?"

They can probably hear her in the café. "Lorelei, just listen for a minute—"

"I won't keep you from seeing her, but if you want to take time out of your important life, you can come here. Maybe Christmas. Or her high school graduation."

She stalks to the edge of the steps. The rain is an opaque curtain, and there are puddles between the tufts of weeds below. She looks back over her shoulder, fear glittering in her eyes. "Sawyer and I don't need you, your money, or your hand-me-downs, *cowboy*."

She takes the steps in one leap and runs splashing through the rain for the café.

* * *

Reese

I've been trying to call Lorelei for a week, but she won't pick up. "Dammit!" My shout echoes off the high ceiling of my kitchen. I'm tired of leaving voice mails that aren't returned.

I want to know what they had for dinner, how the latest puzzle is coming, what new thing Sawyer has learned. I really want to know that Lorelei's okay. That I'm sorry I upset her.

I miss her.

The forkful of eggs is dry, and I wish for some fry bread to go with it. I look around at the cavernous kitchen. Lately, this house irritates me. I've lived here alone since Bo died, but it didn't feel so empty then—as if the potential for Carson's return helped to fill the empty rooms. But since I returned from Unforgiven, it seems even bigger than ten thousand square feet. It's sterile, echoey, and a bit spooky— like a museum at night. Or a mausoleum.

Hell, in a way it's both. This house is a testament to Bo and his ego. Who needs a house this big, out in the middle of nowhere? It's decorated to my father's taste: ornate, ostentatious, and odd. Funny, you just take it for granted that the house you grew up in is "your" place. Now that it really *is* mine, I realize there's nothing of me here, outside of my bedroom.

This place is haunted, but I'm not claiming its ghosts.

And I didn't see any of this until I spent time in that ramshackle farmhouse held together by not much more than the love of the people who live there.

I get up and pace. This isn't like me. I'm in my element—alone and unencumbered. I have the means to buy anything I desire. But what if what I desire can't be bought? It never occurred to me before.

I glance at my phone. I wanted to talk Lorelei in person, but she's left me no choice. I pull up a text. It's early, but I know she'll be at work, opening the diner.

R: Do you think I'll go away if you ignore me long enough?

Less than a minute later, my phone pings.

L: I hoped.

R: You know me better than that by now.

L: But denial worked for a whole week.

R: I really want to talk. You got the wrong impression. I wasn't playing games.

Nothing, for five minutes.

R: Besides, you have my jacket.

L: Yeah, I was feeling bad about that. Sorry.

R: I think sorry is probably the word we've both said the most to each other.

L: Yeah, sorry.

R: Wait, was that a joke?

L: :/ Maybe?

A grin stretches my lips. I should have tried texting days ago. It feels safer somehow—more removed.

R: I'm not trying to take Sawyer from you. It's just that she has a legacy here, too. I want to show her that.

L: You do know she's six months old, right?

R: Yeah, but I've been reading books about babies. The latest studies show that babies can imprint, like ducks do, so—

L: Seriously? You bought books?

R: Well, how am I supposed to learn about stuff otherwise?

L: Babies aren't a college course. You just do it.

R: Kinda hard when she's there and I'm here.

Silence. I carry my dishes to the sink, rinse them, and put them in the dishwasher. The housekeeper will take care of them later.

L: I have to get to work. Moss is first in line and banging on the door.

R: Tell the old fart I say hi. We'll talk later.

I hope.

I'm halfway up the Tara-style staircase when it hits me; I don't *have* to be here. At least, not full time. The Cessna can get me there in…I don't know. I take the rest of the stairs two at a time, jog to my room, and pull up the flight software on my tablet. The closest small airport to Unforgiven is—there isn't one. The closest airport of any kind is Albuquerque, fifty miles away. Doable, but a pain in the ass. Dammit.

Hours later, I'm on horseback, checking the range conditions. The cross-breeding range study I was discussing with the professor at A&M has challenges out here. Pure genes are hard to maintain, due to the fact that bulls respect cows, not boundaries. I know we could achieve a higher yield, but if I can't keep the herds apart, I have no way of knowing which combination throws the best calves, and without that—

The image of a rusted Realtor's sign flashes in my mind. *Wait a minute.* If I bought acreage in Unforgiven, I could start the experiment there. And since the range is poorer, it would be an even better test. Along with better yields, range cattle have to be hardy. It wouldn't be hard to grub out a landing strip; the Cessna doesn't need much.

The sun seems brighter all of a sudden. Colors leach into the black-and-white existence I've been living the past week. I could spend time with my niece *and* help the business. Given enough money, most things are possible.

The exception to the rule is Lorelei West. My spirits rise on the helium of hope. Lorelei's feisty and she doesn't trust me yet, but I am drawn to her good heart. She'll fight to the death for her town, her friends, her family—even stray dogs. You have to respect that.

Then there's that pink bra that I can't get out of my mind.

When I get back to the house, I'm going to look up the Realtor in charge of the land out near Lorelei's property. Can't be too hard to find. If there are more than two Realtors in Unforgiven, they'd starve.

* * *

Lorelei

I walk out to Einstein one morning to see a big Cat grader at work a hundred yards behind the barn, on the land that used to be ours. Old Man Duggar's kids put it up for sale when he passed away, and that was five—no seven—years ago. Someone must've finally bought it. A wave of melancholy stops my feet, and my hand covers my heart, as if to shield it.

Oh, who am I kidding? I can't even replace our roof, much less amass the fortune it would take to buy three hundred acres. Jerking the door open, I toss my bag into the seat and fall in. Time to go to work.

Around nine, I give our waitress a break and go on refill patrol. Conversation flows around me like a river.

"If we don't get rain soon, I'm gonna have to start hauling water…"

"And I told him, that danged truck ain't worth half…"

"Did'ja hear the old Duggar place sold?"

I stop, midpour. "What do you know?"

Floyd, the big-bellied owner of Floyd's Super Clean Used Cars, looks up from his double order of chili-cheese fries. "Huh?"

"Do you know who bought it?"

"Thought you'd know." He winks. "It's that rich Texan relative of yours."

My stomach drops and the tea pitcher has gotten so heavy I set it on the table. "No."

"Yeah." He shovels a forkful of the gooey, colorful mess into his maw.

I'm not asking more. I walk away. The only thing worse than seeing him shovel it in would be watching him talk and eat at the same time.

Something this big needs verification, and I know where to find the horse's mouth. I walk back to my office and call the *Patriot*.

"Unforgiven's home for news."

"Is Ann in?"

"Hold on."

"Ann Miner." Her voice is as clipped as her manners.

"Ann, this is Lorelei, over at the diner. I was just wondering if you know who bought the Duggar place."

"The sale is registered at city hall." She sniffs. "It's hardly a secret. You could go down there and—"

"Just tell me, will you?" God save us from snotty busybodies.

"It's that Texas oilman. Reese something...I have it right here." Papers rustle.

"Thanks. I know his last name." I hang up. I'm seething, but there's nothing I can do. It's a free country, and God knows he has the money. A wave of awareness swamps me, pulling me under. He will be there for Sawyer's milestones...Oh my God, he'll probably want to walk her down the aisle. I am *never* going to be free of the man. I plop my forehead on my desk. Denial works, but only for so long. My reaction is about Sawyer, my jealousy, and the fear that he could give her more. She could like him more.

But it's also about him. He sees through me. I've been searching for weeks and still haven't found a dark corner deep inside where that knowledge fits. It's odd-shaped and uncomfortable, like a shoe on the wrong foot. You can't ignore it. Well, I'm going to have to find out how, because this is not going away. I wish I could pare down this fact as easily as a hunk of maple. But reality is a much harder wood.

I jump when my phone rings. I look at the screen and am relieved to see Carly's photo.

Her honeyed voice is welcome. "Hey, girlfriend. I'm going stir crazy out here. Let's have a playdate, just you, me, and the kids."

I hear a dryer door slam. "Aren't you supposed to be taking it easy?" Carly has difficult deliveries; her first nearly took her down. Though both little Austin and Carly are fine, the doctor isn't taking chances.

"Hello, I have a cowboy husband, a one-and-a-half-year-old, and a newborn. Do you have any idea of how many loads a day that equates to? I should buy stock in detergent."

I hear the smile in her voice. "Yeah, and you hate every minute."

"We're giving it a couple of months and trying for another. I'm Fertile Myrtle, so I'll probably catch first time around."

"At this rate, you're going to get that baseball team that Austin wants."

"And at this rate, I'll be stepping on my boobs in two years. Come and listen to me complain awhile, will you? Besides, I want to see Sawyer."

"Except Mrs. Wheelwright's only day off is Sunday, and you know I can't leave Momma alone. Why don't you come to my place? We'll put the babies down and give ourselves a spa treatment."

"That sounds like heaven. If I bring the box, will you do my hair? Dark roots are for trees."

"I will if you bring your Wicked Woman red nail polish."

"Deal. I can't wait. If I have to spend much more time with Mr. Testosterone, I will not be held responsible for my actions."

I smile, stupidly grateful for some girl time. "Consider it a date." I hang up. It'll be nice to talk out my feelings about Reese. No, that didn't sound right. Talk to another *mother* about my Reese problem.

CHAPTER 8

Reese

I study the drawings on the architect's table, a sense of rightness falling over me. Compared to Bo's house, the cabin is modest, only twenty-five hundred square feet, but it's beautiful, with huge windows and a wraparound porch. "You've captured my idea perfectly, Dan. When can you start building, and when can you be done?"

The thin-faced, bearded man taps a mechanical pencil against the renderings. "Since I have a source for seasoned logs, it cuts wait time. Say three weeks for the foundation and a few months to build...I can have it ready to move in, say, end of October?"

"I know that's fast, and I appreciate it. But can you shave a week or two off that for a bonus for finishing early?"

The side of his mouth thins out in preparation for a polite no.

"Done by end of September for, say, a twenty percent bonus?"

His eyes widen. "Um. Yes." He clears his throat. "I think that could be arranged, but it's going to cost you lots of overtime."

"It's a deal, then." I hold out my hand and he shakes it. Enthusiastically. "I want to show you the site. I have the location of the house picked out. Are you free to fly out tomorrow?"

"I can clear my schedule."

"Good. Can you meet me out at the airport at seven?"

"Yes, Mr. St. James."

I stride for the door, an excitement rising in me like tree sap in the spring. I haven't felt that in forever.

After I bought the land, brought the fences up to bull standards, and grubbed out the runway, I thought about where I'd live part-time. I could have rented one of those dusty apartments over a shuttered store on the square, but town felt too far away from the Wests. I considered a manufactured home, but I want something more permanent.

I spent hours scanning photos and floor plans on the Internet. I knew what I didn't want—a showy albatross like this one. The more I looked, the more overwhelmed I was: Tudor? Italian? Bungalow? I had never considered what fit me—I was always too busy trying to fit where I was. But when I saw the log homes, the soaring walls of windows, oak floors, and cozy fireplaces, I knew what my style was. It touched a chord in me. It said, *home.*

Oh, I know, a log cabin is more suited to the mountains than the desert terrain of Unforgiven, but I don't care. What matters is that Sawyer will be close and I'll have a roof that suits me over my head.

I'll split my time between here and Unforgiven, but I have a feeling I'll leave my heart there, along with my spare clothes.

And I'll be there tomorrow. I have business to do, but maybe I can wrangle a visit with Sawyer. My heart gives a few heavy thuds. The best part would be getting to see Lorelei, but I won't have a way to get to town. I make a mental note to buy a car to keep there, because I'm not going to Unforgiven and missing her blue-suede eyes and sweet smile.

I walk out of the Dallas skyscraper, grinning like a fool.

* * *

Lorelei

Carly sits on the closed toilet in my bathroom, a towel on her shoulders, her hair glopped up with dye and covered in a shower cap. I set the timer on my phone and place it on the sink. "You've got fifteen minutes to cook, and we'll get that stuff off you."

"Thank you, hon. You have no idea how much I've needed this. Now, give me those claws."

"I needed this as much as you." I sit on the edge of the tub and hold out my hand.

She inspects my ragged nails and shakes her head. "Jeez, woman, have you taken a part-time job at the car wash? Your nails are a disaster."

"No, but if they had a midnight shift, I'd think about it. Fish checked out the roof, and the news wasn't good. The whole thing has to be replaced from the support beams out. Where the money is going to come for that, I have no idea."

Carly squeezes my hand. "You know I'd float you a loan, but Austin just bought another bull, and with the new baby, we're kinda short."

I jerk my fingers from hers. "Carly Davis, whatever made you think I'd take money from you?"

She snatches my hand back and picks up a nail file. "Well, I don't have it to offer, so it's not an argument we need to have, right?"

"Right." I've been over the budget, and even in my sleep, the numbers didn't change.

Carly starts filing. "Okay, let's get to it, because I don't know how long Mary and the babies will nap, and when they wake up, there'll be pandemonium." There's a predatory gleam in her eyes. "Tell me about Sawyer's uncle."

"Ugh." I roll my eyes. "He's the most aggravating, presumptuous, pushy—"

"Cute."

"Know-it-all—"

"Charming."

"Domineering—"

"Kind." A smug cat smile plays around the corners of her mouth. "Oh yes, and fabulously rich."

"Have you not been listening?"

"Yep. And I'm hearing all those words you're not saying."

"Carly Beauchamp Davis, you do not want to go there." My words cut through her soft tone like a shark through chum.

"What?" She looks up.

"Don't give me that rodeo-queen eyelash flutter. You and Mrs. Wheelwright. I swear—"

"Mrs. Wheelwright sees potential, too?"

"I love her, but not as a matchmaker."

Carly sighs and drops my hand but doesn't let go. "Lorelei, why won't you even consider the thought that this guy—"

"Men just let you down. Oh, and I almost forgot the worst thing of all. He's a *liar.*"

"Look, I get it. When you fall in love, you fall hard. There was no way you could have known that danged produce salesman was *married.*"

"God, Carly, don't bring him up, I was mooning over wedding dresses in bridal magazines." Shame burns up my throat and onto my cheeks. "The whole town pitied me."

"Yeah, that sucked." She moves on to the next nail. "But like Nana says, 'One butthole doesn't spoil the whole tote sack.' I know you, girlfriend. You act all aloof and above falling in love, but you'd kill to have what Austin and I have, and don't you try to deny it." She points at me. "You gave up too soon. Maybe it was because it was intimidating, living in Patsy's shadow. Maybe you were afraid of looking the fool again. But guess what? No one ever died from looking a fool. It's time to jump back into the human race, Lorelei. You are denying yourself the best of life. And this Reese—"

"Oh my God, what is wrong with everyone?" I throw my hands in the air. "*Even* if Reese St. James weren't all the things I just told you—which he *is*—even if he weren't *five* years younger than me—which he is—even if he were *interested*—which he isn't…Can't you see? All he wants is *Sawyer.*"

"Oh, okay." She nods, but I know this girl; she's just putting it down. For now. "What's he going to do with all that land he bought?" She takes back my hand and continues filing.

I snort. "How would I know? I'm not his financial consultant."

"Don't you talk to him?"

"Only when we need to coordinate about Sawyer. Mostly through texts."

"Oh, you're *texting*." She sounds like we're in high school, talking about passing notes with the cute senior.

"We were before I found out I'm going to be surrounded by him. Forever."

Her shower cap crinkles when she tips her head and sighs. "But, hon, Sawyer having another relative around is a *good* thing, isn't it?"

Bull's-eye. My phone beeps. "Time to rinse out your hair."

"It can wait one minute." She leans into my personal space. "Sorry, girlfriend. Not buying your logic. You have custody, and no judge in the state would find a reason to turn Sawyer over to him. You have to know that. So what is really bugging you about this guy?"

"I already explained all this." I stand with a sigh, turn on the water and wait for it to heat.

"You want to know what I think?" she whispers.

"No, I really don't." I pull the shower cap off her head. "Let's get that goo off, or the color is going to be more Bozo than"—I read the label on the box—"Fiery Siren."

She bends over the sink and puts her head under the water. "I think you're afraid of liking him."

I twist the cold faucet all the way open, smiling at her squeal.

* * *

Reese

"Are you sure you can land on this thing?" From his spastic grip on the Cessna's dash, Dan is trying to hold the plane together by sheer will.

I lower the flaps to the last notch and cut the speed to

sixty, and the plane dips down within a hundred feet of the grubbed-out airstrip. "Piece of cake. Good thing about the land in Unforgiven is that it's flat."

"I just hope it's forgiving," he mutters, closing his eyes.

I'm not judging. The tan scar in the grass rises to meet the landing gear. "Down in three, two, one..."

He starts at the slight bump of a three-point landing.

"You can open your eyes now."

I taxi, then turn back, shut the plane down behind Lorelei's ramshackle barn, and unbuckle my belt. "Come on, I need to know where you recommend putting the house."

While he's extricating himself, I step over to inspect the new barbed-wire fencing with super-sturdy posts. It looks top-notch. I wondered about hiring local, but the guy Manny and Moss recommended did a good job.

I look to the house, feeling a small pull in my chest that's Sawyer. I smile and turn back to the architect. We walk to a slight rise, about fifty yards from the fence line. "What do you think?"

"Well, it depends on the availability of water, of course, but the drainage looks good. You'll want the house to face north/south, to avoid the exposure to the most intense rays of the sunrise and sunset." He walks ten feet away. "The front door would face that way. Would that be a problem?"

I'd be looking right at Lorelei's house, into what I assume is her second-story bedroom window. There's a warm spot in my chest, imagining seeing her light on at night. Knowing she's safe and close would suit me down to the ground. The warm spot shifts lower. Much lower. "No, um. That's fine." The lawn has grown since I was last here. I didn't check in with Lorelei about visiting, but now that I'm this close, I realize I can't leave without at least seeing Sawyer. "I've got something to do. Will you be okay if I leave you for a half hour or so?"

He unzips a leather portfolio he brought with him. "No problem at all."

I jog for the fence, then realize the gate is at the end of my property, a quarter mile away. I'll have the contractor come back and put one in at this end. I duck between the strands of wire, then jog for the house. I hope Mary is having a good day.

I wonder if Sawyer will remember me. A silly hope. The books I've read say that babies don't recognize anyone except their caregivers until around nine months old. I rap on the wood of the screen door. Swing music floats to me from inside. "Anybody home?"

"Is that Reese?" Sarah's head appears around the kitchen doorway. "Laws, it is. Get yourself in here." She turns back to the living room. "Hey, Mary, we have company."

It's as if time stops in this house. Somewhere around 1970.

"Hello, Reese. So nice of you to come see us." Mary is sitting on the couch, watching a black-and-white movie on the old TV set. Her eyes are bright and aware.

A good day, then. "Hello, Mary. You're looking exceptionally pretty today."

She smiles and pats her hair.

"Here's one of the people you came to see." Sarah carries Sawyer in.

She reaches for me. "Babababababa."

"Yep, it's Baba, come to see you." I gather her up, and she clings to my neck. I stand and bury my nose in the hollow of her shoulder and inhale her sweet baby scent, her warm little body lying trusting in my arms. A rush of love hits me so hard, I have to blink it back. "God, I've missed you, little one."

I sit and play with Sawyer and talk to the women for a half hour. I'd love to stay longer, but I have to go. "I'll be back...I'm not sure when, but soon." I stroke the top of Sawyer's head.

"Babababa." She reaches for me again.

"You know," Sarah says, "we just finished our last jigsaw puzzle, and we're left with nothing to do this afternoon. Do you think you could be a dear and make a quick run to town and get us a new one? I think the Five & Dime has one of a field of tulips."

Mary claps her hands. "I love tulips."

"I flew in. I think the police would take a dim view of me trying to land in the town square."

"You can take my car." Sarah keeps a straight face, but there's a telltale sparkle in her eye. "And while you're down there, could you ask Lorelei to stop by O'Grady's and pick up some French rolls for dinner? I'd so appreciate it."

Though I can't deny the thrill that shoots down my nerves at the chance to see Lorelei, I lift an eyebrow. "Oh, left your cell at home, did you?"

Her eyes go round with innocence. "Now, how did you know that?" She roots in her purse at the end of the couch and holds up her keys.

I walk over and plant a kiss on her cheek. "I'll be back before you know I'm gone."

"Don't rush on our account," Mary calls after me.

I jog out the back door, scuttle through the back fence, and find Dan pounding stakes. "I've got to run to town for the ladies here. Are you okay for another twenty or so?"

"There's plenty of paperwork to keep me busy after this. I'll just sit in the plane."

"Okay. I'll bring you back some of the best fry bread you ever ate."

"I'm sure that's true, since I've never eaten any."

I grab the plans from Dan, then hightail it to town, pushing the old boat of a Chevy's speedometer into the red. I'm lucky and nab a parking space right out front. I tuck the renderings under my arm and remind myself to stop at the Five & Dime, in case Sarah really *does* want a puzzle, then head into the Chestnut Creek Café. A frizz of anticipation I don't want to examine runs along my nerves.

The bell jangles against the door, and the smell of bacon on cool air washes over me. Many booths are filled, but the lunch rush hasn't yet begun. I check the counter, but apparently Manny and Moss are off...doing whatever they do when they're not here. The young waitress is working, and through the serving window, I see the cook, Nevada. Today's shirt reads *I'd say I'd love to stay and chat, but I'd be lying.*

What I don't see is Lorelei.

* * *

Lorelei

Sassy raps on the doorframe of my office. She's standing with Reese, who's wearing a goofy smile and carrying a rolled paper under his arm.

I jolt out of my chair like I sat on a hat pin. My hand goes to my messy ponytail. "What are you doing here?" I glance around the room, seeing the disaster area through his eyes.

"I figured it'd be okay to bring him back, you being related and all." Sassy's sugar-sweet smile doesn't fool me. She's enjoying my nerves.

"It's fine." It's not, but what am I going to do, throw him

out? "Come on in." I pull catalogs and flyers from the guest chair, drop them in a corner, then wave him to sit. To his credit, he doesn't run his hand over the seat before he slides his light-khaki chinos into it. "What's going on?"

"I probably should have called...or texted, but I didn't think I'd get to see you, or Sawyer for that matter, when I flew in."

"You flew in?" I'm surprised, but I shouldn't be. I'm sure a plane is well within his means. If he were an animal, he'd be one of his bulls, running all over what was our land to get what he wants. *And remember, Lorelei, in spite of your butterflies, he's here for Sawyer, not you.*

"Yeah. Like I said, I should have called."

I'd like to reprimand him, but I'd sound petty. Besides, he has such a delighted little-boy smile on his face, I'm curious. "What's with the papers?"

"That's what I wanted to show you." He hops up and steps next to me. "Okay to put these on your desk?"

"If you can find room." I'll be darned if I'm going to apologize for my messy office when he wasn't invited to begin with.

He leans over my shoulder, pushes my monitor back, and lays his cylinder of papers on the desk over my piles of invoices, sale flyers, and order forms. His cologne has to be ungodly expensive, because it mainlines a pheromone bouquet to my brain and loosens the inner muscles of my thighs.

"I wanted to show you these." He unrolls a pastel rendering of a two-story wood cabin with dormer windows and wide steps up to a deep porch.

"You're building a cabin." My stomach jumps like a bobber with a fish nibbling. "On our old land."

"Yep." He pulls off the first sheet, to show the rear view.

Rock columns hold a huge curved support beam above huge windows. A stone patio sports a cozy firepit, with Adirondack chairs around it.

It's so unfair. The fact that he doesn't even notice my sarcasm lights a long-dead fire in my chest. I raise my chin and put a hand on my hip so even a big oilman can't miss the signal. "On the land you bought behind my house. *My* family's land, in the old days."

He keeps his gaze on the paper, but his smile goes tight. His head comes up. The look in his eyes reminds me of a stray, fearing a kick.

I realize that I'm behaving like one of those mean girls, pushing the knife in every chance I get. "Okay, I'm not using the 's' word again. I've said it too much. Instead, I'm going to try awful hard not to do anything I need to be sorry for. Deal?" I hold out my hand.

He shakes it, a half smile pulling the corner of his lips. "I'd like that a lot. I promise to do the same."

But he's never said a mean thing to me on purpose. Well, except that lie about being a cowboy, and his hidden motives. *Be careful of good-looking charmers.* It's a warning I ignored once but won't, ever again.

We realize at the same time that we're shaking hands too long and we both pull back. I look to the plans again, my heart throwing panicky beats. "Where on your land are you going to build it?"

"About fifty yards from the fence line, if that's okay with you."

"It's your land. I hardly think my opinion would stop you from doing you what want." I shrug, and something occurs to me. "Hey, how did you get to town. You flew in, so—"

"Sarah asked me to get her and Mary a puzzle, at the Five & Dime. She loaned me her car."

"Oh. I see." I try to keep my voice nonchalant. Sarah and I need to have a talk. She could have at least called to warn me.

"And you're supposed to stop at O'Grady's on your way home and pick up some French rolls for dinner."

I raise one eyebrow, trying to stay serious. "A critical message indeed."

He has a positively dazzling smile. Between that and the cologne, I'll bet the women melt to a puddle around him. Women who aren't me, anyway.

"She said she left her phone at home."

"Oh. That reminds me. Hang on." I step out of my office and walk to the back door. Trying to ignore Nevada's raised brows, I snatch Reese's coat from the rack on the wall.

When I walk back in, he's studying the plaques on my wall. Blood pounds up my neck and my cheeks throb. I hand him his jacket. "Almost forgot."

He turns and tips his head toward the wall. "You're a ballroom dancer?"

I tuck hair behind my ear. "Oh, it's nothing, just a small town—"

"An invitation to *America's Ballroom Challenge* is hardly small-town. How did you do?"

My eyes on the floor, I squeeze past him. "I didn't go."

"Why not?"

"Let's just say my dance partner let me down." An understatement, but I'm not going into the mortifying details.

He touches my forearm. "How awful for you. I'm sorry."

His voice is butter on an old burn that shouldn't sting after all this time. I step back. I barely survived the last good-looking charmer. I'm not leaving myself open to another.

Why am I mooning about old memories all of a sudden?

"I have to get back to work. We're coming on the rush hour, and Sassy is going to need help."

"Sure, I'll let you go. I have to get back too. I shouldn't have come, but with such a critical mission..." He trails off.

I swear, he's looking at my lips. The walls have moved in, and the AC must be overloaded again, because it's gotten hot in here.

"Well..." He rolls up his plans. "I'll probably be around more often soon. You know, overseeing the construction and all."

"And running critical errands?"

"Oh, speaking of that." He taps the end of the tube to straighten it. "I'm going to need to buy some wheels. Can you tell me where I can buy a decent truck around here? It doesn't have to be new, or fancy."

"The only place short of Albuquerque is Floyd's Super Clean."

"The name is Floyd's Super Clean? Really?"

"Floyd's Super Clean Used Cars. And when he sees you coming, he's going to bore you a new...I mean, he's going to—"

He laughs. "I like it when you blush. Yeah, I get it. Will you go with me, to make sure he doesn't take advantage of me?"

"No" moves from my brain to my mouth.

"Please?"

He looks concerned. And sincere. Until I remember. "Yeah, because the out-of-towner surcharge is really going to hurt you."

"It's the principle of the thing. Say you'll go?"

I find I want to. But this encounter is proof that I'm not immune to him. And that's not good. I can't afford to be caught dreaming again. I have Sawyer to think about. "Text me when you're coming in next time, and I'll see if I can get away. That's the best I can do."

He bows a bit at the waist, which brings his face way too close. He freezes, his eyes warm on mine. A lightning flash of want crosses his face, but he straightens. "Thank you." He turns and walks out.

It's only then that I can get a deep breath again. Then I realize that I just almost-kinda-agreed to go somewhere with him. And would have let him kiss me, if...Damned cologne.

But I find myself smiling the rest of the afternoon, and that can't be from cologne. Okay, he's sexy, and I'm coming to realize I miss...companionship. That's all it is. Besides, the female he's really interested in isn't out of diapers yet. I'd best remember that.

CHAPTER 9

Reese

"Mr. St. James, I have Mr. James Travis on the line. Could you hold a moment?"

"Sure." Another reason my attorney irritates me. He can't pick up the phone and make a call himself? And his name. Always James—not Jim, not Jimmy or Jimbo. Puffed-up rooster. I rein in Brandy and look over the small herd the cowboys are collecting, down in the draw.

"Reese! How's it hangin', son?"

I always wonder what he's referring to when he says that, but I'm not calling him on it. "Do you have anything on those new mineral lease negotiations?"

"You always were the serious one. It's all business with you."

No, I just don't like you. "No time for idle chat. I've got sick heifers."

"They're bitches when they're sick, aren't they?"

I pull the phone away from his booming, Texas-size laugh

and try not to grit my teeth. If I didn't need him... "The leases?"

"Nah, son, still working on those. What I called about is the New Mexico custody law. It looks like—"

"I want you to drop that."

"What?" He says it like I told him I voted Democrat.

"I'm not pursuing custody. It'd be useless, in any case. Lorelei West is an exemplary mother."

"Carson's blood is worth twice any buckle bunny's. Do I need to remind you that this is the last of the St. James line, boy? Bo would—"

"I hardly need reminding of my own family tree, and Bo isn't here. This is my decision." Catching my anger, Brandy dances under me.

"Well, if you say so, but if Bo knew about this, he'd—"

"You might want to take a look at who's signing your checks. I own Katy Cattle now, *Jim*, and I'm telling you to drop it. Is there anything else?"

"That's it... for now." His words are everyday, but his tone holds the whiff of a threat.

Or maybe I'm reading too much into it, because I don't like him. I click End and shove the phone in my breast pocket. One thing I know; he'll follow orders. He wouldn't have worked for Bo for more than two minutes if he didn't.

I don't have time to worry about him. I've got cattle to cull.

It's a normal day, filled with problems and eventual solutions. But it's also laced with threads of loneliness that are new. After dinner, I'm working at my desk when I glance to the shelf above to the three proud wooden ponies, frozen midprance. Mine, Carson's, and Lorelei's.

When the echo of lonesome in my chest expands, I pull out my phone and text Lorelei:

Looking at my painted ponies and wishing I could have met your father.

Two minutes later, my phone dings.

L: He was a good carver and an even better man.

R: How's Sawyer?

L: Amazing. She's playing peekaboo and sitting up all by herself!

R: Superkid, that's for sure. I miss her. Listen, I'm about caught up here and thinking about flying out sometime this week. What day do you think you can get away for an hour or two to help me buy a car?

Nothing, for five minutes.

L: Any day is as busy as the next. You pick, and I'll just take a lunch hour for a change. Shouldn't take long.

R: How about tomorrow? Can you meet me at the house? The logistics of borrowing Sarah's car will get complicated— two people, three cars.

L: Okay, say ten? It's quietest then. Hey, I saw them breaking ground over there.

R: I'm looking forward to being nearby. You know, to see Sawyer. Maybe I can babysit sometime?

L: Mrs. Wheelwright has it under control.

R: Yeah, but I'm just saying.

L: Gotta go. This is the only time I get to carve.

R: Make it pretty. Good night, Lorelei.

L: Night.

* * *

Lorelei

Ten minutes later, I put down my microtool. I'm twitchy, and if I try finishing tonight, I'm going to ruin the mustang I'm working on. I stand and walk down the stairs, to Sawyer's room.

She's awake and quiet, but her arms are flailing.

It's amazing how I've slipped so easily into a role I thought had passed me by. I remember in high school, lying in bed at night, wishing on stars. I wished for a husband and at least four babies, and...And now it's taken a tragic miracle to make me a mother. God sure does work in mysterious ways.

"Whatsamatter, baby girl? You antsy tonight, too?" I lift her out of the crib. She's getting heavy. Her diaper is dry. "Do you want some warm milk?"

"Mammmmmm ma."

Tears rush to my eyes. "What? What did you say, baby?"

"Mamamamamama." She gazes up at me. Her eyes have lightened a bit over the past several weeks.

I clasp her to me, trying not to squish too hard, but I want to love the stuffing right out of her. She may not know what she's saying, but I don't care. Wetness traces down my cheek. "Yes, I'm your momma. When you can understand, I'll tell you about your other momma." I take a few waltz steps across the floor and twirl, pulling a giggle from her. "Then, when you're old enough, I'll teach you to dance. Ballet, tap, whatever you like." We dance, around and around the corners of the room. I wonder if Reese can dance. Probably not, being raised on a remote ranch.

Well, that was judgmental, and I'd be mad if he made assumptions about me. I've got to work on that.

I dip Sawyer, and her little fingers clutch my shirt. "And then, when some handsome guy comes to take you out, you'll know how." I spin. "You'll show all those girls how it's done."

I didn't get my dream to dance, but maybe Sawyer will like it. Though I'm not going to be one of those mothers trying to push their daughters into their mold. Whatever Sawyer wants is fine by me.

And if it's something expensive, I'm sure her uncle will step up to pay for it. I suddenly realize I'm imagining him in her life long-term. When did that happen? As I look at my daughter's face, that doesn't rankle quite as much as it used to. I want the best for her. And so does he. That much I'm sure of.

I dip her again, and she squeals.

"Okay, enough of that. We're going to wake up Grandma." I kiss the hand that's wrapped around my thumb. "Let's go get some milk, so we can both sleep, okay?"

* * *

First thing in the morning, I call the staff together for a five-minute confab.

"Guys, I've got an errand to run around ten. I should be back before noon, but if I'm later, y'all hold the fort, okay? I could call Carly, but then she'd have to find a sitter, and—"

"Jeez, chick, chill." Nevada shoves her hands in the back pockets of her jeans. "What are we, incompetent?" She cuts her eyes to Sassy, who's picking her cuticles. "Well, most of us aren't, anyway."

Sassy's head snaps up, but Nevada is looking at me again. "Go. It's not like you're indispensable or something."

"Yeah, we can handle it," Sassy says. "We can always call in Carly's nana if we get in trouble."

I pull in a gasp and choke on my own spit. I bend over, coughing.

Nevada pounds on my back hard enough to leave bruises. "You need the Heimlich? I know the Heimlich."

Now I'm laughing and coughing at the same time. "No, I'm good." Carly's nana is outspoken, and her filter blew out years ago. I take a deep breath and straighten. "Y'all want to look for new jobs, go for it. Nana would drive away business faster than rats in the kitchen and you know it." I shoo them away. "Back to work. We have hungry people to feed."

Sassy pushes through the door into the diner, and I turn to see Nevada watching me.

"What?"

"You don't *have* appointments. I've seen you drag in here with walking pneumonia. You okay?" She tips her head.

I know she won't go all Carly on me. "I'm taking Reese St. James out to Floyd's to buy a car. You know Floyd; he can judge a man's wallet by the cut of his clothes. I don't want him ripping off Reese."

She nods. "Yeah, because getting ripped off on a car would have him eating PB&J for a month."

"I—"

"Nope." She holds up her hands and backs away. "Just pointing out the obvious. No skin off my a—nose." She turns, puts her earbuds in, and walks to the order wheel.

I head for my office to get my purse, reminding myself not to be swayed by dark, sexy eyes and a whiff of cologne. I take a moment to lock down my hormones, my resolve, and my office, then head for my car.

When I pull in my drive, his plane is at the end of his little runway, shining in the sun. I had just braked to a stop when he steps out the screen door of my house. A spurt of familiar jealousy hits my bloodstream. He's been hanging with Sawyer, probably for hours. Must be nice to not *have* to work for a living.

He pulls open Einstein's door and folds himself into the passenger seat. "Thanks for doing this, Lorelei. I really appreciate you taking the time."

"How long have you been here?" I try for offhand, but it comes out like an interrogation. He fills the car with his body and that damned cologne. The fit is too tight. He's too close.

"An hour, and wow, are you right. Sawyer has really learned a lot." He sighs. "Wish I could watch it happen in real time."

I back down the drive. His tone is so wistful, I almost feel sorry for him. I only see her for a few hours a day, but he's not getting anywhere near that. I loosen my jaw. "She is the smartest child on the planet. Did you doubt it?"

"With both our family's genes? Not for a heartbeat." He squinches into the door enough to turn a bit to face me. "Tell me about your sister."

I take the two-lane county road that will skirt town and eventually lead to I-40. "She was the star of our family. People say, 'So-and-so lit up a room,' but Patsy really did." My face relaxes into a smile. "Everyone loved her. I think the word is 'charisma.' In high school she was voted most likely to make it in Hollywood."

"She was beautiful, then?"

The road wanders through arroyos and small hills, and I have to watch for critters. It takes me a moment to put my thoughts to words. "Not in the classic sense. She was pretty, but it wasn't her face—it was as if her joy were glitter and a little bit rubbed off on you just by being around her." I shake my head. "That sounds silly to say, but that's as close as I can come to explaining it."

"You loved her very much."

"Of course I did. She was my sister."

It could be road noise, but I think I heard a soft snort.

"Tell me about Carson. Did you guys have that 'twin' thing everybody talks about?"

Now I know it wasn't road noise, because he does it again.

"We were pretty much opposites. I had less insight into how Carson thought than I do Sawyer."

"What was he like?"

He stares out at the road, flickering with heat shimmers. "He was a carbon copy of my father. All brag, all brave, all bluster. He was the *real* cowboy of the family."

"I wonder if he and Patsy were in love, or if they were just together for the baby."

"One of the guys who rodeoed with Carson came to his funeral. He said those two were mad for each other, and even more crazy about Sawyer. Said he figured they'd have gotten around to getting married eventually."

I sigh. "I'm so glad to hear that."

"I can't imagine why Carson wasn't driving." His voice goes low and tight.

"News flash: women drive now." I lift my hands off the wheel for a moment to point at it. "I didn't take you for a chauvinist."

"I'm not. I just don't think the accident would have been fatal if he had been driving."

Fire leaps in my chest. "Are you saying this was Patsy's fault?"

"No, I'm just saying that a bull rider's reflexes are better."

"Because I hardly think a deer can be somebody's fault. Patsy—"

"Look, as usual, I've said the wrong thing, and I didn't mean to. I was just thinking out loud."

I huff impatience. "Well, think silently, then. Patsy was not at fault. The police report makes it clear. You want to find someone to blame, find that deer."

"Okay. Sorry."

And he looks it. When I hit the button, the windows slide down and fresh, dry air rushes in, cutting his cologne. But it fans the wildfire in my chest. "Don't you dare think my sister was some kind of bubblehead who chased rodeo cowboys and couldn't drive worth a lick."

"Did I say that? I didn't say that." His voice is loud over the wind, and a lot chillier. "I do a good enough job putting my foot in my mouth without you trying to shove the other in."

I open my mouth, then close it. Patsy did have more than one cowboy boyfriend since she was on the circuit, and the only reason she went to high school was to see her friends; her grades just squeaked through. But she wasn't a buckle chaser, and I'm not going to explain the distinction to *him*. "I still wonder, though. Why didn't they tell us about Sawyer?"

"I went through Carson's things, looking for clues, but there was nothing. Did you do the same with Patsy's?"

"Wow. I was so busy scrambling to be sure Sawyer wasn't put in foster care. Then there was the funeral, and...I guess I just forgot to track them down."

"Maybe there's something there that will help put your mind at ease."

It would hurt to see the clothes and everyday things that Patsy fully expected to come back to that night. But if there's a chance of an answer, I need to try. "I'll see if I can get in touch with the girl who was babysitting that night."

We ride in silence until I hang a right at I-40. Floyd's is only a mile down the road. I pull into the lot and shut Einstein down. I grab my purse and pat the dash.

"Why do you do that?"

"What?" The door squeals when I push it open.

"Pat the dash." He uncoils from the seat, stands, puts his fist in the small of his back, and stretches.

"With an old car, you have to appreciate the effort."

One of his brows goes up.

"Hey, you buy an old enough car here, you'll see what I mean." Not much chance of that; I'll bet he's never bought an old car in his life.

"Well, if it isn't Miz Lorelei." Floyd saunters up, his pointy rattlesnake-skin cowboy boots clicking on the hot asphalt. "And...haven't had the pleasure, sir."

He knows danged well who this is. "Floyd, this is Reese St. James."

Floyd puts out a meaty hand, and Reese's disappears in it. "Pleased to meet'cha."

Reese looks a bit...surprised. Between Floyd's belly, his big hat, and his bravado, he can be a bit much to absorb all at once.

"Reese is looking for a used car."

"Well, you came to the right place, sure as God made little road apples, I promise you that," he booms, looking Reese up and down. "Country gentleman like yourself, you're gonna want you a truck. I've got a few you'll like the look of, right over thisaway."

I put a hand to my temple. "Floyd, please, dial back on the country bumpkin a bit, will you? You're giving me a headache."

Reese laughs. "Lead on, Opie."

I chuckle under my breath.

Floyd leads us to the back row, populated only by trucks. "You timed this right. Got a shipment in just yesterday. Hardly had time to wash 'em." He parades in front of a mishmash of pickups. "We got everything from little quarter-pounders to quarter-ton. We got almost new to um...classics." He stops in front of a massive black truck that's jacked up so high the hood is taller than my head. "Now, this would suit a man of your stature."

Reese looks at me with a raised eyebrow and that cute half smile.

I blurt, "I always thought men who bought huge trucks were making up for small—er—equipment."

Reese's brows shoot up, and he lets out a long, loud laugh.

Seeing Floyd's red face, I remember he drives a truck that could be this one's brother.

I slap a hand over my mouth. I can't believe I said that out loud.

"Sorry..."

"Well, that sure won't do, then, will it?" Reese strides down the aisle, lingering here and there, and Floyd follows, chattering like a squirrel on Red Bull.

God, it's hot out here on the asphalt. I swipe a runnel of sweat from my temple, and I'm blinded by a laser of light reflecting off a bumper. I stop in front of a gold Chevy Silverado King Cab. The price on the neon poster board in the window would make me flinch, but this isn't for me. "Hey, Reese, what do you think of this one?"

They walk back my way.

"Oh, you've got an eye for trucks, Lorelei. That's a good 'un," Floyd says. "A pick of the litter, really."

Reese looks it over. "I like the color." He walks around it. "What year is it?"

"It's a 2006, but it's got low mileage. It belonged to—"

"Don't even try to tell us an old lady only drove it to church on Sundays." I put a hand on my hip.

He tips the hat back on his head. "Y'all aren't going to believe this, but the previous owner was Reverend Dooley, of the First Baptist. And he *did* drive it to church on Sundays." He grins like it's the truth.

"For real?" I squint at him, but trying to read a used-car salesman's face? Easier to read a coyote's.

He sweeps off his hat and lays it over his heart. "I swear. Got his name on the title in the office, if you want to see it."

Reese walks over and opens the hood. He spends several minutes looking and tapping and shaking things in there.

I lean over and whisper, "Good idea—make Floyd think you know something about engines. He's not acting nervous, but he's a pretty good horse trader."

Reese turns his head, and his lopsided smile is close. Too close. I straighten a bit.

"I do know engines. I could pull, overhaul, and reinstall this puppy in two days. Less, if you'd help me." He drops the hood. "Our ranch is twenty miles from a dealer, and most times, stuff breaks down a long way from the house. I got to where I could fix just about anything with baling wire and bubble gum."

Wow. That'll teach me to assume. "You're starting to sound more like a mechanic than a cowboy."

He winks. "Cowboys are the fathers of invention, darlin'," he drawls in an imitation of Floyd's sales pitch.

Floyd mops his face with a red kerchief. "Hop in and check out the mileage."

"Come on." Reese strides for the driver's side.

I open the passenger door, and stale heat smacks me in the face. I climb up, leaving the door open for whatever cross breeze might wander by.

"He's right. Only 60K on the odometer." Reese's head swivels. "And neat as a pin. What do you think? Worth a test-drive?"

"If only for the air-conditioning."

He leans out the window. "Got keys for this thing?"

Floyd takes off his hat and wipes sweat. "Under the floor mat."

Reese mutters, "Yeah, because a thief would never think to look there." He bends and comes up with a key.

His cologne in this heat shoots to my head...and down to the south forty. God, he smells good enough to eat.

He shoves the key in and cranks it. The engine roars, then settles to a purr.

I roll down the window while he plays with the AC knobs.

"Take her for a spin," Floyd says, backing up. "You're gonna like 'er."

Reese eases the truck out of the space and rolls to the edge of the highway, looks both ways, then floors it. He cuts left and the truck fishtails, then lines out.

"Whoop! He's got some guts under the hood."

My heart climbs into my throat, looking for a safe place in case of a wreck. "Slow down!"

"Why?" He looks over at me with a huge grin. We must be going eighty.

"We are the last survivors to see that Sawyer gets raised, you idiot," I yell so he'll hear me over the wind.

His grin melts and his foot comes off the floorboard. "Oh yeah, sorry." He holds his hand in front of the vent. "The AC works, anyway. I think you can roll your window up." He gives me an apologetic look and places his hands at ten and two on the wheel. We've slowed to two miles below the speed limit.

I feel bad, yelling like a fishmonger. "You called this thing a 'he.' I thought all guys had female vehicles."

"Depends on the vehicle. This here is a guy." He pats the dash. "What would you name him?"

"You going to buy it?"

"If Floyd replaces all the fluids and the belts and takes five hundred off the price."

Another assumption I was wrong about. I needn't have worried that Floyd was going to rip him off. I think for a minute. "Murphy."

"Seriously?" The smile is back.

"Yeah, I'd call it the Murphinator."

He laughs. "You're funny."

"Hey, it's not as good as Einstein, but you can't have everything."

"Why don't you look and see if there's anything you like on the lot." He hesitates. "It's about time you retired Einstein, don't you think?"

I suck in a breath to let him have it.

"I mean, you have Sawyer now, and that little roller skate of yours wouldn't stand a chance in a collision with the big trucks around here." He looks both ways, and finding the road empty, pulls a U-turn and heads back to Floyd's.

I deflate on my exhale. "I've thought of that. But a new roof on the house comes first. I'm really careful—"

"Lorelei." His hand crosses the expanse of seat coming to rest on mine. "Why don't you let me loan you—"

"You don't know me better than that by now?" I pull my hand from under his. "Why do we have to keep having this discussion?"

"Because the money won't mean anything to me, and it'll keep you safe—you and Sawyer."

His look is so warm and sincere, my anger turns to a

warm puddle of goo in my chest like fudge before it sets. His eyes are brown, but not the usual cow-patty brown. They have golden flecks, and...I jerk my head to look out the window. "I know you mean well. And thank you for the offer. But I can't borrow money that I don't know how or when I can repay." I tuck stray hair from my ponytail behind my ear. "Fish has offered to do the labor, which will help a ton, but—"

"A fish is going to reroof your house? A bit out of his element, no?" He lifts an eyebrow and one corner of his lips.

"No, you doofus. Fish is our former cook at the diner and our current cook Nevada's boyfriend. Joseph Fishing Eagle King."

"Ah, I see. Apache?"

"Navajo."

"Nice guy, huh?"

"The best. He quit the café last year to set up a farming co-op outside town, and he employs the youth of his tribe to help. He donates a good portion of the crop to the rez."

"Sounds like a good guy."

Reese pulls onto the lot and parks up by the showroom. Floyd waves for us to come in.

I put the strap of my purse over my shoulder. "You're pretty sure you're going to buy the truck? Because I've got to get back to work."

"Yeah, but I thought we could go out to lunch afterward, to celebrate."

I shake my head. "Even if I had time, there's only the Chestnut Creek"—I imagine eyes crawling all over us there; no thanks—"or the Lunch Box, which—"

"Gives you the runs." His dimples come out in his smile.

My cheeks heat. "Yeah. And unless you count the lunch counter at O'Grady's, those are all the culinary options that

Unforgiven has to offer. But I've got to get back anyway. I've been gone too long already."

His eyes are doing it again. "You work so hard. You deserve a break. I'd like to take you out somewhere. Maybe Albuquerque? What do you say? We'll go dancing."

Dancing. What I wouldn't give to...Wait. "Are you asking me out? Like on a date?"

He shrugs off my shrill tone. "Sure. Why not?"

"Are you out of your...? I'm older than you!"

"Which probably would have mattered back in junior high. Come on, Lorelei, you deserve some fun."

He's just being nice. And is probably trying to butter me up to get to Sawyer. "Sweet of you to ask, but no, thanks." I crack the door and slide out into the pile-driver heat.

He gets out, closes his door, and steps over to me. "Well, I owe you, Lorelei. Thanks for taking the time out." He holds out his hand.

I go to shake, but he turns my hand and kisses the inside of my wrist. It's so personal, so intimate, I shiver. I'm snared by his look, my heart beating like a scared bunny's. Some kind of weird crackling...power passes between us, and I jerk my hand back. Probably just me. "Don't mention it. It's what neighbors do for each other." I turn and tell my feet to get me back to my car.

"And we *are* going to be neighbors," he calls after me.

Like I could forget that.

CHAPTER 10

Reese

I drive "the Murphinator" on the back road Lorelei took this morning. My asking her out was spontaneous, simply an attempt to thank her. But when she asked if it was a date, why did I say yes? I know better. Hookups is all I do, and Lorelei West is *not* that. No matter how nice the woman, after a few dates, I'm jittery and looking for a way out.

I tried commitment once. Remembering the Sharon debacle is like biting into a grapefruit. She was sweet, loving, and attentive. We were compatible. We had fun together. She acted like I was all that with hot fudge on top.

I was imagining a future together and checking out diamonds when a slip of her tongue let me in on a secret that hadn't occurred to me. She wanted my money—I was simply a sugar daddy with benefits.

I've been up-front with women ever since. No ties, no promises. But lately I've come to realize that casual relationships aren't making it—they're only a temporary fix. There's less satisfaction with each one, to the point where lately, they leave me feeling empty and soulless.

I'm stuck between, not happy with hookups and not wanting to be alone. That desert stretch is a lonely, uncomfortable place. It feels temporary. But what's the alternative? I'm interested in Lorelei; I can't deny that. She's like clean, fresh air after being in a smoke-filled room. I smile, remembering her blush. She'd be so right, in so many ways. It's more than her pretty face, or even that pink bra I can't get out of my mind. She's down-deep *good*. Trustworthy, honest, and...man, I'm starting to sound like that used-car salesman, trying to talk myself into taking a chance.

I'm best forgetting about it. If we dated and it went south (as it always does), I could jeopardize my opportunity to have a role in Sawyer's life. Nothing is worth risking that.

I'm right. I know I am. But Lorelei works so hard and makes do with so little. I'd love to make her life a bit easier, but I know she won't let me. Even something smaller, like a new dress, just to see that gorgeous smile and know that I caused it. But she wouldn't allow that, either.

There's got to be something...

* * *

Lorelei

It's after closing time, and everyone's left for the night. I'll be out of here in a few, once I finish tallying the bank deposit. Sawyer's smiling face floats through my mind.

Be home soon, punkin.

I slip everything into the cash bag, toss it in the safe, and spin the dial. I'll take it down when the bank opens in the morning. My stomach growls. Mrs. Wheelwright's making hamburger casserole tonight, probably light on the hamburger. Not one of my favorites, but payday isn't 'til Friday. I glance to the ceiling. "I'm not complaining, Lord. I'm happy with the gifts you've given—"

Tap. Tap-tap-tap.

My head jerks up at what sounds like keys rapping on glass. I pull my purse from the drawer, trying to listen over my banging heart. Nothing to worry about. The doors are locked, the safe is locked, and I have the Unforgiven PD on speed dial.

I walk out of my office, turn off the lights, and peek through the serving window.

Reese is standing at the front door, spotlighted by the streetlight, hands cupped at the sides of his face, peering in.

"Oh, for cripes' sake." I push through the swinging door into the dining area.

He smiles and waves.

I stomp across the shadowy room to unlock the door. "You scared me out of a year of my life, St. James. What the heck are you doing here this time of night?"

"I'm not really sure, to tell you the truth." He pushes past me. "I was due to fly out this afternoon. But that new truck—"

"The Murphinator."

"Yeah. It steered itself over here."

"Okay, but I've got to get home. Mrs. Wheelwright—"

"This will just take a minute." He sets his phone on the nearest booth and taps the screen. "You're too busy to go dancing, so I brought the dancing to you."

Norah Jones's sultry voice fills the room with melancholy.

"Oh." My hand flies to my mouth. "I love that song."

With a soft smile, he holds out a hand. "Dance with me?"

My brain whispers that I look like roadkill and smell like the deep fryer. My feet ignore all that, and I step into his arms.

"Come away with me," he sings, soft in my ear, and a shiver starts at the back of my neck and shoots down my body.

His hand is at my shoulder blade, supportive but not intrusive. He leads me across the floor, pausing, turning, rising, dipping—he dances like an angel. We're gliding, perfectly in sync. I think to ask how, but then I'm too lost in the steps, the song, the blues-filled longing in that beautiful voice. God, how I've missed this.

It's strange, dancing with a man who commands the floor. It's like a tiny pause in your life—a perfect moment, when you put everything down, open up, and relax in his hands. And when you do, two become one. Something strong and sure courses through me. God, how have I lived these years without dancing?

We spin, and I'm smiling like a fool. I show off, chin up, turning this way and that like this season's debutante at her first dance. He dips and spins me, his head tilted at an arrogant angle, grinning down at me. Knowing we're sharing the exact same joy shifts something in me. In spite of our differences, we have more in common than I knew. Happiness is like champagne, bubbles up from my chest. Everything I hadn't realized I've held tight for so long loosens. I can't help it; I giggle.

When the singer's voice trails off, he dips me, deep and low. The light of the streetlamp blinds me, and I am once more in the arms of my shadow partner. I tip my head back until my ponytail brushes the floor. He holds the dip three beats too long. When I raise my head to see why, he's right there. The light is blocked out, and his face is less than an inch away. His lips hover so close that I feel his breath on mine. He holds there, one second, two, three...

Then he lifts and spins me, all by myself across the dark floor.

The moment is broken.

Without his touch, like Cinderella at midnight, I morph back to a footsore, grease-soaked food slinger. But one with just a bit of sparkle. I walk back to him. "Wow, where did you learn to dance like that?"

"My mother loved dancing. Before she died, she made my father promise that he'd see to it that we knew how to dance properly." He pulls a face. "I hated those classes a lot less than Carson did."

I chuckle, imagining the cowboys I know taking dance lessons. Sure, Ty Murray did it, but let's face it; he's a god. "That was heaven. I'd forgotten just how much I missed it. Thank you. Now I've got to get—"

"Wait." He stops me with a raised finger. "Don't move. I have a present for you."

"Reese, we talked about this..." But he's out the door. My feet take a few steps and I twirl. Nice to know I still have the skill, after all these years.

He steps back inside, holding a grocery bag, and carries it to the booth where his phone is. "You were right about the lack of sophisticated fare in Unforgiven, but"—he waves me over and indicates I should sit—"I managed this." He pulls out a pie.

But not just any pie. It's a Maddy Seavers pie. I know, because it has her brand: she puts her initials with pinholes on any pie she makes. Maddy wins every blue ribbon, every year, at every county fair she attends. And she attends a *lot*. "How did you get one of Maddy's pies?"

He bows a bit, then slides into the booth opposite me.

"Turns out, her son works at the Motor Inn, and when I asked…"

"You sweet-talked Maddy Seavers out of one of her cherry pies?" When I stand, he does, too. I head to the counter for a knife, plates, and forks. "I can't believe it. I tried to get her to bake them for the diner, and she told me to pound sand."

"Aw, she's a sweetheart when you get around that gruff exterior."

I set down everything and slide back into the booth. "Gruff? She's been known to run Jehovah's Witnesses off with a bullwhip."

"Then I'm glad her son asked, not me." He combines a preacher-serious expression with a wink.

"Okay, but you serve. I have to call home." I pull my phone from my purse and hit speed dial.

"Hi, Mrs. Wheelwright. I just wanted to tell y'all to eat without me. I'll be home a bit late. I…I'm having a hard time balancing the bank deposit."

"No problem, Lorelei. You take your time. We're fine here."

I hang up to Reese's questioning eyebrow tilt.

I squirm in my seat as he slides my pie in front of me. "It's just that Mrs. Wheelwright is a bit of a…" *Matchmaker* will insinuate this is more than it is—two people eating pie. "Oh, never mind."

He takes a forkful of pie, and his eyes close. "Wow, I did good, huh?"

"None better."

We eat in silence for a bit.

I look up to his studied gaze. "Why did you stop dancing?" he asks. "Your love of it shines from you, and you're a fantastic partner."

Yeah, I put that dream on the shelf, along with others,

like my favorite clothes from high school. They've sat there for years, gathering dust. So what is with me lately, that I'm remembering them? Tempted to try them on? They don't fit me anymore.

But it's not really about the dream of dancing, is it? It's about everything I had tied to it. The feelings. The love. Being one with a man. It was a false dream, but it sure was a pretty one.

Something about the shadows and Reese's deep rumbly voice make this moment intimate, like the world has paused and we're alone in it. The words slip out, unbidden.

"He and I." I worry the crumbs on my plate, then set down the fork. I'm a grown-up, and years have passed. I should be over this. "We were more than dance partners. He was a produce vendor for the diner, and one day we discovered we had dancing in common.

"Going to dance competitions, weekend trips, we grew close. It'd been a year, and he intimated that we had a future together. I was imagining a June wedding and babies, and…" I take a breath. "Then we got the call that we'd been chosen to compete on *America's Ballroom Challenge.* We were thrilled, of course. The town made a big deal of it: articles in the paper, people stopping by, wishing me luck. The reverend even put it in the church newsletter." I shake my head, bombarded by needle-sharp darts of the hints I'd danced around back then.

"We'd planned to meet on Thursday morning at the Albuquerque airport, but I couldn't wait. I drove over Wednesday afternoon and had a spa treatment that the Ladies of the Historical Society bought for me. I felt like the queen of the ball." I have to stop, to swallow the shame in my throat. "I decided to treat myself to a high-class dinner, to celebrate." I squint to blur the picture in my mind. "I went to a swanky restaurant and asked for a table for one. I was deciding if I could afford a glass of wine with dinner as the waiter led me through the tables. In a plush booth in the corner sat my almost-fiancé, sipping champagne with a curvy blonde."

"Seriously?"

"Oh, it gets worse." My face heats, and I'm glad of the dark. "I marched over and demanded an explanation. The blonde was more than willing to give me one. It was their anniversary."

He winces.

"Turns out, I was just his 'road-trip girl.'" I swallow the memory of rumpled hotel sheets and the welcoming arms of a young fool.

"Someone should have borrowed Mrs. Seavers's bull-whip."

"I should have known. In hindsight, the clues were there." I force my shoulders back. I'm not looking for pity. "I drove home that night."

He reaches across the table to touch me but hesitates, and his hand falls in his lap.

"Of course, the whole town found out. I was mortified. The next time the skunk showed up, Moss Jones kicked the crap out of him." I smile and tuck hair that fell out of my pony-tail in that almost-kiss. "That part didn't suck. He wanted to press charges, but Booger, our local cop, said Moss was just carrying out the trash. Never saw the con artist again."

His eyes are steady on me. "No wonder you hate liars."

"Yeah."

"I've got one of those stories." His voice goes deeper. Quieter.

"What happened?"

"My own fault. You're not the only one who can see truth in the rear view. I was actually shopping for a diamond."

He shakes his head. "I guess I should be glad I overheard her talking with a girlfriend on the phone about how she'd redecorate 'the mausoleum' after we were married and how it would be easy not to have to 'deal with' me much in a house that big."

"Oh." One hand covers my heart, the other takes his hand.

He smiles, but there's no humor in it. "Takes one to know one, I guess, huh?"

"I guess." I suddenly realize we're alone, in the dark, and I'm starting to like him too much. I push to my feet and shoulder my purse. "Sorry to run, but I've got to get home. Thank you for all this. It was a sweet thing to do."

He stands. "It was my pleasure."

I take a step, but his hand on my arm stops me. His cologne wraps around me, luring me closer. I tighten my muscles against the gravitational pull.

"I hear there's big doings around here for the Fourth."

"Big for us, nothing special for anyone else. Just fireworks at the football field for the kids."

His fingers trace down the sleeve of my blouse, not touching my skin but making me hyperaware that only thin fabric separates us. "I'd like to go with you and your family, if that's okay."

I step back. "Thanks, but no."

"Not a date. Just as friends. Why not?"

After tonight? The jury in my mind is still out. "I don't want to give people the wrong idea."

"Lorelei. People are far too concerned about their own lives to care about yours."

I snort. "You never lived in Unforgiven."

"Okay, so I can come??" His white teeth flash in the dark.

"Um...no." I might as well admit it's not Unforgiven I'm worried about getting the wrong idea. It's me.

"Can't blame a guy for trying." He picks up his phone and looks down at the pie. "What do I—"

"I've got it." I take it behind the counter and put it in the pie safe. "They'll be fighting over this in the morning."

"I'd say save a piece for me, but I'm flying out first thing. I wouldn't have missed this for anything."

I quash asking when he'll be back. None of my business. "Okay then, I've got to git."

He follows me to the door and holds it open. "I'm not giving up, you know. I haven't been to fireworks in years."

I focus on how pushy and presumptuous he is, to refreeze the soft spot on my heart. I drive home smelling him on my clothes and hoping he has a lot of business to take care of, so he won't return until I've forgotten spinning in his arms. And that almost-kiss.

CHAPTER 11

Lorelei

It's Sunday, the one day I don't have to work. But it's also Mrs. Wheelwright's day off, so sleeping in is out. Besides, it's raining, which means I'm on bucket patrol, putting pans and pots under the leaks in the ceiling in the upstairs bedrooms. By the time I do that, then get Momma ready and help her downstairs, Sawyer is soaking wet and fussing. I get her cleaned up, fix breakfast, do the dishes, then collapse in the armchair in the living room. Momma's on the couch, watching a televangelist preach old-time gospel, and Sawyer is on a blanket on the carpet sitting on her haunches like a dog, cooing baby words. She hasn't crawled yet, but the last couple of days, she's been thinking about it pretty hard.

I slide off the chair to the floor, hold out my hands, and wiggle my fingers. "Come here, pretty girl. Come to me."

Sawyer bounces, lifting onto her knees, then sitting back again.

"You can do it. I know you can. You're a West, and we are the smartest, prettiest girls in the county."

"You know that's right," Momma says.

Well, Sawyer is, anyway. "Come on, Sawyer. You can do it!" I lean forward a bit to try to entice her closer.

She pulls herself up, drools, and sits back down.

Momma looks away from the TV and has to speak up to be heard over the rain pounding the porch roof. "What happened to that Meals on Wheels boy? We haven't seen him in a while."

It *is* odd. I haven't had a text from Reese since he flew out the morning after our dance. I don't think about him except for the rare slow times: when I wake in the morning, when I'm in the bath, when I'm carving, late at night. "Ah, we don't need him, Momma."

"He was nice. I miss his steaks."

I turn to her. "Well, I don't have steak, but I got a really nice chuck roast at O'Grady's for dinner tonight. What do you think about that?"

"I think you'd better watch that baby." She points.

Sawyer is crawling across the carpet to me.

"Oh my gosh. Come on, sweetie, you're doing it!"

She takes three more wobbly crawls and collapses face-first into my lap. I lift her over my head. "It's superbaby!" I twist her right and left, and she giggles down at me. I lower her to my chest, wrap her in my arms, trying not to squeeze her too hard. "Aren't you a big girl?"

Patsy's eyes stare up at me. My chest clamps tight on a lump of emotion, and tears prick my eyes. I didn't know you could feel grief and giddiness at the same time. *Oh, Patsy.*

"Momma, did you see that? She's crawling!"

"Shhh." She frowns at the screen. "That man's fixin' to save that little girl."

I put Sawyer down, and she crawls unsteadily to the wall, where the TV is plugged in. "Oh, no you don't." I steer her back toward the blanket. I'd better stop at the hardware store tomorrow to get baby-proof plugs for the outlets and hooks for the drawers. I sit watching her, grinning. This is big—a milestone. I want to share it with someone, and Reese deserves to know. He'll be tickled. I pull out my phone.

L: Guess what?

R: What?

L: Sawyer is CRAWLING!!!!

R: Seriously? Dang, wish I were there to see it. Hey, FaceTime me!

L: Um. Okay, but it'll be a minute.

R: Standing by. In the meantime, I'll tell my horse about my amazing niece.

L: You're out riding?

R: Told you I was a cowboy. Sometimes.

I walk backward to the bathroom so I can keep an eye on Sawyer and run a brush through my hair at the same time. I check the mirror. Maybe just a little mascara, so my blond lashes don't make me look like I don't have any. I'd like some blush, but it's upstairs, and...Oh, forget it.

Back in the living room, I hit the icon on my phone, and Reese's face appears. He's wearing a cowboy hat, and his stark white shirt is against a blue-sky backdrop. "I don't believe you're on your horse. Show me."

He reaches the phone out, giving me a panoramic view of land that looks a lot like New Mexico. "Your horse is beautiful. Sorrel, isn't it?"

"Yep. This is Brandy. Now, show me the peanut." His goofy anticipatory grin makes me glad I called him.

I turn the camera on Sawyer. "Come on, baby girl. Show your uncle what you got." I pat the floor.

She scoots over to me, this time a bit steadier. She crawls into my lap, and I turn her to sit in my lap, back to me, so both of us can see the screen.

"Wow, Sawyer, you're the champ!" He pumps a fist in the air. "Way to go!"

Sawyer tips her head and reaches for the phone. "Baba."

"See? She knows who I am—that's right, baby; it's Baba." My grin amps to goofy level.

She reaches for the phone again, and I hold it over my head so she can't get it but we can still see him.

"Hey, Sawyer. You wanna go with me to the fireworks next weekend?" He hesitates a few seconds. "You do? That's great. I'll—what's that? I've gotta ask her if it's okay?"

This man is relentless. But cute. To make him stay away, I'd have to be mean, and I'm too happy to be mean right now. "Oh, all right. But Mrs. Wheelwright and Momma are coming, too."

"Sounds great. We can all fit in the Murphinator."

"You really named it that?" I'm too pleased with myself. God, what am I, a high schooler?

"Yep. It is a good name."

"Well, you may not want to park it under the oak out back next time. It's so covered in bird poop it looks like an Appaloosa. Although this rain may be helping a bit."

He makes a face. "If I can borrow your hose, your chariot will be so shiny you'll need sunglasses to ride in it."

"You wash your own car?" I snort.

"Well, not when I can get to a car wash, but I haven't seen one around Unforgiven."

"That's because there isn't one, and yes, you can use the hose." Sawyer squirms out of my lap and heads for the outlet again. "Look, I've gotta go. When are you flying in?"

"I'll be there Saturday. My bull manager is on the road

with the first load of cows, and I want to be there when he shows up."

"Sawyer, no." I pull her fingers from the TV cord. "I've got to go. It's pouring outside and the pots upstairs are going to overflow. We'll see you Saturday, then."

It's good to have something to look forward to. But he's going to get the wrong idea if I don't set him straight.

Saturday. I'll make it clear when I see him on Saturday.

* * *

Reese

I'm lining up on my little runway in Unforgiven when it hits me. I'm going to need to fence it off, or I'll be cow-dodging on landing. Better include fencing around the house, too, or I'll have uninvited guests for drinks on the patio, along with the flies and patties that come with them.

I circle once, to get a bird's-eye view of the construction. I'm glad I talked the builder into using local labor for the grunt work. Maybe it'll help this town in some small way. The foundation is in, and huge logs are lying about like a giant's pick-up sticks. The experts start the timber frame on Monday. Once the walls are up and the plumbing in, I can stay here when I come to town. A plywood floor beats that nasty hotel bed any day. And I'll be close to Sawyer. The porch and front door face away from the road, and the soaring windows and huge patio will face Lorelei's house. That's the better view.

My stomach lifts with my drop in altitude—and at the thought of Lorelei. I see her eyes in my dreams. They hold the promise of...something I can't name.

You can't afford to figure that out, stupid. Relationships end, but Sawyer, she's family, and I can't lose her. I remind myself once more why I'm here. Picnicking with the Wests on the Fourth just makes sense. If I'm going to be in Sawyer's life, it'll be easier if the family is comfortable with me—like a relative or close friend of the family. Besides, I hope to eventually get Lorelei's permission to take Sawyer to Texas for a visit.

I tamp down the buzz in my chest that has nothing to do with the engines.

The wheels bark on the packed dirt, and I taxi back to the big oak at the fence between my land and the Wests'. I shut it down, get out, and walk to the truck. Lorelei was right. The gold paint is liberally splashed with white. A better name would be "the Poopinator." It looks like all the rain did the other night was smear it.

I glance to the construction site. I should go check on it. But the pull of that old farmhouse and the people it holds wins out. I head for the gate I had put in to give me closer access. Besides, I want to see if I can get up in the attic and determine if the roof can be patched.

A semi's airhorn sounds from the road. Our cattle hauler is at the back gate, and Juan's waving from the open window. I glance to the house. Dammit, visiting is going to have to wait. *Sorry, Peanut.* I jog down the fence line to open the gate at the other end.

We make short work of the job, and soon the cattle are munching grass in their new home and Juan is back on the road.

I check my phone. Eleven. I'd love to stop in and visit the ladies, but I've got another errand to take care of first. I hop in the filthy truck and punch in the address that Moss Jones gave me. This negotiation is going to be dicey, so it's better done in person.

I follow the GPS's directions, and fifteen minutes later I bump off the pavement onto a rutted dirt track. There are rows of crops growing on both sides, green and waving in the breeze. After a mile, I pull into the dooryard of an odd, five-sided log building. A hogan, I think it's called.

I shut down the truck and step out into the blistering heat.

The barrel of a shotgun pokes out the door, followed by a tall, rangy man with long black hair and the bronzed coloring of a Native American.

"Whoa, friend." I put up my hands.

"You're not my friend." The gun's barrel doesn't waver. "What do you want?"

"Are you Joseph 'Fishing Eagle' King?" I knew this would be dicey, but I didn't plan on getting shot.

His eyes narrow. "Who wants to know?"

"I'm Reese St. James. I bought land on the other side of town. Lorelei West is a friend of mine."

He lowers the gun. "Nevada told me about you."

"I want to help the Wests. But I need your assistance." I wipe a rivulet of sweat from the side of my face. "Do you have a minute?"

He looks me over, then turns and opens the door. "Cooler in here. Come on in."

I step into one room that appears to take up the entire bottom floor. It's beautiful, with Navajo rugs, leather furniture, and woven baskets on almost every surface. "Nice place."

"Thank you." He leads the way to a counter and pulls out a bar stool. "Sit. Do you want coffee?"

"No, thanks." I sit.

He steps around the island to pour himself a cup from the coffee maker on the counter. "Tell me."

"Lorelei mentioned that you said you would replace her roof if she came up with the money for materials."

"I did. I'm waiting for her to buy them."

"I'll pay for the materials."

He raises one eyebrow. "Does Lorelei know about this?"

"If you're a friend of hers, you know she'd never take a handout. Or even a loan if she couldn't pay it back right away. I swear, that woman weighs one twenty, and one hundred of it is pride."

He nods. "Strong women have reason to be proud."

A silence expands while I try to take his measure. If this gets back to Lorelei, I'm toast. "They *need* that new roof. I'll give you the money to buy materials, but we have to come up with a story of how you came by them that doesn't involve me."

He crosses his arms. "You want me to help you lie to Lorelei."

"Well, I wouldn't really call it a lie exactly—"

"I know what to call it. What I want to know is why?"

"Because I care about the comfort and safety of my niece, Sawyer."

The corner of his mouth quirks. "So now you're lying to me. This does not inspire trust, dude."

I heave a sigh. "And yes, I care about Lorelei…as a friend."

"And you think lying to her is the best way to show that you're 'friends'?"

I'm letting the air quotes pass. "I know it's a huge risk. But…she works so hard and gives so much and that house means a lot to her. To all of them. And from what I've seen, that roof is to the point of falling on their heads."

He carries his mug around and sits next to me. "You have big stones for a cowboy."

I hear Carson in my head, laughing himself silly.

He takes a sip of coffee while he decides. Then he sets the

mug down with a *thump*. "I'll help. But it's got to be a good story, because if she finds out, she'll be almost as pissed at me as she will be at you."

* * *

Lorelei

The morning of July Fourth dawns clear and cloudless with the promise of the day's heat in the air. It's my day off, but I'm up at my usual time, cooking fried chicken and making a peach cobbler. I smile, remembering all the Fourths of July over the years: me and Patsy dancing in front of the band when we were little, holding hands with my date in high school, leaning back against his solid chest to watch the fireworks. Nowadays it's just Momma and me, and last year Mrs. Wheelwright joined us.

Butterflies brush the walls of my chest. This year will be another memory to add to my collection—I can't wait to see Sawyer's face when the first ball of sparkling color lights up the sky. I don't think the fireworks will scare her; she's a pretty intrepid kid.

Reese will be a part of this year's memory, too.

I'm not sure how I feel about that. He's trying hard to be sweet, but I don't trust his agenda. He acts interested. But why? I'm not saying I don't have good qualities; I do. But I'm no Patsy in the looks or the sparkle department, and men always go for those girls. Especially rich men who have their pick.

Oh, that reminds me. I've got to get some sparklers. Sawyer will get a kick out of them.

I check the rooster clock over the kitchen table. Time to get everyone up. It's going to be a big day.

By nine we're through our morning routine. I've coaxed Momma onto the front porch, and Sawyer is crawling in the grass at my feet.

"When's that Meals on Wheels boy coming back?" Momma's rocker squeaks on the warped boards.

"Today, actually." Butterflies start up a cha-cha in my chest, and I smooth a crease in my shorts that I missed with the iron.

"He's interested in you, you know."

"Momma!"

"I may be old, but I'm not blind. The way he looks at you—and that baby." She tsks. "He wouldn't be much of a catch, though. I don't imagine the county pays much."

"Momma. Stop." Heat spreads up my neck that has nothing to do with the temperature.

"Well, it's past time you got married, Lorelei. There are things more important than what a man earns. You have to admit, he's good-looking."

A fact I wish I could forget. "What do you think, Momma? Should we put a bird feeder in the oak tree this year? Sawyer might like to watch the birds."

"Oh yes, let's. Maybe we should get some corn to bring the quail in. Your daddy loved those quail."

"He did." I smile. She remembers Daddy; it's going to be a good day. "Come on, Sawyer, let's try that standing-up thing again." I hold out my fingers, and when she grasps them, I lift her onto her feet, where she sways like an heiress after a night on the town. "Good job, Peanut."

The butterflies spin and twirl when the bird-spackled Murphinator pulls up the drive, stops opposite us, and the window rolls down. "Yay, Sawyer!" Reese turns it off, climbs out, slams the door, and comes running over, arms out. "That's my girl!"

"Baba."

She pulls my fingers and takes a wavering step toward him.

He reaches her, sweeps her up, and tosses her in the air, making her shriek with happiness.

If someone can resist a baby's giggle, they don't live in this house. Momma is chuckling and my face is split in a grin. For the first time, seeing Reese and Sawyer together, I don't feel the pinch of jealousy. She likes him, and he's mad for her. It will be good for her to have a man in her life, a surrogate dad.

He puts Sawyer down and walks up the steps of the porch to take Momma's hand. "Hello, Mary. How are you doing today?"

"Fine as frog's hair. Did you bring steaks, or did you come for Lorelei?"

"Momma!" God, let the ground swallow me right here.

He winks at her. "No steaks today, Mary." He lets go of her hand and walks back down to us. "Good morning, Lorelei. You're looking exceptionally pretty today."

I look down at my cut-off blue jean shorts, off-the-shoulder white blouse, and my favorite Keds. "If this is great, I must look really bad most days." I square my Fightin' Billy Goats baseball cap to block the sun. "Sit down, will you? You're making my neck ache."

"As you wish," he says with a smile as he sits.

"I thought you were going to wash your car yesterday?"

"I was, but I got tied up. The cattle showed up, and..."

"I saw them. They're awful pretty."

"I don't raise them for looks, but I'm glad you think so. You still okay with me washing the Murph here?"

"Have at it."

"It's getting hot," Momma calls from the porch. "I believe I'll go in."

I should get Sawyer inside, but she's having fun playing with the toys on the blanket. Reese walks to his car,
unbuttoning his shirt and pulling the tail out of his jeans.

Oh, wow. He might not be a full-time cowboy, but he's got
the muscles for it. Broad shoulders, swimmers' lats, down
to a tight waist... and I've always had a healthy appreciation
for a butt-cupping pair of Wranglers.

"We'll be in in a few, Momma." Sawyer's slathered in sunscreen and we're under the oak. I'd hate to miss the show.

He tosses his shirt through the window of the truck,
opens the door, pulls out a bucket, rolls up the window, and
slams the door. Then he walks to the side of the house to
get the hose.

Dang, it *is* hot out here.

"Hey, you need sunscreen?" I ask.

"Real men don't use sunscreen."

"The ones who don't want skin cancer do."

He smiles over at me. "I put some on before I left
the hotel."

When I realize I'm staring like a woman at a Chippen-
dales club, I shake my head to clear it. "Come on, baby girl,
time to get you inside." I sling her legs to straddle my hip
and shake out the blanket.

* * *

"It's four o'clock, time to head 'em up and move 'em out!"
Mrs. Wheelwright calls from the bottom of the stairs. "We
want a good seat, right?"

"Coming." I step into my sandals and check the mirror.
I'm glad I took the time to grab a shower and change.
My hair curls nicely over my shoulders, and my sleeveless
tie-at-the-waist blouse matches my eyes. The denim cutoffs

keep me from looking dressed up. Just the right touch. I twirl away from the mirror, tuck my phone in my back pocket, and with my almost-maxed-out credit card and a twenty in my front pocket, I'm good to go.

I walk down the stairs to the kitchen, where everyone's waiting. "Oh, Momma, you look so pretty!" Her hair is a nimbus of sugar-spun silver curls. Mrs. Wheelwright came over early to do Momma's hair.

"You'll be turning all those men's heads, for sure, Mary," Reese says.

In spite of the sunscreen, he's picked up a gold kiss of sun. His hair is slicked back, showing off the strong lines of his jaw. "Did you wash up with the hose again?"

"Yep."

I roll my eyes. "Oh, for cripes' sake. You could have used our shower."

His gold tint suffuses with pink. "I'm good."

I pull the chicken, store-bought coleslaw, and peach cobbler from the fridge.

"You made your famous fried chicken." Mrs. Wheelwright picks up the large container.

"It's Momma's family recipe."

Reese lifts the cobbler dish. "Well, I can't wait to taste it, so let's get moving."

"Hold on." Mrs. Wheelwright raises a hand. "With the car seat, we're not all going to fit in that truck."

Reese frowns. "She's right. I didn't think about that. If it had bench seats in the front, it would work, but..."

"The baby seat is already in my car anyway." Mrs. Wheelwright heads for the door. "Come on, Mary, you're riding shotgun. Bring the baby to the car, will you, Reese?"

Well, didn't she pull that dance off as smooth as Ginger Rogers?

CHAPTER 12

Reese

Hanging with the Wests today has been a blast. I'm shocked to realize I'm more relaxed in that old farmhouse than I am in Bo's showplace. Their comfortable routines are like a long-practiced dance, where everyone has a place and a part to play.

After today I kinda feel like I have a part, too.

Lorelei directs me to the high school—an ugly two-story cinder-block square sitting in a field outside town. I'd mistake it for a prison, if not for the lack of razor wire. The weather-beaten sign out front declares it UNFORGIVEN HIGH: HOME OF THE FIGHTIN' BILLY GOATS!

I wouldn't house goats in that place, much less kids.

But three hours before the fireworks show, the parking lot is full, and cars are queuing up to park in the hard-packed dirt beside it. I pull into the crawling line. "I thought we'd be the first here."

Lorelei raises a brow. "There's not much to do in

Unforgiven. Any excuse for a party." She rolls down her window. "Hey, Ms. Temple!" She waves to an older lady in a wide-brimmed straw hat walking between rows of cars. The woman waves back. "That's my high school civics teacher."

A big farmer in overalls steps in front of the truck and raps his knuckles on the hood. "Hey, Lorelei. Movin' up in the world, huh?"

"Stuff it, Quad. You're just jealous."

"Of that truck, I am."

When he clears out of the way, I inch forward.

A crowd of young girls call, "Hey, Lorrrrelei, nice... truck," then break into giggles.

Lorelei's looking out the windshield. I'd swear she hadn't heard, except for her pink cheeks.

"Friends of yours?"

"Not exactly. Do you like fried chicken?"

"I like chicken any way I can get it." I ease into the next open space, and a battered truck pulls up beside me.

"Good, because we've got plenty."

I shut down the ignition, climb out, and grab the huge picnic basket from the back. It weighs a ton. I wonder how many people she plans on feeding.

"Oh, hey, Nana, Papaw. I thought you'd be comin' with Carly and the fam."

The little old lady comes around the truck beside us. She's in a cowgirl outfit: puffed-up skirt, suede vest, a neckerchief, and a straw cowgirl hat. But instead of boots, she's in orthopedic shoes and thick, flesh-colored tights that bag at her knees and skinny ankles. "Gotta get here early for the square dance demonstration. Me 'n' Papaw... What in sweet hell are you doin', Leroy?"

All I can see is the baggy backside of worn pants. "Settin' up for business."

"Well, get out here and say hello to Lorelei and... Who's the shiny-lookin' dude?"

A flustered Lorelei turns to me. "Reese St. James, meet Nancy and LeRoy Beauchamp, Carly's grandparents. Nana and Papaw, this is Reese, Sawyer's uncle."

I sweep off my Stetson. "Nice to meet y'all."

The woman squints up at me. "Makin' yourself right at home in the family, I see."

"Um. Ma'am?" Now *I'm* getting flustered.

"Aw, I'm just pullin' your dangly parts, son." She slaps me on the arm. "You could do a darned sight worse than our Lorelei. A good solid woman, right here."

The stooped old man straightens from the truck and takes his wife's elbow. "Come on, hon, before these two explode from embarrassment."

They toddle off.

"I'm so sorry. Nana is wonderful, but she's a bit... outspoken."

"You think?" I put my hat on.

"You're lucky. She seems to like you. She didn't cuss you out or anything. Ask Manny Stipple about the time she dumped pea soup over his head."

"I'll take that as a warning. I'm not doing anything to get on that lady's bad side."

Lorelei cranes her neck. "Mrs. Wheelwright was right behind us. Where—oh, there they are." She trots across the aisle, and I follow to Mrs. Wheelwright's car.

Lorelei opens the back door, but I touch her arm. "May I? Peanut's getting pretty heavy." I set down the picnic basket.

"Okay. I'll get the diaper bag."

"Hey, Sawyer, want to go for a horsey-back ride?"

"Baba." She reaches for me, her starfish fingers opening

and closing. After some figuring, I extricate her from the car seat, pull her out, and swing her onto my hip.

She squeals.

"Hang on, little one."

Mrs. Wheelwright and Mary step out. "Woooweee, it's hot!" Mary waves a plastic fan in front of her face.

"Always is at first, Momma. Should get better from here on." Lorelei pulls two blankets from the back seat and slings the diaper bag over her shoulder.

Mrs. Wheelwright reaches to take the picnic basket.

I grab the handle. "I've got it, ma'am. Y'all lead, and we'll take up the drag."

The older ladies walk on, chattering like agitated squirrels.

Somewhere past the stands, a band is tuning up. The smell of brats and beer floats to me.

"We'll try to find a place on the field, but I don't know…" Lorelei is swallowed by the crowd, and I trot to catch up, Sawyer chortling the whole way.

We round the stands, and the football field is a patchwork quilt of blankets, sleeping bags, and beach towels, dotted with lawn chairs and ice chests. "Wow."

"Yeah, told you the Fourth was a big deal around here."

In the middle of the sea of blankets is a raised dais, maybe twenty by thirty feet. In the corner is a band of five playing "Low Places." People we pass are singing along. We follow Mary and Mrs. Wheelwright's wandering path to squeeze into a spot right up front, at the other end of the stage from the band.

"Lorelei. Just the person I've been wanting." A reedy but commanding voice comes from our left.

Lorelei's shoulders hunch an inch, and she turns. "Hello, Ann."

The woman has a long face, skin stretched over strong

bones. She narrows her eyes. "Are you not going to introduce me to your date?"

She reminds me of that mean witch from *The Wizard of Oz*, only she dresses better and her color is more pallid than green.

"He's not my date; he's Sawyer's." She turns to me, her lips in a thin line. "Reese St. James, this is Ann Miner, head of the Unforgiven Historical Society."

She puts out a hand, as if I should kiss her ring. "*And* the lead reporter for the *Unforgiven Patriot*."

Probably the *only* reporter. "Sorry, hands full." I'm not setting down the basket or Sawyer. If Lorelei doesn't like this woman, I trust her judgment.

"I'd like to interview you for the paper. We do that with newcomers."

I tighten my hold on Sawyer, put down the basket, pull a business card from my pocket, and hand it over. "I'm not here full time, but I'm sure we could set up a chat."

"Very well. Carry on." She gives us a dismissive wave and turns to the woman beside her.

Lorelei rolls her eyes and walks to where the others stand waiting. She shakes out the blankets and helps her mother to sit.

I set the picnic basket on a corner and settle Sawyer beside her grandma.

"You two relax. I'll get the meal ready." Mrs. Wheelwright opens the basket.

Lorelei looks up at me and talks over the music. "We only have water to drink. You want a beer?"

The heat and the sun have baked all the juices out of me. "That sounds like just the thing, as long as you have one with me."

"I could drink one."

"I'll get them. The vendors are under the stands, right?"

"I'll come with you. Momma, you eat. We'll be back as soon as we can." She walks past me, chin high. "Might as well let the crowd get a good look."

I'm still figuring how to read Lorelei's moods, but even I can't miss the burr under her saddle. No hiding for this one; she's taking on the curious looks with a glare.

There's a long line in front of the Kiwanis beer truck. I turn to her. "Maybe we should skip—"

"Lorelei." Carly Beauchamp, the owner of the café, waves from the front of the line. I've seen her before, but we've never been introduced. She beckons us forward. "Come on up here."

Lorelei eyes the line. "If we take cuts, there'll be a riot."

"Nah." She puts her hand on the arm of the young buck behind her. "Leonard, would you mind if Lorelei steps in? She's got a baby and can't be gone long." She bats her pretty green eyes at him.

If the kid is legal to drink, his birthday was last week. He snatches the baseball cap off his head and ducks his red face. "No problem, Carly."

Lorelei steps into the line. "Thanks, Leonard. You're the best."

I step up. "Carly, we haven't had a chance to meet." I take off my hat. "I'm—"

"Oh, I know who you are." She leans in, hugs me, and whispers in my ear, "If you hurt her, you're a dead man."

I back up. In spite of her bright smile, I have no doubt that hug was camouflage for the message. Her warning hits me with the crack of a slap. Carly seems sure that we're a couple, and she's not the first. Are they seeing something I've been trying to hide from myself?

Now I just have to figure out how I feel about that. And then what I plan to *do* about it.

I realize I've missed part of the conversation.

"Austin? He's on the field, trying to herd the cats. I swear, Faith runs more than she walks, and Little Austin is...his dad in a diaper. Let's just leave it at that." She swipes sweat off her forehead and moves forward a step.

By the time we get our beers, I've gotten an earful of the local "flavor" (read: gossip). I file it away for future reference and follow Lorelei through the crowd, admiring her swaying hips. The square-dance demonstration is in full whirl, and Mary and Mrs. Wheelwright are alternating eating, feeding Sawyer bits of chicken, and watching the show.

I sit, and since the stage is above us, I get way too much of a glimpse of what's under old ladies' square-dancing skirts. I turn so my back is to the stage. Thanks to the crowd noise, conversation is impossible. So I wolf down the best fried chicken ever and top it off with a double helping of peach cobbler. I ease back on the blanket, enjoying this small-town Americana scene.

Finally, the square dancers leave the stage to thunderous applause.

"The Squeaky Wheels are next," Lorelei says. "They're pretty good. Pat owns the local garage, but he only hires mechanics who play."

"Wow, that must cut back on the interviews."

"Yep. And frankly, from what I hear about their work, I think he weights their musical talent higher than mechanical ability."

I make a mental note to do my own maintenance on the Murphinator. But she's right; the band isn't half-bad. The crowd is getting into it, clapping and singing along. A herd of young kids cluster in front of the stage, swaying, stomping their feet, and doing toddler improvisational dance.

"I can't wait until Sawyer is old enough to dance up front. It's a family tradition."

Her eyes are wistful. And sad. She's remembering her sister.

The sun is a golden ball at the red-rimmed horizon when the band launches into "Rock Around the Clock." Lorelei is sitting, arms around her bent knees, feet tapping.

I lean over and whisper, "In those dance lessons, you learn more than the waltz?"

She looks down her nose at me. "I was raised on the jitterbug in my Momma's kitchen."

I hold out my hand.

"Are you kidding? Get up in front of every single person in town?" She shakes her head.

"Hey, they're talking about us anyway. Why don't we give them some fat to chew?" I waggle my eyebrows.

She shakes her head again. "I don't want to give them any wrong ideas. We're just friends."

"But dancing on the Fourth is a family tradition, right?" I shrug. "And friends can dance, can't they?" I drop the smile and look steady into her eyes. "Come on, Lorelei. I won't make a fool of you."

The band swings straight into Boogie Woogie Bugle Boy, *the* perfect jitterbug tune. I hold out my hand again.

She looks left, then right, then back at me, stubborn in her jaw and her eyes. "You know what? Dancing is *just* what I want to do." Her smile is a bit wicked when she drops her hand in mine. "Be right back, Momma." She flips off her baseball cap. "Lead on, cowboy."

I pull her to her feet, and we step onto the strip of grass between the blanket and the stage. I take her hands, we catch the beat, and when she nods, I pull her into a cuddle back, push her out under my arm, and pull her back in. She's following like she has telepathy, sensing my next move before I make it. She adds flair, kicking out, and I mimic her. She's working it, bouncing the rock steps. I take a chance, and when I sweep up her legs, she throws her head back and flips.

God, she's fabulous.

The band launches into "Ain't Too Proud to Beg," and we don't miss a beat. I'm sweating, out of breath, and loving every second. Lorelei is grinning bright as the sun, her pony-tail flipping and bouncing. And she said her sister got all the sparkle. She was wrong.

When the song ends, she puffs a breath, and her bangs fly up. "I need water."

"Me too." She turns to walk away, but I still have her hand. I reel her back in, then bow a bit over her hand and kiss it. "Thank you for the dance, miss."

I look up into her startled-doe eyes, and time goes to slo-mo. In hers, I see laughter, surprise, and a hint of a frown. I wonder what she sees in mine.

Something warm and sure settles in my chest. I don't know what it is, but it feels just right. A rolling wave of applause breaks the moment. Wolf whistles come from the crowd, and people stomp the wooden slats in the stands. Lorelei turns, and red-faced, waves to the crowd, then drops a small curtsy.

This lady is badass. Admiration tightens my chest, and I wave, then follow her to the blanket, where Mary and Sarah are clapping loudest of all.

God, that was fun. Seeing Lorelei open, happy, and sparkling makes me want to throw away all my misgivings about my relationship issues and kiss her senseless.

But...Sawyer. Yes, Lorelei's different from all the women in my past. Yes, there are happily married couples I know. But how do you trust that this could be different when you've never experienced anything that worked out?

I could live without a relationship with Lorelei. It would be wrenching, but I could do it. But I can't live without Sawyer. I won't.

Lorelei drops to the blanket, and the two women fuss over her. She's glowing. I caused that. I made her happy, and that makes me happy.

Where does that leave me?

Here. It leaves me right here, sitting in the grass with people who are starting to feel like family.

And just for tonight, that's enough.

* * *

Lorelei

In spite of knowing I'll get teased later, I'm not sorry, because for just a few minutes I got to dance on the Fourth in front of the band again. And what a partner Reese is, dashing and bold and as smooth as new silk—in more than just his dancing. I hope Patsy saw; she'd have joined us if she were here.

I needn't have worried that Sawyer would be scared by the fireworks; she loves them, clapping her hands and making *oh-oh-oh* noises until she fell asleep, cradled in my lap. I look around at the wonder on the upturned faces. Even Ann Miner is smiling. I guess on the Fourth, everyone turns into a kid.

I turn to Momma. "Isn't this—what is it, Momma?"

Her face is in her hands, and when I pull them away, her features are twisted in fright and tears are sheeting down her face. "Momma, what's wrong?"

"The storm! We have to get to shelter!" She pushes to her knees and claps her hands over her ears when another bang goes off. "Bruce—where is Bruce? He was just here." She turns to me, and in the light of the latest firework, I can see the terror in her eyes. "Patsy, find your father. We have to go!"

I gather Sawyer to move her so I can get to Momma, but Reese is faster.

He takes Momma's hands to get her attention. "Mary. Mary, it's all right. We're going, okay?" He pulls her to her feet.

"Bruce. We can't leave him in the storm!"

Mrs. Wheelwright says, "You get her and the baby to the car. I'll pack up and be right there."

Reese puts his arm around Momma, supporting her elbow. "It's okay, Mary. Lorelei will find him. Let's get you…" His deep, calm voice fades as he leads her to the edge of the crowd and heads toward the parking lot.

I lift Sawyer and lay her over my shoulder. Asleep, she's a heavy deadweight, and I struggle to stand.

"I should have seen that coming. I'm sorry," Mrs. Wheelwright says, folding blankets.

"None of us could have. She was fine last year." I look at the mess we've left, but I can't carry more than Sawyer. I step carefully around the sprawled blankets and people.

An hour later Momma and the baby are in bed and Mrs. Wheelwright is on the road home.

"I need a drink." I pull open the fridge, hoping, but knowing there's nothing there stronger than iced tea or 2 percent milk.

Reese snaps his fingers. "I brought a bottle of wine for the picnic, then forgot it. I'll get it out of the truck and meet you on the front porch, okay?"

"Sounds like a plan." I take two stemless wineglasses from the "good dishes" hutch in the corner, and not wanting to wrestle with the front door, walk around the side yard and climb the steps to settle in Momma's rocker. The dark is a welcome friend, and my jitters settle a bit.

Reese's white shirt bobs across the yard. The stairs creak under his boots, and he sits in the chair next to me. "You okay?"

"God, what a night." I sigh. "Good and bad."

"I really enjoyed it. Right up 'til the end, anyway." There's the hollow pop of a cork leaving a bottle. "Here, give me the glasses."

I hand them over. "Thank you for your help. You were good with Momma. She settled faster for you than she would have me or Mrs. Wheelwright."

"I think it's probably a man's voice. She's from a generation that looked to her husband for safety and security." He hands me a glass. "Here's to the jitterbug."

I have to smile. We clink glasses. We sip merlot, looking out into the dark yard, each to our own thoughts. The rasping chirp of the crickets and the creak of my rocker unwind me, allowing the evening's peace to seep in. Since the dance, things between us seem…easier. More comfortable.

It makes me lonely somehow, for the life that passed me by. In high school, I imagined sitting on the porch like this with the man I'd grow old with. But that was before I learned that men aren't reliable. And that they don't want women like me, anyway. Guess all the memories of the day have just made me wistful tonight.

His deep, soft voice comes from my right. "Isn't it funny

how the dark makes it easier to talk? It's like you and I communicate best that way. That and texts."

Uh-oh. "Did you want to talk about something?"

"Nope."

"Now that you bring it up, I have a question for you."

"Uh-oh."

"Nothing big. I think we've had enough drama for one day, don't you? I just wondered how you got your scar."

"Yeah, no drama." He snorts and leans back in the chair. "That's only the one that shows." He takes a sip of wine. "Lorelei, if Carson were here, he'd be taking care of Patsy and Sawyer. You know that, right?"

"I never met him, but I assume so. Why?"

"Will you let me contribute to Sawyer's needs? Help with the monthly expenses? It would make me so happy to be able to do something. I owe it to Sawyer. I owe it to my brother."

He and I seem to have settled into . . . whatever this is, but I'm not taking chances. "Look, you're a good man. I know you mean well. But we're fine."

He sighs. "Everyone thinks money gets you what you want. They don't know how wrong they are. It's the opposite, really."

I turn to him and drape my legs over the arm of the chair. "What is it that you want?"

"I want what everyone wants, I guess. A family . . . someone to connect to. To belong with."

"I get that. It's so sad that you've lost everyone in your family."

"Do y'all have cowbirds around here?"

"What? I have no idea. And you just lost me."

"We have them at home. They're brood parasites, meaning they lay their eggs in other bird's nests."

"Wow, that's weird. But—"

"I always thought I was like that. Like I got dropped into a family where I didn't belong. I'm not whining. It's just a fact."

The emptiness in his voice echoes through me. Having grown up surrounded with love and acceptance, I can't imagine his childhood. "That must have been awful. But it's not too late to make your own family. You can marry. Have children."

He's quiet long enough that I think the subject is closed. "Here, give me your glass."

I look down, surprised to find it's empty. I hand it over, and he fills it, then empties the rest of the bottle in his. "You asked about my scar."

"Yeah, I almost forgot."

"Wish I could." He stands and, glass in hand, paces the boards, passing me, then coming back. "I was fourteen when I got tired. Tired of the taunts. Tired of not fitting in. Frankly, I was starting to believe what I heard from my father at least once a week—that you weren't a man if you didn't enjoy pushing the envelope, hanging your butt on the edge of out-of-control. So the next time Carson dared me to get on a steer, I did. After all, how could I know they were wrong if I never tried?"

"It didn't end well."

"I was off in two seconds, under the bull's hooves. The twenty-seven stitches in my head was the easiest part. It stepped on my…" He sits on the porch railing and cradles the wineglass in his hands. "Well, let's just say that after a week in the hospital, I left with a bit less than I came in with. There are no children in my future. At least, none of my own."

I suck in a breath. "Oh, Reese."

"So you've probably wondered why I keep pushing about Sawyer. She's the last of the St. James line, which makes her my miracle."

The lonely in his voice reverberates through me. He knows what it's like to be on the outside, looking in. Odd, but the more he opens up, the more we seem to have in common in a weird, opposite kind of way. Rich/poor, older/ younger, but still, so many similarities. Beneath the obvious outside, we're alike. We both fell for pretty liars and were let down by those we loved. His sadness makes me want to put my arms around him, pull his head down, and...*Stop, Lorelei*. That's just you and those old dreams. He's looking for a family, not you.

And yet turning away from him is impossible. I sit thinking for a few moments. "I'll tell you what. We'll adopt you into our family." I hold up my almost empty glass, and clink it against his. "I always wanted a younger brother."

He makes a strangled sound in his throat. "That won't work."

"Why not?"

He sets the glass on the railing, takes two steps to my chair, drops to one knee, and takes my chin in his hand. "Because what I feel for you isn't the least bit brotherly."

His lips touch mine, a feather brush that's more a question than a kiss. My heart trips over itself, then speeds to a gallop. My old dreams break out of the closet I stuffed them in. He wants me.

I don't know if it's the wine, or the long, emotional day, but I lean in, and without permission from my brain, my lips open to him.

He pulls a startled breath through his nose and slants his head to deepen the kiss.

There's a quickening in me. A small electric current

running from my lips down my nerve endings, lighting them up in a fireworks display better than the one down at the high school tonight.

His hands cradle my skull, and mine are grasping his forearms, keeping me from floating. He backs up before I would have and sits back on his heels. "Wow."

Everything that was floating explodes and falls to earth like the *Hindenburg*. *What in the hell am I doing?* I open my mouth, but no words come out.

He shrugs. "See what I mean?"

How could I not? My breath is coming in pants, and my nipples are tingling. Hardly an appropriate reaction to "family." I stand and walk a few steps, to get some distance. To be able to breathe. To think. "This is not a good idea."

"I would have agreed with you before, but think about it, Lorelei. We're obviously compatible. And it just makes sense. The perfect solution, really. We could become a family. Sawyer would have a father figure around, and I'd be able to help you." He opens his arms, palms up. "It'd be great for both of us. Just think, we could fix up this house. You wouldn't have to work anymore—to do without anymore."

He steps closer and takes my hands. "And since you're older, it probably wouldn't bother you so much not to have more children, right?"

My anger flares, white-hot. My hand hits his face with a crack, and his head snaps to the side. "You have got to be kidding me. I was starting to believe you could want me." My voice cracks like stepping on thin ice. "But now I find I'm just part of a business deal." I put my hands in my hair. "I may be single, broke, and pathetic, but I have no interest in someone who wants me just to get to my sister's baby."

"No, Lorelei, I didn't mean—"

"Get the hell off my porch." I point into the darkness.

"I'm sorry. I suck at explaining. Let's sit down and..."

"Don't make me get my daddy's shotgun." In spite of the fire inside, ice drips from my words.

"I'm sorry. I didn't mean...I'm sorry." He turns, takes the steps in one bound, shoves his hands in his pockets, and his white shirt disappears into the gloom.

I sit in the rocker and watch his truck roll down the drive and out onto the road. It was bad enough when I thought he only wanted Sawyer. Lately, that reason was starting to feel like whistling past a graveyard, and Carly half convinced me it was only in my head.

But Reese just *told* me my intuition was right all along. I tip my head back against the chair and close my eyes. They say there's someone out there for everyone.

Why not me?

In a minute the crickets crank up again. I can hear the words of their song: *fool, fool, fool.*

CHAPTER 13

Lorelei

Hey, Lorelei, I saw you dancing in front of the stage last night. You can flat shake some booty, girl." Lacey Stephens, a high school senior, holds out her coffee mug for a refill.

Her mother jumps in before I can. "Everyone knows Lorelei is a fantastic dancer. She was going to be on *America's Ballroom Challenge*, don't you remember?"

Lacey gives a teen eye roll. "Ma, I was like nine."

Ouch. Fine, give me your worst, people. I deserve it, for being so easily taken in. I step to the next booth.

"I heard you were the highlight of the night, hon." Mrs. Belkins puts her liver-spotted hand over mine. "Don't you let anyone tell you different."

Seeing how she wasn't even there tells me I'm again center stage in the white-hot spotlight of Unforgiven gossip. My stomach flips, because this time I put myself in it. I return the carafe to the coffee maker and head to my office. To hide.

What seemed like such a good idea last night looks very different in the harsh light of morning. Of course, I didn't know then that I was a placeholder. A fill-in-the-blank. A plug and play. It's too embarrassing. My phone buzzes in my pocket.

R: I just wanted to tell you how sorry I am. When I heard the words out loud, I realized what they sounded like. I'm a bumbling idiot, Lorelei. I always say the wrong thing with you. And I hate it, because the words I say to you matter most. But I swear, I didn't—

There's more, but I'm too heartsick to read on. I turn off my phone and toss it onto the desk. It topples a pile of receipts onto the floor. "This office is disgusting." It's needed to be shoveled out for the past decade. Today I'm in the mood to tackle it. I need to stay busy, or I'm going to end up banging my head against the wall.

I roll up my sleeves and get to work.

My crazy dreams are shoved back in the closet, and I've locked the door. I knew better. But that dance—heck, that whole day up to that point was so perfect, I ignored what I knew for what I wanted. I'm glad last night on the porch happened. Better to know where I stand than to bumble along, oblivious. Like last time.

More than an hour later, I slam the drawer on the last of the filing, when I hear voices.

"Damned if I know. I think she's trying to gut the building, but there's too much crap flying around for me to get close." Nevada never has known how to whisper.

"Well, I'm gonna sure find out." I've heard that tone from Carly before. Usually right before she pitched a fit.

"Don't call me if there's an avalanche. I am not a Saint Bernard," Nevada grouses.

"Noted."

I roll the file cabinet out and set it down by the back door.

Carly's hands are on her hips, her toe tapping. "What in Hel-sinki is going on here?"

"I've put off cleaning out this pit for years." I lift hair out of my eye and swipe the sweat that's running down my cheek. "Today's the day."

She steps to the door. "Holy wow."

"I found these between the desk and the wall." I lift a pair of dust-bunny-covered old-lady underpants from the desk with the end of a pencil. "You want to return them to Nana? And please, I do not want to know how they got there."

"Oh, you're in a mood." She drops the underwear into the overflowing trash can.

"I'm not. Just tired of procrastinating." Now that the room is almost empty, I grab the broom and attack the floor.

"Hmm-hmmm. This is me you're talking to, girlfriend." She sticks her head out the door. "Hey, Nevada, make me two grilled tuna sandwiches, a side of onion rings, French fries, coleslaw, and two huge pieces of chocolate cake, to go, will you?"

"Comin' up."

"I'm not hungry. I've got a ton to do, so—"

"Oh, this is bad." She eyes me with a squint. "You go wash up, or you'll scare the customers. Then you and I are eating lunch on the square." She points a finger. "That's an order, West."

I huff frustration and head for the bathroom. What I see in the mirror stops me. The dirt I expected, but the anger burning in my eyes *would* scare customers. And...wait. Something glints in the fluorescents. I lean closer to squint into the mirror. At my hairline, two silver hairs. Only two, but their existence hits my solar plexus like a wrecking ball.

I wince and notice the lines at the edges of my eyes that don't quite disappear when I relax.

I'd hoped to grow old. I just didn't expect it to happen this soon. I wash my face, pluck out the silver, comb my hair, don a mask of normal (or as close as I can get to it), and stomp back into the kitchen.

Carly is holding a big brown sack and tips her chin at two large cups of iced tea on the counter. "You take those and follow me."

She backs up to the door and pushes it open with her butt.

"Lorelei, you little dancin' queen, you," Manny Stipple slurs, trying to bust a move from his stool at the counter, almost unseating himself.

Carly holds up a hand. "Unless you want to wear another bowl of soup, I would not go there, dude."

We march past the suddenly silent lunchtime crowd, out the door, and Carly doesn't stop until we're at the empty bandstand in the center of the town square. She sits on the steps and points next to her. "Sit."

I don't have much choice; she's my friend, but she's also my boss.

She pulls out our massive lunches and lays them out on the bag.

"Holy cripes, Carly, that's enough for four people."

"On most days, maybe, but man problems require extreme measures."

"Why would you think—"

She tips her head. "Do not play with me, chickie. You and Reese were making goo-goo eyes at each other in front of the whole town before sundown, and from the looks of you now, there were more fireworks last night than the ones shot off at the football field."

"Oh God." I put my face in my hands. I can't do

this if I have to look at her. "He made it clean-window clear last night. He wants me—but only because he wants Sawyer. I'm just the nanny that comes with—a package deal."

She picks up half a sandwich. "I don't believe it. I saw how he looked at you when he kissed your hand, like some errant knight or something. God, girl, *I* was a puddle of goo. Now eat."

I pull a corner off the sandwich and nibble. "I forget what a great cook Nevada is." I sigh. "But it gets worse. He told me that we were a perfect couple because he can't have kids, and I'm too old to care."

"Oh crap-balls. No, he didn't."

I just nod. "You're right. Food helps," I mumble around the ten fries I shoved in my mouth at once.

"Stuff away, hon." She takes a bite of tuna, then snags an onion ring. She sits with a thoughtful look while she eats it. "You told me before that he blurts, though."

"Blurts what he really thinks, yeah. I should be grateful that he does, or I'd have made an even bigger fool of myself than the last time."

She wags a finger. "That was all on that cheating scumbag, not you."

"I'm shoveling out that office today as penance, for being so stupid."

"You're a braver woman than me."

"Tell me about it." I wince. "The underwear wasn't the worst I found, but I can't talk about it while I'm eating."

"Yeah, don't. Has Reese called?"

I shake my head and finish off half the sandwich. "He knows I'd hang up. He texted this morning."

Her eyes light. "What'd he say?"

"Don't know. Don't care. I turned off my phone."

"Well, why didn't you tell me?" She holds out her hand. "You hand it over and start on the cake."

"No. You'll just take his side."

She raises an eyebrow and bounces her hand.

"Fine." I pull my phone from my shirt pocket and slap it in her hand like an operating-room nurse.

She wipes her hands on her jeans and hits buttons.

I take my first bite of the mega-size slice of cake and moan. "You need the passcode."

She doesn't look up. "Duh, it's Sawyer."

Great. Now I'm a transparent fool.

She reads, and her eyebrows tent in that *awwwww* expression that's usually reserved for puppies and babies.

I hold up a hand. "Don't."

"Lorelei, he apologizes for screwing up, and—"

"I'm sure he did." I drop the fork. "What the heck would he do if he wants custody of Sawyer and can't get her any other way? He'd suck up, that's what."

"Remember when it was me and Austin fighting and you tried to talk sense into me?"

"I can hardly forget, since your daughter was a result of that mess."

She nods. "You are being as blind as I was, seeing the hurt and not beyond it—to the idiot's intent."

Bitter surges from my throat to fill my mouth, over-powering the taste of sugar and cocoa. "Well, I don't have to worry about making the same mistake, since I'm too *old* for babies." I bury my face in my hands, and the bitterness reroutes its path to my eyes.

Carly hugs me and lets me cry.

"I'm not crying over him, you know." I sniff.

"I know, hon." She pats my back. "I know."

* * *

Reese

"Yes, it's true. Your Baba is an idiot." The small, cheap contraption Sarah called an "umbrella stroller" clatters across the pavement in front of the house. It's just too pretty this morning to be stuck inside. And besides, today the ladies don't seem to know how to act around me. I shudder, imagining what Lorelei told them. Did I really suggest a *merger*?

"No-no-no-no." Sawyer babbles her newest and favorite word.

I shake my head. "I know you find it hard to believe, but you need to trust me on this. I could mess up God's plan given enough time."

I need to fly out this morning, but I'm delaying leaving. Partly because I want to spend more time with Peanut, but also because it feels like running. I might not be the favorite son, but Bo didn't raise any sons who run.

I'm a logical businessman, and yet my personal life is starting to sound like a *Dr. Phil* episode. I went from deciding to leave Lorelei be at the fireworks to kissing her an hour later. But there was no denying it. I was kidding myself, thinking I could fly close to her light and not get singed. And staying away means no Sawyer.

An impossible situation.

"Buh-buh-buh." Sawyer points at a bird flying overhead.

I drop to a crouch beside the stroller. "Bird. That's a birrrrd."

"Buh-buh-bud."

"Yeah, close enough." I stand and push. "I know I said it wrong. I *know* that, okay?" Why didn't I tell her what matters most? That I'm all in. For the long haul, in. I want *her*, not whatever crap I said last night. So why didn't I *say* it?

My stomach falls. What would Lorelei get? Besides money. I knew she didn't give a crap about that, so why did I throw it in? Because when you don't think you have much to offer, that's what you do. "I mean, when I get past what was given to me, what do I have to offer? Me, personally?"

Sawyer lifts her arms to me.

"Yeah, I know you think I'm all that, but your standards are a bit lower than your momma's." I lift her to straddle my hip and drag the stupid stroller behind us. "I can dance. But she's lived without that for years. Let's face it. She told me last night that she was comfortable with me as her little brother." I wince. "But she did kiss me back. I didn't imagine that." I drop a kiss on Sawyer's head. "That was before I screwed up. Royally. I made her feel like I was using her to get something else I wanted. I know how bad that feels."

Sawyer points at something in my field.

"Cow. That's a cow."

"Cuh-cuh-cuh."

"Near enough." I walk on, dragging the clattering contraption. Lorelei isn't a woman you love and leave. I knew that. I remember the warmth between us. The understanding that pulled us together like two halves of a whole. "I need to fix this. She needs to know I want her for herself. Not for you, or her family, or anything else."

Sawyer puts her hands up to pat my cheek.

"Thanks for the vote of confidence, kid. Now I just have to figure out how."

When we get back to the house, I fix lunch for the ladies. Nothing big, just sandwiches for the grown-ups and mashed-up carrots and bananas for Sawyer. "She's changing every day. I hate to leave."

Mary smiles at her granddaughter. "We'll turn around and she'll be in school."

School. The sandwich flips in my stomach. "Where will she go to school?"

Sarah moves the sippy cup onto the high chair's tray. "John Denver Elementary, in town."

"What? The singer?"

Mary nods. "His name is tied to Colorado, but he was raised in Roswell."

"Wow, who knew."

"We did," Sarah and Mary chorus.

"What's the school like?"

"Oh, it's the oldest school in the district. In fact, the building was one of the first brick buildings in Unforgiven."

"Older than the high school?"

"By about thirty years."

And I thought the high school was worn down. "Are there any private schools in Unforgiven?"

"If you're Catholic, there's St. Bart's," Sarah says.

"We're Baptist," Mary says.

If Sawyer were with me, I could arrange private tutoring. But that's sure not happening, and no way Lorelei would take money from me for it. So maybe I can help the school here. After all, we've got four years before Peanut goes to kindergarten. "Sarah, do you know who the head of the school board is?"

"Know him? I'm practically related to him. He was my son's best friend, growing up."

"Could I get his number from you?"

She tips her head and gives me a knowing smile. "You're a good man, Reese St. James. I don't care what Lorelei says."

I duck my head. "That means more to me than you

know. Thank you." I swipe my mouth with a paper towel posing as a napkin. "Well, I'd better git. I've got to be home before dark."

Sarah eyes me. "Mind if I walk you out?"

"Sure thing." I don't know what's on her mind, but I'd bet my prize bull that it's about Lorelei.

"I'll just be on the porch, Mary. Okay?"

"You run on. I'll just do up these few dishes."

I hold the screen door for Sarah.

"You're going at this all backward, you know."

I step off the cement slab, into the gravel. "I beg your pardon?"

"You can't get where you want to be, from here." She crosses her arms.

"I'm afraid you've lost me, Sarah."

"You know, that does not surprise me." She narrows her eyes. "You really are clueless about women, aren't you?"

"I am not conversant in woman-speak, if that's what you mean. You're going to have to explain it like you would to Sawyer."

"No, she's a female." She raises an eyebrow. "She'd get it by now."

"Are you angry with me, Sarah?"

She tosses her hands in the air. "You got it in three. I've known less astute men, but none of *them* are married, either."

I scratch my head and wait.

"You've bungled this so badly."

"Even I figured *that* out. What I'm hoping you can help me with is, how do I put it right."

"Finally, you're asking the right question." She taps her first two fingers to her head. "Typical man, you're thinking with this."

I know only one other thing that men think with, but I'm sure not bringing that up with a woman old enough to be my mother.

She taps her fingers to her chest. "To communicate with a woman, you need to be thinking with this."

I cock my head. "Hearts don't think."

She rolls her eyes heavenward. "And men think they're the superior beings. Lord, the world sure would be different if you put us in charge." Her gaze drops to me. "Well, if you want a chance, you'd better figure it out." She turns, opens the door, and it slaps behind her. The heavy wooden door closes quietly in my face.

I'm glad the flight home will take four hours—it'll give me time to think. I may even hear what my heart has to say. If I'm going to ascend Mount Lorelei, I need a plan, and if it's a good one, I don't care if I have to pull it from my butt. One thing the last twenty-four hours has solidified— last night's kiss crisped any thought of retreat for me. If I'm going down, I'm going down in a blaze of glory. I've found a woman who is worth it.

I'm just past Las Cruces when my phone buzzes. I hit hands-free.

"Mr. St. James, I have Mr. James Travis on the line. Could you hold a moment?"

"Sure." My fingers tighten on the yoke, and I force them to relax. I need this guy.

"Reese, you young steer, how you doin', son?"

Don't think I didn't notice the castration dig. "What do you need, Jimbo?" I know it's petty to slaughter his name, but I can't resist. If you can't take it, you shouldn't dish it.

"Just getting back to you on the division orders on the latest oil wells. You'll have a copy in your in-box in an hour."

"Good."

"And I'm sending a second attachment. I didn't charge you; it's a gift, in honor of Bo and Carson."

"What is it?"

"You'll see. Let me know what you think."

I click to end the call. What the hell is he up to now?

* * *

Lorelei

"Hey, Lorelei." Nevada stands in the doorway of my spotless office, holding out a cell phone. "It's Fish."

"Why wouldn't he call my—"

"Duh."

Crap. I turned my cell off after Carly read Reese's text. I raise Nevada's phone to my ear. "Hey, Fish. What's happening?"

"I am. And you will agree, when I tell you what I have."

He sounds proud of himself. What does it say about me that his tone puts me on guard? "What do you have?"

"I have the materials to rebuild your roof. Free. Of. Charge."

"You take those back wherever you stole them from. I will not be responsible for you going to jail. Do you know what Nevada would do to me?"

"Didn't steal them. They're not new, but they're in good shape. See, the council got funding to build a new tribal building on the rez. I helped tear down the old one last weekend and called dibs on the roofing materials."

The tightness in my chest loosens just a bit. "Oh, Fish. You are my very own angel."

"Tell Nevada that, will you? She's mad at me for buying her a turquoise and silver necklace instead of the new goats she wanted."

"Ah. You should have known."

"Probably. Anyway, I've got to finish fertilizing and chopping weeds out here, but I should be able to get started in three weeks. In the meantime, I'll have the materials delivered to your house. That sound okay?"

"I'll take you anytime I can get you."

"Don't tell Nevada that, okay?"

"Whatever you say, Fish. And *thank you*." I hang up, imagining the heaven of not having to go on bucket patrol upstairs every time it rains.

CHAPTER 14

Reese

The next morning, I open the email from the attorney and scan the division orders. Travis made a great deal here. He *is* a good business attorney, but I really need to find one I can stand. It'll be the first order of business once we get the calves to market in August.

I file the division orders, then open the "surprise" attachment. It's a surprise all right. A motion to the New Mexico courts to modify a child custody decree. Lorelei's decree.

My conciliatory mood crisps in a blowtorch blast of anger. Bullshit. Travis *is* just like Bo, always pushing and manipulating to get his way. I snatch my phone and hit speed dial. When his secretary puts me through, I jump in before he can speak. "I told you, Travis. I have zero interest in pursuing custody of my niece. Why did you go against my express order?"

"Oh, come on, loosen your tighty-whities, son."

I hear the scree of my teeth grinding. "You didn't answer my question."

"Don't worry. I didn't charge you for it. I did it for Bo."

"Jim. He's dead. You don't work for him any longer, and frankly, I don't think you should be working for me, either." I put all the barbed wire I've got into my tone. I hope it makes him bleed.

"Relax, Reese. Think of it as reference material. You may want it someday."

"I won't." The words come out skinny from squeezing out between my clenched teeth.

"You were interested enough to have me look into custody to begin with. What changed your mind? Wait, you don't have a thing for this woman, do you?"

He's gone too far now. "That is none of your damned business."

"Well, hell, son, why don't you just marry her? That'd solve all your problems, wouldn't it?"

Hearing what was basically my logic the other night from *his* mouth makes me want to go take a shower. That must be how I made Lorelei feel. The only difference is that he sees nothing wrong with what he's saying. "I'm trashing this file and ordering you to do the same. Do you hear me?"

"Kinda hard not to, son."

"And since we already established that my father is dead, I think we can both agree that I am *not* your son." I click End, and when I will my clenched fingers open, the phone clatters to the desk. That clinched it. Finding a new attorney just moved up on the priority list.

But right now I need to fix the only part I have control of—me.

* * *

Lorelei

Sunday morning, Momma and Sawyer are both napping and I'm washing breakfast dishes when a delivery truck pulls up in the drive. I step out of the screen door, wiping my hands on a dish towel. "I didn't order anything, Norm."

"Well, you got something, nonetheless." He hands me a box.

I sign for it and take it inside, setting it on the kitchen table. The return address isn't familiar. I use a knife to slit the tape. There's a note on top of a stack of folded clothes. The blouse weakens my knees, and I collapse in the chair, hauling in breaths. My questing fingers find the note:

Dear Wests,

I'm Sybil, a friend of Patsy's. I was babysitting Sawyer the night of the accident. I'm so sorry this is getting to you so late. I dropped all these off at my mom's when I was in town and asked her to mail them to you, but she forgot. I just returned home to find them still here.

I'm so sorry for your loss—Patsy was a gem. I miss her so.

Wishing you peace,

Sybil

I sit, hands shaking, trying to marshal the strength I'm going to need to look through that box. There's a war going on in my chest. The tiny roses on that blouse almost stopped my heart. These last scraps of my sister are going to flat tear me up.

But at the same time, I want any tiny clue to how Patsy was in her last days. I send up a prayer I find something verifying she was happy, because I can't handle anything less than that.

I take a deep breath and stand.

I lift the blouse as gently as if it's made of butterfly wings. I take it to my nose and inhale. The faintest wisp of my sister's scent remains—the smell of sunshine and outdoors. When I pull it away, there's a damp spot, and I realize tears are sheeting down my face.

Next are a pair of day-to-day jeans that are no longer day-to-day; they're precious.

Beneath them is another envelope, addressed to me in Patsy's scrawling hand. The breath whooshes out of my lungs, and I turn it over and rip it open.

Dear Lorelei,

I was just going to show up, but I realized the news could cause you or Momma (or both) a heart attack, so here goes.

I'm madly in love. I have a daughter.

I can see you standing in front of our mailbox, with the door still flopped open, frozen in shock, reading this. Let me tell you the how, and then I'll get to the why.

Carson St. James is a bull rider I met a year and a half ago. From the first, I knew he was it for me, and the miracle is, he feels the same. Lorelei, I know it's taken a long time, but I finally found the guy on the planet that gets me. We laugh, talk, and hours go by. We just "click"— you know?

When I found out I was pregnant, I was worried, but I needn't have been—Carson was thrilled! He treated me like spun glass the whole time I was pregnant, and we got even closer, if that's possible. He cried when he saw Sawyer for the first time.

Okay, okay, I'm getting to the why—why I haven't told you until now. We have been living in a perfect bubble— just him and me, and now Sawyer. Sounds stupid to say, but it felt like the bubble would break if we told anyone; we wanted to revel in our love, and our sweet baby, before we let the world in.

But Sawyer is six months old now, and I'm starting to realize what I've deprived you and Momma of: seeing me happy, my pregnancy . . . Sawyer. I can't go back and change that, but I can remedy my mistake.

We're coming to see you! In two weeks, we'll be at a rodeo in Albuquerque, and if it's okay, we'll come spend a couple days in Unforgiven.

You are going to love your niece, Sawyer Lorelei West.

I'll see you SOON!

Love you to pieces,

Patsy

* * *

That afternoon, a battered flatbed truck with wood piled in the back pulls up the drive. A dark-skinned man parks and steps out. Two younger men pile out next.

I let the screen door slap behind me.

"Are you Lorelei?"

I smile and nod. "Did Fish send you?"

"Yep. I'm Hok'ee. This is your new roof. Where do you want us to stack it?"

"Um." I turn to the barn. I'd love to keep it out of the weather until Fish can get here, but I don't trust the barn to last that long. "How about the backyard?"

"You got it. Come on, guys." He walks to the back of the truck.

"This is going to be hot work. I'll get you some iced tea." I step into the kitchen, get down plastic tumblers, the tea pitcher, and sugar to put on a tray. Something at the back of my mind is nibbling at my consciousness like a hungry field mouse. What is it?

"Who's there?" Momma walks in the kitchen.

"The cavalry."

She steps to the sink and twitches the curtains. "I don't see any horses, and those aren't soldiers."

I put an arm around her shoulders and squeeze. "They're bringing the materials for our new roof, Momma."

"Oh, that's good."

"You go back to your show. I'll take this out to them and be right with you." Luckily, Sawyer is down for a nap. I don't feel comfortable leaving Momma alone with Sawyer, since their attention span is about the same.

I lift the tray, carry it to the backyard, and set it on the picnic table. "Guys, come get something to drink."

"Thank you, ma'am. We'll be there in a few." One of the men grunts, hefting two bound stacks of shingles and carrying them to the shade of the tree. Hok'ee and the other man are sliding materials off the truck.

The sun bounces off the boards, and a heavy weight drops onto my shoulders. Used boards shouldn't be bright blond or blemish-free. Used shingles shouldn't be bound in neat bundles. I stalk to the truck. No way these came from a building so run-down they had to demolish it. There aren't even nail holes in the wood!

Fish is that giving, but not that rich. But I know who is.

A cold ball of ice builds under my breastbone. Last time I saw Reese, I was a business deal. Does he think this is part of his payment for Sawyer? I can imagine what he wants in return. Spoken or unspoken, I'd owe him. I pull my phone and walk around the house to the front porch.

Reese picks up on the first ring. "Lorelei. I was just going to text—"

"I only want to know one thing." Though my words are calm, my hand is shaking, and I press the phone to my ear to make it stop. "What have I ever done to make you not respect me?"

"What? I don't—"

"I allow you free access to Sawyer. I helped you with your truck. I invited you to join my *family*, for cripes' sake." I take a breath. It's hard to breathe around the ball of ice that's moved into my throat. "And since the first time I met you, all you've done is run over me. My rules, my objections, my *feelings*."

"Look, I know I was an idiot last weekend, okay? I've only just today learned how—"

"You haven't learned a thing. Last weekend you only said the truth. News flash—I'm old. No one wants me. I can live with that. But dammit, I get to say what I owe and whose debt I'm in."

"I don't under—"

"The freaking *roof*. Sawyer is older than the supplies that showed up today."

"Lorelei, I'm—"

"Don't you *dare* say you're sorry, Reese St. James, because you're not, or you wouldn't have gone behind my back like this."

"I wasn't going to say I'm sorry." His words are cold, but

they are snowflakes compared to my arctic heart. "I swear, you are the most prideful, stubborn, infuriating woman I have ever met. Sawyer deserves better."

That one is a direct hit, so it takes me a moment to return fire. "I'm stubborn and prideful? Doubtless. But money isn't a necessity in raising a happy, well-adjusted child. And I *will* be the one to raise her." I click End, shove my phone and my fists into my pockets, and stalk to the backyard to tell the workers that there's been an error. They need to put everything back on the truck and take it back to wherever they got it. And if they have questions, they should call Reese St. James.

Hok'ee opens his mouth to say something, but after a close look at my face, nods. "You heard the lady. Let's get it loaded."

"Thank you." I walk out front to pace the porch. If I go in the house like this, I'm going to scare Momma and Sawyer.

Reese tried his best negotiation to get his way, and now he's flat-out trying to buy me. Us. If he wanted me, really wanted *me*, turning this away would be harder. I mean, that kiss on the porch had me hoping that maybe he really did care. Now here I stand, once more the fool.

I know what Momma and Mrs. Wheelwright would say. That I'm letting my pride get in the way of practicality. Hey, I'm nothing if not practical. But living under his roof knowing that it was just another concession in his *negotiation*...I wouldn't sleep a wink under it.

And I *am* prideful, but if he'd spend some time in my shoes and with my checkbook, he'd see that pride is about all I have. Well, that and more self-worth than to allow myself to be bought.

* * *

Reese

Fish called to apologize, saying he'd planned the delivery during the week, when Lorelei would be at work. By the time she got home, it'd be dark and everything would be draped in tarps. But his friends work full time, and the only day they had available was Sunday.

I'm just glad Lorelei wasn't mad at him. This is all on me.

Lorelei thinks I'm pushing, but dammit, whether she admits it or not, she needs help. She *deserves* help.

I haven't heard from her in two days. No answers to my texts, my voice mails go unreturned—probably unheard. It seems all I've done in this relationship is apologize; I am not going there groveling again. This is at least as much her fault as mine.

But I miss her washed-blue eyes. How she's constantly tucking her hair behind her ear. I miss holding her close when we dance. I want to be on her porch, playing with Sawyer. I want to talk to her in the dark.

I want...it all.

And I have no idea how to unravel the knots I've tied myself into. I've screwed up so bad, I don't even know where to start to make it right.

But I'm going to have to try, because I want Lorelei. She's already constant in my thoughts, but I want her in my life, my day, my bed.

My phone buzzes. An Unforgiven number I'm not familiar with. My heart speeds up, and I fumble the phone. Is Lorelei okay? Sawyer? "H-hello?"

"Mr. St. James, this is Ann Miner. With the *Unforgiven Patriot*."

It takes me seconds to calm enough to remember. "Oh, the interview."

I hear pages turning. "I'm looking at my calendar. How does next week look for you?"

Hope rises. A perfect excuse to go to Unforgiven—no. Not until I have a workable plan, or I'll just mess up things again. "I'm...busy for the coming weeks. Can we do this over the phone?"

She's silent for a span of seconds. "Oh, I suppose. Although you'll have to send me a photo of yourself for the column."

"I can do that."

She asks me questions, and I answer, downplaying the oil and the money. "Is that about it? I have a telecon in—"

"Just a few more questions." Papers rustle. "I have it from a good source that you're responsible for a considerable donation to the school district building fund, with enough left over to begin an after-school program at the elementary school."

"What? Where did you hear that?" Shit. So much for anonymous.

"I'm certainly not divulging my sources. Is it true?"

"I'd rather you didn't print that."

"Are you saying it's untrue?"

"I'm saying I don't wish to discuss it." My words are steel tipped, but she's apparently wearing Kevlar.

"I see, although I don't understand why not. This is a huge boon to our community. You should be proud."

"My reasons are my own. I'm asking you not to print it."

"I'll take your wishes under advisement. Thank you for the interview, Mr. St. James. Good day."

I see why this Miner woman is not well liked. And if she prints that, Lorelei is going to think I'm pushing again.

Lorelei

I step in the back door of the café, sweat taking a roller-coaster ride down the knobs of my spine. The weather is blistering—shriveling the grass, softening the asphalt, and shortening tempers. I had to step between Moss Jones and Manny Stipple when they got into it last week and they've been friends for fifty years. Heat'll do that.

I set down the plastic sacks. "O'Grady's was out of avocados, Nevada. We'll have to make do."

"No worries. I'll just use cukes for garnish." She's wearing a bandanna to keep sweat out of her eyes. The poor AC units are maxed out.

"Don't forget to drink lots of water."

She gives me a thumbs-up.

I push through the swinging door to the dining area, stop to pick up the water and iced tea pitcher, then head out on refill patrol.

The smell of Aqua Net hangs over booth five, which is filled with old ladies with coiffed white hair. I forgot, it's Social Security Check Wednesday. They're chirping like a flock of starlings, the latest issue of the *Patriot* open on the table. "Hello, ladies. Does anyone want...?" Reese stares out from the page, looking hot in a business suit and a Stetson. My heart stutters. I set down the pitchers. "Do you mind if I look at that?"

Ms. Dubois has a merry twinkle in her eye. "You go right ahead, darlin'."

The starlings titter while I read.

Wow. The donation amount is undisclosed, but given all

they're planning to do with the money, I'm guessing six figures. My heart softens to peanut butter. He's doing this for Sawyer.

"Seeing how he's your boyfriend, you'll have to thank him for us." One of the women covers her smile with her hand.

"He's *not* my boyfriend." It came out louder than I meant.

"Yeah," Bonnie Carver says from booth four. "Lorelei wouldn't get tangled up with a Texas hotshot like that."

I don't know whether to take that as a compliment or a "poor Lorelei."

"I mean," Mr. Baldwin, an old farmer, says from the counter, "who does this guy think he is, lording his oil money over the hardworking folks in this town?"

"Aw, come on, he's not so bad," Manny Stipple slurs from his spot at the counter.

"What he said," Moss Jones says.

"Big Man St. James rides in like a guy in a white hat, to help out the poor bumpkins. I hear he's not even a cowboy, like he claims," Scooter Bowman tosses in from booth one by the front door.

And suddenly they're off—holding an impromptu town hall meeting. This isn't the first one I've witnessed, but they usually revolve around politics or the Bureau of Land Management or County Services.

"My momma always told me, never trust an oilman. They're as slippery as their product."

"He's too good-looking by half. Why, I told my granddaughter..."

"I mean, what do we know about this dude, anyway?"

"Stop!" When they ignore me, I put my fingers in my mouth and blast them with my signature eardrum-piercing whistle. People flinch, then fall silent. "Look, I have more reason to be angry with Reese St. James than any of you, but fair is fair." I put my hands on my hips. "He's here because he cares about his niece. He's been nothing but nice and polite to everyone. Do you people even remember that he insisted his builder hire only local help? And now he's funneling money into our failing school system and giving kids a safe place to go after school." I lift the pitchers. "And instead of thanking him, you sit here and gossip about him behind his back. Y'all ought to be ashamed of yourselves." I turn, walk through the silent room to the counter, set down the pitchers. My palms hit the swinging door with a hollow boom that would've done Carly proud.

I head to my office, face flaming, realizing I just gave them reason to believe that Reese St. James *is* my boyfriend. But I couldn't let them assassinate his character. He's overbearing and pushy, but he means well.

Like he did with your roof? It's Mrs. Wheelwright's voice in my head.

* * *

I wake the next morning to a sullen sky, the low clouds boiling in tones of slate and charcoal.

I'm in the kitchen fixing breakfast when Mrs. Wheelwright steps in the door, her careful curls stirred by the wind. "The weatherman says we're in for one heck of a storm."

"We sure can use the rain. And the break from the heat."

She walks to the window over the sink and peers out. "I know you're right, but I've got a bad feeling about this one."

"You know summer storms always look scary. Our sky is so big, you can see a storm coming forever."

She sighs and drops her purse on the counter. "I'm probably just unsettled today. I'll go get Mary up and dressed."

"I already changed Sawyer, and she's playing in her crib. I'll get her in a minute. Breakfast is in ten." I crack eggs into the skillet. "Oh, and there are a bunch of buckets and pots up there, in case the roof starts leaking."

"More like when, from the looks of things out there."

A half hour later, when I step out the door, the wind hits me like a slap. I squint to keep churned-up dust out of my eyes. My blouse flutters and slaps against my skin on my walk to the car, and I smell the ozone in the air. I glance to the foreboding horizon, feeling what Mrs. Wheelwright did—"unsettled" is a good word. It's like the wind has gotten inside me and stirred up things there, too. Prickles of worry trickle into my stomach. "You're being a ninny. We just haven't had a big storm in so long, you forgot what it's like."

Still, I wish I could stay home today. Mrs. Wheelwright sure could use the help, because Momma will be a handful with the storm. But I have hungry Unforgivens to feed, besides needing my paycheck to add to my roof fund. I open the car door and glance back—that house has seen more than a century of storms—it'll handle many more.

The wind tries to blow Einstein off the road, and I have to pay close attention. By the time I park behind the café, big drops are splattering the dust on the windshield. I make a run for the back door.

Nevada is wheeling condiments out of the walk-in fridge. "Carly would say it's going to come a gully washer today."

"Nevada Sweet. I do believe you're becoming a country girl." I snatch a half apron from the hooks by the back door and tie it on.

"I didn't say I'd say it. I said Carly would." She flips on

the old transistor radio on the shelf above the grill, and the clash of heavy metal music fills the room.

All it takes is a raised eyebrow and she turns it down. It's an old tug-of-war between us.

I walk into the dining area, start coffee, and raise the blinds. Normally it's bright enough that we don't need the lights, but today I flip them on. No one is waiting at the front door when I unlock it. Smart people, staying dry. The trees of the square thrash in the wind, and it's raining so hard, the drops bounce off the pavement and I can hear it drumming on the roof. Lightning cracks the sky, and the boom of thunder rattles the windows.

Unease skates across my skin. This is going to be a bad one. My phone buzzes, and I lift it out of the back pocket of my jeans.

Reese: I heard you stood up for me. Thank you.

I shouldn't be surprised he heard; this is Unforgiven. Most likely, Manny or Moss called him. My hand is returning my phone to my pocket when I realize that this time I want to answer—I don't want him to misunderstand.

L: You shouldn't listen to Manny Stipple. You know he drinks, right?

R: Right. But I also know I'm not your favorite person. I thought you'd be on the other side, since I did basically the same thing to you—helping without being asked. Why did you do it?

L: Because it wasn't right. You gave a very generous gift, one that Sawyer and all the kids here will benefit from. It was a good thing to do. And yes, you're still an idiot.

R: Can I call you? Please? I'd like to hear your voice.

L: I'm at work. Gotta go.

I do miss him, and the jolt of anticipation I get when I

know he's flying in. I step behind the counter to make coffee in case someone does brave the storm. But I've got to guard my heart. If I can't have a man who loves me for myself, I'd rather be alone.

"Lorelei, you'd better come in here."

The alarm in Nevada's tone gets me moving—that girl took out the leader of a drug cartel—if *she's* worried, I'm scared spitless. I push into the kitchen. "What—"

"Shhhh. Listen."

"This is the National Weather Service. We have issued a tornado watch for all of Cibola County for the next four hours. We will bring you updates as we have them."

Thunder crashes so close, we both duck.

Nevada's got the look of a spooked horse. "Shit. This is not good."

"Oh, come on, city girl. We have bad storms here. We get warnings like that every once in a while." I'm saying it to calm myself as much as her. "It's been years since we had a tornado." Momma. Sawyer. Mrs. Wheelwright. Their faces race around the inside of my skull. "But you know what? We've got no diners anyway, and it's better to be safe than sorry. I'll call Carly and let her know we're closing. You go—get home to Fish."

"Are you sure?"

"Go. And be safe."

"You too." She rips off her apron, grabs her backpack from the hook by the door, and scoots out.

I pull my phone and dial Carly, who tells me to lock up and go home. It takes about twenty minutes to close up and put the cash drawer in the safe. I open the back door to needles of rain blowing sideways, blinding me. I step out, pull hard on the door to close and lock it, then turn and lean into the wind to get to the car. I'm soaked through. A river of water flows down the center of the alley, almost touching Einstein's back tires.

Sawyer—Momma—Mrs. Wheelwright—*hurry*.

I'm cranking the engine before I have the car door closed. I throw it in reverse, and my soggy shoe squelches when I press the gas. Einstein shoots into the flow. I can feel the water slapping the undercarriage as hail drums on the roof. When I turn onto the deserted square, there's a huge branch from one of the old maples blocking most of the street. I squeeze by and pray this is the last one I see.

As I roll out of town, the wind calms and the rain stops. Instead of being relieved, the trickle of ice becomes a flood of slush in my veins. There is a green tint to the light; the sky ahead is black. In the hush, an electric current lifts the hair on my arms, then shoots through my body, making me twitchy in my own skin. I've felt this before.

Twister's coming.

Alone on the road, I splash on, pushing Einstein to the edge of control, scanning the horizon for funnels. "Come on. Come on." I come to a low spot, where water gushes across the road in a brown, raging river. I brake at the top, trying to remember how low this dip is.

Sawyer! The voice in my head is Patsy's.

I floor it and hit the water like it's a solid wall. Only my seat belt keeps me from flying forward. The tires lose traction, then lose purchase altogether. The water pulls and pushes the car off the road.

It stays perpendicular to the flow, and within a hundred feet it jams against the sides of the arroyo, stuck like a fishbone in the stream's throat. I sit a moment, my brain bathed in panic. *Think!*

The rain begins again, and the wind buffets the car. I've

got to get out. I look upstream to the road. Waves splash against the window. Not that way. But I've got to move fast. If more water comes and pulls me off my perch, I'm in deep trouble.

I eye my purse, but it's so heavy, it would pull me under. I grab my phone and stick it in my bra, thankful I paid extra for the waterproof case. When I crack the door, the water rips it from me, pulling it wide. *Hang on, Momma. I'm coming.* I push myself into the flow.

Cold takes my breath, though the rain cascading down my face is warm. I touch bottom; the water is only waist deep. My feet are pulled from under me, and my head goes under. The current is a living thing, tugging at me, pushing, pulling me along. I kick furiously and am almost to the bank when a submerged claw catches my foot, dragging me back. In a surge of adrenaline I kick again, and I'm free of what I hope was a branch. I finally make the edge and pull myself up the muddy bank, backsliding and grabbing roots for handholds. I flop in the dirt at the top and suck in lungfuls of rain-infused air. I'm a football field downstream from Einstein, twice that to the road. I'm exhausted, I've lost a shoe, and my ankle is scored with deep furrows.

Hurry!

I shoot a look around. No funnel clouds. I pick myself up and run/hobble toward the road, grateful that by some miracle I've ended up on the "home" side of that river.

When I make the road, I turn and head down, jog as fast as I can. Water drips off my hair, and I'm shivering, from cold or shock, or both.

Hurry!

A jagged streak of searing white cuts the sky, and I count, like Momma taught me and Patsy when we were kids. Two seconds until the thunder rolls inside my chest. Thank God the storm is moving away.

I'm limping worse, my sock is soaked in blood, but I'm getting closer—just a quarter mile to go...

Finally, I'm to our yard, but I can't see the house for the whipping branches of the white firs out front.

Hurry!

I splash through the water-filled ditch, duck through the trees, and stop in shock. The barn is flattened, but the house—

The yard is littered with the debris, a branch through a window on the porch, and fully half the roof is *gone*. My feet are rooted as I try to absorb the damage.

A baby's cry comes to me on the wind.

CHAPTER 15

Reese

Hey, Reese." Manuel jogs from the barn. "Did you hear? The area around Albuquerque was hit with, like, three tornadoes this morning."

"What?" Alarm jangling down my nerves, I pull Brandy up and dismount.

"Yeah, they say it's a mess over there."

I've already pulled my phone and hit speed dial. Albuquerque area covers hundreds of miles. The odds of—

I'm sorry, but all circuits are busy. Please try your call again later.

I hit the number for the café.

I'm sorry, but—

"Shit." I toss the reins to Manuel and head for the house at a dead run, my heart thudding in time with my boots. I fling open the door and take the grand staircase two steps at a time. In my room, I grab my iPad, pull up my flight software, and check the radar. Socked in. No way I can fly there. I pull up the Albuquerque weather and discover four separate tornadoes went through the area. One touched down in Unforgiven.

I try again even though...

I'm sorry, but all circuits—

Ice cubes of dread clatter in my stomach. My foot drums a cadence, trying to burn off pressure. I've got to get there. To see for myself they're okay. I stand and grab my overnight bag, throw in a week's worth of clothes, and head for the bathroom to pack essentials. I'm not sure how long I'll be gone. It depends on what I find.

God, don't let me find...

The part of my heart I left in Unforgiven tugs like a warmblood horse, urging me to hurry. I zip the bag and head out to let Manuel know he's in charge while I'm gone.

* * *

Lorelei

Sawyer's wail jerks me from immobility. I sprint on rubbery legs for the back door, dodging nail-filled boards and the worst of the glass. My lungs work like bellows.

Hurry!

The screen door is gone and the glass in the wooden back door is broken out, shards scattered across the back step. I hop over the debris as best I can and push open the door. "Momma?" I step inside, realizing when I put my stocking foot down that there's glass here, too.

"Wahhhhhhh!" Sawyer's cry spirals to a hysterical screech.

I run through the wind-tossed kitchen, ignoring the slicing pain in my foot. I splash across the living room carpet to Sawyer's nursery.

She's pulled herself up and stands clutching the bars of the crib, face crimson, wailing. I snatch her with shaking hands and hug her to me. "It's okay, baby. I'm here. Are you hurt?" My voice cracks, and I'm crying almost as hard as she is as I check her head, her legs, her arms, for bumps or breaks. "It'll be okay, Momma's here." Her diaper is soaked, her face covered in snot.

Which means...I glance at the ceiling. Cold sweat washes over me. Except for Sawyer's crying, the house is silent. Upstairs will be dangerous. I can't take Sawyer with me, but putting her down is going to be the hardest thing I've done today.

No, second hardest. The first will be walking up those stairs.

I lay her in the crib. "I'll be right back, baby. I promise."

Tears roll down the sides of her face, and she reaches for me, but I step back. Her wail starts up again.

I glance around the room, pull the thin crib blanket from the back of the rocker and tie it around my red, shoeless foot. Then I limp to the stairs and look up—into blue sky. It shocks me, not because I didn't know the roof was gone, but because of the *wrongness* of it.

"Momma?" I step around shingles and broken boards, shifting them when my way is blocked. A small stream of water runs down the middle, where the steps are worn. "Mrs. Wheelwright?"

I finally make the landing My heart stutters and I close my eyes against a rush of vertigo. Not only is the roof gone, but a good part of the back wall of the house is, too. "Momma, I'm here." The floor is a tumble of boards, sodden clothes, and broken furniture. I carefully make my way to where Momma's bedroom used to be. Heavy roof-support beams are broken and scattered like a giant's pick-up sticks.

A rattle behind me makes me jump.

"Hello! Is someone out there? Help us!"

That's Mrs. Wheelwright's voice, coming from...where the bathroom should be. The door is covered by timbers, tar paper, pieces of shingles, and broken tree limbs.

"Sarah? It's Lorelei. Is Momma with you? Are you two okay?" I scrabble at the wood, trying to miss the exposed nails, but still hitting some.

"Oh, thank God. We're okay, but I can't get the door open."

"Hang on." I dial 911, and they promise to get here as soon as they can. I keep digging, flinging chunks of plasterboard and God knows what all behind me.

Sarah's voice is muffled by the heavy oak door. "We were downstairs, and I knew it was getting bad. I went to change Sawyer, and Mary...she ran upstairs looking for your daddy."

"Ow, dammit."

"Are you all right?"

"Yeah, just found some glass. Tell me what happened."

"I ran after her, but there wasn't time to get her back downstairs before the twister hit. We got in the bathtub."

"Patsy?" Momma's thready voice tells me the toll today has taken on her.

"Hang on, Momma. I'm almost there."

There's a crash from downstairs, then a hysterical squeal.

"Oh, crap. Hang on, Sarah, Momma. I'll be right back." I scrabble back, and heart skittering, vault down the stairs, ignoring obstacles, water, and pain. In the nursery, Sawyer has rocked the crib enough to knock it over, and she's on her back in a puddle of water, screaming.

I lift her, and she clings to my neck like a limpet. I rock back and forth, murmuring nonsensical words to calm both of us.

My brain is like the carpet: soft, spongy, and water-logged. I know I have to do something, but just what is beyond me. I can't leave Sawyer. I can't take her upstairs to that mess. I can't leave Momma and Sarah...I glance up. Water spots have bloomed several places, and the plaster in the corner is sagging. Oh my God, what if the ceiling gives way?

Momma. Sarah, Sawyer. What do I do?

I rush to the bottom of the stairs. "Sarah? Can you hear me?"

"Yes!"

"Do not move. I don't think the floor is stable. Get back in the tub, and stay there. Okay?"

The sweetest sound I've ever heard floats through broken windows. The wail of a siren, getting closer.

Two minutes later a fire truck turns in, an ambulance right behind. They make me wait outside with Sawyer while they go in. An EMT checks us out and tells me Sawyer is just cold and shocky. I have a nasty cut on the bottom of my foot and several shallower ones on my hands. He wraps my foot, tucks Sawyer and me in a blanket, and I sit at the edge of the stretcher where I can see the back door until they bring Momma and Sarah out and I can breathe again.

They are wild-eyed and bedraggled but able to walk to the ambulance. Momma is cradling her left arm and insisting she's not leaving without Daddy. When she fights off the EMT and tries to run back inside, they give her a shot to calm her.

When they are helped into the ambulance, it's a tearful reunion, and I hug them too long.

"All set. Let's go," the EMT tells the driver.

"Wait, I can drive." Then I remember that Einstein is yet one more casualty of this day. I glance to the side of the drive, where Sarah always parks, but her car is buried under a huge oak limb. "Never mind."

I couldn't care less about my car. Today I came so close to losing these irreplaceable people that make my life worth living. I spend the whole ride to the clinic hugging Sawyer, my gaze flicking from Momma to Mrs. Wheelwright and back. The tornado can have the rest. I have everything I need right here.

Thank you, Lord.

* * *

They stitch up my foot, and then I sit with Sawyer sleeping in my lap, my foot up, in the crowded clinic lobby. Momma is sleeping off the shot in a curtained cubicle in the back. She has a few scrapes and a sprained wrist. There wasn't room for us all back there, so Mrs. Wheelwright is with her.

This is where I hear the big picture, from the walking wounded waiting like me.

Tornadoes are fickle, capricious creatures, touching a filthy finger here, then there, destroying one house, leaving ten others standing around it. Downtown was spared except for felled trees, broken windows, and water damage, but many outlying houses were hit, a few reduced to matchsticks. They've opened the high school gym for evacuees, but the thought of cramming in with a bunch of people sours my stomach. I just want to take Momma home, hold Sawyer, sort this all out in my mind, and grieve.

My chest vibrates, and I jump. I forgot all about the phone. Seeing Reese's name on the screen sends a blast of welcome heat. "H-hello?"

"Oh, thank you, Lord. Lorelei, are y'all okay? I heard about the tornado, and—what is it?"

A choked sob made it around my hand over my mouth. "Reese."

A gray-haired lady I don't know stands over me, arms reaching for Sawyer. "Here, hon, give me the baby."

I grip Sawyer tighter.

"I'm Pat Stark's mother—remember me? It looks like you need to talk to that caller. You can trust me. I'll stay within your line of sight, promise."

"Lorelei? Talk to me!" Reese yells in my ear.

"That's so kind. Thank you." I let her take Sawyer, and she lays her over her shoulder so gently, the baby doesn't wake.

"What's going on? Lorelei?"

"I'm here." I stand and hobble to the window, for some vestige of privacy. "I got washed away in an arroyo, then ran home, and oh, Reese, the roof was gone, and Sawyer—"

"Is Sawyer safe?" The terror in his voice echoes in me.

"Sawyer is okay. She was in her crib. But"—I bite my lips, hoping the pain will help me get control—"Momma. Mrs. Wheelwright. They were upstairs when it hit, and they were stuck in the bathroom." I'm pushing the words with all the breath I have, but they come out a whisper.

"Are they okay?"

"Yes. A bit battered and freaked out, but yes, thank God."

"Where are you? I hear people."

"I just cut my foot, and they made me come to the clinic. But, Reese, it's all such a mess..."

"Look. I'm already on my way, okay? I'm eight hours out. I'll come get you. Where will you be?"

"I d-don't know." My voice is wavery and watery. Knowing he's on his way is a massive relief. I didn't realize how adrift I was until I heard his voice. "I tried calling Carly from the ambulance. She didn't answer, and neither did Nevada. I'm not sure—" My throat locks on a wad of loss.

Sawyer wakes on the older lady's shoulder, and seeing it's not me, let's out a heart-wrenching wail.

"I've got to go. I'm sorry, but—"

"Lorelei, listen to me. Hang on for just a few more hours. I'm on my way, and then I'll take care of you. And Sawyer. And everything else."

Silence, for the span of a breath.

"But only if you want me to."

"O-okay." For some stupid reason, his surrender of control breaks the dam inside me, and I'm crying again.

"Lorelei? It's okay, babe. I'm coming. That's all you need to think about right now. I'm coming."

* * *

A touch on my shoulder wakes me. I tighten my arms around Sawyer and open my eyes. Reese is squatting next to me, face inches from mine. There's a mix of emotion in his eyes: sympathy, worry, and a bucketload of tired.

"Hey," he whispers, to not wake any of the sleepers in the chairs around me.

"Hey." I try to sit up, but I'm tangled in the scratchy army blanket, and Sawyer is a deadweight. But she cries if she's not touching me. Even in her sleep, it seems, she's insecure. And who could blame the poor thing? "What time is it?"

"Around four." Reese reaches for her. "Here, I'll take her."

I hand her to him, and he cradles her like she's still a baby, though she clearly isn't. Her legs dangling over his arm makes me realize how much she's grown. He looks into her sleeping angel face and runs the backs of his fingers down her cheek.

He must have been frantic, thinking something happened to the last of his line.

"How's your mom?"

"They're keeping her overnight for observation. Mrs. Wheelwright is with her."

He sits next to me and touches my arm. "Oh my gosh, your foot. You said you cut it, but you didn't say it was bad."

The thick bandage extends from my toes to midcalf. "Looks worse than it is." Just one more obstacle to deal with.

"How many stitches?" He peers down his nose at me; then his eyes soften. "How many?"

"Twenty."

He swallows. "Can you talk about it?"

I shrug. The cotton in my brain seems to blunt the emotion. Or maybe the tears have washed it out. I tell him the story in a flat voice, starting from when I woke yesterday, though it seems a month ago.

By the end, his arms come around me and he presses my head to his chest. His lips brush the top of my head and he whispers, of everything and nothing. Sweet words, full of support and caring, that weave together like a warm blanket, covering my battered heart.

I stay there, inhaling his cologne, and below that, his scent. My mind is blank. I'm empty. Tomorrow, or more like today, there will be everything to face. But for now it's just so damned good to have someone watch my back so I can relax and rest safe. Emotion and sounds fade before a rushing tide of exhaustion.

I'm jostled, and I spring awake. "Momma."

"It's okay. You sleep." I'm leaning against him, his arm around me.

I straighten, wiping my mouth to be sure I didn't drool on

him. "Oh God, I'm sorry. How long have you been sitting like that?"

His arms slide away and he sits up. "Not long. You need to rest."

I pull my phone from my bra. Five. "Not as much as you. You had to have driven straight through to be here by now."

"No big deal. I stay up two days straight during calving."

When I glance around, yesterday crashes in. "Oh, man."

"Yeah. A new day." He lays his big, blunt-fingered hand over mine. His eyes are serious, sympathetic, and sad. "Will you let me help you through it? There'll be a lot to do and— what? What is it?"

"You're being so nice. But you know I don't deserve it." The grief wakes with a wail that I bite my lips to hold in.

"What? Why would you—"

"It's my fault. If I'd listened to you. Taken your loan. Let Fish put the new roof on." It's not easy to raise my gaze to his, but I have no right to whine. Ever again. "Because of my *stupid* pride, my mother was in danger. She could have been killed. They all could have." I look to where Sawyer lies, sleeping like a precious cherub.

"Oh, hon." His arms come around me again, and I bury my face in his shirt and sob. "Oh, baby, don't do that. Please don't." He backs up a bit, and his fingers lift my chin so I have no choice but to look at him. "I listened to the news all the way here. Six houses were wiped out; there's nothing left. It was a *tornado*."

I try to turn my head, but his grip is firm.

"It's not your fault."

"But a new roof would have—"

"You could have had a steel roof and it wouldn't have mattered." He shakes his head. "Houses can be replaced. I'm just damned grateful that you are all alive." He lets go of my chin and pulls me into his chest. "You cry all you want. But don't you blame yourself."

I don't know if he's right or not. But for now I'm taking the pardon he offers. Because I'm not going to make it through the next few days without it. "Thank you, Reese." I sit listening to the strong thump of his heart under my ear. "Thank you so much for getting here so fast."

Sawyer twists in his arms and wakes. "Baba." Two quick inhales. "Baaaaaabaaaaa." In her muffled cry, she tells him exactly how her day has gone.

CHAPTER 16

Reese

A few hours later, Lorelei, Sawyer, and I are eating boxed breakfasts distributed by the Boy Scouts when Carly Beauchamp appears in the doorway of the clinic, searching faces with a crazed look. I point with the spoon I'm using to feed Sawyer. "Carly's here."

Lorelei waves, and when Carly sees her, she barrels across the floor and launches herself into Lorelei's arms. "Oh my God. I just heard. Oh, hon, I'm so sorry." The rest is buried in Lorelei's hair, and when they untangle, they're both crying.

"Baba." Sawyer smacks my arm, eyeing the spoon of scrambled eggs I'm holding.

"Oh, sorry, Peanut."

"I dropped my phone and broke it, and Austin has his with him, trying to gather the stock, and oh God, what a mess." Carly sits in the chair beside Lorelei. "I'm so glad you came for them, Reese."

"I wouldn't be anywhere else."

"How's your Momma?"

"She's got a sprained wrist and scratches. I think they only kept her because she was so distraught."

Carly surveys Lorelei's foot and the crutches propped on the wall next to her. Her eyebrows go up. "And you?"

"Oh, I'm fine." She sets the Styrofoam container on the floor.

I jump in. "Everyone here is full of stories, Carly, but other than what they witnessed, it's all rumors. What did you see on the way in?"

Lorelei's brows go up. "Are y'all okay? Nana and Papaw? Nevada and Fish? The café?"

Carly sweeps her thick red hair behind her ear. "We're fine. We may need a new roof…" She shoots a rueful look at Lorelei.

"It's okay. You can say the word around me."

"Papaw's still is gone. Literally. But they're fine, and so's their house. I haven't been able to get hold of Nevada. The coverage is spotty out there. But one of Austin's hands lives out that way and told us they're okay, too."

Sawyer has finished her eggs and half of mine. Where does she put it?

"The café is a mess."

"What?" Lorelei grabs her hand.

"No, it's going to be okay. But we're going to be closed for a week or so for repairs. One of the trees from the square came down, and half of it is in the dining room."

"Oh, no," I say.

Carly waves a hand. "We're insured—don't worry. No one is going to miss a paycheck. But listen…" She lowers her voice and darts a look around. "We lost five townspeople to the storm. Everyone's in shock. They're talking about a combined memorial service for all the victims."

Emotions flash across Lorelei's face. Too many, too fast to catch them all. But the last one smooths the lines between her brows. "I think that's a great idea."

"We just thought, you know, if we could all grieve together, it might help."

Lorelei turns to me. "Will you stay?"

"Of course. I'm here as long as you need me. I'll just get us a room—"

"You most certainly will not." Carly's tone cuts through mine. "You are not taking a baby to that nasty fleabag. Not when the Davis Hotel's door is open." She nods to herself, as if it's settled.

Lorelei frowns. "You're sweet, Carly, but we're not putting you out. You have two babies and—"

"And they'll love having Sawyer to play with. Come on, you know how big the homestead house is. You're welcome as long as you want to stay. Your momma, too."

"Mrs. Wheelwright already said she's taking Momma home with her. But her house only has two bedrooms."

Lorelei looks to me, as if unsure. It's clear the past day has done more than rocked her foundations; they've fallen out from under her. I want to step in and make decisions, but I know when she gets her feet back under her, she won't thank me for that—she needs more. She needs to know she can trust herself. And if I can help her with that, maybe she'll come to trust me.

I slip my arm around her shoulders and squeeze. "You do whatever you think is best, hon. I'll get myself a room."

"Not. Happening," Carly says. "Did you think I didn't mean you, too? But don't think I'm doing you a favor. Austin will probably put you to work."

I give Carly a grateful smile. "Thank you. This means a lot to me."

Lorelei grants me a tentative smile. "That's good."

"You two do what you need to do. Peanut and I have inspectors to call, clothes to buy...Oh, that reminds me." I pull a small notebook and pen from my back pocket. "Write down your sizes."

Lorelei blushes. "Oh, I'm fine."

"You can't get into your house for days, at least. What are you going to wear?"

Carly raises a brow. "Lorelei. Cardinal rule. Never discourage a man who wants to spend money on you."

"Okay." But her mouth turns down and her head drops. "We're going to need something for the memorial." She scribbles on the notebook and hands it back to me.

"Done."

"Wait. I need to write down stuff for Sawyer."

"Nah." I swing Sawyer up into my arms. "She'll help me pick everything out. We'll be good."

Carly looks at Lorelei. "Are you done eating? Can you go now? Austin has the kids, but he needs to get back to work."

Lorelei nods. "I just need to check in on Momma and let them know where we'll be." She holds her arms out for Sawyer.

I hand her over. They touch foreheads, Lorelei whispering the whole time. Then she kisses her cheek and hands her back. "She screamed when anyone but me came close yesterday, but she's fine with you."

I hold out my thumb, and Sawyer curls her hand around it. "That's because I'm her Baba. Right, Peanut?"

"Baba." She pats my chest.

In spite of everything, I can't help my grin. God, I love this kid. "That's what I'm talkin' about."

"You don't have a car seat." Carly roots around in her bag and pulls out her keys. "Take mine out of my car. We've got extra at home. We'll meet you in the parking lot."

"Thanks, Carly. I'll pick up another when we're out shopping today." I stand.

"Wait." Lorelei puts a hand on my arm, pulls me down, and kisses my cheek. "Thank you." She looks hard into my eyes to underscore her words, then lets me go.

"I'll be in touch." I make myself turn away and walk out. I know she's putting her trust in me. I only hope I can be deserving of it.

Hope fires in my chest, and a vow forms in my mind: *I'll never betray you.*

* * *

Lorelei

I say goodbye to Momma and Sarah. On the way out, I catch a crutch on the lintel and would have gone down if Carly hadn't caught my arm.

"I'm taking you home and putting you to bed. You've done enough for one day."

"I wish I could argue, but I'm wiped."

She leads me to her mommymobile, staying close. "Lorelei, why do you feel guilty?"

I jerk to a stop. "How did you know?"

"You apologized to Sarah." She unlocks my door and helps me in, puts my crutches in the back seat, then stands, arm on the door, waiting for an answer.

"Because I am guilty. If I'd allowed the new roof to be put on...Don't look at me like that. Reese already lectured me."

"Well, good on him. I'm liking this guy more all the time."

"But how do you get something you know here"—I point to my head—"to your heart? I can't seem to do it."

She pats my hand. "It'll come, hon. I had to learn to forgive myself, too, remember? But look at me now. Happily married and two sweet babies." She takes the seat belt from me and snaps it in place. "You're not responsible for everything, you know. God had the biggest hand in this."

"I know that's right. But still..."

"Give it time, Lorelei. Just try to let it go for now."

I chew on that while she walks around the car and climbs in. "I don't know how to do that."

"I know you don't." She puts the key in and starts the engine. "But maybe it's time you learned, huh?"

I stare out the windshield all the way to her house, testing the idea. Trying to figure out who I would be if I weren't taking care of everything.

We pull into her muddy drive and bump our way through the ruts to the house. She puts it in park and pulls the key. "Now, hand me your phone."

I pull it from my bra.

"Classy, West, classy."

"Hey, if I'd tried to bring my purse, I'da drowned."

She looks up a number and hits speed dial. "Reese? Where are you? Oh. Just wanted to let you know we're at my house now." She recites her address. "Yeah, I'm putting her to bed. We'll see you when you get here."

I feel like a zombie, only my brain doesn't work as well. Carly leads me through the living room, kitchen, and down a hallway, to the first door. "I doubt you're going to want to wear my underwear, but I'll bring you down a top and some shorts so you can get out of those clothes." She tucks me in, fully dressed, in an old iron bedstead draped with a Navajo blanket.

My head hits the pillow, and I'm gone.

* * *

The bed dips and squeals, waking me.

Reese is sitting on the edge with a tender smile. He reaches to tuck hair behind my ear. "You look like a little girl when you sleep."

I rub my eyes. "What time is it?"

"Seven. I came to get you for dinner."

I jolt upright, then groan when my muscles make me pay. "I can't believe I slept most of the day away. Where's Sawyer?" I hate the fear in my voice. "I don't mean you wouldn't take care—"

"Shhhh." He touches my arm. "After what you've been through, you're allowed to be worried. But she and I had a great time shopping."

I notice a zipper bag hanging from the closet door, with an expensive store name on it. An Albuquerque store. More bags are piled on the dresser. "I'll pay you back for all—"

He puts a finger over my lips. "We'll talk about that later. You don't have to think about it now."

I want to argue, but sometime in my sleep, I decided to take Carly's advice and just let things go—as much as I'm able—for now.

He's looking at my mouth. A flush surges from the juncture of my thighs, rising to my face. His finger traces my cheek.

I lean into his touch, wanting to lose myself in a soft emotion far from the brutal ones of the past thirty-six hours. To take the comfort he offers and relax safe in his arms. The yellow light of the lamp on the dresser falls on his stubbled cheek, doing little to cover the strong bones beneath. I trace the scar running from his eyebrow to his hairline.

He closes his eyes, and a muscle jumps in his jaw.

"You know loss, too."

"Yes." He opens his eyes, and I see a deep well of suffering in them.

Like to like; the pain in my chest pulls me to his. We meet in the middle in a bittersweet kiss. Something in my chest turns over, releasing a rush of tenderness.

It's been so long since I've let myself feel that.

His hand comes up under my hair, and he turns my head to deepen the kiss.

My almost-fiancé was a raging fire—a flash of burning heat that consumed us both. Here, then gone. Reese is more like a campfire, flickering in a hypnotic dance that you can't turn away from. The warmth of that fire spreads from my chest. I want more.

"Hey, you two. Dinner's—"

We spring apart like two teens caught by the porch light.

"Never mind." Carly stands in the doorway, arms crossed, with a knowing grin.

"We're coming," Reese says in a slow, sexy voice, not looking away from me.

Carly walks down the hall.

He's not embarrassed at all. I, on the other hand, feel like my face is going to spontaneously combust.

I finger comb my hair and try to get a grip. Letting go a bit is one thing. A few more minutes and I'd have been danged close to shedding clothes. And that shakes me to my core. I don't *do* that.

"Let's go." Reese stands, then bends and scoops me up.

"Stop! I have crutches."

He smiles down at me. "I like this better."

God, I've got to weigh a ton. I need a shower. I need a toothbrush. I need some morals.

I make an effort to weigh less as he carries me through the hall and through the kitchen to the dining room, where he sets me on a chair.

On the table is a platter of beef empanadas, refried beans, and Mexican rice.

Austin is at the head, Faith in a high chair next to him. Carly is at the other end, with baby Austin in her lap. Reese sits next to Austin, and Sawyer is in a high chair between us. She's clean and a wearing pink onesie that reads *Step aside, Barbie, there's a new doll in town.*

"Cute shirt, baby girl." I kiss the top of her head. "Missed you today." My stomach growls, protesting no lunch. "Wow, what a spread, guys. You didn't have to go to the trouble."

"We didn't. Reese cooked." Austin spears three empanadas onto his plate and passes the platter.

I turn to Reese. "I knew you could throw a steak on a grill, but this is real cooking. Seriously?"

He passes me the dish. "Wait 'til you see my flan for dessert."

I close my hanging jaw, spoon out a helping of empanadas, and pass the plate to Carly.

"Hey, no stereotypes around here." Austin passes the rice. "I mean, look at my beautiful wife. We both thought she was country-girl-homecoming-queen for years." The look he gives Carly holds a smoking, toe-curling, just-you-wait challenge. "We both discovered she was a lot more'n that."

"Yeah, and you're more than a thick-skulled rough stock

rider—turns out, you're a heck of a businessman." Her smile looks like she took his challenge and raised him one.

How great would it be to have a relationship like that? How much simpler would life be as part of a pair? "This is wonderful. Where'd you learn to cook?"

"It's a secret recipe of Nora, our housekeeper when I was growing up. Since I didn't do 4H or rodeo, I had lots of time on my hands. I kind of gravitated to the kitchen."

I hear what he didn't say, that he was missing his mother. I'm so glad he at least had a woman in the house. "She taught you well. This is amazing. I apologize for sounding shocked."

"It's become kind of a hobby, but I hate cooking for just myself, so I'm glad when I get the opportunity."

By the time we're done with dessert (his amazing, authentic flan) and are drinking coffee, all three babies are nodding off and I'm not far behind. "Carly, Austin. Have I told you how much I appreciate you having us stay? It's like by being in an unfamiliar place, my brain doesn't keep going back to the horror of yesterday. And that means more to me than you know."

"The pleasure is ours," Austin says.

"The kids are having a blast together, and I'm loving it." Carly sips coffee.

"Well, I'll take my turn babysitting tomorrow. It'll be nice to hang with the kids and relax."

"If you see corralling three little ones as relaxing, I'll take you up on it."

"But for now," Reese says, wiping his mouth with his napkin, then standing, "I'm putting you to bed."

When he lifts me out of the chair and his cologne fills my head, I decide I love this mode of transportation.

He turns at the door. "I'll be back for Sawyer, and then I'll clear the table."

Carly hops up. "You most certainly will not. And we'll put Sawyer to bed with our crew."

Austin lifts Faith's head from the high chair tray. "You cooked, Reese. I'm on the dishes." He unclips the tray and sets it aside.

"Thanks." He carries me through the kitchen and down the hall.

I feel useless, but just for tonight, I'm not going to let it bother me. "Wait." I catch the doorjamb of the bathroom on the way by. "I need to make a pit stop."

"Sure thing." He turns in and sets me down so my butt is resting against the sink. "I bought you stuff I thought you'd need."

Toothbrush, toothpaste, a brush, and hair tiebacks sit on the counter. "You thought of everything. Thank you." I glance at the shower stall and sigh. "I'd kill for a shower, but the doctor said I have to keep my foot dry until he takes the stitches out."

He pulls open cabinets behind the door until he finds a towel and puts it on the sink. "You can wash up in the sink, anyway. You need help?"

His lecherous eyebrow waggle makes me smile. "No, thanks. I've got this." I push him toward the door. "Oh, Carly left me some clothes in the room. Could you get them for me?"

"Sure. I'll be close, in case you need me." He takes a step out of the door and closes it behind him. In a few seconds he knocks, opens the door a crack, hands me a small stack of clothes, and ducks back out.

I clean up in the sink, dry off, and look at what Carly left me to wear. A pair of jean cutoffs that are a bit big in the hips, but I don't care. It's so good to get out of my filthy jeans. I hold up the top. Lavender cabbage roses on almost sheer material. With ruffles. I pull it over my head and realize the V plunges to my cleavage. I'm not looking a gift horse in the mouth, but if she did this with Reese in mind, she and I are going to have a talk. I yank the material together, but there's no buttons to hold it closed. Holy yikes.

I look in the mirror and decide I can't stand to be clean with greasy hair.

But bending over a sink on one foot is harder than I expected. Halfway through, my leg muscles are shaking and I'm out of steam. It's embarrassing, but I can't stand here dripping shampoo all over Carly's bathroom. "Reese?"

"You decent?" his voice calls through the door.

"That's debatable, but can you help me?"

"Sure. What do you need?" He opens the door.

"I'm too tired to..." My leg gives up, and I start sliding sideways. "Eep."

He's there, lifting me so I'm sitting on the counter. "Okay, can you lean over? I'll rinse your hair out."

I try, but my sore muscles scream.

He must see my wince. "Okay, I have an idea." He lifts me off the sink and sits me on the edge of the tub. "If you can kneel, we can do this in the tub."

"I guess yesterday took more out of me than I thought." I shift to kneeling, grasping the side of the tub and hanging my head over.

"Don't apologize. You have limits, same as anyone." He turns the faucets until he's happy with the temperature. "Don't you ever give yourself a break?"

I lean on my elbows, not sure how to answer. When you live on the edge of want, you don't take breaks. Breaks cost—not only monetarily; responsibilities are heavier after you put them down. It's easier to just keep moving forward.

But if I say any of that, I sound like a whiner, so I focus on enjoying the luxury of him massaging my scalp.

His fingers are strong and sure and...sensual. And I like it.

When his fingers slow and shift to a caress, I know I'm not the only one. He combs through the sensitive hair at my nape, and I shiver.

He puts a cup under the flow and spills it over my hair. His fingers follow, combing the soap out. I let myself enjoy it, since he doesn't know what it's doing to me. Too soon, he squeezes out the water, turns off the tap, and hands me a towel.

"Thank you. I feel so much better clean." I twist the towel around my hair and grab the brush to take with me to the bedroom.

He helps me stand. "It was my pleasure." When he straightens, the intensity of his gaze tells me he means it. When I needed him, Reese *came.* Does that mean he's actually a man I could trust? Really let down my walls and trust that he won't hurt me? But he's also the one who suggested a merger, so...

"And can I just say, I approve of Carly's choice of clothes."

I look down, and my face heats. I jerk the edges of the blouse closed again.

But his eyes are teasing, so I decide not to worry about it. It feels almost natural to slip my arm around his neck when he scoops me up. I lay my head on his shoulder, tuck my nose into his neck, and sniff. His cologne mainlines to my brain. Pheromones. I think that's what they call it. Whatever it is, it relaxes my muscles. And my defenses. God, I'd love to spend some time tasting that spot behind his ear...

He carries me across the hall and sits me on the bed like I'm made of glass.

I remember the last time I saw him. I was so angry after

his "business proposal." But I know now I wasn't wrong to hope his feelings for me are genuine—that he doesn't just want Sawyer. Maybe there *is* someone for me, and he's sitting close enough to touch. A thrill shivers down my body and goose bumps rise on my arms.

"Are you cold?" He reaches for the blanket at the foot of the bed.

I grab his lapels, pull him close, and catch his lips. He lets out a soft, sexy moan. The towel on my hair unravels and falls, and I don't care. His arms are holding me close. Safe—another emotion I haven't felt in forever. Desire hits me like a mule's kick. I want more. I'm frantic for more. I'm chasing his tongue, stroking it, running my nails down his back. I need this. I *need* him. I tug at his shirt, pulling out the tails, not wanting to take time to unbutton it.

He lightens the kiss and his lips are gone. I open my eyes to his wince.

"Lorelei. I want this. You've gotta know I want this. But—"

"Never mind." I back up, embarrassment spreading through me like hot oil. "I'm sorry."

He takes my upper arms and gives me a tender smile. "Again with the sorry. You're grieving. You're exhausted. This is a natural reaction to the hell you've been through." He rubs his hands up and down my arms. "It would be wrong for me to take advantage of that, much as I'm going to lie in bed tonight and hate myself for not."

God, let me die now. I'm staring at my hands in my lap, wishing I'd pass out or something.

"Hey." He lifts my chin. "When we make love, I need to know it's because you want *me*, not because you need sex. Know what I mean?"

Oh, I know too well. Wanting to be wanted for who you

are. Wanting a man who, out of all the women on the planet, points to you and says, *Her. She's the one I don't want to live without.* And he hasn't said that. I turn my head. "Of course. No problem."

He leans close so his face is level with mine. "I can't wait for that time. *Our* time." He kisses my forehead. "For now, you get some sleep."

At the door, he turns back, and something about his focused look makes me think he's wavering...then he's gone.

I lie there, thinking about the house and touching my memories like precious stones. Patsy, head back, laughing at the dinner table. Mrs. Wheelwright smiling, working a jigsaw puzzle. Momma looking up from her TV show when I walk in and remembering it's *me*.

A realization blooms in my mind, and I curl into a ball. Patsy's clothes. Her note. They were on the top shelf of my closet. The closet that doesn't exist anymore.

I want to thank God and curse him at the same time. The tornado exploded my life, taking what was left of Patsy, right along with our house.

The question is, what new life will I build with the pieces? What will it look like?

I fall asleep smelling Reese's cologne on my skin and I dream of a knight riding up on a white horse. I reach for him, and he leans down to take a baby from my arms.

CHAPTER 17

Lorelei

Dawn, two days later, brings the day we've all dreaded. The day of the memorial. Reese drives us in his truck. He looks like he stepped out of *GQ*, in a black Western-cut suit and new dress boots. His black Stetson sits in my lap.

I'm wearing what he picked out for me: a short-sleeved black knit dress, the hem just below my knees. It fits perfectly and probably cost more than I make in a month. The shoes are black peep-toe satin with low steady heels. Heel. I can only wear one.

Sawyer is in the baby seat he bought and installed in the back. She's in a pretty pink dress. He said he tried for somber, but no one sells black baby clothes. I'm glad. She'll be a spot of happy color on this sad day. "Did I thank you for all you've done for us?"

I see half his smile in profile. "Only about twenty-two times."

"Baba." Sawyer waves her arms.

He checks her in the rearview mirror. "I'm here, baby girl."

"Stop flirting with your uncle." I'm convinced Sawyer likes him more than me. I'm good for food, diapers, and comfort, but Reese is her magic man, tossing her in the air and entertaining her for hours at a time. He never seems to tire of playing with her on the floor or reading her favorite book, complete with character voices. It stings, but not as much as it used to. She's had so much taken away, I don't have the heart to deny her.

It's a quiet drive across town to the First Baptist Church.

Reese keeps his eyes on the road, but I see the tension in his arms, his big hands tight on the wheel. "I know I have horrible timing, but I wanted to ask you something, and there won't be time the rest of the day."

"What is it?"

"The café is going to be closed at least a week. They won't let you into your house. My cabin doesn't have plumbing, much less air-conditioning, and if you've ever stayed at the motel, you'd know it's not fit for a baby." He takes a deep breath. "Will you come to Texas and stay with me?"

I'm too surprised to answer. I hadn't thought past getting through today.

"I'm getting to know where you grew up. I'd like to show you where I did. Someday, when I'm gone, all that will be Sawyer's."

I hold in a sigh. I'd love to go with them, but wanting never got me anything. "Why don't you take Sawyer for a few days and go home?"

His head whips around. "What? No. I want you to come. Both of you." He reaches for my hand, but I pull it into my lap. "Lorelei, I suck at saying things right. But please, listen with your heart. You'll understand what I mean."

Do I dare trust my heart? The last pair of handsome brown eyes trampled me and left me broken in the road on the way to what he wanted. When Reese's gaze catches mine, I can't help but see in their chocolate depths that he does want me to come. Me.

I haven't been farther than Albuquerque in a decade.

"Please?"

A change of scene would be good—getting away from the heaviness of this place. Maybe that way I'd be able to remember happy times again.

And maybe by seeing the place that shaped him, I'll understand him better—to know if I can trust him. Much as I don't want to admit it, I'm physically, mentally, and emotionally exhausted. "All right, we'll go. Thank you."

His heavy exhale tells me he's been holding his breath. "No. Thank *you*."

* * *

Reese

I sit beside Lorelei in the front pew of the packed First Baptist Church. Carly convinced Lorelei to let Sawyer spend the service in the nursery with the other little ones. I left her with her favorite toy, the stuffed goat I got her the day I met her. I hope she's not crying, but I can't be two places at once, and right now Lorelei needs me more.

Lorelei's mother isn't here. Sarah was afraid it would upset Mary, reminding her of her husband's funeral.

This isn't a traditional service. With the exception of a benediction by the minister, it's been just people talking, telling memories about their friends and neighbors who were lost. Many stories are funny, all are plainspoken and heartfelt, and there is laughter mixed with tears.

People really *know* each other here. They don't pretend to be perfect or anything but what they are: hardworking small-town folk who care about one another. There's a lot more to this ragtag little town than appears on the surface. Lorelei is lucky to have grown up here.

After an hour, the minister breaks in. "Folks, this is wonderful, and I know many others are waiting to talk, but might I suggest after a closing hymn we adjourn to the reception hall? It's past noon, and there will be food and fellowship there."

Those waiting in line shuffle back to their pews.

"Please turn to number one hundred twenty-three in your hymnals."

I turn to the page and smile. Our churchgoing trailed off after my mother died, but even I know "How Great Thou Art." The congregation's voice soars to the high vaulted ceiling, seeming to magically bind us together. Lorelei sings in a halting alto that gets wobbly toward the end. I put my arm around her and hand her a tissue. She leans into me for a moment before straightening. I'm so alert for signs of her feelings, I hold the small gesture to my heart.

Yes, she wanted sex the other night. I want her to want more than sex; I want her to want it with *me*. If that means walking around randy as a young buck until she's sure, I will.

The song trails off, and after apologizing to God for thinking about balls in church, I stand and help Lorelei to the elevator. It takes a long time, because almost everyone stops to ask about her foot, to ask after her mother, Sawyer, or the house.

When we've made it only halfway down the aisle,

Lorelei's face is rigid and she's so pale, I can trace a blue vein at her jawline. "I'm sorry, y'all. I don't mean to cut you off, but I need to get Lorelei to where she can sit. Could you excuse us, please?"

The crowd parts, and we make our way to the elevator. I feel their stares crawling across my back like curious ants, looking for a way in.

When the elevator doors close, Lorelei leans against the wall and sighs. "Thank you. I don't know how much longer I could have stood there."

"Why didn't you excuse yourself? Everyone would have understood."

Her eyes slide closed. "Because that's what I do."

"Well, I'm your guard dog for the rest of the day. You've been through a lot, and your reserves are about gone."

"I knew giving you permission to help was going to make you bossy." Her eyes are still closed, but her mouth has a shade of a smile.

I drop a quick kiss on her lips before the door slides open. "I serve at your pleasure, miss." I bow a bit.

"Like I believe that," she mutters as she clumps by.

But her voice has a humorous lilt that sends hope fizzing through the tight parts of my chest.

* * *

The next day the sun's reflection is a blinding laser in the rearview mirror. I turn it so I can check on Peanut, in the back seat. She's napping. We left Unforgiven before dawn, and it's been a long drive. But I've enjoyed every minute. I was worried Lorelei would change her mind when I took her to visit her mother, but both Sarah and her mother insisted she go.

Twelve hours with Lorelei in an enclosed space has made me realize how odd it is to see her stationary. She's always in motion—working, taking care of people and things. It's like when you spot a hummingbird resting on a branch. It's a rare and precious thing.

I've also found ways we're different. She likes crunchy, salty road snacks—I like chocolate. She's picky about soda fountain drinks (says the machines very seldom get cleaned) and gas station restrooms, so she changes Sawyer in the car. I prefer back roads; she likes freeways.

We've also learned how we're alike when it comes to the big stuff. The importance of education and a teacher who recognizes how each child learns best. That character is who you are when no one is looking and that best friends who marry have the best chance of staying married. We discussed these things in general, not specifically about us or our little family. "Only two hours and we'll be there."

She turns to the back seat. "Hear that, Sawyer? We're almost th—she's asleep."

"She's been so good."

Lorelei turns to watch the grassland rolling by the window. "It's much flatter here, and there's more grass and trees. You must get more rain than—" Her phone rings, and she frowns at the screen. "The insurance company." She swipes the screen. "Hello? Yes, Lester, what have you found out?"

The next two minutes is mostly *yes* and *uh-huh* until she hangs up.

"What's the verdict?"

"Good news and bad news." She sighs. "The house is fixable, and the repairs will be covered under our policy. But we can't live in it until they're almost done, due to mold remediation. It could be six *months* before we can go home."

She sounds like a street orphan.

"Einstein is a total loss. And because he's old, the payout won't be enough to buy a replacement, unless it's older."

Of course. She wouldn't have spent extra for a replacement policy. I want to jump in and offer to help, but I know how she'll react. All the ground we've gained today will be lost. "Hey, you're on vacation, remember? All that will wait until you get home."

I hate her worried frown.

"You want to stop in Langtry? You can see Judge Roy Bean's bar and we can grab something to eat."

"If it's okay with you, I'd rather just keep going. I'm about done with riding."

The tired in her voice reminds me of what she's been through, emotionally and physically. I reach for her hand. "You got it."

It's full dark when I turn onto the long drive that leads to the house. The overhanging trees are spooky in the headlights, and Sawyer is crying in the back seat. "We're here, baby girl. Hold on, and we'll get you out of that thing in just a minute."

I pull through the iron gates, up the circular drive, and park at the front door. I'm glad I called ahead; the fountain is tinkling in the plaza and the house blazes with light.

"Holy wow." Lorelei's eyes are big in the dash lights. "You didn't tell me you lived in a Spanish palace."

I shut the truck down, step out, and extricate Sawyer from the car seat. She quiets in my arms. "Bo didn't know subtle." I look up at the second floor's huge arched window displaying the massive crystal chandelier in the dining hall. Palazzo-style windows march down to ground level, showcasing towering rooms. "It does kinda smack the eye, huh?" I settle Sawyer straddling my hip and wait for Lorelei to get out her crutches. "Let's go inside."

* * *

Lorelei

I knew the St. Jameses had money, of course, but I pictured country-club rich. I underestimated by a personal jet, legacy opera seats, and several polo ponies. He leads me up the buff-colored stone risers, through the leaded glass doors, and into a front hall with marble floors and several arched doorways opening off to the left. There's an honest-to-god *Titanic*-style staircase on the right that could accommodate five grown men walking shoulder to shoulder. The newel post is topped with a carved lion's head, caught midroar.

"Come on, the kitchen is back here. I'll get you two something to eat, and we'll relax."

Like I'm going to relax anywhere inside this house. My crutches creak loudly in the empty space. We pass a golden stand with a ceramic vase on it full of fresh white lilies—real live flowers, not plastic. I'm going to have to watch Sawyer. She crawls at the speed of light and is curious about everything; she could easily break something irreplaceable.

The kitchen is at the end of the hallway. It's more utilitarian, but no less imposing, with stainless fixtures and a Sub-Zero fridge. Nevada would give all her snarky T-shirts for this kitchen.

"Oh good, the housekeeper bought the baby stuff I requested." He slides Sawyer into a shiny new high chair that looks like something from Star Wars. He scoots her up to the huge marble island with a grill in the middle, spotless copper pots hanging above.

He rubs his hands together and looks to me. "What would you like?"

I shrug. "What do you have?"

"Not sure. Why don't you have a seat and let's check it out."

He steps to the fridge, which isn't a walk-in, but when he opens the doors, it's a near thing. It's packed with fresh ingredients. "As long as you don't want fancy, we're good."

"Sawyer and I have about the same taste, and fancy isn't it. Huh, baby?" I chuck her under the chin. She looks as dazzled as I feel. "How about eggs?"

"That I can do." He pulls out a carton of eggs and sets it on the counter. "How about scrambled for Peanut and omelets for us?"

"Sounds good. I'll mix some formula for Sawyer, and I'll have milk."

"I'll get it." He turns, and in the light from the fridge, I can see the shape of his torso through his shirt. Nice.

"Fully leaded, two percent, or goat's?"

"Just regular old milk, I think." He hasn't been here in four days. How much food had to be thrown out because he wasn't here to eat it? Rich or no, wasting food is a crime. He's entitled—but not to me. I'd best rein in my hormones and remember that.

He lifts what I'm sure is a brand-new sippy cup from the counter and when I hand him the formula powder, he mixes it, secures the top, and hands it to Sawyer.

While he cooks, I ask what it was like to grow up here. He must've had a blast, playing hide-and-seek with his brother.

"Yeah, the seeking part took a long time. But once we got old enough, Carson spent most of his time at the stables and working cattle with the hands. I read a lot." He smiles to try to hide the wistfulness of his words.

"You didn't do any of the cowboy stuff?"

"Oh, sure. You couldn't be Bo's son and not. I love riding. I just like mounts that don't try to kill me."

"Shows who got the brains."

"Thanks." He ducks his head to focus on whisking eggs. "You two have got to be tired. We'll save the tour for tomorrow."

"I vote for that."

We chat through dinner about everything and nothing: his cabin progress, my dancing, everything but the life I'll have to pick up in Unforgiven in a few days.

Afterward, what we own doesn't take him more than one trip to the truck.

"Um." I stand in the kitchen doorway. "Wouldn't it be easier if I stayed down here? I mean, those stairs..."

"No bedrooms down here, sorry. But don't worry; I've got you." He grabs our bags of clothes and essentials and jogs up the stairs two at a time. I look around the massive hall. "I don't think we're in Kansas anymore, Toto." I turn to see that Sawyer has fallen asleep in her high chair, head thrown back, mouth open. I crutch over. "Thank God for you, baby." I kiss her forehead. Her sweet baby smell anchors me. I didn't know I could love a human like I love this one.

Reese trots into the kitchen. "How about if I take the princess up and come back for you?"

"I can get myself up there."

"You can. But it would mean a lot to me to spoil you, just for a few days. Will you let me?" His gaze is warm, his expression sincere.

And I decided before we left to let go a little. "Yes." I smile up at him.

"Super. I'll be right back." He lifts Sawyer out of the chair. Her head lolls on his shoulder.

"But she's never slept in a bed. I worry—"

"Don't. I've got it covered. Be right back."

By the time he returns, I've hopped three steps up and am resting, breathing like a buffalo. I don't have my strength back yet.

"There's that stubborn woman I know." He takes the crutches from me and leans them against the banister. "Com'ere."

My arms don't ask permission; they reach for his neck, and he lifts me. "This is going to be harder, you know. We could end up with broken necks at the bottom."

"Oh, and here I was picturing myself as Rhett Butler, sweeping you up the stairs."

I giggle. I must be tired.

At the top, he's barely breathing hard. "Oh, Rhett." I bat my eyelashes at him.

"I'm not done yet. I believe this is where…" He gives me a smoking look and lowers his head for a kiss. I take his mouth, doing my best to reenact Scarlett's passion. Only after two seconds, it's not an act. My fingers are in his hair and I'm willing him to drop me on a fluffy bed and ravish me.

He pulls his head back and grins. "Hey, we're pretty good at this." He carries me down the hall to a room dominated by a canopy bed, trailing flowered chintz. Sawyer is in a crib against the wall. The opposite wall is all window, a French door in the middle. He sets me on the bed.

"Wow."

"I'll get your crutches. The bathroom is through there." He points to a door opposite the bed.

I lie back into what, from the loft, has to be a goose-down comforter.

In a few moments, he steps back in the room and props the crutches against the wall where I can reach them. "I'm right next door. If Sawyer cries during the night, don't get up. I'll hear her."

"Thank you, Reese, really." I spread my arms over my head in a huge stretch.

"I want you and Sawyer to like it here. It doesn't feel like such a beautiful empty cage tonight." He squeezes my hand, then turns and is gone.

I look around at all the luxury, trying to imagine what it would have been like to grow up here.

It would take a remodel and a huge family with a dozen kids to warm this cold place. It makes me want to grab Reese and Sawyer and take them back to Unforgiven, where I could show Reese what love is all about.

Wait, what? I jolt upright, surprised by my thoughts. The next second, I'm surprised to find it's not really a surprise. I started down this slippery slope a while ago, didn't I? Yes, I want his body. But it's more. I want to wrap him up, soothe all his sore places, and make up for his unloving past.

I look inside, but it doesn't take long for me to see; these feelings are deeper than temporary. I need to be careful. While I've been occupied, my heart eased closer to the edge of falling for Reese. And if he's not for real, this long fall could end with a splat.

CHAPTER 18

Lorelei

Daybreak pours in the windows, waking me. Sawyer is fussing. I use one crutch to hobble to the crib. She's wet, of course. Everything I need to change her is on the dresser, next to the crib. What didn't Reese think of? I can't remember to bring the diaper cream from the bathroom to her bedroom, let alone—grief slips like a butter knife between my ribs. Home won't be waiting when we get back, just a hollowed-out shell of memories, broken and scattered to the wind. Where will we live until the repairs are made?

"Well, all that doesn't get you out of a wet diaper, does it, Miss Sawyer?" I balance on one foot, leaning against the sturdy crib in my old T-shirt and underwear. "You are such a good girl. You bounce back from everything. I could learn a lot from you."

When she's changed, I look at that huge bed with longing. It would be fun to snuggle with her in all that acreage...It's only three steps. "You think we can do this?"

She reaches for me. "Momma."

"I'll take that as a yes." I lift her, and still leaning on the crib, settle her on my hip, then reach for the crutch. "Hold still, baby. We be motoring." One precarious hop at a time, we make it—barely. I fall facedown on the bed. Sawyer rolls over with a sweet giggle. "Oh, you think that's funny, do you?" The crutch is under me, and I wrestle with it, trying to pull it out with all my weight on it.

"What the heck are you doing?" Reese stands in the doorway, hands full with a loaded breakfast tray. He sets it on the dresser and rushes over.

I fight the crutch, aware that my nylon-covered butt was waving in the air. Blood throbs to my face.

"Why didn't you wait for me?" He tugs the crutch from under my bare leg.

I roll over, pulling down my shirt with one hand and grabbing Sawyer's ankle with the other to keep her from crawling off the bed. "I could do it. I *did* do it." I scoot to the head of the bed, pull up the covers, and pull Sawyer into my arms. "You don't knock?" I'm decent, except…I'm not wearing a bra. I steal a glimpse down, Yep, the girls are outlined in strained cotton. I tug at the shirt, wishing I could start this day over.

"I thought you were still asleep." The redness in his cheeks tells me he noticed the titty show. He turns back to retrieve the tray.

The smell of fresh-brewed coffee wafts my way. "If that's good coffee, you're forgiven."

"It is. But *you* may not be. What if you'd dropped her?" He reaches for Sawyer.

I don't let go. "I don't need advice from a guy on how to—"

"What, your sex gives you some mystical unshakable understanding of how to care for her? Keep her safe?"

His face is tomato red, and not from embarrassment. "Four months ago you were no more a mother than I am."

His words hit me with the sting of a slap.

His lips pull back in a wince. "I'm sorry. I didn't mean that."

"Oh, yes you did." I pull myself up straighter. Momma would snatch me bald for my sharp words. "It was the vehemence that was a surprise."

"Look, I'm sorry. I was imagining what could have happened." He takes a breath and lets it out in a long whoosh. "You're a great mother. Anyone can see that."

My bad decisions drop into my brain like hail, each hitting with a thud hard enough to leave a bruise. There are a lot of them. "No, you're right. I shouldn't have tried it." I pull my shoulders and my horns in. "I told myself I was going to give up my pride and ask for help." I shrug, the rush of emotion making my sinuses prickle. Dammit, I'm not going to cry again. "But I suck at it."

"I gotta admit, you do."

His smile crashes my pity party. He's right. Besides, it's a gorgeous day, and fighting isn't a good way to start it. "Yeah, I do. I'll keep trying."

"That's settled. Drink your coffee before it gets cold. Can I have the peanut?"

"Sounds like a fair trade." I hand her over.

The mattress dips when he sits and settles her in his lap. He lifts a small bowl of oatmeal and a rubber-coated spoon from the tray. "Just the way you like it, Your Highness."

Sawyer reaches for the spoon.

He fends off her hands. "Oh, no you don't. I don't feel like cleaning this off the walls."

Reese tips a spoonful into her mouth as Sawyer puts her hand in the oatmeal.

"She's pulled that one on me before. I should have warned you, she's fast."

She lifts a handful to her mouth. Some of it even makes it in.

"I can see a bath in your future, kid." He grabs the linen napkin and swipes her hand and face. Then he gives her a few Goldfish to occupy her hands.

"This coffee is great. Thank you for waiting on us." I take another sip. "What do you have planned for today?"

"I thought I'd give you two a short tour of the ranch. I had them bring the four-wheeler around front."

"That'll be fun, but you don't have to entertain us. I know you have work to do."

"Actually, this afternoon, I was hoping to get your advice."

"Sure, on what?"

"Furniture and stuff for the cabin. I have no idea what to get."

"Are you kidding? This house is amazing." So not my style, but amazing just the same.

He spoons more oatmeal to Sawyer. "I had nothing to do with it. When my mother died, Bo brought in a decorator and redid the whole thing." He looks around the beautiful room.

"Wow. That must have felt like he was wiping your mom out of your life."

"Everyone deals with grief differently, I guess." But his eyes are sad. That betrayal cut deep.

"I liked your house. Everything was comfortable. The kind of place you walk in and feel at home. I don't think a fancy designer could give me that."

I know he's just trying to make me feel better. The only thing new in that house was the washer, and that's because the twenty-five-year-old one died five years back.

"I'll be happy to look at whatever, but I'll warn you, interior decoration is not my area of expertise."

"Your taste has gotta be better than mine. I don't even know what I like." He looks around again. "But I know this isn't it. And I didn't know that until I hung out at your house." Sawyer heads for the edge of the bed and he grabs her. "You want down?"

He holds Sawyer and lets her slide down the comforter until her feet touch the floor. She clings to the bedspread and stomps her feet. "I do believe this one is going to be walking soon."

"I've thought she was just waiting for the right moment."

Sawyer takes a sideways step, moves her handholds and takes another. She giggles and takes another.

"Wow, you go, baby." I'd love to sit here and chat longer, but I have got to get to the bathroom, and he's seen way too much of my booty already today. "I need to get up and um…"

"Oh, of course." He leaps off the bed, sweeps Sawyer in his arms, and dangles her upside down. "I'll get the princess ready, okay?"

She squeals with laughter.

"Okay, but if you do that much more, you're going to be cleaning up oatmeal. I'm just saying."

He swings her upright. "Come on, Sawyer. Let's go get ready." He steps to the dresser, pulls out a pink frilly top and knit shorts I've never seen. "We'll give your momma some privacy." He bounces to the door like a prancing horse, making Sawyer giggle. He steps through, then turns back. "You yell when you're ready and I'll take you downstairs. Agreed?"

Unless I scoot down on my butt, I don't see any other way. "Agreed."

I could take a bath in the bathroom sink. I almost do. I manage to wash everything including my hair and get dressed without falling once. I can't wait to get back on my own two feet. "A few more days," that's the very earliest the doctor would venture a guess that the stitches could come out. Reese said he'll take me to his doctor here and have it checked.

When I stump out to the hallway, Reese and Sawyer are walking by, Sawyer holding his fingers.

"Momma!"

My heart soars. I'm so grateful for this miracle baby. "Well, hey, look at you, Peanut."

"She takes after her daddy in the athletic department." Reese is beaming. "I'm taking bets. I say before she leaves, she's got this walking thing down."

"That's a bet I wouldn't take." God, I miss holding her. All I can do is stand and watch.

"I want to show you something." He swings her up into his arms.

"Down."

I crutch over to pet her, but she's squirming. "That girl knows what she wants, Baba."

He sets her on her feet but holds her hands. "I think she got that from your side."

I smile. "Probably."

"We're just going here." He steers Sawyer into the doorway next to our bedroom.

He doesn't have to tell me it's his. It's all business, from the modern desk shoved against the wall with the huge computer monitor to the whiteboard over it, covered in multicolored forward-slanted print, a combination of reminders, coordinates, and breeding notes. There's a map, which must be for flying, because it's full of concentric circles, with no roads. The single iron bed is, I'll bet, his from when he was a kid, neatly made with a bright Navajo blanket.

But what pulls my attention is the three galloping wooden ponies on an otherwise bare shelf over the bed. One is a fanciful Appaloosa, painted with pastels. The other is in Indian war paint. And the one of mine, he bought from the five-and-dime. "I know which is yours." I take two hops to the shelf.

"Which?"

"This one." I lift the pastel Appaloosa.

"How did you know?"

"I can see your mom lifting it out of the dime-store window, thinking, 'Oh, this is so Reese.'"

His eyes are suspiciously shiny, and he just nods. Sawyer leads him away.

The rest of the room is as empty as a sinner's soul. It shows me Reese's life more clearly than anything he ever told me. This room is the opposite of the rest of the house, almost monk-like in its austerity.

My heart aches for that little boy. For the man with gobs of money and an empty place where his family should have been.

Sawyer leads him past me, and I grab his sleeve, stopping them.

When he looks up, I kiss him. A sweet, tender kiss, to tell him he's not alone.

I straighten, but he doesn't move, a confused surprise painted on his features. "What did I do to deserve that?"

"By being who you are."

"In that case, I'll try to do that more often." He smiles and lets Sawyer tug him away.

* * *

Reese

By the time we're done with the grand tour of the ranch, in spite of the ATV's burpy engine, Sawyer is asleep in Lorelei's lap, her sun hat askew. "I think between the sun and the excitement, we managed to wear her out." I pull onto the cobbles of the circular drive.

Lorelei's love for Sawyer surrounds her like an aura. "Another first in a day of firsts."

"I have to admit, I never thought you'd let me put her up on Brandy."

"I trust you."

"Do you really?"

Her brows come down and she shifts a bit in her seat. She knows I'm asking about more than a horse. "I've trusted you to help with negotiations with my insurance company. I trusted you to bring us here. What more do you want?"

More than she's ready to give. But now's not the time to bring that up. I pull up to the door, shut down the engine, and turn to her. "Trust me to fix you dinner, no questions asked?"

Her brows relax. "Oh, heck yes. As Momma would say, my stomach's gnawing on my backbones."

I carry Sawyer in, going slow so Lorelei can keep up. I lead her to the great room, where the spectacular sunset is showcased in the two-story windows.

"Oh wow. I like this room."

I try to see the room from her perspective: the prow-window wall, the fieldstone fireplace that stretches to the wood-beamed ceiling, the pool table, the huge bar. "I do too. It's over-the-top, but at least it's comfortable." I lead her to the buttercream leather couch in front of the windows. "You sit here."

I pull pillows and Sherpa throws from the back of the

couch to make a nest for Sawyer on the wood floor and lay her in it. "This way we won't have to worry about her rolling off the couch. Can I get you a drink? Wine, maybe?"

"You know, wine would be really nice." She sits and props the crutches against the end of the couch. "I'm sorry—"

"No, you can't help."

She shakes her head. "I really am bad about this, aren't I?"

I drop a kiss on her forehead. "You are. But I'll try to get you used to being spoiled this week." I head for the bar.

"I don't know what to do with myself. How to be... stationary. Useless."

"Stationary is not useless. You make the room brighter just sitting in it." I scan the wine rack behind the bar. "Red or white? Say what you want about Bo, but he always kept a good wine cellar."

"Doesn't matter, except not dry, please. The sweeter the better."

"Ah, I have just the thing." I pull a bottle at the bottom and wipe the dust off. "My mother loved sweet wine, too. Bo put in a few bushes for her, just so she could have elderberry wine."

"Wow, homemade?"

"Yep. We still make a couple of cases a year, though there hasn't been anyone here to drink it in a long time."

"It sounds wonderful."

I pull the cork and wrinkle my nose at the cloying smell. "I'll take your word for it." I take down a small stemless globe glass and fill it halfway.

"Let me guess. You're a beer man."

I open the fridge and grab one. "Lone Star all the way, baby." I carry the drinks to the couch and sit beside her.

She's staring at the baby sleeping on the floor, a sheen in her eyes.

"What is it, hon?"

"I'm wondering how and when we should tell Sawyer about her real parents."

I catch a breath at the "we." It could be an unconscious slip, but could it be that she's picturing me in her life in that future "when"? "I think we should always be talking about them. Then they'll be real people to her, not just bedtime-story characters."

"I have to admit, I already tell her about Patsy, even though I know she doesn't understand."

A pang of guilt hits. What with all the stuff going on, I haven't thought about Carson in days. I make a note to conjure a bunch of good memories to tell Sawyer. Not made-up, exactly, just...a bit rose-colored. "We'll do that. We owe it to all three of them."

I hold my bottle up to the clouds outside the window. "Here's to Patsy and Carson. Wherever they are, I hope they're together, smiling down on the three of us." I take a long swallow, wishing there really were an "us." Hoping there can be.

"Hmmm, this is amazing." She licks her lips, holds the glass up, and swirls the almost-purple contents. "As rich as summer sunshine." She sips again.

"It's probably pretty potent, too." But it's her that's potent. As her tongue darts across her lips, she mainlines into my blood. My cock leaps to attention, and I have to shift to make room in my Wranglers.

We sit for a bit, sipping and watching the last of the sun slip below the edge of the world.

"We haven't seen anyone but the cowboys since we got here. When do I get to meet your amazing cook, Nora?"

There's a heartbeat's hesitation, when even the dust motes stop dancing at the sound of her name. Old pain is a dull knife. "She's not here any longer."

Her head comes up at my tone, and her eyes darken. "Tell me."

"After the accident…" I turn the bottle in my hand, just to have something to focus on. "I couldn't climb the stairs for weeks. They made up a bed for me on this couch and left me to heal." I shrug. "To be fair, Bo had a business to run, and Carson had school.

"Nora cooked my favorites, to get me to eat. She sat with me for hours, telling me stories. I guess she felt sorry for me. It helped take my mind off my … problems."

"How old were you?"

"Fourteen."

Her nose wrinkles. "Not an easy time, even in the best of circumstances."

"True. In all those hours, she and I got to be friends. When I could walk, she took me into the kitchen and taught me to cook. Something about the mindless repetition of cutting vegetables and following a recipe calmed my mind." I pull in a breath. "I owe her a lot."

"What happened?"

"Bo happened. When I healed, he wanted things back the way they'd been, me out working cattle when I wasn't in school." I look out at the shadows gathering around the mesquite outside the window. "I said no. We had a terrible fight. He said she'd turned me into a momma's boy."

"Your *father* said that?"

I nod. "One day I came home from school and Nora was gone. He wanted to teach me a lesson, so he fired her."

"No wonder you speak of your father the way you do."

"He was a hard man."

She reaches over and takes my hand. "Pardon me for speaking ill of the dead, but he sounds like a real buttwipe."

The juvenile word pulls a laugh from me. "He was."

She glances around. "But he was obviously a good businessman."

"Nah. All this came from oil money. The cattle business didn't start making money until I took over." I bend and turn on the lamp beside the couch. The window in front of us becomes a mirror.

She smiles. "Score one for the college boy."

"Did you ever want to go to college, Lorelei?"

"Me? No. I did okay in school, but I never saw myself as a career woman. I'm happy running the diner." She nods. "I'm good at it."

"Carly is lucky to have you."

"Hardly. I'm as common as table salt."

I cock my head to see if she's kidding. She's not. "Whatever gave you that idea?" She's so pretty when she blushes.

"I just do what needs to be done. Like millions of people do every day."

"No, they don't. Your sister and my brother went off and rodeoed."

She smiles and gets a faraway look in her eye. "Oh, but Patsy, she was special. I wish you could have met her. If she'd stayed home, she'd have been like hitching a thoroughbred to a vegetable cart."

"You're no cart horse."

"Maybe not, but I take to the traces better. Patsy couldn't—it would have broken her spirit."

"And you think you're not special." I shake my head. "I wish you could see yourself like I see you." I turn and take her face in my hands. Her eyes flick between mine, as if afraid to hear what I'll say next. "It hurts me that you don't see how very special you are. You know your mind and do what's right, no matter how hard it is or how long it takes. Your heart is bigger and softer than any thoroughbred's—

you give and give more, and when you run out, if someone
needs it, you give more. You don't trust easily, but I've seen
you with Sawyer and your mother; when you love, it's all
the way. You're not table salt; you're salt of the earth, and
this country was built by strong women like you. I'd give
anything to earn the love of a woman like that."

Tears tremble on her bottom lashes, but she lets out a shaky
laugh. "You always say the exact wrong thing. How did you
suddenly manage to find *just* the right thing to say?"

"I don't know. I'm on unfamiliar ground here." I bend to
kiss her wine-stained lips. I taste the sweetness, but then she
opens to me, and I delve deeper, to taste her.

She gives way beneath me, and soon we're lying side
by side, pressed together in all the places that matter. I
put my arm under her head and, with the other, pull her
closer. My cock strains, trying to get through clothes to
her warmth. I've waited so long for this...

Slow down. The small corner of my brain not mesmerized
by her taste, her smell, whispers a warning. She's been
through a lot, and she doesn't trust me all the way yet.

Oh so slowly, I break the kiss, and she whimpers. I back
up until her face comes into focus. Her eyes are sleepy, her
face slack with passion.

"Please." She grabs the lapels of my shirt and pulls me
into another kiss. Her leg comes over mine, and her heel
digs into my butt as she grinds against me.

My turn to groan. *Slow.* This will not be a generic back-
seat hookup. I'm going to make this special for her. Though
it may kill me. It's been a long time. But this woman is
going to be worth the waiting. I catch her fingers when they
move to the buttons of my shirt and I lock them in mine, pull
them to my chest, and try to show her, with my mouth, how
much she means to me.

Then, suddenly, I know exactly what to do. Exactly what she needs. "Will you trust me?"

She frowns, as if trying to understand the simple words. "If I haven't made that clear by now—"

"Shhhh." I brush a kiss on her lips. "I don't want you to do anything. I want to do it all." I raise an eyebrow in challenge.

"But I want—"

"And you shall have it. Eventually. Lie back. Relax." I check to be sure Sawyer is still asleep, then slide my fingers inside Lorelei's blouse to touch her bra before I unbutton the top button. I smile when I recognize the pink one. I kiss behind her ear, and she shivers. I work my way down, kissing and undoing buttons. She squirms. Thank the gods for front-clasp bras; one twist and her breasts spring free, delicate, ivory, and just right. I take a nipple in my mouth and make love to it.

"Please." She pulls my head up to kiss me. "Now." Her movements are frenzied with want.

"Not yet." I say it to calm myself as much as her. My cock is a pulsing steel rod. I move down, worshipping every bit of skin I can reach. I unzip her pants and pull them down her long, slim legs. Her delicate musky scent draws me, and I breathe hot over her mound. She moans, shifting beneath me.

I spread and taste her, flicking my tongue over her most delicate hollow, and she strains up to meet me. When I touch where I so want to be, she moans and bucks wildly against my mouth in an orgasm that goes on and on.

I lie down beside her, finger combing her hair and watching her come back to me.

When her breath and her heartbeat slow, a sexy smile stretches her lips. "My turn."

CHAPTER 19

Lorelei

I come awake all at once, aware that I've forgotten something. When I open my eyes, it slams back. Reese is in the bed beside me, eyes closed, hair tousled. In sleep he looks younger, innocent. Except for those sexy lips and the morning-beard shadow.

My heart pumps softly, as if last night eased its need to pound. I feel slack, empty of all the stress, fear, and pain of the past weeks. Good sex can do that to a person.

Only it's more than that.

Last night my guard came down and surety snuck in, burrowing deep into my heart. I *can* trust this man. I know it like I know my own name, and not only because he's great in bed. I worked hard, ignoring all the clues the past months, not believing he could want me: an easily overlooked woman, not much more than a waitress. But all that time, I wasn't looking at the man in front of me; I was looking back. And that's not fair. Not fair to Reese *or* me.

I still can hardly get my head around the fact that a man like *this* wants me, but I'm done doubting it. It's like religion. I don't have to understand all of it to believe. I find I'm ready to have faith.

"What are you smiling at?" He sounds like I feel, sleepy-sated.

"Same thing you are, I'll bet." I stretch, hearing complaint from every tendon and muscle that got a workout last night. And this morning.

He reaches for me and I lean into him without hesitation. His arms come around me and he puts his face in my hair and inhales. "God, you smell good in the morning."

"You are delirious from lack of sleep." I kiss him, morning breath and all.

"Hmmm, you taste good, too." His palm slides down to cradle my breast.

I should be shy, a bit embarrassed. We did things last night that I've never thought of, outside romance novels. I realize now that my almost-fiancé was deficient in more areas than just honesty. Reese's cock is a hard rod against my thigh. I reach to slide my fingers up the velvet shaft and he moans, "You better mean that."

"Oh, I'm dead serious."

I kiss him, deep and languid.

"Baba!" Sawyer has pulled herself up the bars of her crib and smiles her cheery morning smile at us.

Baba groans. "Love you, kid, but your timing stinks."

I try not to giggle and fail.

"I'll change her. But you keep laughing and you get no coffee, woman."

He rolls over me to get to the edge of the bed. I can't resist squeezing that tight butt. "Shutting up now."

* * *

The days are spent in a blur of camaraderie, baby time, and incredible sex. I'm floating on a cloud of forgetfulness and hormones. Overnight, it's like we've stopped focusing on the things that separate us and look instead at each other and appreciate the things we have in common. We exist in a bubble, the three of us. Kind of like . . . a family.

Reese takes us to town to the doctor who presided at Reese's and his brother's birth and patched them up their whole lives. While he takes out my stitches, he tells stories of the St. James boys. I'm laughing so hard, I don't notice any pain.

Carrizo Springs isn't a whole lot bigger than Unforgiven, but thanks to oil, much more prosperous. They even have their own Walmart. I put up only a token protest when he buys more clothes for Sawyer and me. We need them, and he enjoys it so much I don't want to seem ungrateful.

But as the day to go home approaches, my mind returns to my real life. This has been heavenly, but I have to remember that I've only borrowed Cinderella's slippers the past week. The slippers stay here. I go home to reality.

* * *

We're in the kitchen on Thursday afternoon, watching Sawyer scoot around the floor, when Reese turns to me. "What would you think about flying back to Unforgiven tomorrow? It would be faster, and I'm hoping I can set up a meeting at A&M on the way home."

"We've kept you from business the past week, haven't we?" With the exception of phone calls and meetings with his cowhands, he's spent the whole time with us.

He gives me that soft, sexy smile that's for me alone. "I wouldn't have had it any other way. This week has been perfect."

But I hear what he isn't saying: perfection is, by definition, a temporary place. I'd love to get home faster, but small planes aren't as safe as an airline. What if something happened? I shake my head. "I don't feel good about taking chances. The past months have shown me that the world is a lot scarier than I wanted to accept."

He touches the side of my face, softness in his eyes. "This life doesn't come with guarantees, hon. You can't live your life afraid because of the past."

His words strike a chord, echoing my thoughts of just a few days before. I shut myself off from men because of what one did in the past. But still...a worm of worry squirms in my chest.

"After all, Patsy and Carson were killed in a truck, right? You are less likely to die in a plane—"

Sawyer's squeal freezes us both for a heartbeat. Then we're following the sound into the hall. Sawyer is walking, one hand on the wall, two steps from the gold vase full of lilies.

"Sawyer, stop!"

She doesn't. She reaches the stand, trips over the base, loses her balance, and grabs it. It rocks, gyrating, trying to decide.

I run and launch myself at her, hitting the marble floor with a thump that knocks the wind from me. I roll to cover her as the marble stand and china vase come down.

Reese grabs the stand, keeping it from hitting me. "Got it!"

But the vase hits the floor in a shower of shards, water, and lilies. I cover Sawyer's face with my hands as the splinters explode around us.

She takes a deep breath and wails, "Maaaaaamaaaaa!"

Reese is there, hands roaming over us both. "Are you all right? Lorelei? Say something."

I doubt he could hear me over the baby's cry, but it doesn't matter, because I can't get air in my lungs to speak. I lie there, my mouth opening and closing like a fish out of water.

"Lorelei, please, are you cut? Are you hurt?" His voice is almost as frantic as Sawyer's.

I push the baby to him, and he lifts her, scanning her for cuts before clasping her to him, patting her back, and telling her everything's going to be fine.

I work at trying to get my lungs to unlock. Slowly, breath by breath, they loosen. "I'm okay," I wheeze.

He sweeps a palm over the floor, clearing the glass, then sits beside me, Sawyer in his lap. "You hit hard. You're not hurt?" His hand runs over my hair, pulling it back from my face. "You're bleeding."

I put fingers to the sting on my forehead. They come away with a smear of blood. "It's just a scratch." I sit up. "Is Peanut okay?"

"Thanks to you. You run fast for someone who just got off crutches."

"Fear is a powerful motivator." I stroke Sawyer's head. "I guess when she decided to walk, she did it all at once."

"Those West women don't mess around when they make up their minds."

Sawyer has wound down to sniffles. Reese pushes off the wall to stand. "I'll get some formula for her. You stay here and breathe. I'll be right back."

I'm not arguing. The adrenaline dump has cleared, leaving me weak and a bit shaky.

He crunches through the mess to the kitchen.

He's back in a few minutes holding a broom and offering me a hand up. "Go slow."

I stand and get a panoramic view of the mess. "Oh, Reese, your beautiful vase!"

"It's no big deal."

"But it had to be way expensive." Guilt and prices are flying around my skull.

"The first one was. Carson and I broke it throwing a football around when we were in high school. Bo about wore us out."

"He *hit* you?"

"Yeah." He says it like he'd say "we're out of milk." "This one is only a copy. The original *was* expensive. I know, because Carson and I had to do extra chores for three months to earn the money for it." He puts an arm around me. "Can you walk?"

I take a step. I've been limping since the stitches came out, the skin feeling like a too-tight sock. "Actually, I think running stretched it." I take another tentative step. "I'm good."

He leads me back to the kitchen, sits me at the table, and pours me a glass of elderberry wine, then steps out to the hall and sweeps up the mess. He's just dumped the dustpan and put up the broom when Sawyer sees a bird fly by the window and points. "Buud! Buud!"

Reese breaks into a huge grin, takes her hand, and smacks his with it. "Walking and talking in one day! That's my girl." He turns to me. "She and I worked on 'bird,' back before the storm, but it was just buh-buh then." He shakes his head. "It's amazing how much she's changed since we've met her."

"I know. She's outgrown everything she wore at six months." I run my hand over the dark-brown hair she got from her father. "I woke up thinking how it's time I stopped looking back and started looking forward. She's one of the biggest reasons why." I kiss her head. "God has taken so much from you and me—but he's also given us this miracle. I need to remember that and be grateful."

He takes my hand. "I have a double miracle. He brought me you."

Everything is too new. I'm not ready for this. "I'm going to work on facing forward, but let's just enjoy where we are and not look too far down the road, okay?" I lean in and kiss him, to reinforce that this isn't a negative.

"I like where we are, too." He smiles and stands. "Almost time for the big girl's nap. Now that you can get around a bit better, do you want a tour of the parts of the house you haven't seen before we put her in the crib upstairs?"

"I'd love that." I lift my wine and stand.

He swings Sawyer into his arms, drops her onto his hip, and hands her the sippy cup like he's been doing this for years. When he leads us through the high-ceilinged dining room, I understand why he eats in the kitchen. Heavy damask gold curtains, delicate china in a massive breakfront, and a clawfoot burnished table that would seat twenty. "Wow, did your parents entertain a lot?"

"They did before my mom died. I don't think it's been used more than a handful of times since then, and only for business dinners." He looks around, like he hasn't seen it in a while. Maybe he hasn't. "The joy went out of this house with my mother."

It sounds like she was the heart of the family, not Bo, for all him being loud and bigger than life. I wonder what would have been different if she'd lived. Reese would have been more accepted, for sure. More secure in the gifts he was given. "I'm so sorry, Reese."

He leads me through a library with high shelves full

of red leather-bound books, none of which look like they've ever been off the shelf. Then he turns in at the next door.

"This was Bo's office."

I step in and try not to show my horror. Animal heads of every size and shape cover the walls. On every mantel, table, desk, and in each corner sits a fully stuffed animal: fox, lynx, even a full-grown cougar, mouth open, fangs displayed. "The poor things." The dark sadness of this room pushes against my chest.

I shoot a glance to Sawyer, but thank the Lord, she's too focused on playing with her sippy cup to notice the animals.

"Yeah, not my favorite room, either."

I step to the huge stone fireplace, to see better the portrait above it. "Is this your father?"

"Yep, that's Beauregard Brigham St. James."

The man reminds me of old photos of Teddy Roosevelt, with a big walrus mustache and small eyes behind glasses, but the ten-gallon hat and string tie are pure Texan. He's not at all what I expected...except the eyes. They look mean as a feral pig's. "You must favor your mother."

His father glares down at us, amping up the oppressive atmosphere. A shudder rips down my spine. I don't need to guess what this man would think of his son bringing home someone like *me*.

The sippy cup falls from Sawyer's hand, hitting the hearth with a crack that makes me jump. She doesn't notice; she's nodded off on Reese's shoulder.

He bends to retrieve the cup. "Bedtime for this one. Let's go upstairs." At the bottom of the stairs, he stops. "Want me to come back down for you?"

"Nope. I need to get my stamina back." I take the first

step, testing, then another. "It's fine." It feels so good to be self-sufficient again.

But I'm slow, and by the time I've reached the top, he's put Sawyer down in her crib and he's standing in the hall. "Come on to my room. I've got something to show you."

In his room, he grabs a rolled tube of papers in the corner, unfurls them on the table.

Seeing his wooden horses, I remember. "Oh, Reese, I'm so sorry."

His head comes up. "Why?"

"I was making you a horse. For a cabin-warming gift." The image flashes: my room was destroyed along with everything else on the second floor. "It's gone now, along with all my woodworking tools." My voice comes out shaky. Anything that didn't get sucked out will be rusted, damaged from all the water.

He takes the step to me and wraps me in his arms. My hands go around his waist, and I lean into him, absorbing the comfort and safety.

"They can be replaced."

I shake my head and step back. They were my father's. *Face forward. Face forward.* "What are these?"

"The plans for the cabin. I thought maybe seeing them would help you come up with decorating ideas."

We spend a half hour talking of rugs and curtains and paint and searching the Internet for photos he can use when shopping.

"Why don't you redecorate this house, too? You've mentioned that it isn't your taste."

"It doesn't seem worth the trouble."

I glance at the cabin plans he seems much more invested in. I wonder if he sees this. "You seem really isolated out here. Don't you have any friends?"

"Sure." He shifts in his chair. "A few guys from college and I get together a couple of times a year, to play golf, drink, and relive the good old days."

"But what about—"

"I have the business and acquaintances involved with that. It's harder to make friends after you leave school, you know? You're lucky to have a friend like Carly."

"I am. I love the heck out of her. But there are limits; she's my friend, but she's also my boss. I have to be careful not to cross that line. I think maybe you can't have no-holds-barred friendships like you did as a kid when you're an adult." I play with the edge of the notepad.

"Well, we have each other as family now. Maybe, with time…"

He's staring intently at me, that warm campfire flame in his eyes. The one I want to snuggle up and get close to.

"Maybe…" I lean in and kiss him deeply, holding nothing back.

We spend the next hour exploring the possibility—in his bed.

I'm almost asleep when he says, "I have a surprise for you, but before I tell you, you need to know that it's okay to tell me no."

I come alert. He knows that whatever it is, is pushing. "What?"

"I had the contractor put on another crew, and they've been working around the clock. The cabin isn't done by any means, but there's AC and running water. If you want, you and Sawyer can move in there. You know, until your house is done." He gets up on one elbow, a worry line between his brows. "But if you'd rather stay with Carly or at the motel or anywhere else, that's fine, too."

"Seriously?" A layer of sadness I wasn't even aware

of slips from my shoulders. I've felt so displaced, so homeless. Carly has been a love to offer to put us up, but all I've wanted was home. To be close enough to see the house every day, to see the same trees and hills, to drive the same roads to work. It would be like getting some of my old life back. "You are the most thoughtful, most wonderful..." I'm kissing his face all over, and he laughs.

I sober and back up, to see him better. "No, really, why the heck aren't you dripping in women?"

"A woman explained it to me not long ago. I'm pushy and arrogant and entitled."

I roll on top of him, and my hair falls around us. "All true, but you do have a *few* good qualities."

CHAPTER 20

Lorelei

The real world meets me at the dirt airstrip the next morning. In the distance, it's almost toylike, the wing struts and propeller flimsy as a kid's rubber-band airplane. Ants of worry scurry around my stomach. Reese and his manager, Manuel, are schlepping our borrowed suitcase from the truck across the field. I'm holding Sawyer, trying to keep up.

"Bud!" She points to the plane.

"Reese."

He's chatting with Manuel.

"Reese!"

He stops. "What?"

"I'm not sure about this." It seemed safer when we talked about it yesterday...in abstract. In reality? It's a big gulp.

He tells Manuel to go on and turns to me. "Hon, it's fine. I've flown a hundred thousand miles. I've never had a problem."

"In that plane?" I nod toward it. "Because then you should probably replace things. Or get it serviced, or whatever you do. I'll just drive—"

"It was serviced yesterday, by my personal mechanic. He's the best. And Cessnas have been around since 1916 for a reason. They are stable and safe." He steps over and puts his arms around Sawyer and me. "You don't think I'd risk the most important people on the planet, do you?"

"But—"

"Lorelei, look at me."

I glance up from my feet.

"I am a terrible bull rider. I stink at flowery words. I'm only a passable cowboy." When he looks at the plane, pride shines in his chocolate eyes. "But I'm a damned fine pilot." He squeezes us. "Trust me? I won't let anything bad happen to you or Sawyer."

I have no doubt about his abilities. But there are things beyond his control.

He drops the hug and steps back. "It's a beautiful day; the wind is almost still. Perfect conditions—oh, and I've got these." He drops the backpack he has slung over his shoulder and pulls out tiny headphones. "These are for Peanut. Noise canceling, to protect her hearing. You and I each have a pair in the cockpit." He smiles, holds them out, and waits.

This is so like him, thinking ahead, thinking of everything for our safety and comfort.

Face forward. Just because bad things have happened one after another doesn't mean they're going to keep happening. A pool of sureness rises from my core, drowning the worry ants. I'm a West woman, strong and steady hearted. I look down at Sawyer. "You want to fly in the airplane?"

"Buud!" She points.

I take the baby headphones from Reese. "Lead on, Buud Boy."

Four hours later, we touch down with barely a bump on the dirt runway on his land. Seeing the house's devastation from the air hit me like looking into an opened skull. It brought back that day in technicolor. And reminded me to be grateful for what I still have.

"See? That wasn't so bad." Reese's voice is scratchy through the headphones.

It was scary at first. I think I left permanent finger impressions in the armrest. But once the ground stopped falling away and we leveled out, my stomach settled. It was beautiful, seeing the land from a bird's perspective. I speak into my mic. "You were right. You're a great pilot. It's so pretty up there. I had no idea."

I can't see his eyes behind the dark sunglasses.

"I mean, I've flown, but never in a small plane. It's more real. More immediate."

"That it is." When he shuts down the engines, the silence almost hurts my ears. I'd gotten used to the roaring of engines and air. We take off the headsets and he shows me where to stow them.

"I'll get sleepy Sawyer and her seat out, then the luggage."

We talked on the flight and worked out a game plan. Bouncing ideas off him and getting his opinion about the repairs on my house helped—for once I'm not worried about what I didn't think of. We'll take the Murphinator, and he'll drive me out to Floyd's to buy a car. Then back to the cabin, to get settled.

The only problem I haven't settled is Sawyer. Thank God for Carly; she's offered to take Sawyer during the day until I find a babysitter or get her into daycare. I have to be at work in the morning. Reese can stay until tomorrow, but he has an appointment at the university next Friday. I appreciate everything he's done, but it's time for me to get on my feet and take charge of my life again. To decide where we go from here.

I want Reese in my life, but as a boyfriend, not as my

own personal genie, to grant my every wish. I pull luggage out of the back while he wrestles with Sawyer's car seat, discussing the logistics of it with her the whole time.

Boyfriend. The word makes me smile.

* * *

My phone alarm goes off the next morning, and it takes me a moment of feeling around on the floor to find it. By the time I do, I've remembered where I am. It's black as the inside of a cave in Reese's cabin. I ease out of bed, careful not to wake him. I feel my way out of the room, touching bare wood two-by-fours, the cement floor cold underfoot. The cabin has running water and electricity, but not much more. The interior walls are open, baring the bones of the construction, wiring, and pipes. I make it across the hall without stubbing anything and flip on the light in the bathroom. The fixtures are in, and the shower pan, but no walls, which would make showering a voyeur's dream, if not for the black plastic hung around it. Reese had appliances delivered, and the bed, a crib, a playpen, and a card table with chairs are the only furnishings. Sawyer is living in that huge playpen until this place is finished. It's dangerous enough for a grown-up. The thought of her wandering around wires and nails and...I shudder.

But I'm grateful for Reese's gift—a roof over our heads.

I throw on my clothes, wash my face, brush my teeth, and walk out to what will be the great room to stand looking out the huge windows, scanning the dark for the hulking shape of my ruined house. As we came up the drive last night, something clicked in me and my world righted. I practically ran from this place a week ago, hoping to outstrip my memories. It didn't work, and I'm surprised to discover that

I no longer want to. They're broken and battered, but these are my roots, my family's legacy.

Home.

Sarah and Momma promised to come to the diner for breakfast. I can't wait to hug them both.

I go back and kiss Sawyer goodbye, then stand at the edge of the bed, wanting to do the same with Reese, but I don't want to chance waking him. I turn to leave.

"Hey."

A little thrill goes through me at the sound of his voice. I turn back. "You go back to sleep. You're going to need it; Peanut will flat wear you out today."

His hand finds mine in the dark, and he tugs. I step over and bend for his sleepy-but-oh-so-sexy kiss. It makes me want to shuck my clothes and snuggle back into bed. And him.

"You have a good day today."

"It'll be crazy. I'll stop at O'Grady's for milk and stuff on the way home, but I'll bring dinner from the café, so we don't have to worry about cooking. Don't forget, Sawyer doesn't step foot out of the playpen unless you take her outside." I let go of his hand.

"K." His slur tells me he's already on his way back to dreamland. "Love you."

I freeze, rocked by waves of shock, and a roller-coaster dip of apprehension.

A soft snore comes from the dark.

Is that old wives' tale true, that you don't lie, talking in your sleep? I'm so not ready for this. I've just admitted *boyfriend* to myself... but love? Nuh-uh. Not ready.

I'm going to try to forget he said that.

I close the door softly and walk to my new car: a white, almost-new Chevy Spark. I'd have gotten something way older, but Reese pointed out that with Sawyer, I needed something safe and dependable. He's right, but it was hard to fork over more. I need a bigger cushion in my bank account than I have right now. I have to admit, though, it's so good to get behind the wheel and not have to send up a prayer that it starts. I've got to think of a name for him, but my to-do list weighs more than a dentist's lead apron.

And the reopening of the Chestnut Creek Café after a week of repairs is going to have everyone stopping in to see the changes and catching up with one another. It's going to be crazy.

I'm surprised when I unlock the back door of the café to see the lights blazing. "Hello?"

Carly comes through the swinging door from the dining area and wraps me in a big hug. "You're finally back! Man, I've missed you."

"You have two babies at home and you're here before dawn? What is wrong with you?" I squeeze her back. "I missed you, too."

"We need to get caught up, girlfriend, and once everyone shows, it's going to get nuts." She steps back and winks. "I want to hear all the juicy details." She walks to the grill, grabs a half apron, and ties it on over her jeans. "I'll make breakfast. You go get us coffee, okay?"

God, it's good to be home.

I step through the door and look around. The black-and-white checkerboard tiles are the same, as are the gold scrolled letters on the door. But the booths have been recovered in shiny red leather, a white chevron stripe on each section. The bamboo roll-up window shades have been replaced with red-and-white striped canvas roman shades. "I like what you've done with the place," I say through the serving window.

"I know, nice, huh? I figured the insurance was paying, so why not?"

I start the first pot of coffee, then scoop and stack setups for more.

"Okay, so spill, sister." She cracks eggs and slaps frozen hash browns on the grill.

By the time I give her a recap of the past week's events, breakfast is ready. She pushes open the door with her butt and sets the plates on the counter. "Holy cripes, Lorelei, that house sounds fantastical, like out of a movie."

"It is. Just like a movie set. In the lights, it looks perfect, but it's really just fabric, wood, and paint with no depth." I sit on one of the stools and pat the next, for her to sit. "It's expensive and beautiful and cold, and oh so lonely."

"You feel sorry for him." She eyes me over the rim of her coffee cup.

"Reese is kind of like that house. On the outside, his life looks all glamorous, something to envy. But I wouldn't trade my life here in Unforgiven for his mansion and all the trimmings. No way." I pick up my fork and play with my scrambled eggs. "He's so alone, Carly. His father and brother made him feel 'less than,' an outsider in his own family. Can you imagine?"

"You're in love with him." She doesn't say it as a question.

I remember Reese's sleepy admission this morning, "It's too early for that..." I take a sip of coffee and consider. "But I *really* like him. You know? Oh, Carly, he's so thoughtful and kind, and it's like Sawyer has put color in his world. They're mad for each other."

She tips her head and studies me. "And do you believe now that it isn't just Sawyer he wants?"

I give her a shy smile. "I'm starting to."

She grabs my hand. "I'm so happy for you, Lorelei. After that...dingleberry you had last time, you *so* deserve every happiness."

The lock rattles, and the back door opens. "Hey, who's the buttwipe who parked their little marshmallow in one of our spots back here?" Nevada steps in. "Carly? What in hell are you doing here before the sun?"

God, I've missed this place. I carry my half-eaten plate of food to the kitchen and set it on the counter. "Com'ere, you foulmouthed little headbanger." When I hug her, Nevada stands, hands at sides, bearing it until I let go. "I think you just named my new car. Marshmallow."

"A good name." Carly pushes through the door.

"Okay, now that you're both here, I have an idea." I lean against the counter. "What do you think about a grand reopening?"

"I think it's a great idea. Except we open in"—Carly checks the clock over the serving window—"ten minutes."

"I'm thinking bigger. Every business on the square was affected by the storm, either a little or a lot." I cross my arms over my chest. "I'm talking a blowout party. We decide on a day, and all the businesses on the square offer special prices to bring people downtown, then a dance that night. Whatcha think?"

"I think you should have sex more often. You think better." Carly nods.

"Lorelei got *laid*?" Nevada takes a step, and just when I think she's going to hug me, she puts up a fist to bump instead. "Way to go, boss."

My face flames, but at the same time, it's kind of nice to be inside the relationship banter for a change.

Carly bumps my shoulder in silent support. "We could use it as a fundraiser, too, for families who didn't have insurance."

There's a knock at the front window. Moss and Manny are standing, hands cupped around their eyes, peering in.

"Looks like we're back in business." Carly pushes off the counter. "Let's do this."

* * *

The next week is the grand reopening celebration, and if the other merchants are half as busy as we've been, it's a huge success. All our employees are working open to close, and even so, we can hardly keep up. Between the breakfast and lunch rush, Sassy cruises by carrying a tray loaded with dirty dishes.

"Hold the fort for a minute, will you, Sassy? I've got to get some fresh air."

"I'll try, Lorelei, but don't be gone too long."

"I won't." I hold the door open for more customers, then step out.

We couldn't have ordered a more perfect day. The August sun is baking, but a bit of a breeze flips the edges of the sunshades that dot the town square. Under them, vendors with home-baked goods, quilts, artwork, and Native crafts are on display, and the Lions Club beer truck is doing a brisk business.

Scars of the storm are everywhere. City maintenance chainsawed the dead trees, and the ones that are left are almost stripped of leaves. But the bandstand survived, and the high school kids draped everything in twinkle lights for the dance tonight.

We've survived the railroad spur closing, I-40 being rerouted away, and Route 66 falling out of the public's eye—it's going to take more than a tornado to kill my hometown.

I say hi to locals passing, then lean against the building, pull out my phone, and type.

L: It's a gorgeous day. Downtown is packed, and I heard

we've already raised over 5000 for charity. This party is going to be epic. I wish you could be here.

R: Not as much as I do. Damned negotiations are taking forever. Even if I flew out now, I couldn't get there in time. We knew it was a long shot.

L: Yeah, but…Sawyer says she misses you. We haven't seen you in a week!

R: Only Sawyer?

L: Okay, I admit I was looking forward to dancing tonight.

R: I'm being used. You just wanted a dance partner.

L: And the bed is too big.

R: See? Used. I knew it.

L: :p

R: Sorry, gotta go. I'll call later, k?

L: k.

I slip the phone into my pocket. The old saw about absence and fond hearts is true. It's funny; I've never had a man around full-time in my life, but after living with Reese for a week, I miss him like crazy. There are a million things a day that I want to tell him, to ask his opinion about. Every night after Sawyer is asleep, I sit on the patio with a jelly glass of his elderberry wine, wishing his deep rumbly voice would come out of the dark.

I'm nervous about it, but I've even started imagining a future with him. It's distant and fuzzy-edged, but these days I'm daring to hope.

The cabin is gaining comforts by the day. The walls are in, and the flooring should be complete when I get home tonight. Reese gave me a credit card number and free rein to buy furniture, but so far I haven't. I've spent a lot of hours on the Internet, researching, but actually purchasing will cross some invisible line, and though my finger hovers, I haven't worked up the courage to hit that button. But I want to.

This in-between time in our relationship is equal parts impatience and indecision, fun and fear. But damn, I wish he could be here tonight.

* * *

Reese

I pocket my phone and pull the door to the john.

James Travis is washing his hands at the sink. "Don't worry, boy. They're tighter than a nun's asshole, but we'll get them to come around to our terms, you'll see."

I wince at the slur that makes me want to take a swipe at his gleeful smile. My father was a hard man, but at least he had a little class—why did he pick this guy for a best friend? I've been researching new attorneys, but with Lorelei and Sawyer here for a week, then me there, I haven't had time to interview any yet. "Can you finish up the meeting without me? I've got somewhere to be."

His bushy gray eyebrows rise. "You got that hot aunt stashed at home? I hear she's a looker."

I jerk straight. How does he know Lorelei was here? Someone in my employ has a big mouth. "Really don't see how that's any of your business, and you'll keep a civil tongue when you talk about Lorelei West."

He wipes his hands on a paper towel, then holds them up. "Hey, I think it's a smart move. You can't beat 'em, bed 'em. That's what I always say."

Before I think, I'm across the room and his tie is twisted around my hand. "I warned you."

His fat face turns crimson, and his mouth opens. I get

a close-up spider veins on his nose and cheeks, care of his other best friend—Jim Beam.

He's not worth it. I let go and give him a little shove away from me. "You disgust me. If you weren't my father's friend…"

He's breathing heavy, and he backs up until he's against the wall. "You little pissant."

A sly look slides onto his face. "Don't you talk to me about your father. You couldn't carry his jockstrap." His lips curl from his teeth, making him look like a fat raccoon caught raiding a trash can. "Your father thought you were useless; did you know that? Little whiner. He was half-afraid that after the accident you'd be batting for the other team." He throws the paper towel toward the trash and misses.

"I guess that West woman figures the money makes up for the lack of"—he glances to the zipper of my pants—"other things."

My hands fist, longing to pound that arrogant face. "You're fired."

"You can't fire me. I've worked for a St. James for over forty years."

"And as of now you don't. You got a problem with that, call my father and take it up with him." I turn and stalk for the door. "I'll have my new attorney stop by and pick up every record of the St. Jameses' business dealings." I push the door open, and it bangs against the wall. "You make sure it's all there."

I stride to the meeting room, and all heads rise when I open the door. "I'm sorry, we're going to have to reschedule. I've just fired my attorney. My new attorney will be in touch."

Then I'm jogging down the hall and out to my truck. If I can get in the air within the half hour, I may make that party.

CHAPTER 21

Lorelei

I'm kneeling on a booth cushion in the shadowy diner, chin on my hands, watching the couples dip and sway in pretty circles under the fairy lights in the square. Pat and the Squeaky Wheels are belting out their rendition of George Strait's "I Just Want to Dance with You."

Looks like even Nevada couldn't resist. Fish holds her like she's made of crystal, and her love-struck expression tells me they're *both* getting lucky tonight.

I sigh.

Something touches my leg, and I whirl.

A three-year-old towhead is tugging on my pants leg and rubbing his eyes.

I press a hand to my chest to hold in my banging heart. "Mason, you're supposed to be asleep."

"I'm firsty."

I smile down at him. "Well, we can't have that." I stand and lift him into my arms, taking in his sleepy-kid smell.

He wraps his arms around my shoulders and lays his head on my chest.

Every babysitter within ten miles is at the dance, so I agreed to watch the little ones. There's a dozen of them, including Sawyer and Carly's two, sacked out on sleeping bags or in car seats on the floor. I had help when the kids were awake, but once we got them settled for bed, I shooed everyone out.

I dance the little guy across the floor, spinning and dipping until he giggles. "Shhh. We don't want to wake everybody." I pour milk in a little plastic cup, and he takes a couple of sips, then hands it back. Probably just woke up in a strange place and wanted reassurance. He's asleep by the time I lay him back down.

I check the clock over the serving window. The dance will be over in ten minutes. I resume my perch on the booth cushions. A slow song is next, matching the melancholy shade of my mood. The wistful chords tug at my heart, making me wish again that Reese could have been here. We'd be dancing, one of his hands cradling mine, the other at the hollow of my back, claiming me. Another sigh.

Stop it, Lorelei. In the old days, this was your life: watching through the glass at other people having fun. This is just one night. Reese said he'd be back in a couple of days, and…I notice a man in a cowboy hat, his back to me, watching the dancers and talking to the woman next to him. When she turns and points to the café, my heart does a tap dance against my ribs. He turns. I'd know that strong jaw anywhere.

He's here! I scramble off the cushions and bounce for the door. When he pulls it open, I launch myself into his arms, knocking off his hat. "I can't believe you came," I say in an excited whisper and kiss his face all over.

He hugs me tight. "This makes it worth the trip." He squeezes me, then bends to pick up his hat.

I hold my finger to my lips, take his hand, and tiptoe around the pod of sleeping children to the kitchen. I can watch them through the serving window. "Did your meeting end early?" In the fluorescents, I get a good look at his face. "What's wrong?"

"Nothing. I'm just dead tired."

But I know his face so well. Behind the tired, there's pain. "Tell me."

He puts his hands in his pockets. "I fired my attorney today."

"Why?"

"A bunch of reasons really. It's been coming on a long time."

He pulls a hand from his pocket and rubs his eyes, reminding me of Mason earlier. "You poor thing. The dance is over soon, and when all the kids are gone, I'm taking you home and putting you to bed. I'll even let you sleep, this time." I stand on tiptoe to give him a quick kiss. But he opens his mouth and takes me in, and I'm lost to everything but him. He rocks me back and forth in a stationary dance, and his cologne fills my head, the scent that my brain equates with security, support...and sex.

"Lorelei, where are—oh, hello, Reese." Carly's in the doorway, wearing a huge grin.

He breaks the kiss but doesn't let me go. "Hi, Carly. You're looking fetching tonight."

Her curls bounce when she does a step-turn, and the rhinestones flash on her jeans pockets. "Nothing like a night out to take you back to your rodeo-queen days. And all the mommas hereabouts have you to thank for that, Lorelei.

You're a love for watching the kids." She steps over and kisses my cheek.

"Are you kidding? It's me that owes you. You've been watching Sawyer every day."

Austin sticks his head in the serving window. "I cut our calves out of the herd out here, hon. You ready to go?"

"My kids as cattle. That's what I get for marrying a cowboy." Carly smiles. "Head 'em up, move 'em out, big guy."

By the time we get the kids matched with their parents, the café locked, and we hit the road, it's after midnight. I settle Sawyer in her crib at the cabin while Reese looks around. "They've gotten a lot done."

"The Sheetrock is done, and they say the floors will be done tomorrow." I walk to the fridge, pull out a beer for him, and carry it to the card table.

"When is the furniture going to be delivered?" He sits, twists off the cap, and takes a long swallow.

"I've got some stuff picked out, but I was waiting for your opinion."

"Hon, I told you, you don't need my approval. If you like it, I'll like it."

I brush a crumb off the pebbly surface of the table. "It's expensive, Reese. I don't feel comfortable making decisions that big with someone else's money."

"I've told you before, the money doesn't matter."

Easy to say when you have more than you need. "I'm just not used to it, that's all."

"I'll look at what you've picked out tomorrow, if that'll make you feel better." He takes a swig of his beer. "Right now, I'm beat."

"How long can you stay?"

"I've got to fly out tomorrow morning."

"You came all this way for one night?"

"I'd go farther than that for one night with you." My skin heats with his smoking gaze.

I stand and hold out my hand. "Then why are we out here wasting it?"

He turns the lights out on the way to the bedroom, and the darkness wraps around us, shutting out the world.

He undresses me slowly, running his hands over every bit of skin as it's exposed. Then he lays me on the covers and tastes. Parts of me flick on—parts I didn't know could be turned on: the backs of my knees, the arch of my foot, between my fingers. With the lack of sight, my other senses sharpen. A hot, empty place builds inside, urging me to hurry.

He kisses me, deep and slow and lazy, like he has more time than one night and intends to take it all. It takes way too much time for him to strip and join me.

He proceeds to teach me things about myself. How the scrape of his beard stubble over my nipple can bring my back off the bed. How a hot breath in my ear can make me spasm. How a giving, reverent touch can open parts of me I didn't know were closed.

When I'm squirming and begging him with my kisses and my tongue to take me, he spreads my legs wide, so my heels are off the sides of the narrow bed. I hear the crinkle of a condom wrapper, and then he's there, slipping just the head of his throbbing cock to the edge of me, whispering, "Now?"

"Oh please, now."

He laces our fingers together on either side of my head, then plunges into me.

I suck in a breath and my fingers clench on his.

Slow, so slow, he withdraws, until he's at the edge of me again, then holds. Holds. Holds.

When he plunges again, I lose all control. My heels are on the bed, and I rise to meet every thrust, kissing him wildly, willing him faster. Faster. Faster.

A titanic orgasm starts high and rolls over me, spasming my body and exploding my mind. His mouth takes in my scream and he thrusts.

I feel his release, and my body takes it, milking him for more.

Then we're falling, locked together, perfectly in sync, as one.

There is only the dark and the sound of our quieting breaths. He cradles me as if I'm as fragile as a child's wish.

His lips touch mine in a delicate kiss that somehow tastes like promises. "A tragedy brought us together. A baby made sure we stayed that way. So much has happened in the past months, I feel like our new family has been forged from fire." He kisses my forehead. "I've never been happier than I am right now."

And with his words I realize that despite the pain of the past months, neither have I.

* * *

Reese

There's a buzzing, like swarming bees in my brain. Lorelei's face is illuminated, squinting in the light of her cell phone.

"What time is it?" I mumble.

"Four." She lifts my arm off her chest.

"What? Why?" I grab her wrist when she sits up. "You don't get up 'til five." It's dark, and the bed is a warm nest, made for snuggling—and more, going by the strength of my woody.

She sits up and drops her feet to the floor. "That was before I had to get Sawyer ready and drive her across town to Carly's."

I groan. So much for picking up where we left off last night. "You don't need to, you know."

"Yeah, I do. If I don't open on time, they'll beat down the door." She flips on the dime-store lamp on the floor and reaches for the clothes she laid out last night.

"No, I mean you don't need to work anymore." The past days have changed things. What I thought was forever beyond my reach is no longer a mirage—it's real, solid, so close on the horizon, I can almost touch it. "I still think we should get a nanny for Sawyer, but if you're opposed to that, why don't you stay home with her?"

"What are you talking about?" She hooks her bra, then shrugs into a white blouse.

I push myself up on one elbow. "Don't you see? You don't *have* to work. You can have the luxury of being a full-time mom."

She frowns. "What makes you think I want that?"

"You told me yourself that Carly can't watch Sawyer forever, so rather than stick Sawyer in day care, picking up germs and bad habits and who knows what all, she could be hanging with you, at home. You could spend more time with her and be there for all the big moments." I shrug. "Win-win. What could be better for you both?"

"What on earth are you talking about?" She stands and pulls her jeans up with jerky movements. "I have to work."

"Hon, that's what I'm saying. You don't." I sit up. She's worked so hard her whole life. I've looked forward to easing that burden, to spoil her with the luxury of time.

"I like to work." She tucks her shirt into her jeans.

"Okay, then, you could go to school, get your degree. With that, you could—"

Her eyes narrow. "I *like* being manager of the café. I'm good at it."

"Of course you are." I have got to learn the language she speaks, because I mean well, but most times I end up chewing my boot. "But now you can be anything you want. You're smart enough. You want to be a doctor? An attorney? We'll make it happen."

Her brows come down. "I see. What you're saying is that a manager of a café isn't good enough for you."

No way I'm getting back to sleep after this. I stand and reach for my pants. "Dammit, that's not what I'm saying." She's really pissed. "You twist my words and make me sound like some elitist ass. I'm not."

"Well, let's recap…" She steps into her shoes. "In the past five minutes you've told me"—she ticks off my transgressions on her fingers—"I should stay home with Sawyer, eating bonbons and teaching her skills she's never going to get stuffed away in a germ-filled tenement, and barring that, I should become a brain surgeon." She plants her hands on her hips and glares.

"I did not, and you know it." Now she's trying to piss me off. If she wants a fight… "I thought you'd appreciate being able to relax and not holding the weight of the world on your shoulders for a change. What's so bad about that?"

"It's not. But as usual, *you* dictate what I should want. Who made you the purveyor of what is good for my life?"

"Okay. You like being a café manager. Great. If that makes you happy, I'm happy. But what about Sawyer? Look, Unforgiven is a great town, but let's just say there's a reason I chose your school system to donate to, okay?"

"Oh, really? My career isn't good enough, and now my hometown isn't? I'm relegating Sawyer to growing up poor white trash because she goes to day care? For your information, I grew up in this school system, and I did just fine." Her voice spirals. "Wait, let me guess. She's be *so* much better off if she had a fancy nanny teaching her proper manners, followed by a snooty private school. Or better yet, a home-school tutor. Yeah, *that's* it. She could grow up a cultured elitist snob, hanging out at the country club with all the other trust-fund babies." She puts a finger to her flushed cheek. "Oh, wait. We don't have a country club in our back-woods burg. Whatever shall we do?" She raises her finger and her voice. "I know, we'll move to Texas, where things are so high class and wonderful. Of course that house is as cold and sterile as a hospital operating room, but what the heck? She'd do great there!"

Sawyer wails in the other room.

Lorelei's shoulders slump, and a desperate look of sadness replaces anger. "I always dreamed a man would come along who would see past Patsy's sparkle, to see me. To want me for exactly who I am. I thought I found him. Apparently not."

This morning has gone to shit. And I'm not sure why, or how to fix it. "That's not fair. I'm trying to make your life easier, and you make it sound like—"

"Oh, my hero." She wrings her hands. "It's a miracle I survived until you came to rescue me from the dumpster." She stalks out of the room.

I grab a T-shirt, pull it over my head, and follow, stubbing my toe on the cement floor. "Sonofa*bitch*!" I hop to lean against the bedroom doorjamb, clutching my foot.

"Tsk, tsk." Lorelei unsnaps Sawyer's pants in spite of the fact that the baby is flailing, kicking, and crying. "Is that any way to talk in front of a future debutante?" She looks down. "Sawyer, quit already. We've got to get you ready."

I hobble to the crib. "You go get ready. I'll change her." I grab a diaper and reach for the baby.

"I've got it." She snatches the diaper from me. "You've done quite enough already." She catches Sawyer's feet and positions the diaper under her.

"What the hell, Lorelei?" I'm slow to anger, but damn, this is too much. "Now I can't change her? Will it always be like this? Me getting the tag ends with her, when you're done and gone off to your little day job?"

Sawyer lets loose, peeing on herself, the diaper, and the bedding. "Really, little girl?" Lorelei looks up at me, eyes glittering with malice. "Oh, it's my *little* job now? Amazing what comes out when we get right down to it."

"Yeah, it is. I didn't know how you thought about my home. My upbringing. My family."

She pulls out the diaper with one hand, a wipe with the other. "Shit. I do not have time for this." With efficient movements, she wrangles the baby, cleans her, pulls the tabs, and secures the diaper. "I haven't mentioned your family. But now that you bring it up, I've gotta tell you, you're sounding a lot like your father. Your way or the highway." She grabs a top and shorts from the garbage bag of clean baby clothes on the floor.

"Oh, that's a low blow. And you have no idea what the hell you're talking about." At my shout, Sawyer ramps it up to that high-pitched baby screech that runs fingernails down my chalkboard nerves and vibrates my eardrums.

"It's okay, baby girl. He'll be flying off to Oz soon, where the streets are paved with gold." She says it in a lilting nursery-rhyme voice and pulls the shirt over Sawyer's head, then lifts her and bounces her to soothe her. "Oh yeah, you're not mean. You don't decorate with dead animals. But you're like a landslide, overcoming opposition with your money and your charm."

"Goddamn it, I don't *have* any charm!"

She clutches Sawyer to her chest. "Finally, something we agree on."

The future I could almost touch has vanished overnight. Being a loner is preferable to twisting yourself in knots to be someone you're not or apologizing for who you are. "You knew I had money from the very first day. I can't change that. Excuse me for trying to make yours and Sawyer's lives better." I stomp to the bedroom. "I've got to go." I throw my clothes in my duffel, grab my stuff from the bathroom, and heave it in. In two minutes, I'm out the door. In fifteen, I'm taxiing down the bumpy dirt runway.

I've got four hours of flying time to figure out how I went from *I love you* to turning into my father.

I'm *not* like Bo.

Am I?

CHAPTER 22

Reese

I'm in the barn cleaning stalls, because filthy grunt work is about all I'm good for right now. Two days and still no word. I've thought eighteen thousand times about calling her, but since I don't know how that argument started to begin with, I stand a good chance of making it happen again. And that could cause damage I can't fix.

How did she get the idea I wanted to change her? I want her just the way she is. Except, obviously, not mad, and closer. She's a wonderful mother to Sawyer. How could I imagine that I'd think any different?

And while I'm shoveling shit, I might as well admit that I'm wounded. If she was looking for a chink in my armor, she found it. I've tried to look at my behavior through her eyes, and it hurts to recognize I see Bo in how I reacted.

I put aside the pitchfork and walk to the house.

The front door opens with a click that echoes down the hall. I glance to the empty gold stand, remembering that perfect memory of Sawyer's first steps. Missing her and Lorelei tugs at my heart.

I glance left, to the formal living room, where my mother's portrait hangs over the mantel. Her eyes seem to follow me as I walk past the door. I stop and go back.

The room smells of lemon furniture polish and floor wax. I drop onto the ornate French Provincial couch and study her. The story is that Bo wanted her to pose on the grand staircase in a formal gown for that portrait, but Mom refused. Instead, this is the mother I almost remember: a handsome woman with soft eyes, sitting in front of the fire in a high-collared white blouse and a Pendleton plaid wool skirt, her favorite papillon pup at her feet. She studies me back.

"What, Mom? What am I missing?"

No answer. Which is probably a good thing. Neither ghosts nor crazy runs in our family.

I pick up the cut-crystal egg in the ornate stand on the coffee table and hold it up to the light. It probably cost more than Lorelei makes in a month. I focus past it, to the window's light and the dust motes dancing in it. They will pile up on the floor and the furniture. Someone will come by and dust them away, and they'll begin falling again.

Suddenly the air seems heavy. Dead—as if it's been trapped in this room for decades. The house is silent, save the ticking of the ornate grandfather clock in the corner. It gets louder, ticking the seconds into minutes. Minutes to days, days to decades...

I can't breathe.

I shoot off the couch and stalk to the dining room. The drapes hold the air in here, too.

Why didn't I leave this place long ago? Worse yet, why didn't it even cross my mind to do so?

Because I didn't really understand what home meant

until I stepped into Lorelei's well-lived-in farmhouse. Home may be a place, but it's only walls and a roof to hold your *people*.

I want more. Way more than this.

I need to understand what it is about me that pisses Lorelei off. My money? Yeah, she's been uncomfortable with it, but it wasn't the money she was yelling about the other day. What did she call me? A landslide. I decide what I want and then go get it.

That's true. It's what makes me a good businessman.

It also makes me like my father.

Both Carson and I were pushed, bullied, and herded to what Bo wanted. We were St. Jameses, a reflection of—and on—him.

Carson went along.

I rebelled.

But did I really? I didn't rodeo or drink whiskey or make crude remarks, but funny how the career I chose complemented Bo's empire nicely. Was my rebellion a capitulation? When you're indoctrinated from an early age, who's to say what was your idea and what was just an acceptable alternative?

But I can't get distracted by tangents. The past can't be changed, and this isn't about me. It's about Lorelei. She tried to tell me all this from the first day I met her. But I thought I knew what was best. For her, for Sawyer. I muscled in, threw money around, and expected things to go my way. How is that any different from Bo?

Lorelei

Two days since Reese stomped out and still no word from him. I'm glad. Okay, not really, but I'm thankful for the time to think. I was angry. I regret saying he was like his father. Insinuating his life is like his house—cold and empty.

I'm guilty of having lost my temper but not of saying anything that isn't true. I just wish I'd said it a little gentler. A little less angry.

In a vacuum, I don't know if he thinks we're fighting, or if we're over. Hell, I'm not even sure which outcome I'm rooting for. On one hand, he is the first man who saw past the waitress, the caregiver, the doer, to *me*. I finally believed that was who he wanted. But if he wants to change me into whatever his idea of a St. James woman is, we *are* done.

"Hey, Lorelei, you gonna bogart that coffeepot, or can we have some?"

When Moss holds his mug out, I realize I've been standing and staring out the front windows far too long. "Oh, yeah. Sorry." I pour. "You want a refill, Manny?"

"Sure."

I pretend I don't see the flask of white lightning he tips into it before offering the mug.

He studies me as I pour. "Where's that old, polecat, Reese, today?"

Moss smacks his friend in the arm. "Shut up, ya idjit. I told you they were broken up."

"Oh. I forgot."

I roll my eyes to the stamped tin ceiling. I love many things about this town, but personal business traveling at the speed of light isn't among them.

Manny's eyes are full of bloodshot sincerity. "He prob'ly did something stupid, but he means well. I'm sure of it."

I wish it were that simple. "Good, then you can go out with him."

"I'm just saying, you should give a guy a chance, you know—"

"I now know why they named this town Unforgiven."

Moss perks up at his favorite subject. "You do?"

"Men. You figure it out." I slam the coffeepot on the warmer and steam for my office, where I won't get any more work done than I have the past two days.

Should Sawyer and I move out of the cabin? They've started demolition on the second story of my house, so we'd be living downstairs amid dust and chaos, but we're gone before dawn and home after dusk, so we wouldn't be in the workers' way. Not a great one, maybe, but it's an option. Plan B.

My bruised heart keeps thumping, the pain a constant reminder that I'm living in limbo. I don't want a plan B. I miss Reese. Sawyer keeps asking for her Baba.

I miss us.

Maybe I should be the one to call. What would I say? Nothing has changed.

But…

An hour of vacillating later, I am interrupted by Sassy sticking her head in my office. "There's a guy out here asking for you."

My heart taps a hopeful dance, and the corners of my mouth lift. "Reese?"

"Nah. Some guy I've never seen before."

I sigh and push to my feet. Probably a vendor's rep, trying to poach my business. I push through the swinging door to the dining room. The stranger sticks out of the crowd. He's young, with slicked-back hair and expensive shoes. And he's the only one in a suit.

"Lorelei West?"

"Yes."

"Do you live at 305 Solomon Lane in Unforgiven, New Mexico?"

Alarm jangles down my nerves. "That's none of your business. Who are you?"

"Process server for Travis & Partners." He hands me a folded piece of paper.

Heart banging, I open what looks like a legal document and scan it as he turns away. Summons...Form numbers, legalese, blah, blah CUSTODY: Sawyer West.

Knees shaking, I stumble back, steady myself on the counter, and skip to the signature at the bottom. Reese St. James.

"Lorelei? What is it?" Moss catches my arm. Then he looks down at the paper. "Why that chickenshit piece of Texas trash."

There are black spots floating at the edge of my vision. I just stand there, trying to gulp air. This cannot be happening.

Manny leans over. "What? What's that paper?"

"Reese is going to try to fight Lorelei for custody of Sawyer."

"Nah, he wouldn't," Manny says in a disbelieving tone.

"He did." Moss, cradling my elbow, walks me over and pushes through the door to the kitchen.

Nevada looks up from the grill. "Moss, what the hell are you doing back here?"

"Get her some water. She's in shock."

He deposits me in the chair in my office. "Put your head down. You don't look so good."

I'd argue, but despite my lungs straining, I can't get enough air. I put my elbows on my knees and pull out the trash can, just in case my stomach decides to bail my lunch.

He wouldn't.

He did.

There must be a mistake.

He said he loved *me.*
Sawyer!
I launch to my feet. "I have to go."

"Whoa there." Moss pushes me back down.

Nevada shoves him out the door and sets a bottle of water on the desk.

"I have to get Sawyer." I sniff, and my fingers clench the open air. "I have to see her. Touch her. Ohmygod, what am I going to do?"

"Hang on." Nevada pushes my shoulders to keep me in the chair. "You'll kill yourself behind the wheel like this. Besides, she's with Carly, and she'd never let anyone have Sawyer. She may talk all sweet, but she could take The Rock when she goes all momma bear, and you know it." She pulls a tissue from the box on the desk and hands it to me.

That's when I realize tears are sheeting down my face, dripping off my chin. "He *signed* that form. He knows what it would do to me. How could he *do* that?"

Rhetorical question. Because he did it. Which makes him worse than my first choice in men. My almost-fiancé just used me. My stomach is a cauldron of simmering emotion: hurt, betrayal, and a building anger. "He's rich. You know he can hire the best attorneys out there. Hell, he already hired them." I must be in shock, because my brain moves like a drunken sloth, and my hands have the DTs.

Nevada parks her butt on the desk. "He's from Texas. This is New Mexico. Our courts gave you custody. He'd have to find a damned fine reason to reverse that, and he won't be able to, because there isn't one." Nevada's voice is calm, but her eyes dart, as if looking for someone to take over with the crazy lady.

My mind scrabbles, running a highlight reel of every second Reese was around. The vase! Could that be construed to be neglect? But it happened at *his* house. The tornado? Because I didn't let him put on a new roof? Have I done anything...*not* done anything I should have?

"Carly? I think you'd better get down here." Nevada's talking into her phone. "Yeah, bring the kids. You'll see when you get here."

Rage bubbles over the edge of the cauldron, and the panic clears from my brain. I pull open the drawer and snatch my phone. I may not have much of my mind right now, but he's going to get a good piece of what's left.

* * *

Reese

My phone rings in the pocket of my shirt. I pull it...Her name on the screen makes my stomach drop and my mood rise. I swipe the screen. "I'm so glad you called. I've been—"

"How *could* you?" Her voice smacks my eardrum. "You don't like me, fine. Dump me, but this...is the lowest, shittiest..."

Was that a *sob*?

"I don't give a crap that you have more money than God. You're not getting your way this time. I'll fight you. I'll fight you 'til I have nothing. Then I'll steal what I need to keep fighting. You're going to be sorry you messed with this country girl, you lousy, lowlife, stinking *liar*."

Click.

I stare at my phone like it's going to explain whatever the hell just happened. This isn't the argument from the other day—something has sent her ballistic, but what? I feel like a guilty kid, except I didn't do anything.

I'd text, but I have no way to know if she'll read it, so I hit redial. It goes straight to voice mail.

My mind grabs and discards reasons, possibilities, and solutions, but it's impossible. I don't have enough information. How do I get more? Remembering, I pull my wallet from my pocket and retrieve the number for the café I wrote on a scrap of paper.

I dial.

"Chestnut Creek Café."

"Nevada. It's Reese St. James. What is—"

"You are lucky you're not here, dude. I've killed before, and I damned sure can do it again. I can't believe you have the balls to call here after—"

"Wait! After what? What happened?"

"Do not insult my intelligence. You know damned well what."

"Dammit, I *don't*. Will someone please tell me what the hell is going on?"

"You're going to pretend you don't know Lorelei was just served with the custody papers you sent? Papers *you* signed?" She makes a disgusting sound, like she's getting ready to spit. "You don't deserve it, but I'll give you a piece of advice. Don't show up here. Every man jack around will be watching out for you. You mess with our people, you're going to find out firsthand why this town was named Unforgiven."

Click.

Travis. That sonofabitch. He not only served the papers I told him to tear up, he forged my name? I take off in a jog for my truck. He's gone off the deep end to pull something like this. I know the man—it isn't so much that I fired him, but the way I fired him. His ego has gotten in the way of his brain. James Travis and I are going to have a *talk*.

I have the truck running by the time my brain kicks in. My knuckles go white on the wheel. This is what he wants. If I give him half of what he deserves, he'll have me arrested. And Bo hired him because he's a pit bull in the courtroom— *he'll* end up looking like the injured party.

As much as it would make me feel better to confront him in person, there's a better way.

The perfect irony. I'll take him to court. I'll have him disbarred. I'll have *him* thrown in jail.

I shut down the truck and stalk for the house. I've got bigger problems. I've got to straighten this out with Lorelei. It hurts me, imagining how she must be freaking out.

She's not going to believe a word I say. After all, I promised to back off before and didn't.

I'm going to have to find a way, though, because I was kidding myself; once you find the love of a fine woman and a family, there's no going back to being a loner.

Somehow, I've got to convince her that I have enough love for her to surmount everything in our way...even my own stupidity.

CHAPTER 23

Reese

I touch down on San Antonio's Stinson Airport runway, taxi to the main building, shut the engine down, get out, and chock the wheels.

I've spent the last three days beating myself up. After a ton of shit-shoveling, I finally have a plan that I can live with.

I hate the plan. I'm not even sure I'm capable of carrying it out. But it's the only way that stands a chance of convincing Lorelei that I love her for *her*—no strings attached.

And that stipulation means I'm taking a chance. The biggest chance of my life.

I may never see Sawyer or Lorelei again.

Just thinking it makes me nauseous. I pull the door to the airport lobby, grateful for the cool slap of air. My new attorney stands from the couch and strides forward to shake my hand.

"Mr. St. James, good to see you again." Paul Conroy is tall and thin, brown haired, and baby-faced young. But I did my research: top of his class at UT, on track to be the youngest partner in the history of one of the most esteemed attorney firms in Houston before leaving to start his own practice. Smart, hungry, and not afraid to take risks. Just what I'm looking for.

"Name's Reese, and thanks for coming out here to meet me. You saved me an hour of San Antonio traffic."

He gives me a confident smile. "As of today, you are my biggest client. I'll drive to your ranch if you want me to."

"I'll have you out and show you around one weekend. In the meantime, shall we get started?" I lead him down a corridor to a conference room that the airport manager allows me to rent by the hour. We sit. I pull out papers. He pulls out a legal pad and pen. "As I said on the phone, we have several items to discuss. The first is my ex-attorney; then we'll get to the important part…"

* * *

Lorelei

I wake in panic, seeing another unfamiliar ceiling. When my seeking fingers touch Sawyer's warm, chubby leg, I let out a sigh and relax. I'm in Carly and Austin's downstairs bedroom. They offered a crib for Sawyer upstairs, but I can't sleep if she's not close enough to touch. I know it's silly. It's not like Reese is going to sneak in the house and kidnap her. But my heart and my instincts have taken over. Besides, Sawyer keeps the bed from being too damned empty.

I don't know what I would have done without Carly. She showed up that awful day last week, drove us out to the cabin, helped me gather my stuff and lock the door. I roll over and look out the window. The pink-tinted clouds on a backdrop of baby blue—it's going to be another gorgeous scorcher. And it's Sunday, my day off.

I tickle Sawyer awake, then roll out of bed. Such a happy kid. Looking back, pre-Sawyer, my life before her seems so long ago. She's my constant reminder that my mantra is more important than ever. *Face forward.* Another tornado touched down—this time a personal one—and it tore up my life. But I have Sawyer. She's my anchor and my joy. I catch her hand and kiss it. If I can give her one-tenth of what she's given me, I'll have succeeded as a mom.

When Carly walks into the kitchen, I've got coffee going and Sawyer in a high chair eating Cheerios and bananas in yogurt.

Carly's curls are rampant, and she's wearing an old chenille bathrobe that was probably white at one time. But even in no makeup, she's gorgeous. "What're you doing up? This is your day to sleep in." She puts the back of her hand to a yawn.

"I'm making breakfast for everyone. Where's Austin?" I open the fridge door and pull out the egg carton and a block of cheddar.

"Oh, he's long gone. He's picking up a bull in Santa Fe this morning, and he's so excited about the bloodline, he hardly slept last night."

"And I'll bet you thought up some way to distract him."

Redheads blush so easily.

She shoots me a smug smile and pulls from the cupboard a mug with *Unforgiven Feed & Tack* on the side. "First, coffee. Then I've got to get the kids up and ready." She pours, gives my cup a warm-up, and returns the pot. "Are you coming to Nana's with us today? You know she'd be thrilled to have you."

I take down a mixing bowl and crack eggs into it. "I know, and I appreciate the invite, but I think Sawyer and I will take some flowers out to the cemetery. Then I want to run by the house and see how they're progressing."

She steps close and squints. "How're you doing?"

"I called a family law attorney in Albuquerque. I have an appointment on Tuesday." I beat those eggs hard enough to make their mommas dizzy. If I stay focused, minute to minute, I'm fine. It's when I have spare moments, quiet, alone moments, that the hole in me expands. I miss him. And I hate myself for missing him.

"You deserve to be happy, Lorelei. I don't know why you have such dismal luck with men."

"Maybe I'm naive. I say yes to the ones that smarter women see through." Or maybe those are the only ones who want me.

Her head is shaking before my words are out. "We all thought the first one was for real. And I was personally rooting for Reese." She waves a hand. "Until they both proved to be lying manipulative scumbags, of course."

Of course.

* * *

Two hours later, I pull into the cemetery and drive to our plots. I release Sawyer from the car seat, and she tells me her latest, greatest word. "Down."

I lift the bouquets from the seat, take her hand, and we toddle our way to the graves. Daddy's long headstone has a blank spot next to his name: a place for Momma's in a time hopefully decades from now. "Hey, Daddy. I'm looking out for Momma, just like I promised you. You rest easy now." I lay the bouquet on the grass by the stone.

I lead Sawyer to Patsy's grave. The disturbed sod pushes a thumb into my bruised heart. It's not quite level but getting there. "Hey, Patsy. I brought Sawyer to visit." She plops down on the grave to pull handfuls of grass. I kneel beside her and prop the last bouquet against the stone. "She's such a happy, wonderful child. You should be so proud..." I have to pause until my throat unlocks. "You don't have to worry. Your daughter is *not* going to be raised anywhere but with me, right here in Unforgiven." I jerk out a weed. "I *swear* it to you."

I give in and cry for the dead. And for us, the left behind.

Twenty minutes later, I pull into our rutted dirt drive and up to the back door of the house. When I realize I'm avoiding looking at the cabin, I force my gaze up the slight hill. I wonder how much progress the workers made to the interior this week. "None of your business," I mumble, and unsnap the seat belt. I free Sawyer from the car seat.

"Down."

"I can't, Peanut. We're going into the house, and I shudder to think what you'd get into."

She points to the cabin. "Baba."

I catch her hand. "No Baba, hon." If I have my way, we'll never see him again. Any man who cared so little about Sawyer that he'd try to rip her from my arms...If he's hurting, he can just look in the mirror.

"Baba." She sticks out her lower lip.

I hand her the car keys as a shiny distraction and carry her to the house. I called the contractor on Tuesday, told him to halt work on the upstairs and focus on getting the ground floor livable. We can't stay with Carly forever, and the sooner Sawyer and I can move in, the sooner we can start to create a new normal. Whatever that looks like.

The smell of hot mildew hits when I step in the door. The kitchen welcomes me with its shabby, familiar self. God, I've missed this house. The living room is empty, furniture having been carried off to the dump, and they've torn up the carpet. The baseboards are gone, and there's fresh plaster at the bottom of the walls. When that's done, they can lay the heartwood pine floor I chose. I'm still trying to decide on new furniture. I can only do a little at a time before getting overwhelmed, but I'm grateful for the insurance money that allows me to afford it.

Sawyer drops the keys, jerking me from my reverie. I shoot a look up the stairwell, but I'm not ready to go there. Will I ever be able to walk up those stairs without seeing the hole—to the house as well as my life?

Well, that's nothing I can figure out today. I pick up the keys, then bounce Sawyer on my hip. "You ready for our picnic?"

I'm not sure how much she understands, but she nods anyway.

"Okay, you can help." I carry her back to the car, set her on her feet, and take a sippy cup from the diaper bag. "Here, you can carry this." I put the strap over my shoulder, grab the quilt off the seat, and the grocery bag from the floorboard. "Let's go."

I lead the way to the front yard, blazing a trail through knee-high grass sprinkled with weeds, flowering a pretty yellow. "We'll pretend we're in a jungle." I spread the quilt under the red oak that's sheltered four generations of West picnics.

We sink onto it, the crushed-grass smell rising clean and fresh to my nose, reminding me that the world goes on, despite my personal drama. Note to self—be more like the world.

After slathering Sawyer in sunscreen, I open the grocery bag and lay out our lunch: cut-up fruit, ham and cheese cubes, Goldfish for dessert. I'm not adopting a baby-focused menu, but this was easier. There's a thermos of lemonade for me, water for Sawyer.

Sawyer has fallen asleep when a sedan pulls up to the far gate in Reese's fence. A tall man gets out, looks around, then unlocks the gate, pulls in, and closes the gate behind him.

Warning bells clang in my head. He has a key. Clean-cut in dress pants and an open-collared shirt, he sure isn't a worker. Architect, maybe?

I get to my knees to peer over the grass. He disappears around the cabin, only to return minutes later. He puts a hand up to shade his eyes, looking down the hill to the house. I duck. When I look up again, he's on his way to his car. Dang it—he's seen Marshmallow.

Well, what do I care? It's got nothing to do with me. Might as well get used to it. Reese will be living there soon. Unless he sells out, which gets my vote.

When the car turns left at the road, a lump of cold forms at the bottom of my throat, like a swallowed ice cube. Despite my willing him to move on, he pulls into my drive.

I stay crouched, then realize that when he finds me, I'm going to look like an idiot, hiding in the grass. Besides, West women don't run. I stand up as he gets out of his car, a thick file folder under his arm. "Are you lost?" Well, that's stupid. If he has a key to the gate, he's exactly where he wants to be.

He walks to the edge of the grass, then wades in. "Are you Lorelei?"

"Who wants to know?"

"I'm Paul Conroy, Mr. St. James's attorney." He holds out a hand.

My muscles jerk taut, shielding my bones. And my guts. "Get off my land." The words are frosty, having come from behind the ice cube in my throat.

"Miss, you don't understand. I'm—"

"I've had enough of Mr. St. James's legal business." I point a shaky finger toward his car. "Leave. Now."

"I understand your anger, but that travesty was not perpetrated by Mr. St. James. It was—"

"You don't get it. I do not *care*. Do I need to get my shotgun?" Daddy never owned one, but this city dude doesn't know that.

His baby face twists. "Could you please just hear me out?"

"No."

He squares his shoulders and his face firms to authoritative lines. "Ma'am, I'm sorry, but I can't leave until I give you some things."

Whatever it is doesn't have to touch me. He'll leave and I can forget all this. "Give it here."

"You can read them at your leisure, but I'll give you a quick summary." He hands me the folder. "Mr. St. James has set up two trust funds: one for you and one for the baby."

I scan the top page and suck in a breath. This is more money than I'd need to live on for twenty years. I flip to the next stapled pages. Sawyer gets the same amount. Enough to raise her and for a Harvard education, should she choose it. And I'm the trustee.

"He can't buy me or his niece."

"It's your choice, of course, but the funding is complete and in your name regardless. It's irrevocable."

That jolts me. "What about custody? Is he going to fight me?"

He points to the envelope. "In the back, there's an envelope with your name handwritten on it. Maybe that will answer your question." He reaches into his pocket. "Here is my card, should you have any questions. Thank you for hearing me out."

He takes the stomped-down trail through the grass, gets in his car, and drives away.

I flip past the legal documents to the envelope with my name on it. In Reese's handwriting.

I could tear it up, never read it.

But can I live with the *why*?

This envelope is Pandora's box in a great disguise.

True. But my last relationship ended in me running away in shame. I took it on, but that shame wasn't mine, dammit. Haven't I grown up at all? My emotions are agitated. Like sand in the surf, they rub my nerves raw. I have to know.

I sink onto the quilt, feeling like I've drunk from a firehose—it's too much to take in. My brain is waterlogged. I slit the envelope and pull out the heavy ivory sheet.

Lorelei,

I didn't send that paperwork. I didn't sign it. It hasn't been filed with the court. It never will be. My ex-attorney forged it, then sent it, in retaliation for me firing him.

But I didn't write to tell you that.

You were right. In many ways I am like my father. I promised that I wouldn't push you—then I started the land-slide. But that's not why I wrote this, either. I don't expect you to forgive me. You may not even care.

I wrote this because I couldn't live with myself if you thought that you weren't wonderful exactly as you are. You are strong and honest and the best mother Sawyer could ever have. I have no doubt that Carson and Patsy are looking down and smiling, knowing Sawyer will have everything she needs to grow up just like her new mother.

See, you taught me so much, not by what you said but by who you are: caring, giving, loving. Seeing myself— my life—through your eyes made me ashamed. I'm making changes going forward, but you probably don't care about that, either. And that's okay. I just couldn't live with myself if you thought less of yourself because of something I said.

I am the man you thought I was. Inside, I am. But when I open my mouth, that doesn't come out—something stupid does. I know you saw the real me hiding inside. I know it because a woman like you wouldn't have loved me otherwise. No matter what happens, I'll always be grateful for that, because you showed me that man is good just as he is. Not a hard-ass, not a hair-on-fire cowboy, but good, just the same.

You and I didn't get the chance to start small, like most couples do. All the "get to know you" essential things. We didn't get to because we started big—Sawyer big. I never got to know that you love your job for a lot more than the money it brings in; it's a part of who you are.

That's it. That's what I wanted to say.

My new attorney has given you the trust paperwork. It's not meant to change your mind or landslide you. It's free and clear. There are no strings, no qualifiers, no hidden agenda. If you don't want to take it from me, consider it from Carson. He'd want this.

If you'd rather, I'll sell the property—your family's former property. If you want to buy your legacy back, you now have the funds to do it.

Regardless, I'll continue to love you. Forever.

Reese

* * *

"Holy plot twist, Batman," Carly says.

It's dark, the kids are in bed, and we're sipping wine in their great room. "Tell me about it."

"I'm no lawyer, but this sure looks legit." Austin flips pages. "What are you going to do?"

"I'm not taking his money."

"Why not?" He drains his beer. "There aren't any strings that I can see, and the way it's set up, if you never touch it, that money just rots there. No way for him to pull the money back. You'd be crazy not to."

"I'll keep Sawyer's. It'll fund her college if she wants to go. But I don't need his money."

"I don't think he did it because you needed it, Lorelei." Carly is sitting on the floor, one arm hooked over Austin's knee.

"I want to believe that, but..."

Carly picks up the letter. "Are you telling me you don't believe that he loves you? After this?" She waves the paper, and it rustles in accusation.

"I'm telling you it doesn't matter."

"Really? Love doesn't matter?" Austin tips his head. "No, wait." He holds up a hand. "I've got one too many Y chromosomes for this discussion. I'm gonna grab another beer." He stands. "I'll be upstairs, studying bovine bloodlines. At least I'm competent to have an opinion in that arena." He bends to give Carly a kiss.

"See you in a bit, babe." Carly rests her back against the couch and raises an eyebrow at me. "I remember the first time I met Reese. We were in the beer line at the fireworks, remember?"

Trying to forget that day has been a dismal failure. I nod.

"You were oblivious, but I saw how he looked at you. Like you were a sweating glass of ice water and he was dying of thirst in a heat wave." She takes a sip of wine. "I could see the road you two were on. That's why I told him I'd do some serious damage if he hurt you."

"You *didn't*." How did I miss that?

She nods. "Sure did. And when I see him, he'll find out it wasn't an idle threat. But don't get me off the subject. I saw that day that he loved you. He may not even have known it yet, but when he looked at you, his face went soft. Kind of happy-drunk, you know?"

"You're reading too many fairy tales to your kids."

"Nope. Know how I know? Austin had that look when he saw me get crowned homecoming queen. When he saw me at the back of the church in my wedding dress. The day Faith was born." She tips her head. "Kinda between dreamy and poleaxed."

"Whatever, Cinderella. He's only ever wanted Sawyer. It was his goal from the first—"

"Yep. He's crazy about that baby." She puts her wineglass down and pushes to her feet. "Just one more thing before I go upstairs and seduce my husband." She tips her head and her smile is so sad. "I couldn't help but notice. That letter wasn't about Sawyer, it was about *you*. If all he wanted was that baby, why is that letter about you?"

CHAPTER 24

Lorelei

Carly goes up to bed, leaving me alone, and I'm not enjoying the company. I walk into the kitchen and empty the last of the sangria into my glass. Can't let it go to waste. Carly's right. I can't use Sawyer as an excuse any longer. Or the fake custody papers. Or my grief or his money. Every excuse I've pulled has been shot down, like clay pigeons at a skeet shoot. The only excuse left is me.

Why am I searching for reasons not to try again?

I think better walking. Carrying my wine, I walk into the great room, through to the dining room, back through the kitchen, then repeat, my feet following the circular path of my thoughts.

I'm afraid. Of course I'm afraid. But that's not an excuse, because I'm sure Reese is, too. Yet he had the guts to write that letter, and it might as well have been written in his blood. He laid it out on the page, holding back nothing.

Yet I'm holding back. Why?

My parents taught me to take care of my responsibilities and obligations. Momma, by how she lived, and Daddy, through his integrity and his love for us. I don't regret the challenges, because they made my shoulders strong and taught me to rely on my own two feet and hands. That saved me after my first disastrous love affair.

Independence is good. To a point. But I took it further.

I watched friends and acquaintances fall in love, marry, and have families. I troweled over the hole of being left behind with a spackling of pride. I was better than those weak people who needed a spouse. I didn't need anyone. I've worn my pride like Joan of Arc's armor. For years. Looking back, I wonder if my attitude drove off men who might have been interested if I hadn't held myself so separate. So superior.

And then comes a man who's seen the good, the bad, the ugly of me. Reese was right. We haven't had time for the small things, but we've sure had a chance to see the big things. Even so, he stood up, pointed to me, and said, "This one. I choose this woman."

And suddenly the road I'm on has a fork. I can see a long way down the road straight ahead. I should, because it's the same as the road behind me—only one set of footprints. I can stay in my golden armor of superiority, looking down on the lesser beings.

Or I can take it off and choose the other road, the one I can't see very far down.

The choice is simple: the solitary life I know or the human-cluttered messy one I've disdained but secretly always wanted?

Now that it's in black and white, the choice seems easy.

The whirlpool in my mind slackens, ebbing into swirls of calm. Peace rises floating from my heart to settle on my face in a smile.

* * *

Reese

I sit in the kitchen after breakfast, watching the sun come up and feeling like I've been in suspended animation since my attorney called to tell me the package had been delivered yesterday afternoon. Ringer on high volume, my phone mocks me from the table. What is she thinking? God, I'd give a lot to know.

The phone rings so loud I almost fall out of my chair. Then I nearly brush it to the floor, trying to grab it.

"H-hello?"

"Hi, Reese."

She sounds so sad. Oh shit. That can't be good. I rush in. "Lorelei, I'm so glad you called. I've been—"

"Can I talk first?"

"Sure?" What I've been sitting here wishing for is happening. Given her tone, I'm not so sure I want to know what she's so eager to say.

"I was so worried I would screw this up that I wrote you a letter. Is it okay if I read it to you?"

My hand is shaking so bad it makes her voice cut out. I put the phone on speaker, place it on the table, and clasp my hands in my lap. "Of course."

There's the sound of paper rustling. "Reese. The first time I met you, I called you a liar. But I need to be honest with you. See, *I'm* the liar." She pulls a deep breath in through her nose. "I've been jealous and petty and made all kinds of excuses why you and I couldn't be. I hid behind my pride and acted like I didn't need you." Her voice wobbles, and she sniffs.

"It's okay. Just tell me." I'm dying here.

"That's what I'm trying to tell you..." Her voice spirals. "I love you. I want another chance to...Please don't give up on me. I'm prideful and stubborn, and..."

I hear her crying, and God may damn my soul, but it makes me so happy. "Lorelei, where are you?"

She sniffs. "I'm at Carly's. I've got to get ready to go to work, but I had to—"

"I'm on my way. I'll see you in five hours. Faster, if the Cessna will do it." I lift the phone to my ear like it's going to bring her closer, wishing I could touch her. "I love you. I want us to be a family—you, me, and our miracle baby."

"I do, too. But we still have so many things to work out."

"And we'll start. As soon as I get there, okay? In the meantime, close your eyes. Can you feel me, holding you?"

She gives a watery chuckle. "No, silly. I want the real thing. Hurry."

* * *

Lorelei

I'm at work, but I'm like a caffeinated squirrel, starting and stopping and leaving things half-undone. I told Carly about the call with Reese before I left her house but forbade her to come down here. If she wants reunions, she can watch the Hallmark Channel. I'm nervous enough already.

I check my phone again. He is probably...two minutes closer than the last time I checked.

"Holy crap, Lorelei. Get outta the kitchen, will you?" Nevada, in a backward baseball cap and her BITE THE COOK apron glares at me. "You're making *me* nervous already." She shoos me away with her spatula. "Seriously. Go away."

I push through the door to the dining area. Sassy makes a cross with her fingers to ward me off. "You already broke two glasses, dropped a tray of dirty dishes, and threw coffee grounds on the floor. No disrespect, but you need to not touch anything else today, okay?"

The midmorning diners ogle me like I'm a new exhibit at the zoo.

"Fine. I'm going to get some air." I walk out, wrapped in whatever dignity I have left. I feel naked without my pride armor, but I dropped that in the dumpster out back on my way in.

I'm trying not to get ahead of myself, but a zillion questions zing around my mind. I wander down the sidewalk, nodding to townspeople I pass. I'm almost to the dime store when the Murphinator squeals around the corner onto the square opposite me. There isn't a parking space in front of the café, so he makes one, taking the no-parking zone.

My head forgets its questions—my heart takes over. And my heart is all in. I love this man. I run down the sidewalk, my feet hardly touching the ground.

The truck rocks when he throws it in park, the door opens, and he steps out. He's sexy in jeans, a white broadcloth shirt with the sleeves rolled, and his Stetson. He's looking to the café as he takes the step up at the curb.

"Hey, cowboy!" I launch myself at him, wrapping my arms around his neck and my legs around his waist.

"Whoa!" He laughs. We fall back against the truck and he wraps me up in his arms while I kiss his face all over.

It's what golden retrievers do.

EPILOGUE

Lorelei

NOVEMBER, THE FOLLOWING YEAR

Our refurbished farmhouse swarms with people; the yard is full of kids in long pants and jackets playing tag or just chasing one another for the joy of it. The smell of crushed autumn leaves and grilling meat comes to me through the open window over the kitchen sink. I pull a tray of deviled eggs from our new stainless-steel fridge and close the door with my butt.

"Let me have those." Nevada takes them from me. "You go enjoy the birthday girl. We've got this."

"Yeah, get lost, Momma." Carly's nana stirs a pot on the stove, a cigarette with a long ash bouncing on her lip.

"I'm going." I turn away, not wanting to know where that ash ends up. "Don't start without me. I've got to grab her present from upstairs." I walk through the living room but get stopped by clusters of people.

"Where did you get those window treatments?"

"I love your Momma's room down here. So homey."

"Great idea to extend the living room out to where the porch used to be and build on a new porch. It's modern, but not cold, like something out of a catalog, you know?"

"Thanks…Thank you…Glad you like it…" I keep moving until I get to the stairs. The shadows in that stairwell have ceased to haunt me in the past month. Reese turned Momma's old room into an office for himself, and we moved Momma downstairs, where she should have been all along.

In our room, I step to the closet and reach to the top shelf, way in the back, and bring down two gift bags, one gold, one pink, spewing glitter and tissue paper. I smile, not even caring that I'll be cleaning up glitter until next summer. I turn and check the mirror to be sure I don't look too harried. The royal-blue sweater Reese gave me shows off my eyes, and excitement colors my cheeks. It's not every day your daughter turns two. I turn and take in the room that became ours when the house was finished.

My grandmother's cast-iron bed, covered in her wedding-ring quilt, is centered in front of the huge arched window we had put in. Reese's briefcase and overnight bag are next to it; he's flying out for business in San Antonio tomorrow. He sold the Texas house and an acre it sits on to an oilman friend of his. He's keeping the cattle ranch, but this is his headquarters.

I glance out the window, to the cabin. Reese decided to turn it into a day care for babies of the working mothers in Unforgiven. And it's free to anyone who can't afford to pay.

But in the evening it's all mine. The West Dance Studio opened six months ago, and I'm up to two classes a week. Seems there are folks in Unforgiven who want to learn to waltz. And rumba. And I'm considering bringing in someone to teach ballet to the little ones.

"Lorelei! We're starving here" comes from below, and I turn and walk out.

Reese walks into the kitchen holding a platter of hot dogs in one hand, hamburgers in the other. "It's food, people. Come fill your plates!"

Twenty-five people can't all fit in the dining room. They spill into the living room, the kitchen, and out the door.

"Momma? Sarah?" They step in from the living room. Momma looks wonderful in her new dress. She smiles at Sawyer.

"Here, I've saved you seats." I pat the chair backs.

"Here's your place, princess." Reese lifts Sawyer into the chair at the head of the table, where I'm standing.

"Okay, Baba. Cake?"

He laughs. "After lunch. Then we'll have cake."

Carly's kids and the other little ones take the rest of the seats.

"I'd like to say grace first, if that's all right," I say, and the room quiets. I take Carly's hand in my left and Reese's in my right. Reese takes the hand next to him, and soon we're a long completed chain.

"Dear Lord. We're here today to celebrate the birthday of a very special girl. A girl who brought us together and, in spite of ourselves, made us a family. Thank you." Reese squeezes my hand. "Thank you for all of our friends in this house and our loved ones who are with you. Watch over them, and us. We ask this in your name, amen."

I raise my head and see the tears in my eyes reflected in many others'.

I blink them back. "One more thing, before we eat."

Groans.

"Oh, come on. The kids are behaving better than you grown-ups today."

More groans and a few chuckles.

I take the bags from the pantry, where I stashed them on a shelf. I hand the pink one to Sawyer and the gold one to Reese.

"It's not my birthday." But he's already rooting in the sack.

"Horsie!" Sawyer pulls out the pony I carved for her. It's painted sky blue, with puffy white clouds and flowers in its mane and tail. "Momma, horsie!"

Reese leans over and whispers in my ear. "Next year, what do you say I get her a real one?"

We discuss decisions nowadays and make them together. Parenting as a team is *so* much easier. I smile up at him. "We'll see."

He pulls out his present. "A horsie." But he says it quietly, laced with awe. I carved him a cow pony out of cedar and left it unpainted, because the striations of color in the wood were so beautiful. The only touch of paint was a white heart brand on his rump.

He grabs my hand. "Dig in, everyone. We'll be right back." He leads me out the screen door. It slaps behind us.

I shiver at the chill in the air. "Brrrr."

"I'll warm you up." He spins me around, leans me against the house, and kisses me.

God, this man can kiss. Before I know it, my hands are in his hair and we're both breathing heavy.

He backs up. "Warm now?"

"Almost." I try to pull him down for another, but steps back.

"Thank you for my horse. It's the most beautiful one ever." He looks down. "I have a present for you, too."

I smile up at him. "Not a horsie, please."

"Not a horsie." He reaches in the pocket of his Wranglers and pulls out a ring.

Not just a ring. A huge sapphire in a raised filigree platinum setting. It catches the light and flashes rainbow diamonds up the siding. I want to reach for it, but I don't dare. "Ohmygod."

"It was my mother's. We've taken it slow and worked on the little things. Built a solid foundation." He looks up, his melted-chocolate eyes on mine. "But I don't want to wait another second. You and Sawyer are the loves of my life. Would you do me the honor of becoming my wife, Lorelei?"

"Ohmygod."

He stands holding the ring, worry in his eyes. "Is that ohmygod yes or ohmygod no?"

"Ohmygod yes!" I bounce on my toes while he slips the ring on my finger. I thought it would look strange on my stubby finger, but it doesn't. It looks like mine. I turn my hand to study it from another angle. It's a perfect fit.

Just like him.

Austin Davis and Carly Beauchamp have been in love for as long as anyone in Unforgiven, New Mexico, can remember. But after Austin puts his rodeo career before Carly one too many times, Carly declares their relationship over—for good. Now this cowboy is ready to do whatever it takes to win her back. But Carly's hiding a secret—one that will test the depth and strength of their love.

Turn the page for an excerpt from
The Last True Cowboy

Available Now

CHAPTER 1

CARLY

Addiction sucks. I should know. Papaw has his White Lightning. Nana has her Bingo-jones. My addiction has sad green eyes and my name tattooed across his left pec.

But my wedding-dress dreams *always* come in second to his rodeo. There's even a term for it: Rodeo Widow. Except to earn that title, I'd have to be *married*.

Squinting through the windshield glare, I shift the knob on the steering column to third and press on the gas, but the speedometer doesn't budge. Dang it, at this rate I'm going to be late for the breakfast shift. Papaw bought the truck new about the time I was born, and Nana named it "Nellybelle." Said she stole the name from a car on some TV show—Roy Somebody. All I know is, I'm stuck driving the beater, so Nana can drive the Camry to Bingo.

I'm less than a mile from the paved road when clanking starts under the hood. It sounds like the hammers of hell in there. I take it out of gear and lurch to the side of the washboard road and watch the dust billow up in the rearview mirror. "Now that's just craptastic." I'm no mechanic, but I've been driving since before I could reach the pedals. I know what a thrown rod sounds like. Nana would say, "Nellybelle's sleeping with Jesus." My luck she'll want to have a funeral.

I grab a rubber band from the glovebox and lasso my hair into a thick ponytail. My hair is more strawberry than strawberry blonde, meaning if it takes longer than ten minutes to catch a ride, I'll look like Elmo. With freckles. Luckily, Papaw left a gimme cap behind the seat. I slap it on, throw my purse strap over my shoulder, open the door, and slide into the hot morning.

Once I hit the blacktop, odds are somebody will stop. One good thing about living outside of Unforgiven, New Mexico, all your life is that sooner or later someone you know is bound to come by.

I hear it before I see it. Quad Reynolds's truck materializes through the heat-haze off the blacktop. It's almost as ancient at Nellybelle (may she rust in peace).

He pulls alongside me and yells out the window, "Where's your car?"

Now the Reynoldses aren't among Unforgiven's best and brightest, and given a population of 1,500, that's not a high bar. Quad was the first of his clan to get a high school diploma, mostly thanks to kind and long-suffering teachers passing him along year to year like a white elephant gift. People can't help what they're born with (or without), but Quad has had a thing for me since third grade. He's also got body odor and dandruff so bad his eyebrows flake. I stuff my hands in my back pockets and walk up to the window. "I broke down. Can you give me a lift to town?"

"Heck yeah. Climb in." He unhooks the bungee cord that holds the passenger door shut. "Wait." He holds the door closed with a hand on the window frame. "You're not gonna make me eat those foldy-overy things again, are you?"

Exasperation puffs from my lips. "They're crepes, and no one made you eat them the first time. Besides, I took them off the menu." Mostly because no one ate them. I keep trying changes to the menu to improve business, but so far, the only thing that's gone over is Ratatouille. And only because I told them the name is French for "hash."

"Oh good." The door moans when he pushes it open.

I climb into the cab, right into his yearning look. "When're you going to throw over that no-account cowboy and fall for me, Carly Sue?"

"Believe me, I'm considering giving him up."

"Well, I'm available, but you better hurry 'afore some woman snatches me away."

Not going there. I'm no mean girl. "I'll take it under advisement, thanks." I turn so the springs quit pushing on my butt bone and so the bungee doesn't scrape my shins.

He drapes an arm over the steering wheel, and the breeze washes me in the smell of day-old sweat. "Where is Austin now, anyway?"

"Let's see. What day is it?"

"Thursday. No. Wait. Friday."

"He's in Las Cruces. Three-day rodeo at the county fair this weekend."

He shakes his head. "That boy can ride. I'll give him that."

Yeah. That's the problem.

Austin and I fell in love in first grade. I looked across the craft table and recognized a piece of me, staring back.

Something about him just clicked with me. It was the same for him, and like two jigsaw pieces, we snapped together. We never have come undone. Until now.

This time, I mean it.

Quad's truck rolls into the sleepy-with-morning town. The street curves around Soldier Park, with its peeling bandstand and obligatory Civil War cannon. The Civic Theater is finally playing last month's blockbuster for anyone who hasn't made the fifty-mile trek to Albuquerque. Austin took me to The Civic on our first real date, in junior high. I don't remember what movie, because we ended up making out in the balcony the whole time.

A few pickups are parked in front of the Lunch Box Café, owned by our main competitor and archnemesis, Dusty Banks. He puts the grease in "greasy spoon," but I guess some people enjoy that. We cruise past too many windows blotted out by paint or covered in butcher paper.

Unforgiven has faltered for years, tripping and stumbling to the edge of default. Doubly unlucky, we're not only at the end of a defunct railway spur, but we're on Route 66—the abandoned part.

Quad pulls up in the last angled parking space outside Chestnut Creek Café. It's the end of the road, literally. The converted railway station has been my second home for every one of my twenty-nine years. Papaw bought it back in the '50s, when the spur shut down, and named it after the place where he asked Nana to marry him (he hides his romantic streak well). He cooked, and Nana worked the cash register. Nowadays, Papaw works more at his side business (the still) and Nana keeps the local Bingo parlor in business. But hey, they earned a rest. They'd planned to turn it over to my mom and dad, but a drunk driver on Interstate 40 crashed that dream when I was just a baby.

"Thanks for the ride, Quad." I reach for the bungee cord but he's quicker, leaning over my lap, giving me a close-up of his "ambiance" and his bald spot. I hold my breath until he's on his own side again.

"You bet. Now, get out in that kitchen and rattle those pots and pans." He chuckles and slaps his thigh, raising a cloud of red New Mexico dust.

I don't bother to remind him that I'm not the cook. I just slide out and hold the door shut so he can re-hook the bungee.

The gingham curtains and the old-fashioned gold lettering on the glass door raise a faint haze of pride in my chest. The bells on the door jingle as I step inside and the café wraps itself around my heart, welcoming me with breakfast babble and the smell of bacon. I inhale a deep breath of home.

"Hey, Carly." Moss Jones raises his coffee cup in a salute, his grizzly-brown beard full of crumbs.

"Mornin', Moss."

Lorelei, my friend and our longtime waitress, swishes by, balancing four plates and three orders of toast. "You're late, Carly Beauchamp."

"Yeah, tell me about it." I push through the swinging door to the kitchen and head for my office. "Hey, Fish."

The name on our cook's driver's license is Joseph King, but he'd rather be called by his Navajo name—Fishing Eagle. He's got a dozen eggs, a rasher of bacon, and a boatload of hash browns crowded on the grill and a spatula in each hand. "Carly, can you grab me more bacon?"

"Sure." I pull open the door to the walk-in refrigerator.

"And some more eggs?" His voice is muffled by the heavy door.

I've just finished that when Lorelei sticks her head through the serving window. "Fish, you got those grits for table five?" She sorts tickets on the order wheel. "Hey, Carly, would you mind setting me up for coffee?"

"Sure." I push back through the swinging door to the dining area. I'm the manager and heir-apparent, but most days that washes out to being the gofer. After grabbing a cup for myself, I pull coffee and filters from under the counter and start scooping and stacking enough set-ups to last through lunch.

Conversation flows past me like a river.

"We even went down to the courthouse in Albuquerque, but they didn't know, either. I'm gonna—"

"So, I tell him, if you think you're going to the bar tonight, you've got—"

"Last week's rain washed out the road. I can't even get to my field, much less—"

My phone blats the opening notes to Blake Shelton's "Austin" and my hand jerks, slinging coffee across the counter. "Crap on a cracker." I'd let it go to voice mail but I've been dodging his calls for two days and if I don't answer soon, he'll sic Nana on me.

Nana loves Austin. And she's not alone. Every girl in Cibola County adores him. Every mom wants to adopt him. And no dad wants him anywhere near his daughter.

Acid scalds my stomach lining. I pull my phone from the pocket of my jeans, mash the button, and prop it between my cheek and shoulder. "Hey."

"Hey, Tigger."

In two words, I'm opening to him like a morning glory to the sun. I've read that twins have a special language that only they understand. Austin and I are like that. We're hard-wired into each other's feelings like a Vulcan mind-meld, without the weird face-touching thing.

In those same two words, I know he's hungover. I can

see him partying with his buds at some trashy bar the night before. I should—I've been there for enough of them. But that was in the glory days, when Austin was winning buckles and I was Cibola County Rodeo Queen. We lived for the road, sex, fair food, sex, and the dream we could make a living on barrels and rough stock.

That bubble burst when I had to come home and help Nana and Papaw with the diner. Yeah, I miss it, but you've got to grow up sometime. But Austin still hasn't. To be fair, he *is* making a living at it, if you consider having just enough money for rodeo dogs, gas, and his next entry fee "living."

Which reminds me. "Don't you 'Tigger' me. We need to talk, Austin Davis."

"Aw, come on, darlin'. Don't be mad. You know I can't stand it when you're upset."

His drawl flows over me with the sweetness of Sunday morning sex. He knows I love his voice. It eases through my cracks, loosening my muscles and my resolve.

"I'll be home for Sadie Hawkins on Friday. We'll talk then."

The litany he's recited too many times burns the sweetness to ash. "I'm serious. I can't go on like this." I drop the coffee scoop to hold the phone in both hands, as if he could feel the painful squeeze. "The girl gets to ask for Sadie Hawkins. I'm not asking you." I click the end button, wishing for the old days, when you could end a call with a satisfying slam.

In high school, the Student Council thought it'd be fun to include the whole town for Sadie Hawkins Day. Every year since, it's a blowout party in the town's square. Austin and I have been to every one of the past fourteen of them.

Streaks are overrated.

My ears prickle as I realize the diner is filled with an unnatural silence. I turn. Every eye in the place is lasered on me like I'm some rare zoo animal. My face blazes, which only makes me madder. I hate to blush. Redheads don't do it well.

"Aw, come on, Carly," Moss says, too loud in the quiet room. "You say that ever' time."

I slap a hand on my hip. "Really?" God, the nerve.

"Really," June Stevens says from booth number three.

Several heads nod.

Dropping the phone in my shirt pocket, I stomp for the kitchen. "This place has the privacy of a glass outhouse." My palms hit the door with a hollow boom and I stride for my office. At least that door has a satisfying slam.

* * *

An hour and a half later, morning work done, I'm sitting, drinking coffee and cataloging my troubles…the biggest of which has a bad-boy grin and one really fine butt. If I sit here any longer, I'm going to tip into sulkiness. And I'm not a sulker. It's time to tackle the trouble I *can* do something about. Wheels.

The café is hopping with the early lunch crowd, and Lorelei has a reinforcement. Sassy Medina, a new-to-town girl with a pretty smile and good references.

Lorelei spies me and hustles over. "Would you hold the fort for a few, Carly? I've got to run down to O'Grady's for tomatoes and we're almost out of Spam."

"Sure. Just be sure Jerry gives us the discount."

She rolls her eyes. "Thanks. I've only worked here seven years, so I'm likely to forget that."

"Yeah, yeah, just go." Grabbing a half apron from under

the counter, I tie it on and drop a book of order tickets in the pocket. Coffee pot in one hand, sweet tea pitcher in the other, I go on refill patrol.

At the first table, my second-grade teacher, Ms. Simons, says, "You stand your ground, Carly. Austin will wise up and marry you. You just wait and see if he doesn't."

The high-schoolers in the booth at the window titter and ask if Austin is officially available for the dance. As far as I'm concerned, he is.

At the counter, the town drunk, Manny Stipple, explains with beery sincerity why Austin deserves another chance.

At twenty-nine, my biological clock has stopped ticking— it's tap dancing on my ovaries. Every girl from my high school class is married and having babies, except me. Well, me and Rose Hart, but she wears men's clothes and is taking hormones to grow a beard. She goes by Roy now.

I'm just about to lose it when my posse spills through the door, trailing strollers, diaper bags, and toddlers. Julie, Jess, and I ruled the homecoming court, and we've managed to stay close through marriages (theirs), kids (theirs), and break-ups (mine). We were all great friends, but Jess and I—we had a special bond. Back in junior high, she decided it wasn't fair that I didn't have a sister, so she stepped up for the job. We've been tight ever since. I love me that Jess.

They take booth number one and settle, passing out crayons and Goldfish. I drop menus on the table and we chat while they decide. Jess rubs her stomach as she studies the daily specials on the board above the order window.

"Jess, are you preggers again?"

"Can you believe it?" She smiles at me with a glow reserved for pubescence and motherhood.

My biological clock bongs a funeral dirge.

She eases her toddler over, scoots down, and pats the bench next her.

Lorelei walks in the front door, her arms full of bags.

"I want to hear all the nasty details, I promise. But right now, I've got to fix a problem. Can I borrow someone's car?"

Jess's perfectly plucked brows draw together. Even in motherhood, she keeps herself up—if you ignore the spit-up stain on her silk shirt. "Take mine." She reaches in her diaper bag, pulls out her keys, and tosses them to me.

"Thanks, hon. I'll be back before you're done with lunch."

Her son wails, and she waves me off.

I unlock the door of the SUV, shift a stuffed Minion to the passenger seat, and climb in. The hot air is infused with eau de Kid. Discarded juice boxes and crumbs litter the floor. My mood falls like a rock tossed into a dry well. It's not that I need a vanful of kids to feel complete. I have a full life. But dang, my dreams aren't all high-and-mighty. All I want is to raise a big family in a small town, with the love of my life. Cutting Austin loose will mean cutting loose of all my dreams. But I'm sick of hoping and praying and attempting long-distance mind manipulation.

Maybe I can convince him to come home, take over his dad's ranch, and start our business.

Yeah, that's the maybe I hoped for last year.

And the year before that. And...I blow out a breath. I'm not getting anywhere sitting here, sweating and counting spilled Goldfish. I fire the engine, put the car in gear, and head out of town.

Floyd's Super Clean Used Cars sits all by itself, two miles out of town on the road to Albuquerque. Cars are cheaper in the big city but I don't have that kind of time. Turning into the almost-deserted lot, I park and head for the '50s-style glass-fronted building. Metallic air conditioning greets me, along with a gum-snapping salesman. Ignoring his howdy, I stride for the back office to rustle us up a new truck. Who am I kidding? Rustling is about the only way we could afford a new one. If I don't find a way to compete with the Lunch Box... *One problem at a time.*

The owner hasn't changed a bit from our high school days. Well, except for the paunch. "Jeez, Floyd. Really?"

He drops a nasty girlie magazine in a drawer and his cowboy boots from the desk. "Hey, Carly." His eyes scan the parking lot. "You looking to trade in the mommy-mobile, huh?" He drops a wink. "Austin know about this?"

I cross my arms. More crap I do not need. "You know very well that's Jess's car."

One corner of his mouth lifts. "Ah, so it is. What can I do you for, Carly?"

"I need to buy a used truck."

"What happened to Nellybelle?"

"She took a dump on the way to work this morning."

Floyd stands, sweeps off his cowboy hat, and lays it over his heart. "Please extend my condolences to your dear Nana."

"Cut the crap, Floyd. I need wheels." I do some quick math in my head to figure what I can afford. "And none of that south-of-the-border stuff you slap a cheap paint job on to make it look saleable."

He puts on a hurt look. "Darlin', you know that when I do have the occasional 'international trade,' I save it for the tourists."

Except the only tourists in Unforgiven are ones who made a wrong turn on the way to Albuquerque. And they sure aren't looking to buy a car. "Just show me what you've got."

He leads the way to the almost-empty lot. "We're a little short on inventory. We had a big blowout sale here last week. You prob'ly heard my commercials on the radio." He puffs out his chest and steps to a dusty compact with burnt paint.

I heard them. But again, not a mean girl. "That won't work. You know it's too small to carry Papaw's . . . product."

"And fine product it is, too. Been known to sample it a time or two myself." He wanders to a battered Dodge Caravan that, from the look of it, could be the first specimen that came off the assembly line.

"It'll hold six, with room left over for a golden retriever." He gives me the sleazy salesman grin and waggles his bushy eyebrows.

The sticker on the window is in my price range, and I'm desperate. But I haven't fallen that far yet. If Austin sees me in that, he'll think . . . well, I don't want to think what he'll think. What the whole *town* will think. *Poor Carly, wannabe mommy.* My face blazes hotter than the 102-degree air. "Floyd, this will not do. I'm not looking for anything special, just a better-than-beater truck that'll get me to work, and Papaw can borrow now and again for deliveries. How hard can that be?"

He takes off his hat and scratches his head. "Honest, Carly, that's all I've got right now. Next shipment of used cars isn't for two weeks."

"I don't have two weeks, Floyd." I hate the whine in my voice, but I really am desperate.

He squints into the sun. "I do have something. But it's not what you're looking for."

Neither is the Mommymobile. "Let's see it."

I follow Floyd's waddle to the shop behind the showroom. "If you're gonna try to sell me something you're working on—"

"Nope. Just storing it to keep it out of the weather." He strides to a sheet-covered mound in the center of the bay, lifts the edge, and pulls it off with a magician's flourish.

"That's not a car."

"Damn, Carly, your powers of observation are downright acute." He drops the cover in a corner and slaps the dust off his hands. "This here's a 2005 Honda Shadow Spirit VT750."

The motorcycle is low to the ground, but it's not a cruiser; you'd sit almost upright on it. It's got chrome pipes running down the side and a cushy seat that steps up to a tiny passenger seat with a short sissy bar. But it's the paint job that makes me fall in insta-love. An eye-popping royal blue, with lighter blue flames rippling down the tank. Thoughts zip through my brain like summer heat lightning.

My grandparents would have a fit. I get it; my parents died on a bike.

He names a price lower than I'd have guessed.

It sure wouldn't work as Papaw's delivery van. But it's cheap enough that maybe he could buy a truck, when Floyd gets more inventory.

"It's got low mileage." Floyd must see something on my face, because he's got a greedy gleam in his eye. "Prettier'n a speckled pup, ain't it?"

I nod. My brain flashes to the picture on the wall outside my bedroom. I've seen that photo every day since I've been old enough to toddle down the hall. A frozen moment, of parents I don't remember. My dad, in greasy jeans and a white T-shirt, sitting on a Harley with ape-hanger handlebars, grinning at the camera. My mom, draped around him wearing shorts and a halter top. When I was little, I got the happy. As I got older, I got the sexy. My mom is smiling, but her nails make indentations in the T-shirt—like she wanted to rip it off and do him, right there.

They died on that motorcycle. But even that was romantic—they went together, her arms wrapped around him. Neither had to face a long life of being alone. The thought makes me shudder.

That photo whispers to me at night, telling me bedtime stories of speed and laughter and love. When I think of my parents, it's that stop-action moment that I feel in my gut. Young, full of the future, and mad for each other. That's what I want.

That's my dream.

I found the guy, but that dream depends on Austin to make it come true. Here sits a dream I can make come true, all by myself.

But Nana and Papaw...No, you know what? I've worried about what people would think all my life: I've worked my butt off, being what everyone expected Carly to be: Austin's girl, the dedicated granddaughter who quit rodeo to take over the diner. Well, everyone is going to have to stand back—I'm going to put what *I* want first for once.

Floyd is still standing there with his face and his stomach hanging out.

"You'd give me more off, if we bought a truck too, right? A volume discount?"

He rolls his eyes to the rafters. "Lord, I give to your church every Sunday, but I hadn't planned my business to be nonprofit."

I give him my best Rodeo Queen smile. "If money's tight, maybe you should drop your magazine subscriptions." Floyd's a negotiator, but he's got nothing on the grandkid of a Cajun bootlegger.

His fat mouth twists. "Oh, all right. Fifteen percent off the bike for a package deal." He squints across the bike at me. "You got a license to ride, Carly?"

"Yep." I got it back in high school, and never dropped the endorsement. I pull my wallet from my back pocket. "How much you want to hold it?"

Floyd holds up his hands. "I've known you since kindergarten. Your word is good enough for me."

* * *

That evening, Lorelei is driving me home. We've passed Nellybelle's corpse and are almost to our turnoff when my phone blares "Austin." I check the time, then power off the phone. He must be getting desperate if he's calling this close to his event. I look up to see a flash of pity crossing Lorelei's face.

"Friday is Sadie Hawkins. You may ride over with Nana and Papaw, but you know darned well that when Austin shows up and bats his eyes, you'll end up two-stepping the night away—first in the town square, then in his bed." She turns into the long dirt drive that leads to my house.

I rest my arm on the open window and let the breeze blow out my thoughts. "Not this time."

She doesn't roll her eyes, but it's a near thing. "So, what, you gonna dump Austin and go out with Quad?" She pulls in the dooryard.

"Nah. When Austin really understands how important it is to me, he'll agree to make this his last season."

"If you say so. I'll be by in the morning to pick you up for work."

"Thanks, Lorelei, I appreciate the ride." I slide out, slam the door, and wave as she backs up.

The screen door shushes over the worn green linoleum that's been here so long there's a thin spot next to the sink. The smell of liver and onions smacks me in the face.

Nana is at the stove, poking the contents of a cast-iron skillet like she's got a live rattlesnake in there. If it weren't for the liver smell, I'd half believe she did. Nana's always been quirky and outspoken, but the past few years, as she puts it, her "give-a-shit gave up the ghost." She now says whatever she's thinking, to whomever. We had her tested; it's not Alzheimer's. It's more like Old Folks Tourette's.

She removes the perpetual cigarette from the corner of her mouth, taps the ash on the coffee can ashtray on the counter, then returns it to her lip. "Well com'ere an' give me a hug, sugar."

She watches me cross the floor with the forever squint she's gotten avoiding smoke from that cigarette. Her gray hair is pulled into a messy bun on the top of her head, stray bits standing straight out, defying gravity. Nana's hair used to be red, like mine. They say she was a looker in her day.

"What's the matter?"

Ducking the cigarette, I put my arms around her short frame. Her skin is like biscuit dough, white and pillow-soft, and she smells of smoke, onion, and sweat. The smell of love, and home. "You won't want to hug me when I tell you that Nellybelle died." I kiss her cheek.

"I heard." She rocks me a few seconds, then releases me. "Ah, fuck it. The old nag outlived her usefulness ten years ago." She turns back to the stove. "Now go wash up. Dinner's in fifteen. Emma Jean's pickin' me up, an' I can't be late to Bingo."

Instead, I head for the office where an ancient desktop computer perches on the rolltop desk. It takes forever to fire up. Papaw refuses to replace it, or to get faster internet service, contending that it's bad enough that they make him pay for TV when it used to be free. With Papaw, all change is seen as a conspiracy.

When I finally get to Google, I type, "Motorcycle riding tips."

Luckily, I won't have to start from scratch. My memory flashes film clips from high school, when Austin taught me how to ride the county dirt roads on his little off-road Yamaha. He'd yelled "Shift!" in my ear until I figured out the sound of the revs winding up. And when it got hot, we'd stop at Chestnut Creek to skinny-dip and wind up each other's revs. We had no responsibilities. No expectations. Life rolled out in front of us, and we screamed along, flat-out, never thinking ahead.

God, I miss those days.

I jot several websites on a scratch pad from Haley Feed & Tack, fold the sheet, and put it in my pocket. I'll do research at the diner tomorrow, where they don't haul in pixels via mule team.

By the time I've set the table, Papaw is washing up at the kitchen sink. "I'm gonna have to use the Camry tomorrow to pick up a load of corn at the feed store."

Nana sets the bowl of mashed potatoes on the table. "Last time you did that, we had that squirrel 'pocalypse in the trunk."

"I'm gonna buy it in bags this time. Can't fit as much in that way, but..." He crosses to the fridge, opens the door, and roots around for ketchup.

I pour three glasses of iced tea. "I stopped by Floyd's, but he had a blowout sale last weekend, and didn't have anything worthwhile. He says he'll have some trucks in next week."

Papaw plops the ketchup in front of his plate and lowers his long, thin frame into the chair with a grunt.

His knee must be bad today. Probably not a good time to bring this up, but he'll know soon anyway. I set the gravy boat on the table and sit. "Looks good, Nana." In keeping with our mealtime hierarchy, I pass the platter of fried liver to Papaw.

"Thank you, missy."

Nana fills hers, then passes each plate to me.

Papaw says grace.

Might as well get it over with. "I bought a motorcycle at Floyd's today."

ACKNOWLEDGMENTS

Thank you to my critters, Kimberly Belle and Fae Rowen, who always throw me a line when I'm in the Pit of Despair (aka: the middle). Shout out to my biggest cheerleader, Miranda King. Double thank you to my plot-angel, Orly Konig. And as always, a *huge* thank you to my friend and lay-editor, Donna Hopson.

A special thank you to Lorelei Frank for being patient until "her" character finally got her own book!

Thanks also to my super-agent, Nalini Akolekar of Spencerhill Associates, and my power-editor and knitting buddy, Amy Pierpont.

ABOUT THE AUTHOR

Laura Drake grew up in the suburbs outside Detroit. A tomboy, she's always loved the outdoors and adventure. In 1980 she and her sister packed everything they owned into Pintos and moved to California. There she met and married a motorcycling, bleed-maroon Texas Aggie and her love affair with the West began.

In 2014, Laura realized a lifelong dream of becoming a Texan, and is currently working on her accent. She gave up the corporate CFO gig to write full time. She's a wife, grandmother, and motorcycle chick in the remaining waking hours.

You can learn more at:
   LauraDrakeBooks.com
   Twitter @LauraDrakeBooks
   Facebook.com/LauraDrakeBooks

Looking for more hot cowboys?
Forever has you covered!

COWBOY STRONG
by Carolyn Brown

Alana Carey can out-rope and out-ride the toughest Texas cowboys. But she does have one soft spot—Paxton Callahan. So when her father falls ill, Alana presents Pax with a crazy proposal: to pretend to be her fiancé so her father can die in peace. But as the faux-wedding day draws near, Alana and Paxton must decide whether to come clean about their charade or finally admit their love is the real deal. Includes the bonus story *Sunrise Ranch*!

COWBOY COURAGE
by Carolyn Brown

Heading back to Texas to hold down the fort at her aunt's bed-and-breakfast will give Rose O'Malley just the break she needs from the military. But while she may speak seven languages, she can't repair a leaky sink to save her life. When Hudson Baker strides in like a hero and effortlessly figures out the fix, Rose can't help wondering if the boy she once crushed on as a kid could now be her saving grace. Includes the bonus story *Wildflower Ranch*!

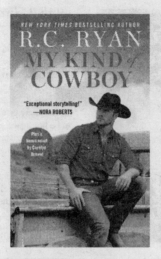

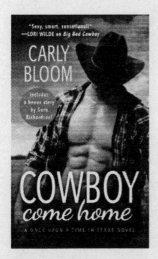

COWBOY COME HOME
by Carly Bloom

As far as Claire Kowalski is concerned, Big Verde, Texas, is perfect, except for one thing: the lack of eligible men. Some days it feels like she's dated every single one. It's too bad that the only man who ever tickled her fancy is the wandering, restless cowboy who took her heart with him when he left her father's ranch years ago. Just when she's resigned herself to never seeing him again, Ford Jarvis knocks on the door. Includes a bonus story by Sara Richardson!

FIRST KISS WITH A COWBOY
by Sara Richardson

With her carefully ordered life crumbling apart, shy and sensible Jane Harding welcomes the distraction of helping plan her best friend's wedding. When she discovers that the boy who once tempted her is now the best man, however, her distraction risks becoming a disaster. Toby Garrett may be the rodeo circuit's sexiest bull rider, but his kiss with Jane has never stopped fueling his fantasies. Can this sweet-talking cowboy prove that the passion still burning between them is worth braving the odds? Includes the bonus story *Cowboy to the Rescue* by A.J. Pine!

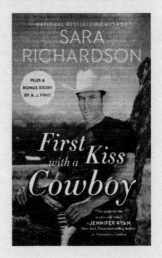

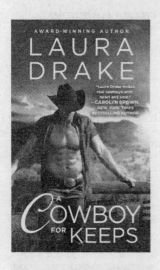

A COWBOY FOR KEEPS
by Laura Drake

Not much rattles a cowboy like Reese St. James—until his twin brother dies in a car accident, leaving behind a six-month-old daughter. Reese immediately heads to Unforgiven, New Mexico, to bring his niece home—but the girl's guardian, Lorelei West, refuses to let a hotshot cowboy like Reese take away her sister's baby. Only the more time they spend together, the harder it is to deny the attraction between them. Opening their hearts to a child is one thing—can they also open their hearts to a chance at happily-ever-after?

MY ONE AND ONLY COWBOY
by A.J. Pine

Sam Callahan is too busy trying to keep his new guest ranch afloat to spend any time on serious relationships—at least that's what he tells himself. But when a gorgeous blonde shows up insisting she owns half his property, Sam quickly realizes he's got bigger problems than Delaney's claim on the land: She could also claim his heart. Includes a bonus novel by Carolyn Brown!

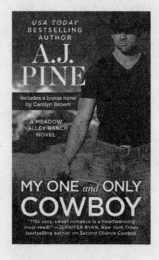